THE MOMENT OF TEMPTATION
HAD COME. IF SHE TURNED TO HIM,
IF HE TOUCHED HER, HE
WOULD SUCCUMB.

"Matilda," said Stephen.

"Not here," she said.

"Then, for the love of God, say where."

"In my bedchamber."

"That would be madness."

"This is madness, Stephen. I shall be
waiting."

"If we are discovered,..."

"Then we must say to ourselves—for I
doubt we should be allowed to say it
together—'It was worthwhile.'"

They rode through the forest. They fell in
with the rest of the party. Then they
rode back to the castle....

THE PASSIONATE ENEMIES

a novel by

Jean Plaidy

FAWCETT CREST • NEW YORK

THE PASSIONATE ENEMIES

Published by Fawcett Crest Books, a unit of CBS Publications, the Consumer Publishing Division of CBS Inc., by arrangement with G.P. Putnam's Sons

ISBN: 0-449-24390-7

Printed in the United States of America

First Fawcett Crest Printing: April 1981

10   9   8   7   6   5   4   3   2   1

CONTENTS

The King Decides to Marry 9

The Wedding and Coronation 31

In the Imperial Bedchamber 55

The Poet's Eyes 61

Homage to Matilda 79

The Reluctant Bride 105

The Lovers 123

A Surfeit of Lampreys 143

Hugh Bigod 165

The King's Mysterious Malaise 175

The Queen Commands 193

A Troubadour's Song 205

Matilda's Triumph 213

Matilda's Prisoner 233

Flight from London 257

The Funeral Cortège 271

Escape Over the Ice 279

Departures 291

The Last Meeting 305

The End of an Era 315

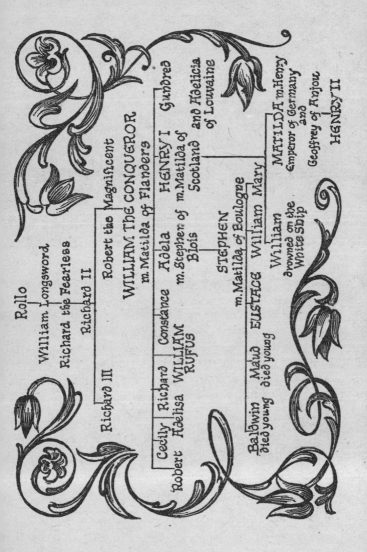

Rollo
|
William Longsword
|
Richard the Fearless
|
Richard II
|
Richard III
|
Robert the Magnificent
|
WILLIAM THE CONQUEROR
m. Matilda of Flanders

Cecily Richard Constance WILLIAM Adela HENRY I Gundred
Robert Adelisa   RUFUS   m. Stephen of m. Matilda of and Adelicia
                                    Blois   Scotland   of Louvaine

STEPHEN
m. Matilda of Boulogne

Baldwin Maud EUSTACE William Mary
died young died young   drowned on the
                        William White Ship

MATILDA m. Henry
Emperor of Germany and
Geoffrey of Anjou
|
HENRY II

The King Decides to Marry

"A King cannot have too many children, if they be bastards," mused the King. "It is only the legitimate ones with which he should be sparing. Too many legitimate sons can cause friction, as in my own family. But bastards can be thrown a castle or two, honours, titles and they may boast throughout their lives of their royal connection, and be loyal often, for a man will be loyal to that of which he is proud. But even so a King should have more than one legitimate son, for in what sad case he is if by evil fortune he should lose his heir."

And this was precisely the evil fortune which had overtaken him, King Henry I of England, and since he had lost his only legitimate son he had become irascible, ready to burst into anger at the slightest provocation, to the terror of those who served him. Before this tragedy, although he had been capable of acts of cruelty, he had been known, harsh and ruthless though he might be, as a just man.

There was none who could soothe him as easily as his nephew Stephen and indeed it was whispered that he might make Stephen his heir. This would not have been viewed with great disfavour for this young and handsome man was affable to all no matter how humble; he knew how to charm and never hesitated to, even when there seemed little to gain from it but the affection of those who, if the King willed it, would be his subjects. Stephen practised charm on all so that when it was turned on those who could bring him great good, it seemed to be used naturally and without sly motive.

Since the death of his wife, two years before, Henry I of England had sought comfort in wild animals and women. All through his life these pastimes had afforded him more pleasure than any others and he had pursued them with a verve which never flagged and had resulted in many a fine deer or wild boar being brought to the royal table and the most desirable ladies of England to his bed. As a result of his indulgence in these pursuits he had developed indigestion, and innumerable young men and women claimed him as their father. While he deplored the former he delighted in the latter.

Never before in his life had he felt so restless as he did at this time and the cause of the unwelcome change in his nature was the recent tragedy when his son William, on crossing from Normandy to England, had been drowned in that fated White Ship which had struck the rocks just out of Barfleur; and another son and daughter of the King (though these were of the numerous illegitimate brood) had gone down with him.

And here was Henry, fifty-two years of age, master of both England and Normandy, a widower, without a son to follow him to the throne.

Henry loved order in his life. There were some who said he should have been a clerk. Indeed the French had nicknamed him Henri Beauclerc. He loved learning and favoured scholars. He had no intention of dying yet but he wanted to make sure, as his father the Conqueror had, that he had a son to follow him.

Henry knew that he must come to a decision and he could enjoy no peace until he did. True, he could temporarily forget his dilemma in his pleasures and it was always a joy to ride out to the hunt and stop at some castle where a loving chatelaine would be eagerly waiting for him; but with the light of morning would come the depressing realization: fifty-two years old and no son to follow him.

One of his relaxations was to go through his household accounts in which every penny must be accounted for personally to him. This was a task he had reserved for himself whenever he was not absent fighting in Normandy. Alas, he had spent a great deal of his life as King fighting Normandy for there would always be barons there to oppose him and, while his nephew, William the Clito, lived, men would rally to his banner and try to take Normandy from Henry. That was something he accepted. It was these cruel blows of fate which exacerbated him beyond endurance. His wife had given him only two children, a son and a daughter, and then after several barren years had died; his only son was drowned in the prime of his manhood on the White Ship; and he, Henry,

10

who had arranged his household and his armies with precise efficiency had suddenly found that fate had dealt him a cruel blow which had at one stroke ruined his careful plans.

The figures of his accounts danced before his eyes. He saw that his Chancellor of the Chaplains had had his simnel cake and his measure of clear and ordinary wine; he had had his thick wax candle and his forty pieces of candle with his five shillings a day. His watchmen had had no more than their four candles, their food and one and a half pennies a day. All members of the household from the Chancellors, who were the chief of all departments, to the most menial serving men had had their dues and one set of figures neatly balanced another, so that there was nothing of which he could complain.

He put aside the accounts and shouted to one of his pages to bring his nephew Stephen to him.

Stephen immediately responded. One did not keep the King waiting at any time, but in the last weeks one responded with even greater alacrity to his commands.

The King's mood softened a little at the sight of his nephew. Stephen grew more like his mother every day and Adela had been Henry's favourite sister. Married to Stephen of Blois she had been in a position to help him in odd little ways when he was planning his conquest of Normandy and Henry was glad to be able to repay her by taking her son under his wing. He had given Stephen estates in England so that he was a rich man; he had found a bride for him, none other than the dead Queen's niece; and since the death of his son, Stephen was constantly at his uncle's side and none would have been surprised if the King had not declared him his heir.

Now the King smiled affectionately at his good-looking nephew.

"Ah, Stephen," he said, "be seated."

Stephen bowed and sat as requested on the faldestol close to the King's chair.

"You find me in ill mood," said the King.

"You have had much to plague you," replied Stephen in that gentle soothing voice which charmed so many.

"'Tis true. I dream of the White Ship. I can't forget it, Stephen. She was so beautiful, that ship. The finest in my fleet. I hear the cries of the stricken...."

"It is so soon as yet, sir. You will grow away from it."

"That may be, but I cannot help but ask myself what I have done that God should so forsake me."

"You have been a true and just King, sir. God will remember that."

"Then why did He take my only legitimate son from me?"

"His ways are mysterious," answered Stephen. He tried to suppress the lilt in his voice. Was he the chosen one? Was that why William who stood in his way had been removed?

"Mysterious indeed," said the King. "For years my Queen was barren. Why could I not get children with her? 'Twas no fault of mine. Others could bear my children. Why not the Queen?"

"The Queen was ill, sir. In health she bore you two fine children, William...and Matilda...."

Stephen lingered over that name. Matilda. It was more than six years ago that the King's daughter had gone to Germany for her marriage with the Emperor but Stephen had never forgotten her. He often wondered whether she ever thought of him. If he could have married Matilda....What a wild dream that had been. He ought to have known that as the third son of the Count of Blois he would then have had no chance of marriage with the daughter of the King of England. But if Matilda had never married, if she were free, now that the King's only son and his heir William was dead, Henry might have given Matilda to his favourite nephew. Stephen was carried away by regrets. What a prospect! Marriage with that fascinating virago. There had been a great bond between them. He had scarcely been able to prevent himself from attempting to seduce her. She would have been willing enough. But she had been only twelve years old when she went away, young in years, but knowledgeable in the ways of the world. Matilda was one of those who appeared to be born with such knowledge. He wondered often how she had fared with her old Emperor—forty years her senior.

Wild, imperious, handsome Matilda and gentle, equally handsome, charming Stephen—what a pair they would have made. And she believed so too. She had wanted him as he had wanted her. He remembered their encounters in detail. They had not been physical lovers. Their passion had not taken them as far as that. There was too much at stake. Matilda in spite of her desire for her fascinating cousin had been delighted at the prospect of becoming an Empress. Matilda wanted power more than she wanted love. She was after all the granddaughter of the Conqueror—as he, Stephen, was

12

the grandson. They would both consider consequences before they indulged in follies. He had often thought of what could have happened to him if he had followed his inclinations and seduced his cousin. What if he had got her with child? He could picture the King's friendliness turning to wrath; and Henry had the family temper although he was under more control than those of his father and his brother Rufus had been. Matilda was a bargaining counter in her family. The marriage had meant an alliance with Germany against the French. The Emperor, much as he wanted a son, would not wish that son to have begun his life within his little bride before she came to him.

Stephen sweated at the thought. The King's justice was swift and implacable. The favoured nephew would no longer be cherished. He could see himself imprisoned for life, perhaps deprived of his eyes—for doubtless the King would consider that just reprisal: his eyes for Matilda's virginity. It was a picture that had been in his mind since the days when he had sported with his cousin.

But he had escaped disaster. He and Matilda had sighed for each other and made love by words and looks—no more; for each had been fully aware of the pitfalls before them; and Matilda for all her passionate nature had no wish to lose the Empress's crown any more than Stephen had to lose his eyes.

"Matilda is an Empress now," said the King. "Were she not in Germany, the wife of the Emperor, and had she stayed in England she would have been the heiress to the throne."

"A woman...." began Stephen.

"Ay, a woman."

"Could a woman hold together a country like this? Could a woman hold Normandy together?"

"Matilda could," said the King.

"Ay, Matilda," echoed Stephen.

Henry closed his eyes and the lines of bitterness and irritation showed clearly when his face was in repose.

"I used to think," went on the King, "that Matilda should have been born the boy."

"She has a great spirit, sir."

"William...." The King's voice grew tender. "William was a beautiful boy, though over gentle, perhaps. He reminded me of my brother Richard. Richard was of a like nature. Kindly, good—all men loved him. William was like that. And he died, Stephen...as Richard died. Sometimes I think that some men are too good for this world."

13

"It may be, sir. William was good. Yet he was a fighter."

"So was Richard. My father had great hopes of him. Secretly I think he was my father's favourite."

"Had your father lived longer," went on Stephen, softly flattering, "you would have been that. I wish the Conqueror could have lived to see your greatness, sir."

Henry said: "I have done my best—often in great difficulties."

"You are a great king, sir. Unrivalled...." Stephen looked obliquely at the King and decided to amend the flattery. "Save by one, the great Conqueror himself."

"None of us can hope to rival him, Stephen."

"No, sir. He was a man to whom conquest was the meaning of life. He had no real life outside it. It was the Conqueror's way of life, but mayhap it is not the best way. A man's life is not enriched by battle and nothing but battle. The exercises of the mind make great men greater. You, sir, have astonished the world with your scholarship and you have taken your pleasure and given much to others—surely love, sir, is a more worthy object than war."

Henry smiled benignly. Trust Stephen to cheer him up. He had been asking himself in his latest mood of depression whether God was punishing him for his lechery and Stephen in that golden voice of his was calling it giving pleasure to others while taking it himself, an exercise in relaxation that he might fight his worthy causes with more energy than he would otherwise have had.

"Stephen," said the King, "you are a great help to me. I rejoice that you are at my side in this hour of tragedy. Kings are denied the mourning that humbler men can indulge in."

"'Tis true, sir."

"And when a King is left without an heir, he must needs plan."

"You have one legitimate child, sir."

"Matilda! Empress! Nay, Stephen, she could not be Queen of England and wife to the Emperor at the same time. The people would not have it. They would suspect that Germany was trying to take England and make a vassal state of her. Nay. Matilda is Empress of Germany."

"Do you regret her marriage, sir?"

The King hesitated. "It brought me great good, as you know, Stephen. The King of France hates the match; therefore it must be good for me, must it not? Yet had I not made

14

it she would be here and by the saints, Stephen, I would have trained her to rule this land and made her my heir."

"But as you so rightly say, sir, it is too late. She is the Empress."

"It is this solemn fact, Stephen, which has brought me to this decision."

Stephen was afraid to look at his uncle for fear he should betray his eagerness.

It was coming now. He was certain of it. The King was going to tell him that, because he was the son of his favourite sister, his beloved nephew whom he regarded as his own son, who had fought gallantly at his side in Normandy, who had shown himself to be liked by the English and a young man malleable to the King's will, he would name him his heir.

This, thought Stephen, is the greatest moment of my life. Why should I not be King of England? Am I not the Conqueror's grandson? Of the three sons who survived great William, Rufus was dead, Robert a prisoner in his brother Henry's hands, and Henry was fifty-two without a male heir. So why should not the son of the Conqueror's daughter take the coveted crown?

It was almost as though fate was playing into his hands. Fate had married Matilda to the Emperor of Germany so that she could not be Queen of England (and how would the people react to a woman on the throne?). William, the King's only son, had been drowned in the White Ship. And he, Stephen, had been sent at an early age to the English court; he had won the King's favour; he had a grace and charm of manner which had brought many to his side.

This was his great moment. He could almost feel the crown on his head.

Time seemed to slow down. So many thoughts pushed themselves into his mind with the rapidity of lightning.

"Yes," said the King, speaking ponderously as though to give greater effect to his words, "I have given this matter much thought. It is not a step to take lightly. But I am no longer a young man, Stephen. I have lived through fifty-two winters. It is a goodly age, and although I am still in the full flush of my vigour I must perforce look facts in the face. A kingdom without an heir is a kingdom which breeds trouble. Long before I die the people must know that there is another to step into my shoes. I trust you, Stephen. You have proved yourself to be a good friend to me and this country."

Stephen could scarcely suppress his excitement.

"My lord, I will serve you and this land with my life."

"I know it, Stephen. You are a good boy. If I had a wife and got her with child it would be a year before a son could be born. I should be fifty-three years of age, Stephen."

Stephen nodded sagely. "How wise you are, sir. I have most admired your love of truth. You always looked it in the face and admitted to what you saw. Sir, it is a quality I most admire. I strive always to emulate it."

The King inclined his head.

"So," he went on, "I have decided to marry again. Now...no waiting. By the saints, there is no time for dallying. I must get my bride to bed and with child without delay."

Stephen was speechless. For once he could not find the right words to say.

The King did not seem to notice. "Yes, I shall marry at once. I must have a son. The Kingdom must have an heir. I trust you, Stephen. When my son is born you will swear on sacred bones to me that you will uphold him if I should die before he is of an age to defend himself. I know you would do so, but I shall need your oath...and that of all those who serve me. Yes, Stephen, I have come to this decision. There is nothing for me to do but take a wife."

Stephen bowed his head, still not speaking. How could he trust himself to do so when he had seen his hopes shattered, his greatest ambition shown to him as to be as nothing more than a dream.

Stephen rode from Westminster to the Tower Royal, that magnificent palace which Henry had given him at the time of his marriage. In the Chepe the merchants recognized him and bowed their deference. He knew that they believed he could well become their king. Many a merchant's daughter smiled at him from a window. Stephen's liking for attractive girls was well known, and so courteous was he in his approach, so kindly even when the *affaire* was at an end, that his amatory adventures were regarded as a kingly pastime to be indulgently accepted rather than deplored.

Past the wooden houses with their thatched roofs to the great stone fortress between the Chepe and Watling Street— a palace, a king's residence but not to be the home of a king, he thought bitterly.

In her solarium his wife was seated with her women working on a piece of needlework. She looked up with pleasure

16

as he entered, so did the rest of her ladies, some of whom had at one time been on intimate terms with him.

He gave no indication of the bitterness in his mind which the blow to his hopes had aroused. He waved to the ladies to be seated for they had all risen with the exception of his wife to curtsey.

"Pray do not disturb the charming picture you make," he said smiling, but his wife knew that something had disturbed him for she was well aware of his changing moods and she dismissed her women that she might be alone with her husband.

"Stephen," she said, "you have had bad news."

"Have I betrayed it, then?" he asked.

"Only to me who know you so well," she answered.

He sat down on the faldestol and leaned his head against her knee. She touched his luxuriant hair and was happy because in this disappointment, whatever it was, he had come to her.

He was thinking: My meek Matilda. She is a good wife to me. I would that they had given her a different name though. Matilda! Small wonder that when I hear that name I must always think of that other Matilda. But she excited him not at all, this dear good little wife of his, and never had, even in the early days of their marriage.

"You come from the King," said Matilda, gently.

"Ay, from the King."

"Stephen. He is not displeased with you!"

"Nay. I am still his good nephew. He has told me that he intends to marry."

She was silent. She understood perfectly. Stephen had been disappointed of his hopes. Only she knew how he had longed for their fulfilment. She herself had regarded that state with apprehension, for if he were King of England she would be Queen and she knew that her nature was such as to shrink from such a position.

Gently she stroked his hair. She said: "If he married, he might not get a son."

Stephen turned his head, took the hand which caressed him and looked up into her face. "It is what I tell myself. He is an old man. Yet he is lusty still."

"The Queen could not latterly get children by him."

"Nay," said Stephen gloomily, "but others could."

"Let us wait and see. It may well be that he will not get a child, and if he does not...."

17

"If he does not," said Stephen, "who knows?"

He was gay suddenly; he was convinced now that the King was too old to get sons. Stephen's was an optimistic nature and he could always bring himself to believe what he wanted to happen.

"He loves you dearly," said Matilda. "You are as a son to him."

"I should have the people with me," said Stephen. "But Matilda, if he does not get a son, and it seems likely that he may not, he will always hope to get one and he will not name his successor because he will go on telling himself that his successor will be his own son."

"He will realize in time. You know him well. He is a man who must have his affairs in order."

"But if he were to die suddenly as his predecessor did."

"Then Stephen . . . you would be there to take care of the future."

"A younger son of my mother! Why, my brother Theobald would come before me."

"The English would never have Theobald. You have been here so long, you have made yourself popular with the people. They would choose you, Stephen."

"Yes, he said, "the people would choose me." His expression clouded temporarily. "Oh, but Matilda, how I wish that he had not decided to marry. How much better if he had named me as his successor and taught me all the ways of kingship, which is what I have dreamed he would since William died."

"Be patient, Stephen."

He smiled at her. "I needs must. I am a lucky man. I have the King's favour. I have my hopes; but my greatest treasure is the devotion of my loving wife."

Words, she thought, charming words. And before the day was out he would be sporting with his newest mistress and telling her she was the most important woman in his life. Life was hard for some women. She knew that good Matilda, her aunt for whom she had been named, had suffered in the same way as she did. The King had been affectionate towards his wife; indeed they were said to have been in love at the time of their marriage—the Queen certainly had been with the King—and she had to endure his faithlessness. Was it the fate of women?

Perhaps a convent upbringing did not prepare one for the ways of men.

18

She herself had spent her childhood in the Abbey of Bermondsey—the dear peaceful abbey where a young girl dreamed her dreams of romance, for she had known all her life that when the time came she would leave the sequestered life for that of marriage.

Her mother had made this clear to her when she had told her of the unhappy childhood she had had with her sister the Queen, when they had been sent first to Rumsey and then to Wilton Abbey to be under the care of their tyrant aunt, Christina, the Abbess.

She had visited the King's Court with her mother on one or two occasions and there she had made the acquaintance not only of Stephen, her future husband, but of her cousins William, the heir to the throne, and his sister Matilda. She had thought Stephen charming from the moment she had seen him and had been so happy that he was to be her husband. She had not known then that the charm she had thought was especially for her was for everyone and it meant little except that Stephen had a gift with words and he liked to say what he thought would best please people—which was not necessarily what he meant.

She would never forget that other Matilda—a little older than herself—forceful, handsome, demanding the attention of all the others. She had been rather glad when she had heard that Matilda had made a brilliant marriage and had gone to Germany to be an Empress. Even as a child she had had uneasy feelings that Stephen might have preferred the bold flamboyant Matilda to the self-effacing one.

There had come the happy day when she had been betrothed to Stephen, to be followed by sad ones due to her mother's death. The Countess of Boulogne had been well one day and dead the next, and strangely enough she had died in that Abbey of Bermondsey where Matilda had received her education. She was buried in the Abbey and Matilda had made many a pilgrimage to her mother's grave.

As for her father she had scarcely known him. He had been much older than her mother and it seemed to her that he was always away from home fighting with the crusades.

But she had her husband—the handsome Stephen—and she should be happy, for even though she had learned that he was not the hero she had made of him in her dreams, he was still the most attractive man at Court and, if she did not attempt to interfere with his pleasures, the kindest of husbands.

19

Now she set about soothing him, pointing out the chances against the King's producing a son. She reminded him that the King's daughter Matilda was safe in Germany.

"To whom could the King turn," she asked, "but to you?"

Henry decided that he would pay a visit to the man whose cleverness he respected more than that of anyone else in the kingdom, Roger, the Bishop of Salisbury. The journey would offer the pleasures of the chase and he could savour once more the joys of the New Forest, that beloved hunting ground of many memories.

Roger was a man of the world, a man of charm and tolerance in spite of the fact that he was a churchman. He had been discovered by Henry in Caen where he had called attention to himself by the speedy manner in which he could get through Mass. This had amused and pleased Henry and it had occurred to him that there was something more to the man than a small living in a remote spot warranted.

He had offered Roger advancement which the priest had gratefully accepted and Roger had left his little Normandy town and come to England with the King. Advancement had rapidly followed, for Roger had shown himself to be a very astute statesman and although he had become Bishop of Salisbury he was more than a man of the Church. He was one of Henry's chief ministers and during the King's many absences in Normandy had played a leading part in the control of State affairs.

Roger was also one of the richest and most influential men in the country; and it was with him that Henry decided to discuss the steps he would take to put his plan into action.

The journey to Salisbury was pleasant, enlivened as it was by hunting on the way and stopping at the castles of his loyal subjects who did all they knew to cheer him. There was a banquet always awaiting him; and among the company he invariably found a beautiful lady to enchant him; so he forgot temporarily how ill life had served him and his irascibility scarcely showed itself.

The New Forest was full of memories and the greatest of course was of that fateful day when his brother William, known as Rufus, had ridden out to the hunt in the full vigour of his health and had been carried back the next day a corpse in an old cart. Henry could still live through those emotions of twenty years ago.

He could clearly see that battered body, bloody and mud-spattered with twigs and grasses caught up in it—parts of the forest which many said had killed him. How many men had Rufus commanded to lose their eyes, their ears, their noses because they had dared trap and steal one of the King's deer. How many had cursed Rufus—and his father before him—because their homes had been taken from them and they left penniless because the King needed a great forest in which to follow the sport he loved. It was said that the spirits of those men haunted the forest and looked constantly for revenge.

In that case he, Henry, should be wary, for although he had brought justice to the land and many praise him for it, he had done nothing to change the cruel forestry laws and the curses of the dead men would fall on him as they had on his dead brother and father. Strange that he, like them, cared nothing for this. The chase of wild animals was as much a passion with him as with other members of his family and nothing must stand in the way of it.

He remembered that ride to Winchester when he had battled for his future and his crown had depended on the speed of his arrival there. He was the younger brother and there was an elder one—Robert, Duke of Normandy—and he had known that there were Normans in Normandy and in England, too, who would think that Robert had a greater claim to the throne than he had. By good fortune and the making of many promises—which alas he had found it impossible to keep—he had succeeded in taking the crown and keeping it for twenty years. Moreover he had taken Normandy from his brother who now languished in a Cardiff prison; he could say that since that fateful day in the New Forest, when Rufus had met a mysterious death, he had achieved a great deal.

Never had he felt so secure—although of course he must expect further trouble in Normandy—and then at the height of his triumph the White Ship had foundered and he had lost his son and heir.

So here he was brought back to the melancholy fact which was after all the reason for his visit to the Bishop of Salisbury.

Roger was waiting to greet him at his palace and at his side was Matilda of Ramsbury, Roger's mistress. Matilda was a very beautiful woman and the King eyed her with approval. He did not blame Roger in the least for openly keeping such a mistress although there was a law that members of the clergy were not to marry and many who had done so before

21

this law had been brought into force, had been excommunicated, driven out of their livings and forced to beg for their
bread.

This had caused the late Queen much distress and her
pleading for the displaced clergy had irritated her husband
who could do nothing about the matter, for it was one of the
conditions of his reconciliation with the Church. What had
aroused the Queen's indignation was the fact that rich and
powerful churchmen like Roger openly kept their mistresses,
flagrantly ignoring the demands of their calling; and Roger's
nephew Nigel, who had been made Bishop of Ely, was married and made no secret of it.

Henry had never been able to make his wife understand
the necessity for compromise. Matilda was too good; that had
been her great failing. Well, now she was dead and here was
another reason why he must consult with Roger without delay.

"It does me good to see you, my friend," said the King, and
kissing the beautiful Matilda warmly, he added: "And you
too, my dear. I see that you have taken good care of my
friend."

They went into the palace talking merrily and everyone
was relieved to see the good mood of the King.

There was a splendid banquet, for Roger lived in good
style, and minstrels entertained them for a while but the
Bishop was well aware that the King was impatient to talk
seriously and so it was not long before he had carried him
off to his private chamber.

"Roger," said the King, "I am beset by my cares. You know
full well how I have felt since the tragedy."

"Alas, my lord."

"I must get an heir. If my daughter Matilda were not in
Germany I should make all swear fealty to her, but a woman,
Roger! How would a woman fare?"

"If any woman could rule a realm that woman would
doubtless be the Empress, my lord. She showed great spirit
and was indeed what one would expect a daughter of yours
to be."

"The country needs a man. Why has God so forsaken me,
Roger, by taking my only son?"

"God works in a mysterious way," said Roger piously, remembering briefly that he was a member of the Church.

"You think I should accept this Divine decision. You think
I should appoint—say, my nephew, as my heir?"

Stephen! thought Roger. God forbid. He knew that Stephen would not favour him. Certainly it must not be Stephen.

"Nay, my lord, I don't think you should despair."

"How so? When I have no son... to follow me and no wife by whom I could get one."

Roger understood his lord. He wanted him to suggest he do what Henry had already made up his mind to do. Well, that suited Roger. Get the King married; let him get a child and that child be educated by the Church, which meant the Bishop of Salisbury. He would be moulded into a future king with a correct appreciation of Roger and his family. There was Roger's son, Roger le Poer, born of his dear Matilda; there was his nephew Nigel, already Bishop of Ely; and there was another nephew Alexander, and Roger had the bishopric of Lincoln in mind for him. Roger wanted a powerful ring of the members of his own family, all dabbling in state affairs, all working for the administration under the King of course, who would bring not only good to the country but to the family as well.

He said therefore: "My lord, you could take a wife."

The King's expression lightened. "I confess it has been in my mind."

"The idea of marriage may be distasteful to you," said Roger soothingly, "but you will do it, I doubt not, for the good of the kingdom."

The idea of marriage distasteful! The thought of a new woman could never be that. Roger knew it but he wanted to placate the King who was not his usual shrewd self. Henry needed wooing from this irascibility which was beginning to be turned on all those about him—even favourites. The prospect of a marriage with a young and attractive woman would help a great deal.

"Yes," said the King, "I would marry that I might give the country an heir."

"The question arises, whom would you marry?"

"That is what we must discover."

"The bride should be young, my lord."

"Well," replied the King, "I am not so young myself. I have a fancy for a mature woman, one in her late twenties. A widow mayhap who has already proved herself capable of bearing sons."

A widow! A strong-minded woman of mature age. A new influence on the King. No, thought Roger. A young girl would be better. A young girl who could be moulded.

"A young virgin would be more to your taste," said Roger.

"They can be a little tiresome," said the King. "I am not of an age to do much wooing."

"Nay, the girl would be overawed by your rank, by your greatness. Older women can be shrews."

"The Queen was never that."

"Ah, but you moulded her to your ways. She was a virgin untried in all ways when she came to you. You were able to make of her what you wished."

"She had a mind of her own, Roger. She did not agree with me in all things." He smiled wryly. "The Church for one thing. I can't tell you how horrified she was when she heard of your living here with your Matilda."

Roger nodded. We want no more of that, he thought. Most definitely a young girl for the King.

And because he had expected that marriage would be a prospect which would soon come into the King's mind he had already thought of a possible bride for him.

She was young, some eighteen years of age, a fair virgin of not too grand a house so that she might be overawed by marriage with the King of England and grateful to the man who had helped to arrange it.

Roger began to talk of the allure of young virgins and he and the King exchanged accounts of their adventures as they had done on other occasions, but with the prospect of marriage before him the King found the talk amusing and stimulating.

During the discourse Roger mentioned the girl he had had in mind since the question of the King's remarriage had occurred to him.

"I hear the Duke of Brabant has a beautiful daughter," he said.

"The Duke of Brabant?" repeated the King thoughtfully.

"Some seventeen years of age, a delicious virgin. I have heard her referred to as the Fair Maid of Brabant. She and her family would be overcome with joy to be united with the royal house of England."

"What do you know of this maiden, Roger?"

"Only that she is young, ready for marriage and can trace her descent to Charlemagne."

"She does not sound impossible," mused the King.

Roger was amused. Negotiations should begin without delay. The King should have his young bride and this would mean an end to Stephen's hopes, which was exactly what Roger wanted.

In the court at Mainz the Empress Matilda was thinking of England. She had done little more since she had heard of the death of her brother William in the White Ship. Often she wished she were home. Often she thought of her cousin Stephen. Was he thinking of her, she wondered, or had he contented himself with his meek little wife? Was he roaming the countryside sporting with mistress after mistress—and doing so, did he ever give a thought to his cousin Matilda?

Matilda lay in her ornate bed—the Imperial bed—and thought of her husband—poor doddering Henry! What could one expect from a man nearly sixty years of age, although her father was in his fifties and by all accounts as virile as ever. How unfortunate that she, Matilda, should have been given a husband teetering on the edge of senility.

There had been no child of the marriage. That did not surprise anyone. If her father had known that the White Ship was going to founder would he have given her to Stephen? From all accounts Stephen was ingratiating himself with all those who could bring good to him. Clever Stephen! Handsome Stephen! How flattered he would be if he knew how often she remembered him!

"It is only because, Master Stephen, I am married to this impotent old man and as the Empress I am not allowed to take lovers," she murmured. "It would be treason I believe and I have no desire to be done away with. If I had had other lovers I would have forgotten you, as you, libertine that you are, have no doubt forgotten me in your numerous love adventures."

To speak to him as though he were there was a great comfort. In spite of the fact that it was nearly seven years since she had seen him, she could picture him clearly.

Heaven help me, she thought, I must have truly loved that man.

Why? she asked herself. It was because they were so different. She had criticized him, argued with him and would often have liked to fight him physically wounding him, so greatly did he irritate her. But fighting with Stephen would have been more stimulating than being affectionate with anyone else. She had often wondered what it would have been like to make love with Stephen.

So near they had come to that...dangerously near. But

25

always it was Stephen who held off. That was another difference in their natures. Stephen was cautious as she never would be. Stephen thought before he acted; she never did. When her fury was raging she never stopped to think of consequences. Stephen's temper was always in control—or almost always. That smooth tongue of his continued saying charming, soothing things which he did not mean. Deceiver, she thought. And yet people loved him for it.

She had loved him for it. She remembered the clever manner in which he had brought peace in the schoolroom, simply because he did not want to be involved in strife. Stephen wanted people to love him, to find him charming; he could not bear to have even one person dislike him, whereas she, imperious, demanding, cared not whether people loved or hated her as long as she had her way. "I am strong," she used to argue, "you are weak, Stephen. You want to rely on the friendship of others. I can stand by myself." "You will see, when you are older, who is right and who is wrong," Stephen had retorted. "You will learn that it is never wise to make enemies."

How she longed for those verbal battles, which had given such spice to the old life. She could see herself with flashing eyes and Stephen lolling elegantly on a faldestol laughing at her with veiled desire in his eyes.

She wanted to go home. She wanted to see Stephen again.

She looked up at the frame of the bedstead which was elegantly carved and inlaid with metal and enamel. It was very grand, this bed in which it had been hoped that she would bear the Emperor a son.

She was pleased that this had never come to pass. It never would now. She had often wondered what would happen to her if her father died, for now that William was dead she, Matilda, was the heiress of England, or would have been had they not married her into Germany.

As the wife of the Emperor she would never be accepted as Queen of England. She could imagine the barons and bishops putting their heads together and deciding that to bring Matilda back to England and make her Queen would be against everything they believed to be right. In the first place she was a woman and they would consider it beneath their dignity to be ruled by a woman. In the second place they would not accept the wife of the Emperor as Queen of England. They would suspect Germany of trying to unite the two countries. No, never while the Emperor lived....

Of course he would not live for ever.

While she lay in bed Henry came into the chamber. Poor old Henry, he sat down heavily on the faldestol, seeming a little breathless, his eyes somewhat vague as they often had been for some time.

He looked at his beautiful young wife and his eyes brightened a little. She was a very handsome girl with her long hair flowing about her and those proud flashing eyes.

He half rose from his stool.

You foolish old man, thought Matilda scornfully, you haven't the strength.

"My love," he said, "not yet risen."

"Nay," she answered. "I will rise when I have a mind to."

"Yes, yes." She had made it clear on her arrival in Germany when she was little more than twelve years old that she would have her way. Then he had been very willing to indulge her. A beautiful, clever child wife and he an ailing man even then.

She compared him now with Stephen and she felt the familiar mingling of longing and resentment.

"News from England," he said. "I thought you would like to hear it, my dear."

She felt angry. News from England and it went to him. Her father should send news to her. Was she not his daughter? But she was merely the Empress. She was a woman. She was going to show people that a woman could be as forceful, as shrewd a ruler as a man.

Yes, a ruler. She had always wanted it. A ruler in her own right. A ruler of England. That was what she had always wanted. How she had railed against being born a girl. She would have been a better ruler than William ever could. Poor William. But one must not say ought against the dead because that brought ill luck. Yet had she been the son instead of the daughter, she would never have been so foolish as to get drowned on the White Ship for she did hear that there had been far too much merry-making on that ship before it set sail and that many of the crew had been drunk. But ever since the death of William she had had in her mind that one day she would go back to England and be its Queen.

The stumbling block was the Emperor—poor senile old man—for while he lived she must stay here. Her consolation was that he could not live for ever.

The forests of England seemed greener than these; she longed to be riding through them. The deer there were more

27

fleet, and boars more wild; the minstrels' songs were more appealing; the people were more gay. That she should think so was, she knew, a symptom of homesickness. Well, she was homesick for England and obsessed by a desire to claim her dues. And more than anything she wished to see Stephen.

"Stephen," she would say, "I am a widow now. There is no longer the need for caution...."

She could imagine his response.

And if she were indeed the Queen! She pictured his kneeling to do his homage. Their eyes would meet; there would be understanding between them. You are my lover, Stephen, she would convey to him, but never forget that I am not only your mistress in the bedchamber but in the State also.

Exciting dreams—and this old man stood between her and them—and even when there was news from England her father must needs send it to the Emperor, not to his daughter.

"You are breathless, Henry," she said. "Has this news so excited you?"

"Nay. You know what my breathing is like."

Yes, poor old man, she thought. Soon I doubt not it will cease to be at all. Then I shall be free.

She nodded as though with compassion. "This news from England. What is it?"

"There is to be a marriage."

"A marriage? Who is to marry then?"

"The King no less."

"My father? He is an old man."

The Emperor smiled. "He is some seven years younger than I."

For a moment her eyes were cruel. She wanted to say: "And that is too old for marriage." But she curbed her tongue.

"It is but two years since my mother died."

"It is a reasonable time for mourning. And since your brother's death...."

She nodded. Since her brother's death! The foundering of the White Ship had had its effect on all of them, and that which had brought despair to her father had set hopes soaring in his daughter's heart.

"So it is the need to get an heir," she said and there was a constricted feeling in her throat which had its source in bitter anger. He would marry again, get a son, and that would be the end of Matilda's hopes.

"Of a certainty," replied the Emperor. "For what other reason should he wish for marriage? He has chosen the lady."

"And who is she?"

"Adelicia of Louvaine."

"I know nothing of her."

The Emperor smiled again. "Your father would not think it necessary to ask your approval, my love."

"Adelicia of Louvaine," she repeated. "Is she young? Is she likely to give him an heir?"

"You may rest assured that as far as these mysteries are known to men the answer to that is yes."

She wanted to rage; she wanted to throw her pillow at this old man. It was always difficult to control her violent temper. Stephen had laughed at it, Stephen who was always calm and amiable.

She said: "I will rise now. I must offer my congratulations to my father."

The Emperor nodded. "We must both do that."

Unsteadily he rose. He looked at her and she thought he was coming to the bed. She drew her thick brows together in a frown and he turned away.

She would shout at him in a moment. She was so infuriated. Her father to marry! What if the new bride proved fertile! She could have many sons. And Matilda, who had been one step from the throne, would be pushed so far back that she could never hope to reach it.

The Wedding and Coronation

Princess Adelicia of Louvaine knew that something important was about to happen for envoys from a foreign land had arrived at her father's castle and there had been much serious talk between them and her parents; that the matter concerned her she was also aware and when a Princess became a matter of State this could mean one thing, and that was marriage.

She had been expecting it for she had passed her seventeenth birthday. That she was not already married was doubtless due to the fact no suitor had yet been considered worthy of her. Her mother had descended from great Charlemagne himself, a fact which she neither forgot herself or allowed her family to

Her sister was watching her covertly, but Adelicia pretended to be absorbed by her needlework, for which she was famed. Such work as she did with silk and gold thread was considered to be a woman's greatest asset. In the long ago days when she had been no more than five years old her governesses used to say to her: "Now, Adelicia, that will not do. You will never have a grand husband if you do not persevere with your needle."

She wondered why husbands should set such store by fine needlework; and if that was all hers looked for, he should be well pleased. The standard she had worked for her father to carry during the battle was said to be a masterpiece.

Her sister said: "They say the messengers have come from England."

"From England," repeated Adelicia. She knew of England, of course. Who did not? The King of England was often in Normandy which he had taken from his brother. The King of England, who was also the Duke of Normandy, was one of the most powerful men in Europe.

"I wonder on whose behalf they come," went on her sister. "It cannot be for the King, though he is recently widowed, for he is a very old man, too old for marriage."

Adelicia said: "Why should you suppose they come to talk of marriage? Could it not be of other matters?"

"Nay, 'tis marriage. All say so. And that means you, Adelicia, for you are the eldest. My turn will come next."

Adelicia shivered slightly. It was alarming to contemplate giving up all that had been home during one's lifetime to go away to a foreign land.

She returned to her stitching .

"How you can go on working at such a time I can't imagine," said her sister impatiently. "If a husband were to be offered to me I would be so excited."

Adelicia smiled. Inwardly she was far from calm, but of what use would it be to give vent to her feelings? She must wait and see. At that moment a serving woman appeared and said that the Duke, her father, wished to see her without delay.

Calmly she laid aside her needlework and rose.

Her sister watched her with round eyes. "I can't wait to hear, Adelicia," she said. "Promise to come straight back and tell me."

Adelicia went sedately to her father's apartment.

"Come in, daughter," he said.

Her mother was there too. The Countess took her in her arms and kissed her ceremoniously.

She is pleased, thought Adelicia. So it must be someone worthy of her blood.

"My dear child, a great honour," murmured the Duke. "But be seated."

Godfrey of Louvaine was tender. It was sad, he thought, that girls should be taken from their homes. But this was life and it happened to all. He loved his eldest daughter dearly. He cherished the beautiful standard she had made for him and often regretted that rulers such as himself must be forced to leave their homes so often in order to protect or regain their patrimony. Men must go away to fight and women must go away to marry. It was, alas, the accepted order of things.

He stroked his smooth cheek—a habit he had acquired thirteen years or so before when he had shaved it. He was even now known as Godfrey Barbatus because before the year 1107 he had worn a luxuriant beard. He had made a vow that he would not shave this beard until he recovered Lower Lorraine which had belonged to his ancestors. Now his smooth face proclaimed to the world that he had regained that which had been lost to his family.

"My dear child," he said, "you know that envoys have been arriving here at the castle. They come from England and you may have guessed for what purpose. You are a child no longer and it has long been my wish, and that of your mother, to find a husband for you."

"A *suitable* husband," said the Duchess.

"He must indeed be worthy of our house, and so we are now well pleased."

Adelicia waited in trepidation.

"You have guessed, daughter," said her mother. "They come from England and there is only one whom we could consider."

Her father put in: "The King of England is asking for your hand."

"The King of England! But he is an old man."

"He is a king," said her mother reprovingly.

"Fifty is not so old," said her father soothingly. "And the King of England is a man who has kept his youth."

She was afraid. An old man! What had she heard of him? He was the son of the Conqueror who was spoken of throughout the land with awed respect.

She wanted to fall on her knees and beg of them to allow her to stay with them, so frightened was she at the prospect of going to England.

She looked from one parent to another but neither would meet her appealing gaze.

"It is a brilliant match," said the Duchess. "There is to be no delay. The King is very eager for the marriage to take place at once."

"He has heard excellent reports of you," said her father.

"Of a certainty he has," reported the Duchess. "What else could he hear of such a well brought up girl? The documents will be signed and the wedding take place without delay. That is the wish of the King."

Adelicia turned to them, her eyes wide, but they pretended not to notice her panic. Her father said: "The King was a good husband to his first wife. How much more so will he cherish one who is so much younger and more beautiful." He came to her and stroked her hair. "All will be well, dearest

33

child. It is necessary that you marry and this is an excellent match. It could not be better. You will be happy with the King of England."

"You will be his Queen," said her mother. "And I doubt not that you will soon be the mother of his heir."

That was what frightened her. She had only vague ideas as to what must precede her giving birth to an heir, but what she knew terrified her.

Solemnly her parents kissed her.

It was like the sealing of a bond. This meant that she must be handed over to her husband and that all the ceremonies that must go before that final event, after which there could be no turning back, were about to begin.

So she was to go away to England. Her parents were rejoicing because the King of England on the signing of the contract had promised a magnificent settlement.

"What a generous man!" cried the Duchess.

Her husband replied that the King of England was known to be one who liked to see every penny accounted for, and even those who admired him most had never called him generous.

"Then," replied the Duchess, "it is even more admirable, for in this he shows clearly that he appreciates our daughter."

The King was in no mood to wait for the marriage. He was going to call at the castle and take his bride back to England.

The Duke was wary. "Should he be allowed to take our daughter away without first marrying her?" he asked.

"On such a settlement, yes," retorted his wife. Did the Duke think that he would have paid so handsomely for a wife when he had no intention of making her such! Besides, all knew that the King was ageing. He must get an heir soon if he were to get one at all.

So it was arranged. The King should come to Louvaine in person and when he left Adelicia should go with him. His people would insist that the marriage ceremony took place in England, so the Princess would travel back in his train and as soon as they reached England the marriage would be solemnized.

"Is it to be so soon then?" asked Adelicia.

She was assured that it was, and preparations immediately began throughout the castle.

Her sister had discovered a little about the bridegroom,

34

for there was a great deal of whispering in the castle and she was not averse to keeping her ears alert for what was not intended for them. She wondered whether it would be wiser to tell Adelicia or leave her to discover for herself, but finally decided that it would be better for her sister to be prepared.

Adelicia had always been such a dreamer and as she sat over her needlework had imagined herself as one of the romantic figures which she created with her tiny silken stitches. Adelicia was indeed not unlike them in appearance, for she was the beauty of the family; her long golden hair made a delightful frame for her beautiful features and her wide blue eyes looked out placidly from her oval face. Adelicia had always been the peacemaker in the family. Whatever her fate she would meet it stoically but, reasoned her more worldly-wise though younger sister, she should be made aware of what she might have to face. So as they sat in the window seat looking down to the winding road which led up to the moat and drawbridge, her sister said to Adelicia: "I know for whom you look."

"He will come soon," said Adelicia. "He will come riding at the head of his company."

"Indeed so. That is what all the preparations are for. There will be such a banquet. Our father does not entertain a king every day and one who will be his son-in-law. Why he must be as old as Father himself. Is that not odd? A son-in-law as old as his father-in-law."

"I doubt not it has been so, many times before."

"Oh, yes, old men like to marry young girls. I wonder what it will be like, Adelicia, married to an old man."

"They say he is young for his years."

"But what years! Fifty-two years of age! Oh, Adelicia."

Adelicia did not answer.

"They say women like him, and he likes women well. So there is little doubt that he will be fond of you."

"I shall hope to please him."

"You will. You know you are very beautiful, Adelicia."

"Let us hope that he will think so."

"He'll be blind if he does not. They say it is time he married for so much does he love women he will get more and more bastards if he does not."

Adelicia said sternly: "You talk with impropriety."

"I speak the truth, sister. Listen. Do you hear horses?" She was at the window. "It is! I believe it is! Look at the standard!"

Adelicia needed no admonition to look. She could not take her eyes from the riders; they came nearer and she clearly saw the man at the head of them. He was by no means young—had she expected him to be?—but he was not ill-favoured.

Nearer and nearer they came.

There was tension throughout the castle, the sound of running feet and voices shouting to each other.

"It is the King of England."

The drawbridge was lowered. Adelicia saw her mother in the courtyard; in her hand the great goblet which was brought out for only the most honoured visitors. The Duke stood beside her. And there was the King of England seated on his horse, looking noble and big in his armour, taking the cup of cheer and welcome from her mother; and her father himself held the King's stirrup while he dismounted.

So the King of England came to the castle of the Duke of Louvaine.

Her women dressed her with greatest care, chattering as they did so. They put on her long blue gown with the hanging sleeves and the beautiful embroidered band which she had wrought herself, around the long skirt; they combed her long hair and she wore it flowing about her shoulders. Never had she looked so beautiful, whispered her women.

Her mother came to the chamber to take her down to the banqueting hall and there in an antechamber she came face to face with her future husband.

He was less tall than he had seemed from below. He was of medium height and broad-chested; his plentiful black hair was flecked with white; there was a steadiness about his gaze which was comforting. He looked younger than his fifty-two years and there was a charm about him which was reassuring.

Certainly he was not the bridegroom of her dreams; how could he be, this ageing widower? But he was less forbidding than the picture her tortured imagination had conjured up, and she was grateful for that.

He took her hand and bowed; his eyes took in each detail. She is beautiful indeed, he thought. Reports have not lied. But his heart sank a little because she was so young and clearly inexperienced. He was too old, as he had said, for over-much wooing. He preferred a mature woman, eager and passionate as himself. He could name a few. Nesta was at

36

the head of the list—wild incomparable Nesta, Princess of Wales, who long ago had been his beloved mistress even before his first marriage. He would have married Nesta had it been possible; but when he had been a young prince with nothing but his hopes dependent on the generosity of his supporters, he had been in no position to marry, and after he had seized the crown it had been necessary that he should marry his Saxon princess, Matilda of Scotland. He had always been mindful of the fact that he was a king first and his crown must come before all else.

It was for this reason that he must now marry, to get an heir; had he acted according to his inclinations he would have continued to make merry with his mistresses. But he must get a son. He was growing old and there was not much time left for begetting. Moreover, it had been hinted by his priests that, as each day he took a step nearer to that one when he must answer for his sins, he would be well advised to curb the merry life of sexual indulgence which he had followed since his early teens, all through the years of his first marriage until this time.

Dreary old age! When a man must be concerned at having no heir and at the same time curb his pleasures on earth lest he should find himself, through this indulgence, debarred from sharing those of heaven.

He should be grateful that the girl was a beauty. Slender, as young girls were, she did not look like a breeder of men. She must be. That was the purpose of the marriage. She was pleasant to look at; he liked her docile looks in a wife, though he would have cared for more spirit in a mistress.

He kissed her hand tenderly; he felt her tremble slightly. Poor child, she had nothing to fear from him. He wondered if she had heard of his reputation with women. No doubt she had—or would—and be shocked by it. Poor little simpleton, she would not know that he would be kinder to her out of his experience of her sex and his fondness for it than a more moral man might have been!

"You are beautiful," he said. "I am sure we shall be happy."

She did feel happier.

She sat beside him at the banquet and he talked to her about his Court and life in England. He told her too, of his sorrow when his son William was drowned on the White Ship; he did not mention that two illegitimate children of his were drowned at the same time. Tears filled her eyes and her sympathy made her feel drawn towards him.

"You will comfort me for my loss," he said. "You and you alone can do it. We will have a fine son ere long and then I shall cease to mourn."

She nodded and her fear of what this would mean was replaced by her desire to soothe him.

"Would we could be married this day," he said. "But I am a king and there are times when kings must needs be governed by their subjects. They will wish to see me married. And my Archbishop must perform the ceremony. But have no fear, I shall lose no time in making you my Queen."

Adelicia's parents were delighted with the impression their daughter was making on her future husband and pleased that she did not regard him with the abhorrence they had feared. Adelicia had always been a good and obedient girl but even she might have felt some rebellion to be taken from her home and given to an old man.

There was much feasting and revelry through the castle and in due course the cavalcade set out for the coast and embarkation to England.

During the journey the King had become more and more enamoured of his bride, but as it would have been most unseemly to take a mistress while his prospective bride was travelling in his suite and he was unaccustomed to going so long without the solace of feminine company, the waiting was indeed irksome.

He had found his bride not unintelligent. She lacked the erudition of Matilda, his first wife, but then few women had received the education she had had. He himself had always favoured scholars and was indeed a scholar himself. He had been the only one of his brothers to take kindly to book learning and because of his proficiency in this field had earned the name "Beauclerc". Adelicia could never be the companion Matilda had been; but she was perhaps more meek. He did not expect she would excite him as his mistresses did; nevertheless lovemaking with her would be a pleasure; and in view of the fact that there would be this dedicated purpose behind it he was eager to begin.

He had begun to charm her with his conversation and subtle compliments; and by the time they reached Ely, she was eager to do all that he wished. He could, of course, have taken her to his bed before they reached Windsor and the actual marriage ceremony took place.

That could be dangerous. What if he got her with child as

he so hoped to do at the earliest moment and met his end before the ceremony. There would be a disaster; and the child would be just another of his bastards.

No. If he were to take her to bed before and during the tedious journey to Windsor, then a ceremony there must be.

He sent for his priest and told him of his dilemma.

"My lord," was the answer, "the marriage must be solemnized with all ceremony due to the King and his new Queen."

"I know it, I know it," said the King with a return to that irascibility which all had dreaded and which had abated considerably during the wooing period. "But you know my ardent nature. Would you have me anticipate the marriage vows?"

"My lord, you would perjure your soul. And the Princess is no ordinary woman to be taken at your pleasure."

"I know that well, man. So there must be a ceremony. Oh, nothing to make a noise about. A few words said over us. Come. No more arguments. Arrange it."

And so it was arranged.

There at Ely the words were spoken and Adelicia became the wife of Henry I of England.

He found her submissive but not responsive; it was as he had thought.

Still, she was beautiful; she was young and appealing; and once she had a healthy boy growing within her he would be content.

The royal party made its way from Ely to Windsor and there waiting to greet them at the castle was Henry's old friend and chief adviser, Roger, Bishop of Salisbury. With him was his beautiful mistress, Matilda of Ramsbury whom Adelicia presumed to be his wife. She was a little puzzled because she had been under the impression that the clergy were not permitted to marry.

Roger was respectful; the beautiful Matilda was kind and as there had been so many strange revelations in her life during the last months, Adelicia accepted this as yet another. The laws of England must be different from those in her country.

Matilda carried Adelicia off to her apartments and there, with the assistance of a few women, helped her change her habit and prepare for the banquet which would celebrate their arrival.

Adelicia was struck by the outstanding beauty of Matilda

and could scarcely take her eyes from her; she seemed awkward in her presence and very, very young.

"You are going to be very happy," Matilda told her. "The King will be an indulgent husband if you do all you can to please him."

She was comforted.

In the meantime Roger had accompanied the King to his chamber and they talked alone together.

"The marriage," said Roger, "should take place without delay for you are an impatient man, my lord."

"Did you think, Roger, I would wait for the ceremony? We are already bedded."

"To my lord's satisfaction, I trust."

"She is a child, Roger. No more."

"I believe you are not averse to a young virgin."

"Virgin she doubtless was and is so no longer. I trust by now that the seed has been well and truly planted."

"It is a matter for rejoicing, my lord. But the ceremony?"

"The priest married us at Ely and every night since, she has been in my bed."

"So there was a ceremony. That pleasures me for there are spies who watch our movements. I doubt not there would be indignation from the Duke of Louvaine were he to hear that his daughter had lost her virginity without gaining a marriage contract."

"Nay. I married her, but I'll do so again for the sake of the people. It would never do for it to be set abroad that there had been no ceremony. There would always be those to declare that the child which I pray is now growing within her, were a bastard."

"The marriage must take place without delay and since Windsor is within my diocese I claim the right to perform it."

"And old Ralph of Canterbury?"

"He is in his dotage. Nay, I'll marry you here and there should be no delay, for the child the Queen gives you must be born within the correct space of time after the nuptials which have already taken place."

"Oh, never fear. When she tells me she is with child, I'll rejoice no matter if the child arrives a little soon for decency."

"Then I will make all preparations for the ceremony," answered Roger.

It was hardly to be expected that the Archbishop of Canterbury would stand by while Roger of Salisbury snatched his privileges from under his nose.

Roger, who was an extremely ambitious man, was, however, determined not to lose one point in the battle for power. To marry the King and his new Queen would establish him in the eyes of the country as not only the most important man of the State—under the King, of course—but of the Church also.

It had been before Christmas when the party had arrived at Windsor and the King wished the matter to be settled before the season's celebrations began.

"My one concern," he said, "is that the ceremony be performed with expedition."

But by this time, the news that Roger of Salisbury was to perform the marriage ceremony had spread throughout the country and Ralph and his adherents began to raise their protests.

The Archbishop's envoy arrived and demanded an audience with the King. Henry was exasperated but realized the need to placate Ralph. "You must explain to the Archbishop," he said, "that I have made these arrangements because he partially lost his speech when he was overtaken by a fit which paralysed his lips to some extent and I believe that he would willingly forgo the irksome task of marrying us and that Roger, in his health and strength, would willingly perform the duty for him."

Ralph laughed this explanation to scorn. All knew of the ambitions of Roger of Salisbury. All knew that he was living openly with his mistress. It was not fitting that such a man who was living an immoral life should perform the marriage ceremony for the King and Queen, and moreover it was improper because to conduct such a ceremony was the prerogative of the Archbishop of Canterbury and no other.

The King's ill temper flared up. He was heartily tired of Archbishops who thought because they were head of the Church of England—under the Pope of course—that they ruled the land. He had come through one quarrel with his Archbishop of Canterbury, Anselm, and he was not going through another.

Ralph immediately called an ecclesiastical council, the object of which was to decide whether the ceremony should be performed by the Bishop in whose diocese the royal pair were residing, or by the Archbishop of Canterbury who declared he had jurisdiction over all dioceses.

Meanwhile the King chafed. He had devoted himself to Adelicia, taking no mistresses, and he daily expected to hear that she was with child. Delay irritated him.

Adelicia was getting to know the Court. There was Stephen, the King's nephew, a handsome and very charming man who was gracious to her; she liked his wife Matilda very much for she was gentle and pleasant and told Adelicia how well she understood the strangeness she must be feeling now.

"Stephen is a courteous gentleman and has never shown aught but kindness to me," Matilda told her, "but I well remember the first weeks of Court life after my marriage and how strange it all was after the Abbey where I was educated."

Adelicia replied that she too found it very strange, but the King was kind to her and she would in time grow as contented with her lot as Matilda was with hers.

Matilda did not tell Adelicia how she was tormented by the infidelities of her husband as it seemed very likely the Queen would be in due course by those of hers, for once Adelicia was with child, Matilda knew that the King, having done his duty, would seek his pleasure in other quarters.

The commission finally decided that the honour of marrying the royal pair belonged to the Archbishop of Canterbury.

Ralph was triumphant and immediately set out for Windsor. Roger was angry. This meant more to him than performing a ceremony. It was a set-back to power. His goal was to see his family in all the important positions in the country and with a doddering old Archbishop as the Primate, he had believed he was already at the head of the Church.

Henry placated him. "Never mind, Roger. The old man has right on his side. And the council is behind him. He'll have to perform the ceremony. There's no doubt of that and I cannot put it off any longer. We shall have to have the Queen crowned though. That will be at Westminster and I promise you you shall officiate at that ceremony."

Roger was appeased.

Ralph d'Escures made his painful journey from Canterbury to Windsor.

He had not been the same since his seizure and found travelling a great burden to him. Nevertheless he was not going to allow that upstart Roger of Salisbury to usurp his place, which was what he was trying to do on every occasion.

42

It was scandalous that Roger should live openly with his mistress. The King should order him to dismiss the woman. Perhaps it was not easy for a man who had had more mistresses than any in England to ask a subject to dismiss one. But kings were kings and allowed such a licence, though it was to be deplored; while churchmen who defied the law of Holy Church deserved excommunication.

Roger with his Matilda of Ramsbury and their sons and his nephew, who had a wife, made their own laws of which poorer members of the clergy were not allowed to avail themselves. Ralph wondered that the King, who was so meticulous in many ways, should allow this. It must be because he valued Roger and was eager to give him special privileges; moreover being nothing more or less than a lecher himself, he looked leniently on that sin in others.

Ralph regarded himself as a virtuous man because he had not been tormented for many years by any desires for women. Now that he was paralysed and his speech was impaired, a poor old man on the edge of the grave, naturally he gave no thought to such matters—except to condemn others who made them a too important part of their lives.

The King must get an heir. All agreed on that since God had seen fit to punish him by taking his only legitimate son—and small wonder. How could God have driven home the lesson better than by taking the one legitimate son of a man who had indiscriminately scattered illegitimate ones throughout the kingdom?

The Archbishop approved of the marriage and hoped God would forgive the King his past sins and favour him with a child, but he was not allowing anyone but himself to perform the ceremony.

Arriving at Windsor he was exhausted and must take to his bed. The King visited him there and reproved him for making such a journey when his health was in such poor state.

"My lord," gasped the Archbishop, speaking so that the King had to come close to hear, for his speech was at the best of times slightly slurred and when he was tired, very much so, "I know my duty."

"I had thought to spare you," said the King. "The Bishop of Salisbury in whose diocese we are was very ready and willing to perform the ceremony."

"I doubt it not," said Ralph grimly.

"Now you are here, if you should not be well enough to rise from your bed on the morrow...."

"I shall be well enough," replied the Archbishop firmly. "I have spent many hours on my knees asking God to bless your union with a child."

"I thank you," said the King, for he supposed that a man of Ralph's piety would be more likely to soften God's heart and so ensure a favourable answer to the petition than one such as himself. "I am confident I shall be so blessed. The Queen is young and I believe will bear many children."

"She is a good and pious lady," replied Ralph, "and there seems no reason why *she* should not be favoured." Ralph sighed. He was thinking of the scandals about the King. "My lord," he said, "you should pray earnestly and long...and humbly. You have fathered so many in a manner which would not find favour in God's eyes."

"Yes. He has given me many children whom I love dearly. You know my son Robert of Gloucester...." The King's voice softened when he spoke of his favourite son, Nesta's boy, the fruit of early passion such as he could never hope to reach again. "What a fine son he is! God smiled on me on the day he was born."

"He frowned on the night when the White Ship went down taking with it your only legitimate son."

"Ay, and two of the others whom I loved dearly."

"God is not mocked," replied Ralph. "Forget not that the sins we commit must be paid for."

"I paid for mine when I lost my William."

"It is for God to say whether you have paid in full."

A plague on this pious old churchman! thought the King. Why must they always prophesy evil? It was the same with Anselm. They thought themselves so good that they could see nothing but the sins of others. Men like Ralph and Anselm had nothing to be proud of. In the King's eyes, men who did not desire women—ay, and satisfy their desires—were in some measure less than men. They had no desires and preached piety over those who had. Small wonder that he wanted to see merry men like Roger the Bishop of Salisbury in the Church, men who knew what it was to desire a woman. And what a woman Matilda of Ramsbury was! She reminded him in some ways of Nesta.

He was in no mood to listen to more of Ralph's preaching. He rose.

"So," he said, "tomorrow you will conduct the ceremony."

The ceremony was performed in the chapel at Windsor and all wondered whether the aged Archbishop of Canterbury would survive it. So distorted was his speech that it was difficult to hear what he said; and during one or two moments it seemed that his tottering footsteps would falter.

The King fumed inwardly and thought what a nuisance the old man was; but he had learned, as his brother Rufus had before him, that trouble could be incurred through quarrels with the Church. He had anxieties enough. Normandy hung like a millstone about his neck. His brother Robert was incarcerated in Cardiff Castle, which was no less than he deserved, for if ever a man invited disaster that man was Robert. But Robert's son, William the Clito, still roamed Normandy and at any moment an insurrection could spring up in support of him. The governing of England, the holding of Normandy—these were troubles enough. Henry wanted no more bickering with the Church. So this old man must perforce do what he considered his duty while Roger chafed because of what had been denied him.

But there was Adelicia beside him, and she was beautiful. He wished that he could feel more enthusiasm for her. She was too young, too meek and acquiescing. Often it seemed that she was doing her painful duty. Perhaps she was. Poor girl, a stranger to the passionate ecstasy in which he had revelled with so many—but chiefly with Nesta, the incomparable mistress, now married to Gerald de Windsor, a husband he had found for her twenty years ago when he had married his first wife Matilda. Theirs had been an enduring relationship. They had made no demands on each other. How many mistresses had he taken over the years? How many lovers had shared her bed? It mattered not. She was for him, and he was for her, the best they had ever known in all their wide experience.

It was not meet that while he said his marriage vows to this young girl he should be thinking of a woman as old as himself. If God were watching he might decide that for such impiety he should have a barren marriage.

Have done with thoughts of other women. Pray that soon his Adelicia should tell him that the signs were evident.

There was feasting to celebrate the marriage; the King sat at the head of the table, his bride beside him. Roger was on his other side.

Roger was a little silent and seeking to placate him the King said: "I thought we should not get through the ceremony. I swear he nearly fell more than once."

"Doddering old idiot," grumbled Roger.

"Still my Archbishop," replied the King. He turned to the Queen. "Tomorrow, my love, to Westminster and there you shall be crowned, Queen of England in very truth."

"I thank you, my lord," said Adelicia, warmly.

The King took her hand and placed it on his thigh.

"This," he said to Roger, "is my beloved wife. God has been good to me."

"And may he continue to bless you."

"He will, I doubt not," said the King. "Soon you will see the fruit of our nights. My Queen longs for this no less than I. And we pray continually for this fulfilment."

"As all your good subjects do. And with such love between you and God's blessing, ere long you will surely have a healthy boy."

"Amen," said the King. He added: "You shall crown us both at Westminster, Roger. I dearly wish to see the crown on that fair head."

Roger smiled his triumph, spirits restored. He had failed to officiate at the King's marriage but that would be forgotten when at the important ceremony of crowning, he was the one to place the crown on the Queen's head.

Ralph lay on his straw exhausted by the day's activities. At least he had the satisfaction of knowing that he stopped that upstart from usurping his place.

He was thinking of the days of his youth—a preoccupation which increased as he grew more aged—and how peaceful those days seemed in comparison with the present day. But then he had been first a humble monk and after that a prior and abbot of the Abbey at Séez. Then he had come to England and finally, because he was a man of cheerful disposition, he had become popular. There had been some who thought he was too ready to laugh, a quality which somehow detracted from a man's piety, but since he had proved himself a man of high moral character, what might have been termed a certain frivolity was forgiven.

It was only since his seizure when he had found it so difficult to perform his duties and suffered acutely from many handicaps that he began to be irritable. And now as he lay on his bed he thought that he, being so old and infirm, could

46

not have much time left to him and he doubted he would live long enough to see the King's heir, which was what this marriage was for.

One of his servants came to him in some haste.

"My lord Archbishop," he said, "the royal party have left for Westminster."

"So soon," cried Ralph.

"My lord, the Queen is to be crowned without delay and it is said that Roger of Salisbury will perform the ceremony."

"Never," cried the Archbishop, rising from his bed. "There is only one who must do that."

"You are unfit, my lord."

"Do not advise me on whether or not I shall do my duty. Send my servants with all speed."

The blood was pounding in his head, his limbs were shaking, and the room circled round him as it did when he rose too hastily.

He cared not. He said to his servants: "Help me to dress without delay. Have everything ready for our departure. We leave for Westminster at once."

Breathlessly the Archbishop entered the Abbey. There was a gasp throughout the spectators as he walked, swaying a little yet clearly resolute, towards the altar.

Roger had reached that stage in the ceremony when the crowns had been placed on the heads of the King and Queen and Ralph was so angry that many thought he would die on the spot.

He approached the King. He cried out and his anger gave him some extra power because his words were distinctly heard by all those close to the King.

"Who has placed this crown on your head?"

Henry was abashed. Who would have believed that this sick man could so quickly have followed him. He had deliberately arranged that the ceremony should begin very early so that it would be over before there was time for repercussions. Evidently they had not been quick enough for Ralph. Crowning was an even more important occasion than the marriage, and Henry should have known that if the Archbishop had been so determined to perform one he certainly would not willingly allow any but himself to officiate at the other.

Henry was aware of the trouble that could ensue. It had been rash of him to attempt to placate Roger in this manner.

He murmured: "If the ceremony has not been performed in a proper manner, it must then be done again."

The Archbishop retorted, his eyes flashing: "Indeed, my lord, it must be done again."

And with that he lifted the strap which was fixed under the King's chin and by which the crown was held in place so that the crown fell sideways onto the King's shoulder.

There was a gasp of dismay from the spectators.

The Archbishop then took the crown and placing it firmly on the King's head proceeded with the Coronation.

Consternation followed. There were also people who saw omens—good or bad—in every event; and the fact that the King had had his crown taken off his head seemed like a bad one.

"Nonsense," said the King, who like his father preferred to see good in omens. "This is a good sign. I lost my son, and though momentarily I lost the crown from my head, it was replaced. So shall my fair young Queen refill our royal cradle. Ere long our marriage will be fruitful I promise you, for I am a young man again, through my Queen, and I know that ere long she will give me the son I crave."

So there was rejoicing throughout the land and celebrations at Court; but, although the King and Queen prayed each day that there might be a sign, there was none.

Why, oh, why, do my mistresses conceive and not my wife? the King wondered.

Henry's temper, which had improved since his marriage and the hopes of getting an heir, now became easily frayed once more. He was restless. It was a month since the official marriage and there was still no sign that Adelicia was pregnant. It was not as though they had not attempted to get a child before that. Ever since that marriage at Ely he had spent each night in her bed. And still no sign! It was ironical that he had feared they might not have the official ceremony in time.

Roger had returned to Salisbury and taken his Matilda with him. He missed their company. Stephen was amusing and his wife, another Matilda, was pleasant enough; his troubadours and minstrels did their best to entertain him but he was restless. He wanted to be young again. He was still a healthy man, but he was beginning to suffer from the irritating little ailments which came with encroaching age, and his digestion was not of the best. It was not that he was a

48

man who overate or drank excessively. Indeed he was moderate enough—except where his favourite foods were concerned. He admitted to a certain greed over lampreys which his cooks knew how to stew and serve deliciously; and he sometimes took more of this dish than was advisable—but he was abstemious in most things. It had always been women and the chase—never food and drink which had pleased him.

He enjoyed the company of Stephen, but Stephen had changed slightly. He knew his nephew must have had hopes of succeeding him. He did not blame him. Such thoughts would have entered his own mind had he been in Stephen's position. And now, for all his affection, Stephen could not help being secretly pleased that the Queen did not astonish them all by the speed with which she had conceived. This must needs put a barrier between them. Well, he could scarcely blame Stephen for being ambitious.

The sooner a son was on the way the sooner everything would be settled. Stephen would then know that he could no longer hope. But in the meantime the situation was a difficult one and there had begun to come into the King's mind a fear that the Queen might be barren.

There was one man who could usually entertain him. This was Luke de Barré, one of his best warriors, who was at the same time a poet. The verses Luke wrote were of such a nature as to amuse the King; he had known Luke since their boyhood and they had always been good friends.

Now he sent for Luke and commanded him to sing some of his latest songs.

Luke complied, and although occasionally the songs were a little ribald and now and then contained sly allusions to the King himself, Henry was amused and forgot his irritation.

While Luke sang to the company a messenger arrived. He had ridden at full speed from the Welsh border. He had brought grave news. The Welsh were marching on Chester. The Earl of Chester had recently died and it was due to this that the Welsh had revolted.

The King rose from his chair.

"There is nothing else to be done," he said, "than for me to leave for Wales without delay."

Adelicia was tearful.

It was so short a time since they had been married.

The King took her face in his hands and kissed her ten-

49

derly. "Who knows," he said, "perhaps by the time I return you will have some news for me. If you should have it, send to me wherever I am. Nothing could put me in better spirits."

"I will, my lord, and I will pray day and night."

Prayers! he thought with some impatience. Of what avail were they? Babies were got in warm beds not draughty chapels.

But let her pray. She was a good sweet child, and longed to give him what he wanted as fervently as he wished for it.

"It grieves me to leave you, my fair Queen," he said.

But already he was thinking of Wales—the home of Nesta. He was remembering how, when he had heard that his presence was needed in Wales his blood would tingle and his spirits soar; and in fact when Matilda had been alive he had invented trouble in Wales that he might have an excuse to ride to Carew Castle.

Adelicia stood at the turret watching him ride away. He turned to lift a hand to her in farewell.

"Oh, God," she prayed, "let me be with child."

It was no difficult task, old warrior that he was, to subdue the Welsh. The enemy retreated before him and he marched as far as Snowdon. It was not long before they were ready to accept him as the victor. He insisted they pay him tribute—always something which pleased him. He loved money as his father had before him. Money, land, possessions to have and to hold and never lose grip of them—for they meant power. Rufus had been the same; only Robert had been the foolish one of the family; and look what had happened to him: his patrimony lost—the beloved Dukedom of Normandy—and himself his brother's prisoner. He took hostages from the Princes of Wales—their sons—and by so doing he was sure that the tribute would be paid.

Now he could call at Carew Castle and be sure of a welcome.

He was amazed by her just as he had always been. She was no longer young but seemed to have lost none of her allure.

"You amaze me, Nesta," he told her. "Every time I see you I seem to have forgotten how desirable you are."

"You should remember," she told him.

Gerald de Windsor was complaisant. How could he be aught else? Who had given him his rich lands? Where would

Gerald be if he had not had the good fortune to be selected by the King as husband of his beloved mistress?

So when the King called Gerald must play the generous host to his sovereign and not only relinquish the place of honour to his lord but his bed also.

"Also," said the King, "I become young again with you."

She lay back on her bed smiling at him.

"We were meant for each other, Henry. You know that."

"If I had not been a King. . . . Were the best times before I became King?"

"The best time is always now," she said. "That is the secret."

She became philosophical. "My dearest King," she went on, "you should regret nothing. Our love has always been removed from dull domesticity. Would it have been the same if we had been together every day and night?"

"I am taken away so often. Each time I should have returned to you with the utmost eagerness. I should have thought of you while I was fighting."

"And lost your wars because of it."

"Nay, fought the harder that I might the sooner return to you."

"You must learn, my beloved, that fate does not give us all we ask. Our love has been a joy to us both and neither ever had a lover like the other. But how should we have known this perfection of each other if we had not had so many others to set it against?" She laughed at him. "Come, be gay. Soon you will have ridden away. Tell me of your new wife. She is a beauty, I hear."

"She is a pretty creature."

"Then because I love you, I rejoice for you."

"There is no rejoicing save when I am with you. Yours is the only bed in which I long to be."

"You always spoke so gallantly to me, Henry, but I did not always believe you. Come, be truthful. Is it not an enjoyable task getting this fair creature with the heir of England?"

"'Tis no easy one."

"Virgins they say do not conceive as easily as those who have borne children before. You must curb your impatience. Ere long a messenger will come riding to Wales with the news that the seed is sown."

"Why do we talk of other children when you and I have our fine sons to warm our hearts?"

"Because, my lord, these children cannot be the heirs to the throne. But I beg of you, cast aside your cares. This night you are here and I am here so let us not waste the precious hours with regrets. Rather let us rejoice because tonight at least we are together."

And there she was, as beautiful as ever, the most desirable woman in his life. He forgot all else—there was nothing, nothing but Nesta, his beloved.

If he could but stay in Wales how joyous he would be. But of course he must remember always that he was a King with a kingdom to protect.

He rode through the valley with his men behind him, his standards fluttering in the wind, his mind full of memories of Nesta, and he was promising himself that before he left her native land he would have another night with her.

The fighting was over. He had done that for which he had come. There was no reason why he should not mingle some pleasure with the serious business of subduing the Welsh. He would rest here awhile; he would feign to be occupying himself with state business, which he would in a measure, and at night he would be a guest at Carew Castle, and his bed would be that of the custodian's wife.

It was while he was riding through English territory that he felt the arrow strike his chest. It was well aimed; but for the fact that he was wearing heavy armour it would have pierced his heart.

"By God's death," he cried, "it was no Welsh hand that shot that arrow."

He ordered that the arrow be picked up and given to him. He held it for some time looking steadily at it. It could have happened so easily. If he had not been wearing steel, if the arrow had found a chink, he could be lying on the ground now, as Rufus had lain. He had a vision of his brother when they had brought him to the lodge in the churl's cart—the poor muddied, bloody body of King William Rufus. Rufus had worn no armour. He had been hunting. There had been no protection for Rufus against the assassin's arrow—if assassin it had been. There would always be a mystery about Rufus's death but someone must know; and he, Henry, had had everything to gain from it.

The incident of the arrow was disquieting. So near death—such a lucky chance that he was seated on his horse when he might have been lying on the ground dead.

How vulnerable were kings—ore so than most men.

He must remember that. He should not have been spending his nights with Nesta. There was no time to lose with his true and lawful Queen. They must get a son. He decided that without delay he would go back to Adelicia. Who knew—by the time he arrived she might have some good news for him.

Alas, it was not so.

In the Imperial Bedchamber

In the Imperial Court at Utrecht, the Empress Matilda eagerly awaited news from England. She had heard that her father's marriage had so far proved fruitless and she laughed to herself.

How she wished she were there! How she would love to have seen Stephen's disappointment when he heard that there was to be this marriage. How she would have jeered at him.

He had hoped to inherit the crown. Stephen! Not even the eldest son of the Count of Blois! She would have teased him had she been there, laughed at his pretensions, maddened him until he wanted to seize her, shake her and then make love to her. Those had been the exciting days, and how she missed them.

Here she was married to an old man who bored her. She had to take great pains to keep her temper, yet she did for the most part, because it was wise to do so. He adored her, his handsome young wife, his clever wife who could advise him on so many occasions, for it was the sad truth that the once great Emperor was becoming somewhat senile.

Often she wondered how long he would live, and what would become of her when he died. The people here were pleased with her. She was always very careful when in public to behave with gracious charm; it was only with her immediate servants that she allowed her violent temper its range. They went in fear of her rages; and if they as much as whispered a word of them outside the household they were punished for it.

Often she laughed when she heard herself described as a good wife and a gracious Empress. She liked to think though that she had a hand in ruling the country, and the more feeble her husband grew, the more powerful she became.

Poor old Henry, he had changed since their marriage ...though even then he was a poor old man. And when he died what would become of her? That was the thought which was always uppermost in her mind. What if this Queen Adelicia was in truth barren? What if there were no son and heir? The King of England would remember that he had a daughter, for surely she was next in succession.

A Queen! Would they accept a woman? She would see that they did. What excitement to be back again. To watch the effect she would have on Stephen, poor Stephen, who loved her—and to whom she was far from indifferent—cheated of the crown and married to the wrong Matilda!

It was small wonder that she eagerly awaited the news from England.

In the Imperial bed she yawned and glanced at her sleeping husband. He was more repulsive in his night attire than in his imperial uniform. He was getting so frail. Surely soon she must be free.

She dozed a little and dreamed of England. She awoke startled and saw that the Emperor had risen from his bed.

She lay still, watching him. He walked to the window, groaning.

She leaped out of bed and said to him, "Henry, what ails you? Are you ill?"

She laid her hand on his arm; he was trembling.

"Matilda," he said, "my wife Matilda."

"In truth it is I," she said. "Could it be any other here in your bedchamber?"

"I cannot sleep," he said.

"Your nights are always restless. Come back to bed. You are cold."

"Cold with fear," he answered.

"Of what should you be afraid? We are well guarded. The people are not displeased with their Emperor and they love their Empress."

"Not of the assassin's blow, Matilda. Perforce I should welcome that...if I were prepared."

"Henry, you are ill."

"Sick of mind," he answered.

Yes, you poor old fool, she thought. I have long known that.

"Come back to bed for I find it cold, if you do not. Come back and talk to me."

He allowed her to lead him back. She lighted a candle and set it down on a stool near the bed.

"What has set you wandering from your bed in the night? Fie, my lord, did I catch you on your way to visit a mistress?"

His horror was apparent. "You could not believe such a falsehood."

"Nay, nay," she soothed him. And she thought: You impotent old man, you cannot satisfy one woman let alone more. "I did but seek to lighten the conversation. Tell me now what ails you."

"I am very weary of this life," he said. "I would I could depart from it but I must make my peace with God and that will take me many years of repentance. I pray God that I may have time to expiate all my sins."

"You have expressed your penitence. Rest assured it has been granted to you."

"My dear Matilda, you cannot guess the extent of my wickedness."

"Tell me of it if it eases you to talk."

"You know that my brother Conrad and I plotted against our father, the Emperor."

"Many sons have done this."

"It was an evil thing to do."

"Mayhap not. If you brought good to your country by usurping the crown, that could not be wrong."

"A son against his own father!"

"Many sons have rebelled against their fathers, Henry."

"And what will their punishment be in Heaven?"

"That I cannot tell you, never having rebelled against my father and gone to Heaven."

He did not seem to hear her. He went on: "When my brother Conrad joined the revolt against my father I was at his side."

"You were led astray by your elder brother."

"Nay. I was ambitious—more so than Conrad. I was determined to become the Emperor and because Conrad had led an expedition against my father I was proclaimed his heir. But I could not wait, Matilda. How ambitious I was in those days. You know what I did. It is common knowledge. I trapped him, trapped my own father. We met and were reconciled. And then when he was in my power I forced him to abdicate that I might take the Imperial crown. Poor old man, I imprisoned him and he escaped me and there was war between us until his death."

"It is long ago and best forgotten," said Matilda. "You gave the country many years of peace."

"I took the crown from my father."

"And were a good Emperor to your people."

"I often think of the bloodshed in Italy when I marched there and forced the Pope to come to terms."

"The investiture matter had to be settled and that you did."

"There was much bloodshed. Sometimes in my dreams I see the corpses piled up high."

"All rulers must needs go to war."

"I was ruthless. I was cruel."

"As all rulers must be."

"You seek to comfort me, Matilda. You have been a good wife to me. Never shall I forget when you first came to us...a handsome child. You were but twelve years old."

"And you were forty years older than I!"

"Poor child. And you seemed not afraid."

"I am not easily frightened," replied Matilda. "You indulged me, too. Apart from the fact that you made me speak German and act like a German, you were good to me."

"I would we had been blessed with sons."

Matilda was silent thinking, you were over old for that. And if I had had sons I should never have been able to leave Germany. I should have been here all the days of my life when my heart is in England.

"Try to sleep," she said.

"It is not easy. I like not the darkness of the night. In the dark I see pictures of the past. It is only by daylight that they disappear."

"Then I will leave the candle burning."

"And talk to me, Matilda. While I talk to you I am better. You comfort me when you tell me that you have not been unhappy here."

She lay down watching the flickering shadows throw grotesque shadows on the walls. He talked a little and she answered drowsily. She was not sleepy but her thoughts were far from him.

He cannot live much longer was the theme of these. Then I shall be free.

Freedom! She had watched the birds wheeling in the sky;

58

how effortlessly they flew. That was how she wished she could fly...back to England.

"Are you asleep, Matilda?"

Oh, God, she thought, is he going to start again? Go to sleep, you senile old man. I have had enough of you.

He sighed and was quiet. She lay still, thinking of home. What was happening there now? Adelicia was sleeping beside her husband—poor barren Adelicia. And Stephen was with his Matilda, or with some mistress more likely. She knew Stephen.

She wondered whether he had forgotten her. If he had when she returned to England he would soon remember. But how could she return while she was tied to this old fool of an Emperor?

Tonight though when he had stood shivering by the window and she had lighted the candle and looked into his yellow face she had thought she had seen death there.

Soon, she prayed. Let me have my freedom. Let Adelicia remain barren. Let the King, my father, in his despair of never having a son, remember that he has a strong and clever daughter.

Let all these things come to pass. Let me go to England...and Stephen.

The Poet's Eyes

The King was growing melancholy again. Surely Adelicia would become pregnant soon? Why was it that in spite of his efforts she remained barren?

He was growing more and more irascible. So much seemed to irritate him that all his servants were afraid to go near him. Adelicia was unhappy, wondering whether she was to blame because she could not give the King the son he so urgently needed. Each night the King came to her bed but he was beginning to show that his performance there was in the nature of a duty.

He was finding fault with everyone and everything; and it was during one of his restless periods that he decided to send his daughter-in-law back to her father.

He liked his son's widow. She was a charming young girl. Another Matilda. There were too many Matildas: his dead wife; his spirited daughter; Stephen's wife; and they reminded him of the past when he had a healthy son and had been content enough even though his wife seemed to have stopped childbearing at too early an age. And in particular did his daughter-in-law, her head downcast, her thoughts of her young lost husband making her melancholy, bring home to him his dilemma.

He sent for Roger that he might talk to him of his desire to be rid of her.

"'Tis not that I do not like the girl, Roger. She is a fair and gentle creature; but to look at her is a constant reminder of William and how he met his death on the White Ship, and then I begin to think, Roger, that God has deserted me. He took my son and will not give me another."

"You are impatient, my lord."

"As I must needs be. Look at me. Do you not see an ageing man?"

"I see a man in the prime of his life, sir. The Queen longs too passionately for a child, it may be, for I have heard wise women say that often if the longing is too intense the seed will not take root."

"It is no fault of mine, of that I'm sure. I've bastards enough to prove I can get a woman with child."

"Bastards enough," repeated the Bishop. "And never fear, an heir to the throne will come in time."

"In time," screamed the King. "Am I a young man to have time to spare?"

Roger could see that his master was getting near to one of his irritable moods and he sought to soothe him.

"You sent for me to discuss the future of your daughter-in-law, I believe, my lord."

"Ay, Matilda. A sweet girl. But every time I look at her I see the White Ship. The sight of my son's widow does nothing to ease my pain."

"Then she must needs be sent away where you do not see her."

"Where shall I send her?"

"Back to Anjou, back to her father."

"I will do it, Roger. But wait. She came with a big dowry. Methinks Fulk would receive his daughter back with open arms if that went with her."

"Ah, her dowry," sighed Roger. "It was such a fine dowry. Fulk was pleased to ally his family with your royal one, and was ready to pay dearly for the honour."

"Which he did," said the King. "But the marriage was of short duration; he will want to marry his daughter to another. She is a child still."

"He will look for the return of the dowry," said Roger.

"He will have to search diligently for it and then he will never find it."

"I thought not," said Roger; and he laughed. The King smiled with him, ill humour temporarily banished.

"Nay," said the King. "I shall send Fulk his daughter but not the dowry he paid that she might marry my son. She married my son, did she not?"

"In all truth she did."

"Then I kept my word. I gave my son to his daughter and he gave the dowry to me."

"He will be incensed."

"Let him be," said the King. "Do you think I care for the Count of Anjou?"

"A useful province, my lord."

"Useful yes, and it was well that there was an alliance between us. Now there is peace in Normandy. My son has died; Fulk's daughter is his widow. Therefore I shall send her back to her father, but her dowry stays with me. She had her brief glory, poor girl. She will remember all her life—and so will Fulk—that she could have been a Queen of England. That was worth a dowry."

"It is, sir. Even when there is no hope of her ever attaining her ambition."

"Then, Roger, arrange it. Tell the girl I regret her going. I will see her myself. I like her well, she is comely and pleasant. But her presence grieves me solely because I remember that she is a widow, and whose. She must go . . . but dowerless, Roger. The girl departs but the money stays."

Henry took a tender farewell of his daughter-in-law, raising her in his arms and kissing her.

"It grieves me, my dear daughter, that you should leave us," he said. "But to remain here is too much of a reminder to us both. You will go home to your father and I doubt not that in due course he will find you a husband whom you can love, to whom you can give children; and who will make you forget this unhappy part of your life."

She thanked him for his goodness to her and he appeared genuinely sorry to see her go. But when she was no longer here to remind him of his loss, his temper did not improve. Nor would it, said those about him, until he had a son.

When Fulk of Anjou welcomed his daughter he believed that the enormous dowry he had paid to the King of England at the time of the marriage would be returned with her.

He was furious when he understood that the intention of the King of England was to keep it. He had paid that sum of money to see his daughter Queen of England; the fact that fate had intervened and her husband had been drowned and she had lost her opportunity was no reason why he should be asked to pay for what he had not received.

"The King of England is a miser," he cried. "He is like all that breed. His father was a man who stretched out and took all within his reach and never let go of anything on which he laid his hands. They are a miserly acquisitive breed and I want my money back. And if he thinks he can cheat me,

63

he must be taught otherwise. Henry of England shall learn it was an evil day when he decided to cheat Fulk of Anjou.'

Anjou was the most powerful province in France, and the history of Fulk's family was as romantic an epic as that of the great Dukes of Normandy whose first Duke Rollo had ravaged the French countryside so determinedly that the French King had been obliged to bestow Normandy upon them.

The founder of Fulk's family was Tortulf the Forester who had lived in the ninth century. He was a hunter and an outlaw and his home had been the woods. He became renowned for his skill in hunting wild animals and fighting valiantly those who came against him. It was said of him that he feared nothing but ill-fame.

At this time the Danes were ravaging the fair lands of France as they were those of England, and Tortulf threw in his lot with King Charles the Bold and together they repulsed the Norsemen. For his reward Tortulf asked for land and this was granted him. He had a son, Ingelger, who joined him in battle and was as skilled as his father. Together they won that land which was called Anjou.

The greatest of their line was Fulk the Good who brought peace and prosperity to Anjou but as frequently happens, a wise ruler is often followed by a foolish one and under the next Duke, Geoffrey Grey-gown, the Angevins lost their power and became mere vassals to the neighbouring lands of Blois and Champagne.

Yet out of this vassaldom there arose like the phoenix great Fulk the Black, a mighty man. He was a man who determined that he would make Anjou once more the most powerful province in France; he dedicated his life to this purpose and as he cared for no man but only for his ruthless ambition he succeeded. Nothing was allowed to stand in his way. He was cold, ruthless, incapable of affection even to those nearest to him, as was shown by his treatment of his wife and son. When his wife was unfaithful to him he decreed that her crime warranted death by burning and he, dressed as though for a festival, himself led her to the stake, and he lighted the faggots and watched unmoved while she writhed in her death agonies. When his son Geoffrey took up arms against such a tyrant and was beaten, he insisted that the young man be saddled as though he were a beast of burden and that he grovel at his feet begging for a pardon which he was led to believe he would not receive. As his son must be a future count of Anjou he was pardoned for expediency, not from a fatherly affection.

Like most men of his times as his youth passed he began to fear the hereafter and contemplating his sins a desire for forgiveness overtook him. While he could face any earthly foe, he was unsure of how he would fare in Heaven. He shared the general belief that a show of extreme piety could wipe out the past so, as many had before him, he took the pilgrimage to Jerusalem and had himself whipped through the streets there. This he endured with stoical courage but when he returned to Anjou by no means mended in his ways, believing that the severity of the scourging had settled the score for future as well as past sins.

These were the ancestors of that Fulk whom Henry had placated by the marriage of his son to Fulk's daughter; and whom he now flouted by returning that daughter without her dowry.

It was not to be expected that the proud and powerful Count of Anjou would meekly accept such treatment.

Fuming in his castle he wondered how best to discomfit Henry of England.

There was one who, many would say, had a greater right to the crown of England than Normandy; and that was the Conqueror's eldest son Robert. Robert, who had done battle with his younger brother Henry and been defeated, was now his brother's prisoner in Cardiff Castle, but he had a son, William the Clito.

If William were victorious in Normandy and succeeded in taking what many believed to be his rightful heritage from the usurper Henry, there was every possibility that he might make an attempt on England as well. Fulk was well aware that one of the greatest anxieties in Henry's life was his nephew, the Clito.

Discreetly he sent messages to the young man. Would a meeting be possible? If the Clito would come to his castle he would have a proposition to lay before him which he felt sure he would find very attractive.

William the Clito was in many respects like his father. Good-looking, charming, easy going, he had one great ambition which was to restore Normandy to his branch of the family and to bring about the release of his father, Robert of Normandy (nicknamed Curthose by his father, the Conqueror, because of his short legs) a very charming man, in spite of his feckless ways and the many enterprises in which he had indulged and which had all come to failure. Always there had been those who would follow him in spite of his irresponsibility. The Clito remembered his father with affection and the thought of his suffering in a dungeon, held prisoner by that ogre, his uncle Henry of England, could make him fly into a rage which ended in tears of sorrow.

So when Fulk of Anjou sent him an invitation he accepted with alacrity.

Fulk received him with great respect, which considering his recently alliance with Henry through the marriage of his daughter might have made most people suspicious. But the Clito, like his father, was ready to accept friendship wherever it was offered without asking too many questions.

"My dear, dear Prince," said Fulk, "you find here a man who has suffered great disillusion. I made a great mistake when I trusted the King of England."

"In allying yourself with him you played the traitor to the rightful Duke," the Clito reminded him.

"Alas! Let me explain to you. I love this land, and we have had too many wars. The country needs peace. Your father was unable to give that peace. I believed that Henry could. It was a terrible decision for me to make but I put what I thought to be the good of the country first."

"And arranged a marriage for your daughter at the same time."

"This seemed a wise thing. The young people loved each other. How could I refuse them?",

Fulk narrowed his eyes. Had he gone too far? His daughter had been a child; so young that the marriage could not be consummated at the time of the ceremony. He allowed himself to be carried away by his own eloquence and the sentiments he was whipping up in his cynical mind. "They were happy and then the tragedy happened."

"And it is for this reason..." began the Clito.

"My lord, my reason is that I now realize my error. There is one true Duke of Normandy and that is not Henry. Indeed is he in truth the rightful heir to England? For twenty years and more he has held the crown of England but was he the Conqueror's eldest son?"

"My father was that. He should have had England before Rufus. He should have it now."

"And Rufus is dead and Henry reigns... and some would say he knew something of Rufus's end. And the eldest son of Great William lies a prisoner in England."

66

"It shall not always be so."

"Nay. It shall not. That is something on which we can agree. I want us to stand together. Anjou is the most powerful of provinces. You cannot doubt that. You will find me at your side with all the help I can give you. I want nothing so much as to see Henry routed. I want him turned out of Normandy. That is our first step. Then we shall free your father. We shall consider England."

Clito's eyes shone. Like his father he was better at talking victory than fighting for it. He could see in Fulk's eyes his hatred of the King of England and he knew it to be real.

"We will talk of these matters at length. But first we will eat and afterwards you shall hear my daughters play and sing to you. They are reckoned worth the hearing."

"Your daughter who was the wife of my cousin William?"

"His widow, yes. She is with me now, poor soul. I rejoice to have her back. I liked it not when she resided at the Court of that...miser of England. She has a sister..."

He was watching the Clito eagerly. Young, impressionable—and Sibyl was a charming girl, as beautiful as her sister Matilda.

Clito would have to understand that one of the conditions Fulk would demand for his services was a marriage between Sibyl and the Clito.

He laughed aloud when he thought of Henry's receiving the news. Fulk's daughter, the wife of his nephew, the true heir of Normandy. Henry would know that meant trouble. He would know whose side Fulk was on. He would know that he would not stop at Normandy either. He would have his eyes on England.

The news of the betrothal of Sibyl to the Clito threw Henry into a passion of rage. For a whole day none dared approach him.

Then Adelicia timidly begged him to take care that he did no harm to his health.

Henry looked at her as though he did not see her. How could he explain to this simple girl what was going on in his mind? He had made a mistake. He should have sent the dowry back to Fulk. He had learned early in life that there was nothing so costly as war and it was almost always advisable to take other measures—even those which cost him dear—to avoid it.

Fulk was wily. How dared he marry his daughter to the

Clito! This meant of course that his alliance with Henry was at an end. He was now on the side of Robert and his son and all the considerable forces at his disposal would be turned against his one-time ally.

This was his answer to the return of his dowerless daughter.

If his own William had lived....It all came back to that disastrous loss of the White Ship.

Henry knew that he could not allow matters to drift. Immediate action was necessary.

Stephen was begging for an audience. He came in warily, knowing the moods of the King.

"My lord," said Stephen, "I come to ask what you wish of me. Am I to prepare to leave with you for Normandy?"

The King's anger lifted a little. Of course he must go to Normandy without delay, and Stephen would be with him. Good Stephen.

"It is pleasant to know that there are some on whose loyalty I can rely," muttered the King.

"You will wish to leave at once?" asked Stephen.

Henry nodded. It was the only way. Normandy was the great thorn in his flesh. All his life it seemed he had been fighting in Normandy; and with the alliance with Anjou he had hoped to keep the peace. The worst thing that could happen was that Anjou should join with Clito. And by sending back Matilda without her dowry he had brought this about.

His own shortsightedness was to blame; and how much harder it was to endure tribulation when one feared it was the result of one's own actions.

There had now come into his mind the growing certainty that God was punishing him for his lasciviousness by making Adelicia barren.

He looked at Stephen and wondered whether after all he might not yet be forced to make his nephew his heir. Stephen had suffered a bitter disappointment when Adelicia had become the Queen; it seemed he need not have feared.

"Yes, Stephen," cried Henry, "to Normandy. Anjou must be made to feel my anger. This betrothal of his daughter and Clito can mean one thing."

"My lord," replied Stephen, "are not Clito and Fulk's daughter related? I believe them to be cousins of the fifth degree."

Henry was silent and then burst into loud laughter. "'Tis so," he bellowed.

68

"Then, my lord, the Pope....?"

"Aye," cried Henry. "The Pope!"

They were both silent for a moment and each knew the other was remembering that William, the King's son, and Matilda, Fulk's daughter, had been fifth cousins too; yet no one had denied their right to marry on the grounds of consanguinity. The relationship between them was exactly the same as that between Clito and Sibyl.

"You think, my lord...." began Stephen.

"I think, Stephen, that the Pope will have the good sense to support Henry, King of England, against a mere Count of Anjou. Send for Roger. He can deal with this matter with the Pope. And you are right, nephew, you and I will prepare to leave for Normandy without delay."

Henry took his leave of his Queen with mild regret.

She did not greatly excite him and he had almost given up hope of getting an heir by her. Away from her he could indulge in a way of life more natural to him; there would be pleasant encounters on the way. For if, he thought moodily, after all the endeavours I have made she remains barren, then barren she must be.

Adelicia herself was not entirely sorry to see him go. She had been overshadowed by his urgent need to get a son and it would be pleasant to be rid of it.

She would have the sole occupancy of her bed at night; she could lie and dream about the needlework she would do, or the songs she would learn to play and sing. She would not have to be overshadowed by that dreadful sense of guilt.

She had become very friendly with Stephen's wife Matilda and was fond of her son, little Baldwin, a charming child though perhaps too frail for his mother's comfort.

Matilda was desolate at the departure of Stephen. He had the power to make people love him. He was so handsome and courteous always, although Adelicia had learned that he was not always faithful to his wife.

After they had watched the men depart they sat over their needlework together and talked of their lives. Always Adelicia was looking for the signs which did not come. "Soon," she said, "if there is no indication I shall know it is useless to hope and that in itself will be a relief."

"Poor Adelicia. But the King has been kind to you, has he not?"

"Yes, he has been kind, yet I know that I have been a great disappointment to him."

"The King is too old to beget children. He should blame himself for this lack, not you."

"Yet I do not think he does."

"Of course it is said that he has more children than any of his subjects."

Adelicia blushed.

"You know it," persisted Matilda. "Do not be shy with me. Do not imagine that Stephen is a faithful husband."

"Not Stephen!"

"He has his mistresses. He is like the King in that. One woman does not satisfy them. It is a fact we must needs accept. At least I do not have to watch him with Matilda."

"Matilda?"

"My namesake, yes. The King's daughter. You have heard of that Matilda."

"It must be years since she was at Court."

"She left more than ten years ago. She will be twenty-two years of age now. I saw her only on my visits to the Court from Bermondsey. But Matilda is someone one never forgets. I know that Stephen has never forgotten her. I can tell by the look on his face when she is mentioned."

"But she was so young when she went away."

"I have heard much of her and sometimes when Stephen says my name...Matilda...he says it like that yearningly and I fancy he is thinking of her."

"Oh, how could it be? She was but a child when she went away."

"There was something about her. She was different from others."

"You are jealous, Matilda."

"Am I? I know he has mistresses and I have ceased to think of them. He says they mean nothing to him and I believe him. It is Matilda of whom I think often. I wonder what she is doing in Germany...if she ever thinks of us."

Adelicia shook her head and taking up a needle threaded it with deep blue silk.

"Why Matilda," she said, "you are fanciful. How could he think of this other Matilda now...after ten years...and she a child when she went away? Nay, you have allowed this matter to obsess you as I have the need to get a child. Our husbands have gone. We will pray for their speedy victory and in the meantime we will be as merry as we can for if I

70

am not with child there is naught I can do about that now; as for you, this Matilda who haunts you is far away; she is the Empress of Germany so what can she do to take your husband from you?"

"You are right, Adelicia. Let us decide what we will instruct the musicians to play this night."

A year had passed and the King was still in Normandy. The Pope had been prevailed upon to prevent the marriage of Clito and Sibyl. That at least would show Fulk the kind of adversary he had in the King of England.

Fulk might rage against the Pope who could be so careless about some marriages and so meticulous about others—depending of course on the power of the people concerned. But of what use? The edict from Rome was no marriage, so no marriage there was.

The King should see though that the Count of Anjou could be a bitter enemy even if his daughter were not married to the true heir of Normandy—ay, and to England. And the fighting was fierce.

In spite of his years Henry had lost none of his skill as a general. He had his victories but they were not complete, for all over Normandy the barons were rising against him and the King of France never forgot the enmity he felt towards the King of England.

One matter which wounded Henry deeply was the disaffection of his old friend, Luke de Barré. This boyhood companion of his, whose verses he had been wont to enjoy, had gone over to the enemy. He had decided that the true heir to Normandy was the young Clito and Luke put himself at the service of the young man.

"I would never have believed," said the King, "that Luke de Barré would have turned traitor."

This was even more than the loss of an old friend for not only had Luke gone over to the other side but he was using his talents to help the enemy. His verses had always been admired and Henry could recall many happy hours in the great halls of his various castles when he had sat laughing at Luke while he sang the songs he had composed.

They were witty and to the point and often somewhat satirical, for Luke had always liked to parody the foibles of those about him.

And now he was parodying Henry. It was incredible that he should dare. Some of the songs were brought to the King's

71

notice and when he heard those sly words he flew into a rage, so that his minstrels dared not sing more of Luke's songs until told that it would be the worse for them if they did not.

Some of these were stirring battle songs, calculated to put heart into the King's enemies; they set out the rights of Clito's cause and the wrongs of Henry's; and not only that. When they had been friends they had gone out visiting inns and taverns together, had shared many an adventure with the ladies who frequented such places, and the King's wrath grew when he heard in detail accounts of those adventures put into verse . . . his confidence betrayed by this traitorous man.

He told Stephen what he would do to him if ever he fell into his hands.

"By God's death," he said, "I would make him wish he had never been born."

The Clito had inherited a great deal from his father—not less that which amounted almost to a genius for failure. He was a man who—sometimes through no fault of his own—was never in the significant spot at the vital moment. Henry, with his meticulous planning, his years of experience and the respect and fear he inspired in all those about him, was an adversary as certain to succeed as Clito was doomed to fail.

One by one castles fell into Henry's hands and by Easter time it was clear that the rebel defences were crumbling and that this phase of the war was virtually at an end.

Thousands of prisoners were taken and when Henry heard that the warrior-bard Luke de Barré was among them he laughed aloud.

"Now he will see," he cried, "what happens to those who would mock the King."

That night he paced his chamber asking himself what revenge would hurt his old friend most. To be condemned to death! He knew Luke. He would shrug his shoulders philosophically and make some ode on the beauty of death and go gracefully to his execution. That was not punishment enough.

His eyes. Of course, his eyes! Those beautifully dreamy eyes which the women so much admired and with which he surveyed the world that so excited him that he must record what he saw sometimes lyrically, often satirically.

That should be his sentence. The fate all men dreaded more than any other was to have the light put out and be plunged into a darkness which should last for the rest of their lives.

He himself gave the order: Luke de Barré to be taken to the scaffold and there publicly to have his eyes put out.

The King's kinsman, the Earl of Flanders, begged for an audience.

"What is it?" asked the King.

"My lord, forgive me, but may I speak to you concerning the poet Luke de Barré?"

"Have they not yet carried out the sentence on him?"

"Not yet, and I beg you will order it not to be done."

"Why should you plead for a traitor?" asked the King.

"A traitor he is, sir. But he is a poet more than a warrior."

"Are you saying that I should pardon this man who has insulted me?"

"Nay, sir, but such a sentence.... Allow me to bring him to you. On his knees he will ask your pardon."

"I doubt it not, now that he is my prisoner."

"It was but words."

"Words! Know you not the power of words? At times methinks they are more effective than the sword."

"I beg of you, sir, show mercy on this man."

"No!" cried the King. "I say no! This man, a wit, a bard, a minstrel hath composed ribald songs against me and sung them to make my enemies laugh. God has delivered him into my hands. I wish all to see what happens to those who flout me that others may be deterred from like petulance."

"Sir...."

"Get you gone," cried the King, "or you too will feel my wrath."

Alone the King muttered, "Now, Luke de Barré, you will learn what it means to insult the King."

"My eyes!" cried Luke de Barré. "Not my eyes. Take my life...but not my eyes."

"My lord," said the guard, "it is the King's command."

"My eyes, my *precious* eyes. It must not be. Take me to the King."

"The Earl of Flanders has spoken for you but the King has sworn to show no mercy."

"I will give everything I have...lands, wealth... everything...for my eyes."

The guard did not answer.

All through the night Luke de Barré sat in his dungeon. He had asked for a candle that he might see for as long as he would be allowed to. He asked for writing materials because he must write to the King. But such materials were denied him.

Henry was a hard man. He had always known it. It would have been different with his brother Robert or the Clito. They would have more feeling for their friend. But Henry was the victor. Henry had always been the victor from the moment he had ridden to Winchester and proclaimed himself the King.

They had had amusing adventures together. Two young men whose minds had been in tune. That was what had attracted Henry in the first place. He liked a companion when sporting with women and then they would talk together of deeper matters. There had been a bond between them. Beauclerc had chosen scholars for his friends.

Henry must remember those days of friendship. He must see him.

Yet he had always known that Henry was a ruthless man. Why had he been tempted to write those songs? The words had been witty and he had always been carried away by words. And Henry *was* wrong to take Normandy. The Clito—or his father—were the true heirs.

Henry must know this, for he was a just man. Just, cruel, ruthless....

"Oh, God, let me see the King," he prayed. "Let me talk to him."

He could remind him of the old days, the hilarious adventures, the women they had known, the days of their youth.

But the King would not see him. The Earl of Flanders came.

"I have tried to plead with Henry," he explained. "He stands firm. Your songs angered him greatly."

"Oh, fool that I was. I never thought he could do this to me."

The Earl looked sorrowfully at the poet.

"You made an ill choice," he said, "and now must needs pay for it. Did you not realize that the Clito could never win against the King."

"I thought his cause just."

"And to mock the King! Did you not know that he would never forgive that."

"I thought I could talk to him; he ever loved an argument. I thought we would talk as we used to in the old days."

The Earl shook his head and Luke put his hands over his eyes.

74

"So," he said at length, "there is no hope then."

The Earl was silent.

"My eyes, my precious eyes," muttered Luke. "I will never never part with them until the day I die."

The Earl sought to comfort him but what comfort was there for a man who must for ever grope his way through darkness.

They led him to the scaffold. The people of Rouen had gathered to watch the agonies of this man whose quarrel with the King had become notorious.

Luke de Barré, tall, handsome, his hands bound behind his back, his eyes wild and staring as though they were trying to miss no tiny detail of any scene before their light was put out.

On the scaffold was the brazier; there were the red-hot irons.

"Oh, God, help me," prayed Luke de Barré. "Thou knowest I cannot live without mine eyes."

He spoke in loud tones to the men who guarded him. "Tell the King," he said, "that I shall never forget him, and he will never forget me."

Then with a sudden cry he ran from his guards. They followed him but not with any concern for his hands were bound behind his back and escape was impossible for him. There were many in that crowd come to witness the agony of the King's enemy who felt sorry for the poet. Some of the women would have sheltered him could they have done so, for even now that he was no longer young there was about him undeniable charm.

"Hold him," cried the guard, but no one moved. Then Luke de Barré faced the crowd and said: "I cannot say farewell, my eyes, for thee and I must never part."

Then running fast forward he lowered his head and thrust it against the stone wall.

There was a groan from the crowd as the blood streamed from his head and again and again he threw his head against the wall.

He lay on the ground. The guards bent over him.

Luke de Barré was dying but there were a few moments of consciousness left to him.

He was heard to murmur: "He could not take my eyes from me. I see...I see while life remains, I see." And then: "He shall never forget me...never while he lives."

And so died Luke de Barré before the King's order could be carried out.

When the news was brought to the King he was greatly disturbed.

Henry dismissed depressing thoughts. He had brought the trouble in Normandy to a temporary standstill. There still remained Fulk of Anjou, quiet at the moment because the time was not ripe for attack but smarting from the news that the Pope had given judgment against the marriage of Clito and his daughter.

Henry knew that if he left Normandy the rebels would immediately return. Clito was still free. Anjou was biding his time. So what could he do but stay here?

The news from England was not of the best. The war with Normandy had proved even more costly than Henry had calculated. There had to be taxes which the English loathed.

The crime of debasing the coinage had increased. Often a pound was so reduced by clipping that it was worth only half its value in gold. Henry drew up laws of even greater severity to be used against offenders. Mutilation was the greatest deterrent. No one wanted to lose a hand, a foot, a nose, his ears, or most of all his eyes for the sake of money.

But he was wise enough to know that these measures were unpopular and although the English realized that he had brought a law and order to the land which they had not enjoyed under his brother Rufus, there was a limit to what they would endure.

Life was turning sour for him and it had all begun with the loss of the White Ship. There he was back at the old theme. Adelicia was barren. He was never going to get a child—let alone a son—from her.

Sometimes in the quiet of the night a great depression descended upon him. God had forsaken him...not in all matters. He gave him victory; he gave him wealth; and these were important to him; but he denied him comfort; he would not give him a son and his sins weighed heavily on him.

He had started to think of the old days before he had become King, when he was a penniless Prince, the youngest son of the great Conqueror who had had nothing to leave him but five thousand pounds of silver while his brothers Robert and Rufus had Normandy and England. "But," prophesied his father, "have patience and you shall excel your brothers in wealth and power."

76

And that had come to pass. Yet here he was a melancholy man. He had lived fifty-six years and for twenty-four years he had been King of England. His father would not have been displeased with his endeavours. There was a similarity between them although Henry's lechery was quite alien to the Conqueror's austerity. Henry's father had been a cold man, a faithful husband, who spent so much time at war that there had been little time for love.

Perhaps, thought the King, when a man reaches my age, melancholy is often his companion.

He thought of Adelicia in England. A pleasant, meek creature who had always tried to please him. He remembered how she had interested herself in the animals in his Zoo when she, poor child, was afraid of half of them. She was determined to please him and do all that was required of her which was admirable in a wife. Also, there was one thing she could not do for that was not within her power. And that was all I wanted of her, he thought angrily.

He was finding it hard to sleep at night. He would go to bed exhausted and find even so that sleep would not come.

When it did it would be light, uneasy sleep.

One night he awoke startled because he thought someone stood by his bed. He sat up sweating. He saw a face there...a laughing face with eyes that glittered oddly.

"Ah, Henry, but you remember me. I have sworn that never, never shall you forget me."

"Luke," he said. "Is it you, Luke?"

He stared out of bed, but there was no one there.

He went back to bed uneasy. Was Luke de Barré going to haunt him for the rest of his life?

Homage to Matilda

There was another who was tormented by remorse. This was the Emperor Henry V. Matilda who was the recipient of his nocturnal monologues daily expected that he was going mad.

She often wondered what would happen then. Would they put him away? And what of her? She was without children so she would not be the mother of the new Emperor; she would be of no importance without her husband. If he went mad then she would have no standing at all.

Popular she had been with the people for they were unaware of her arrogant nature as she had always taken care to appear gracious in public. Looking at the senile old man she often thought how unfairly life had treated her. Had her father known that her brother William was to die and he be unable to get legitimate sons he would never have sent her so far away. Would he have married her to Stephen? They were cousins. Bah! Who cared for that? She laughed when she heard that the Pope had refused the Clito permission to marry Anjou's daughter on grounds of consanguinity. There was one law for the powerful and another for the less powerful in such matters.

And now Adelicia was barren and if Matilda became a widow her father would recall her to England, and who then should he appoint as his successor but his own daughter! A woman! She laughed. Let her go to England, let her show the people the stuff of which she was made and they would realize that a woman could be as great a ruler as any man.

But because of this senile old fool she must remain in Germany, a prisoner if ever there was one. It could not go on.

It was by night that his growing obsession became more

apparent. Then he would ramble on about his sins, and how he had betrayed his father. It was a common failing. So many rulers lived ruthlessly during their youth, trampling underfoot all those who stood in their way and then when old age began to overtake them repentance set in. They became worried about the life hereafter and wondered how best they could placate God for their sins and win a place in heaven. To achieve their ambition on Earth they went forth with fire and sword; to reach it on High they went with bare feet and hair shirt on pilgrimages of repentance.

Matilda at twenty-four years of age could laugh at them. She was not yet of an age to fear death or seek repentance.

Her great-grandfather, Robert the Magnificent, after usurping the throne from his brother, and some said murdering him, had become a saint by going on a pilgrimage to the Holy Land and dying there. It was simple. Do what you liked in your youth. Pillage, burn, snatch the crown from your brother's or your father's head. All was well as long as you repented in due course, suffered a few scourgings, irritated your skin with the hair shirt and walked barefoot to the shrine of Jerusalem. The only catch was that you must do it in time. And if you were a warrior it might well be that death came too swiftly and suddenly to give you that time. Then presumably, you were doomed.

Her grandfather—that man whom she had never known because he had died before her birth but who was a legend in the family, the greatest of them all, not excluding Duke Rollo the founder of the Normans or her father Henry I who was known as the Lion of Justice—was one who had never made a pilgrimage to save his soul. He had been too great, too sure of the righteousness of his causes; he had not taken the diadem from father or brother; he had merely snatched it from Harold Godwin of England who many said had no more right to it than he had. She admired her grandfather. She dreamed that one day she would be a Queen as great as any King and the people would say her name in the same breath as that of her father, the Lion of Justice, and her grandfather William the Conqueror.

In the meantime she was married to this stupid old man and while this was the case she was a prisoner condemned each night to listen to his ravings. She had acquired the habit of murmuring sympathetically when she had not heard a word.

It was always the same! An account of the tricks he had

80

played on his father; he and his brother Conrad had risen against their own flesh and blood. "What greater crime is there, Matilda, tell me, than that of the son who takes up arms against the man who sired him?"

She would answer vaguely: "It was a great sin, but many have done the same."

"I feel the burden of my sins heavy upon me. What can I do to gain repentance, Matilda, what can I do?"

She would sigh and murmur something. "Don't distress yourself so. You will be ill." And all the time she would be wondering what was happening in her father's Court and whether perhaps after all Adelicia was pregnant.

"I can know no peace...." the droning voice went on.

Nor I, she thought, while you are here to plague me.

"There must be a way. There must be a way."

How much longer can he live?

He looked frail and his eyes were so wild. Surely his ministers must notice it. They did. They looked at each other significantly.

"Try to sleep," she whispered soothingly.

"There is no sleep...no peace. Heavily my sins weigh upon me."

She would pretend to be asleep but he went on muttering.

If he were dead would my father send for me? she wondered. If he did not I should ask him to.

How strange it would be to go home. Her father would have changed. So much had happened since she had gone. Her mother had died; then her brother; and the King had a new wife. Adelicia, meek barren Adelicia. Remain barren, dear stepmother. It is very important to me that you should.

His mutterings had stopped. Thank God, he was sleeping at last.

She too slept and dreamed that her father had sent for her and once more she saw the green fields of England.

Her cousin Stephen was waiting to hold her horse as she dismounted; he caught her and held her fast as she did so.

She awoke startled. There was a lighted candle in the room. She did not speak but lay quietly watching. On the wall was a long shadow of an ancient man like an evil spirit. Henry? she thought.

He was standing by the bed breathing heavily; his head was bare and he had put on a shapeless garment such as pilgrims wore.

He picked up a staff and she saw him clearly as he walked to the door. His feet were bare.

Where was he going?

At the door he blew out the candle and set it down. She heard the door open quietly and she was alone.

He cannot have a mistress, she thought, and laughed at the notion. He had gone completely mad, she was sure of it. He was walking about the palace in his shapeless garment, his feet bare. Someone would see him, they would bring him back; they would talk to her very discreetly. "The Emperor is mad," they would imply.

And they would put him away and there would be a new Emperor and she would be of no importance because she had no son.

She lay still, thinking.

Could it be that he often made these nocturnal wanderings? Perhaps some of his servants knew it and they kept it from her. He must be imagining that he was a pilgrim. Walking round his palace deluding himself that he was in the Holy Land!

There could be no doubt that he was mad.

She lay awaiting his return. He did not come and at last she slept.

When she awoke he had still not returned.

His ministers told her the Emperor was dead. He had been taken ill in the night. Death, all knew, had been creeping gradually upon him.

She thought of the poor old man rising from his bed and walking barefooted from the room.

"Where is he?" she asked.

They took her to a small room. It was dark, for very little light came through the slits of windows and there were no candles. There was a bed on which lay what appeared to be a body covered over with a cloth.

"It is indeed the Emperor?" she asked.

They told her that it was. He had died in the night. They had been expecting it. The funeral should take place without delay. There were secrets in their eyes and their looks were furtive, but she did not ask for explanations. She did not wish to know.

The Emperor was buried with accustomed pomp and she arranged for a monument to be erected to him in Spires Cathedral.

She asked to be left alone to mourn.

It pleased her to play the stricken widow. She shut herself in her apartments asking herself what would happen next. She knew and she rejoiced in it. What she had thought of as her days of bondage were over.

Her ministers came to see her to express their grief. They had always been respectful to her.

They wanted her to know that they hoped she would stay in Germany. They believed she would find consolation there.

She thanked them and said how she appreciated their kindness to her in her bereavement. "It came so suddenly," she said watching them intently. "Although I had known for so long that he was ailing, I feared his mind...."

They nodded gravely.

They would not want a madman on the Imperial throne. They were genuine in their respect for her. The years of careful behaviour had borne their fruit. Stay here! she thought. Nay. This is a release for you, gentlemen, and no less so for me.

"I think my father may command me to return to him. If he does, as his daughter I must obey him."

But she thanked them and told them that she had been very happy in their land, that she had become German through her marriage. But as yet she was too recently bereaved to know what she wished.

They bowed themselves out.

It was a grand ceremony. She listened to the dirges and thought of poor mad Henry and wondered about him.

He was having a magnificent funeral though and the monument was very stately.

Back to the palace to shut herself in her apartments, to mourn she said; but she meant to wait.

Life had become exciting.

The King had welcomed Adelicia to Rouen and was glad of her company. Perhaps it was because he was getting old but he found it soothing. She was undemanding, full of the desire to please, as though she could not do enough to make up for her barrenness.

He told her it was a comfort to have her with him. He feared he was often irritable but he did not always feel well and sometimes a man wanted to talk and not weigh his words. He could do that only with his wife.

She accepted the compliment happily enough and still continued to pray for a child.

He had given up hope.

When news of what had happened in Germany came to him he discussed it with Adelicia. It was a family matter first, he said, although it could become a State one.

"Matilda a widow and childless! I shall bring her home, Adelicia."

"Yes, Henry."

"I wonder what she is like now? She is twenty-four years of age—no older than you. You could be sisters."

"Poor Matilda. How sad she must be."

"A widow...and childless. Had she had a son it would have made all the difference to her life."

Adelicia sighed, reminded as she was of her own shortcomings.

"Yes, she must come home. There must be no delay. I despair, Adelicia, of your ever giving me a son."

"My lord husband, it grieves me...."

"I know. I know. But it is God's will. And now there is my daughter. At least God has left me one child. I shall make her my heir, Adelicia...that is unless you give me a son even now."

"If I could...."

"Yes, yes, I know. But perhaps this is the answer. A woman, though!"

"Will the people accept a woman, Henry?"

"They will if I say they shall."

She bowed her head.

"I shall send for Matilda at once. She shall join us here, for God knows how long I must remain here. There are traitors everywhere. And when she comes I will have her proclaimed my heir. It seems to me, Adelicia, that this is the answer."

Her eyes shining with excitement, Matilda saw before her the walled city of Rouen. From the distance it appeared like one vast castle; the river Seine shone silver in the sunlight which glinted on the stones of Rollo's Tower. A glow of pride swept over her. This had been the capital of her famous grandfather and now it was in the hands of her father, the only one of his sons who was worthy of him.

She was proud of her ancestry. This was where she belonged—here in the stronghold of the Norman Dukes who

84

had wrested the land from the French and in England too where she had been born and bred.

The years of bondage were over. She had escaped from her poor senile old husband and was a free woman again.

Through the gates and into the town. One or two people looked at her curiously. They did not yet know who she was, but they would. At least they could see that she was a personage of importance; her entourage would tell them that, but even without it they would have known, for she carried herself like an Empress.

The drawbridge was lowered and there waiting to greet her were the King and Queen.

Father and daughter surveyed each other appraisingly for a few seconds, then Henry took her into his arms. He seemed genuinely moved.

"Matilda, daughter, this gives me great pleasure."

"Oh, Father," she replied with feeling, "I have longed so much to see you."

They stood away from each other. Two of a kind, and although they did feel affection for each other they could not help assessing the possibilities each offered the other.

He was thinking: She's a handsome girl and twenty-four, which is marriageable. She has lost none of her forcefulness. Yes, if they would accept a woman that would be Matilda. She has a dignity, a stateliness. She has the air of one born to command.

And Matilda thought: How he has aged! He is indeed an old man. He cannot last many more years. Five. Six. Ten perhaps. Nay, that's too many. He's strong though. A lion in truth.

They were proud of each other.

"Here is the Queen," said the King.

Matilda bowed graciously and Adelicia flushing took her hands and kissed her.

"Welcome," she said. "We have been impatient for your arrival ever since we knew you were coming."

No spirit, decided Matilda. Of no importance. Completely subservient to the King. Perhaps the right kind of wife for him.

The King led his daughter into the castle. Adelicia walked on the other side of her. In the great hall the King's knights were drawn up in readiness to be presented to his daughter. He had clearly meant it to be a solemn occasion.

Henry watching his daughter receive her homage, felt his

spirits rise. What a woman, he thought. Germany had been good for her. She was every inch an Empress. She would not need to learn how to become a Queen.

One by one they came to do homage to her and the King's eyes glowed with pride when Robert, Earl of Gloucester, stood before her. He loved that boy—his own son by his beloved mistress. How often had he said: "Oh, God, why was not Robert legitimate!" If he had been there would have been no anxieties, no need to have made this second marriage which had brought him nothing.

Any man would be proud of two such children. He never liked Robert to be too far from him. It was several years now since he had brought him to Court and founded his fortunes in a rich marriage. Mabel, daughter of Robert FitzHamon and heiress to the rich lands of Gloucester, had proved a good wife; she had given him children who were a delight to the King. Healthy grandchildren. Why had not Robert been legitimate!

He must needs make the best of what he had and Robert was constantly with him. He had proved himself a good soldier and had shared many of Henry's campaigns. It was well to be served by members of the family who owed their prosperity to him. Robert was the result of a fervent passion which his legitimate children were not. He had been fond of his first wife Matilda, mother of this proud and haughty daughter and sad William; but it was the mother of Robert of Gloucester who had meant more to him than any other woman and he was glad that he had this reminder of their love constantly before him.

Now he knelt to Matilda and the King hoped that Robert would always be near her when she needed his support.

When this ceremony was over, Adelicia took her stepdaughter up to the chamber which had been prepared for her, and Matilda said: "I did not see my cousin Stephen among the knights."

"Stephen left the Court some weeks ago," Adelicia told her. "He has gone to Boulogne."

"He married Matilda of Boulogne, I know."

"And he is there looking after her estates. He was with the King in Normandy and now that it is peaceful he has gone to Boulogne."

Matilda felt disappointed. Her greatest anticipation had been a reunion with Stephen—well, perhaps not her greatest. That was certainly the hope of becoming her father's heiress.

But not far off was the hope that the excitement she used to know in Stephen's presence had not diminished.

"I doubt not," said Adelicia, "that he will ere long rejoin the Court. He never stays long from the King's side."

Matilda smiled. She would see him soon. Of course he would not stay long from the King's side. She could guess what went on in his mind.

He too would have hopes of the crown. She was amused. That they should both have the same ambitions—which neither could achieve if the other were successful—would, she believed, add a piquancy to their relations which would make it even more intriguing than it had been in the old days.

Before his daughter had been a week in Rouen, Henry had made up his mind.

He sent for Matilda and made sure that they were quite alone together so that they could talk frankly.

"Matilda," he said, "as you know I am disturbed at having no male heir."

Matilda replied: "My lord, you have a young wife. It may well be that you will ere long have a bonny son."

He shook his head. "I fear not. Adelicia is barren. We have been married six years and not a sign."

"But for some part of that time you have not been with the Queen."

"I have been with her long enough to fear that she is barren. I am married..." he waved his hand "...and so there is no hope."

"I know it must be a matter which greatly distresses you."

"I have never been one to mourn for what God has denied me. It seems to me wise now to cast about for a means of settling my affairs without a male heir."

"You are a wise lion as well as a just one," she said.

"And you are my only child and I believe that therefore as my nearest of kin you should take the place of your dead brother."

Her heart leaped with joy. Was this not the very moment of which she had dreamed for so many years?

"Father," she said, "you could rely on me to play my part."

"I know it. I have seen enough. You are indeed my daughter. I can see my spirit in you and that of your grandfather. I would have no qualms at leaving my crown in your hands."

"That is many years away," she said; and she thought:

Four perhaps. Five. Mayhap less. "I would have time to study your ways, to walk in your footsteps. I would be an apt pupil."

"I believe that. Do not think it is a joyous state to be a King of England and a Duke of Normandy."

"It is a great inheritance, a fearful duty."

"I see you understand. I have had little peace since I came to the throne. Many years of my reign have been spent out of England. That country I have ruled strongly and some might say harshly but all must admit justly. In Normandy I have fought bitterly for many years and I fear shall continue to do so. I should never have allowed the Clito to go free. Where he is, there will be trouble. As my elder brother's son, many declare him to be the heir of England as well as Normandy. I shall never know peace while he lives and he is a young man. His father, my brother Robert, as you know, is in prison in England and my good bastard Robert of Gloucester is in charge of him, so that I know he is in the best possible hands. But there has been trouble and there will be trouble. Clito will never give up his claims and there will always be those to support him. So do not think for one moment that being a ruler of countries merely consists of banquets and pleasure and being acclaimed by the people as one rides through the countryside."

"How could you ever believe I would have such foolish notions? I understood the problems which faced my husband. He was never at rest."

"You have been well schooled. Now, Matilda, I intend to make you my heir but before you can become this I must make sure that the people will accept you. While I live, yes...but if I were no longer here, who knows what might happen. I fear the Clito. I shall command all my knights and nobles to swear allegiance to you. They will need some persuasion."

"Why so?" asked Matilda haughtily.

"Because you are a woman."

"I will show them that a woman such as I am is as good as any man."

"I believe that you will...in course of time. But they do not know that yet. That is why I proposed to assemble them and make them one by one swear allegiance to you."

She nodded.

"Therefore," he went on, "we shall return to England and I shall send out a proclamation that all those whom I summon to London shall come and swear loyalty to you."

"Shall you send to all those whom it would concern?"

"Every one."

"There is my cousin Stephen. I believe he is in Boulogne. Shall you summon him?"

"Of a surety I will. It is very important that Stephen swear loyalty to you."

"He has some slight claim himself."

The King nodded. "Through my sister, his mother. Yes, he is no less the Conqueror's grandson than you are his granddaughter. Stephen has been a good nephew. At one time I thought I might train him to follow me. I think he had his hopes. But that was when the Emperor was alive and there did not seem any reason why you should come back."

"I shall be glad to know that the powerful men of the land accept me," she said.

She would be also equally glad to see Stephen and that she must surely do very soon.

It was September when they crossed to England. Matilda was moved to see again the burnished leaves, the green grass, the grey castle walls of the land she would always consider to be her home.

She rode between the King and Queen, and Henry told her how he had been born here shortly after his father had conquered the country and that it had always seemed to him to be his native land. It was one of the reasons why the people had accepted him. His brothers had been Normans; but he reckoned himself to be completely English.

"As I do," said Matilda.

"It is well to let the people know you feel this," he told her.

And so they came to London where Henry very soon made his intention known. He called together an assembly of the leading members of the Church and nobility. There he told them that in the event of his dying without a male heir he wished them to swear that they would without hesitation accept his daughter Matilda, as their sovereign.

This announcement was greeted with silence.

The King shouted: "This is my will."

Still there was silence.

It was Roger, Bishop of Salisbury, who was the first to raise his voice.

"My lord," he said, "these are troubled times. There are

some among us who fear that a woman, however gifted, would not be strong enough to stand against those who would rebel."

The King frowned and all those present trembled. They had always feared his wrath and since the disaster to the White Ship he was liable to fly into violent rages when he might order any punishment to be inflicted on those who disagreed with him.

For a few moments Roger and the King regarded each other steadily while the flame of anger flickered in the King's eyes. Roger was warning him. He was asking for time, for a private discussion. There they would work out a plan for making the King's will into law.

The King said: "I give you time to think of this matter. But rest assured this is my will and intention and it will go ill with any of you who attempt to defy me."

Crestfallen the gathering disbanded.

When the King and the Bishop of Salisbury were alone together, the Bishop said: "You must forgive my outburst, my lord. I believed that if we had not disbanded the assembly then some might have uttered that which they would find it hard to withdraw. You have chosen the Empress as your successor. Let us now see how we can prepare the lords and churchmen to accept this."

"They will accept it," said the King shortly. "As you all will."

"We shall, my lord, but let the matter be presented in such a manner that it is seen to be a right conclusion."

"It is my will," said the King, "and therefore a right conclusion."

Roger smiled blandly but he was thinking how Henry had changed. He was getting old and the need to establish his successor was imperative. Because his temper had shortened he no longer saw with the same clarity. Always before, his great virtue had been the ability to reason and admit he was wrong if proved to be.

Now Roger realized, even he must walk warily.

"It is your intention that Matilda should inherit both England and Normandy?"

"I do not wish them to be separated."

Roger nodded.

"And," added the King, "we must bear William Clito in mind. We must make it clear that he has no right to Normandy."

They were both silent. As the son of Robert to whom the

Conqueror had left his Duchy of Normandy there could be no logical argument that Clito was not the heir.

"Normandy is mine by right of conquest," said Henry, "as England was my father's by the same token."

"Matilda's descent through her mother will carry weight with the people."

"Ah," said Henry, "the Saxon line."

"You were wise when you married a daughter of Saxon kings, my lord."

"I know it well. The marriage helped me to the throne. Normans and Saxons united to make the English. That was what the people liked to hear."

"Now we will remind them that Edgar Atheling was your wife's uncle and many would have regarded him as the true Saxon King; but the Conqueror took England and brought great good to the land, so your daughter has a right to ascend the throne through her grandfather the Conqueror and through her mother's family the royal Athelings."

"That shall be done," said the King, "but they will know my wish and it would be well if they obeyed it."

"I have no doubt they will," replied Roger.

The Court had moved to Windsor, one of the King's favourite spots ever since his wife Matilda had, during one of his absences in Normandy, occupied herself with making the castle habitable. Matilda had been very interested in architecture as he was and his father and brothers had been; and they had certainly made some fine additions to the castle as they had to their apartments in the Tower of London.

Here the King decided to call together the assembly of nobles and high members of the Church that they might make their vows to Matilda.

The edict had gone out. All noblemen and churchmen above a certain standing were to present themselves at Windsor for the ceremony and any who did not appear would suffer the King's displeasure. What form that would take none could be sure, but eyes, noses, ears and hands were too precious to be risked.

Matilda was delighted with the way everything had turned out, and on the day Stephen arrived at Windsor she was greatly excited.

She saw his arrival, watching from a turret window. He had changed little, she thought, and where he had it was for the better. He was a man now.

She saw his silly little wife with him; courteously he helped her from the saddle and she stood smiling at him foolishly, thought Matilda.

Then he turned and spoke to some of the grooms. They smiled and bowed. Stephen always knew how to please everyone and did not hesitate to use his charm on the most lowly. She watched him come into the castle.

He was conscious of her as she was of him. When they assembled in the great hall and took their places at the board she was aware of his eyes eagerly scanning the company and she knew for whom he looked.

At length his eyes met hers. Oh, yes, the old spark was there; it flashed between them. Matilda wanted to sing aloud; she wondered if he felt the same.

When they had eaten and the drinking horns were being filled he came to sit beside her.

"Welcome home!" he said.

"Thank you, my lord."

"You are still the same exciting Matilda."

"And you have changed little, Stephen. Did you know that I was here?"

"The whole world knows that you are here."

"Yet you were in no haste to see me."

"I came with as much speed as I could muster."

She shrugged her shoulders petulantly. "It took so long. Boulogne is not so far."

"I have estates, duties. I was being harried by the Clito. I could not come until I had driven him off and beaten him...even for you."

"Stephen," she said, "will you swear fealty to me?"

"With all my heart," he answered.

How beautiful was the forest. How exhilarating to ride through in the chase and to know that Stephen was of the party.

They were of more importance to each other than the deer or the wild boar.

He was beside her, and it was not difficult to lose the rest of the party. How handsome he is! she thought. He must be the handsomest man in England! Oh, what joy to be home! How had she endured those weary, dreary years with that senile old man when this handsome knight was here, desiring her, dreaming of her surely, as she had dreamed of him.

"Oh, Stephen," she cried as he brought his horse close to

hers, "how beautiful is England! Nowhere in the world is there a forest like this."

"Because the Empress rides in it—that is why."

"Mayhap you prefer the forests of Boulogne."

"It would depend who was there."

"But this is my forest, Stephen, *my* forest. Look back at the castle. Is it not a noble sight? Did you know it is said King Arthur lived here...and that Merlin built a forest on the heights here. The Round Table was here."

"Legend," said Stephen. "It is of greater moment that you and I are here...together."

"So you feel that to be so."

"I do. And you."

"I am not displeased to be here."

"Then I must be beside myself with joy because my haughty Empress is not displeased."

"They used to call it Wyndleshore because of the winding river-banks. Did you know that, Stephen?"

"I knew it not, nor cared," he answered.

"My mother enlarged it and made it what it is today. Before that it was simply a hunting lodge. I remember seeing it for the first time."

"Do you remember seeing me for the first time?"

"Yes. Our cousin Stephen! Even then I liked you better than my brother."

"I liked you better than the whole Court put together."

She inclined her head, her cheeks flushed.

Then she cried out passionately: "And they married me to that old man!"

"You were so anxious to be an Empress. You put on airs in the nursery the moment you knew you were going to marry him. It seemed the title compensated for the man."

"It didn't, Stephen. I'd rather be a Queen."

"Ay," said Stephen, "and a Queen of England."

She lifted her head and studied him challengingly.

"Stephen, you are going to swear fealty to me. It is for that reason you are here."

"I know it well. The King has made his wishes clear."

"And will you do it?"

"How could I do aught else and not earn the acute displeasure of the King."

"So for that reason, you will swear to serve me?"

"That...and others."

"What others?"

"It was ever my greatest wish to make you happy."

"Oh, Stephen, it was so unfair. To give me to that old man and you that foolish girl."

"*My* Matilda is a good woman."

"A good woman. Did you want a good woman, Stephen? Was that why you wanted me?"

"I wanted you because you were the only one I cared for."

"And now?"

"It seems I am a man who does not change."

"They should have married us, Stephen. If they had, how different everything would have been."

"I should have had a virago for a wife instead of a meek woman who does all in her power to please me."

"But your virago would have pleased you more. Admit it, Stephen...if you dare."

"I make no attempt to deny it."

"I shall be your Queen one day."

"Hush. To say that is to anticipate the King's death. That's treason."

"Is he not anticipating it by calling you all here to swear loyalty to me?"

"In a manner. But he does not believe it will come to pass for many years. Who knows, by that time he may have got himself a son."

"Never. The Queen is barren."

"Trees which have stood barren for years will suddenly bear fruit."

"A barren woman and an old man. I am safe enough. You say this but to plague me."

"I beg you to take care for your own sake."

She laughed at him. "Poor Stephen, you had hopes did you not?"

"At one time, yes."

"And now I have disappointed them."

"You could never disappoint me."

"Nay...nor you me, Stephen. But they should have married us. You have some claim, I'll agree to that. You and I together would have worked well, Stephen. But my brother was alive then. He died too late."

Stephen said ironically, "Would you have had him hasten his departure?"

"There. You plague me again! Oh, Stephen, it is good to be home. It is good to see you. You are not bold enough, cousin. You never were. You were afraid that we should allow

94

our feelings their full rein, were you not? You used to think that if you got me with child you would have lost your eyes. You are not bold enough, Stephen."

"You were but twelve years old."

"Some are mature at that age. If you had not a wife, Stephen, it might be possible now. My father likes you. You are his good nephew. Your mother was always his favourite sister. I believe if you were free he would let us marry."

"But I am not free, Matilda."

In the distance they heard the sound of horses' hoofs. Some of the party were returning. She spurred her horse.

"You must learn to be bold, Stephen," she threw over her shoulder as she rode away.

They had given in. They knew they must; and although they could not imagine serving a woman, since it was the King's will there was no question of disobeying him.

So they came to Windsor and the King congratulated himself and Roger on their astuteness in pointing out how truly English Matilda was while being the granddaughter of the great Norman Conqueror.

They were earnestly discussing the matter of precedence. "I doubt not that the Archbishop of Canterbury will expect to take his oath first," said Roger.

"As head of the Church he will." The King smiled. "I remember well old Ralph's fury when you half-crowned the Queen and how he had to start from the beginning. We want no repetition of such a scene."

Roger grimaced. "Then I must needs swear my oaths after him."

"William Corbeil is not a bad fellow as Archbishops go. He is determined to cling to his rights. Who is not? But I had made up my mind to have no conflict with him such as I and my brother before me had with Anselm. The Church can be a plague to a King as you well know."

"But think what a blessing, my lord, when Church and State work together as in some cases."

"I forget not that you have worked well for me, Roger. Nor ever shall. I would I could set you above William. But it so happens that the Archbishopric of Canterbury has been appointed the first in the land."

"I know it well and let it be. It is not I who will complain. And after me will come your brother-in-law, the King of Scotland. That is as it should be, for he is the highest rank among the layman. So it will be the Archbishop as head of the Church followed by me as your chief judiciary as well as your Bishop, and then the King of Scotland. It is the next, my lord, that gives cause for careful thought."

"I have thought my son Robert."

"'Tis either Robert of Gloucester or your nephew Stephen."

"Stephen is but my nephew, Robert is my son."

"I know well how you love the Earl of Gloucester."

"Love him? Why, Roger, a hundred times a day I look at that young man and say, 'Would to God, you had been my legitimate son'."

"There lies the problem, my lord. For all his virtues he is your bastard."

"Alas 'tis true."

"And Stephen, born in wedlock, is the son of your sister."

"I have a fondness for them both. I confess, Roger, often I have wished that they had been my legitimate sons."

"And now, my lord, who shall precede the other?"

"I am unsure. When Matilda was a wife and not a widow, I should have said Stephen, for Stephen though my nephew is legitimate. But now there is Matilda...I know not, Roger. I will ponder the matter and let you know my decision."

"And when that decision is made the rest will be easy."

They talked of other matters.

When Stephen heard that there was a possibility of Robert of Gloucester's taking precedence over him he was bitterly angry. This would be construed—and rightly so—that the King considered his illegitimate son of greater importance than his nephew. It must not be. He must do all in his power to prevent it.

He allowed his wife Matilda to see his consternation; he knew that he must be wary of others. It would be fatal at this stage to offend the King.

Matilda, however, for all that she failed to excite him, was completely reliable.

"I do not understand how the King can consider it," he said. "It is an insult. I...to walk behind the son of one of his mistresses."

"You know, Stephen, how he loves Robert of Gloucester."

"We all know how he dotes on the fellow. But he is a bastard."

"The King's own son," said Matilda gently.

"Matilda, if the King allows this I have but one alterna-

96

tive...to return to Boulogne immediately after the ceremony."

"It might offend the King."

"I should be in Boulogne before he was able to express his displeasure."

"Do not risk offending him, Stephen."

"I shall care nothing for it if he allows me to be treated so, for depend upon it, Matilda, if he allows this it means that he has put me from his mind as regards...higher things."

She understood him well. She knew of the ambitions he rarely allowed others to see. She knew that he could be cruel. He had been so during his campaigns. He was not so open and frank as he appeared to be. Most men—and women particularly—found him affable but they did not know that there was a purpose behind his actions. They did not know that ever since the death of Prince William, Stephen had passionately longed to become King of England.

They guessed that the idea would enter his head that it might be a possibility, but that was natural enough for he was in the line of succession. They believed though that in his rather carefree amiable way Stephen had no great ambition.

Little did they know, thought Matilda. It seemed that the vision of a crown could change men. Yet was it really change?

There were two things she had always feared. One was that the King would die and that Stephen would take the throne; the other was that the Empress Matilda would return. This last had come to pass and she often wondered what was happening between this woman and her husband.

At least Stephen still longed for the crown; and how could it be his if it were Matilda's?

"Stephen," she said, laying her hand gently on his arm, "be careful."

He covered her hand with his. "You may be sure I shall," he answered her with a tender smile. "I can talk to you of these matters as I can to few others. I can trust you, Matilda."

"Whom should a man trust if not his wife?"

"I should be grateful for you," he said.

She wondered whether when he said those words he was thinking of the other Matilda.

It was with great pleasure that he received his brother Henry at Windsor.

To please his sister Adela, Stephen's mother, early that year the King had invited another of her sons to England where he might have an opportunity of making his fortune. The King had always been on very special terms of friendship with his sister and Adela followed her brother's progress with the utmost interest. She had applauded when he captured their elder brother Robert and imprisoned him; she informed him of the Clito's movements in Normandy whenever she could, so it was small wonder that the King should wish to repay her by helping her children.

Her third son Stephen had become more of an Englishman than a Norman and Adela had believed that he had had a good chance of taking the crown on his uncle's death. Now the Empress Matilda had been widowed that was changed and she deplored the fact that they had not married Stephen to the King's daughter Matilda rather than to his wife's niece. However, that was done and could not be changed, but Henry at least had offered to do something for her fourth son Henry, named after him.

He had written to his sister. "I can now offer your son Henry the Abbacy of Glastonbury. This will be but a beginning. I do not see why he should not in due course hold a high place in the Church."

Adela had been delighted. This was an excellent opportunity for her son, and good for her brother too. She knew that Henry planned to fill the Church with men who would serve him well, and who better than his own nephew?

"If Henry should prove as good a friend to me as Stephen," added the King, "he need have no fears about his future."

Young Henry, who had been brought up in the monastery of Cluny, was eager to accept the invitation and Stephen had warmly welcomed his brother, not only because of the family ties but because he knew that in Henry he would have a supporter when he should need it. He took his brother to his apartment where they might talk in secret.

Henry was astute and he was well aware of Stephen's hopes and fears. Immediately they began to discuss the significance of the order of precedence.

Henry knew of this for the whole Court was discussing it and he was determined with Stephen that it must not be.

"Yet," said Stephen, "if the King should decree that his bastard Robert go before me, what can I do?"

"I think, brother, then you should leave Court at once."

"And not swear fealty to the Empress?"

98

"If you did not do that it might well be the end of you."

"I believe that might well be. The King has been a good friend to me since I came to his Court but if I refused this order—and it is an order—I should so incur his wrath that he might well have me in a dungeon. I can tell you, Henry, that your uncle's rages can be terrible. He could demand my blood or my eyes in one of his rages and I assure you that would be my end."

"Nay, Stephen, you must take the oath of fealty to the Empress Matilda. But if the King should put Robert of Gloucester before you, then you should ask permission to leave Court and go to Boulogne with your wife and child."

"I see it is the only course to take."

"It is a pity that the Emperor died. Had he gone on living...had the King died first...."

"Hush, Henry, now it is you who are being indiscreet. Not a word of that. The Empress is here. She is the King's daughter. That is something we must accept."

He smiled, thinking of her—Matilda the haughty Empress who was so enchanted by him that in spite of her arrogant nature she could not hide it.

How could he be sorry that she had come home, no matter in what circumstances?

In the hall the Empress sat with her half-brother Robert, Earl of Gloucester. How respectful was the Earl. He was certainly pleased with himself, thought Stephen, as he approached them. And small wonder. The King doted on this son. It was said that of all his bastards—and there were more than twenty of them—Robert of Gloucester was the favourite. The King had bestowed great honours on him—lands and a rich wife; it was frequently whispered that one of the King's greatest regrets was that this fine man—soldier and scholar, a combination which never failed to appeal to Henry—was not his legitimate son.

"Here comes our cousin," said Matilda, her eyes watching Stephen with that sensuality towards which he had ever felt a ready response.

"Hail, cousin!" said Robert.

Stephen wanted to reply: "Hail, bastard." But it was not his nature to give way to his feelings; so he smiled in his charming and affable way.

"We were speaking of the ceremony," said Matilda. "How

I shall enjoy having two such as you to kneel to me and swear always to serve me."

Stephen replied.that he too longed for the opportunity.

"See how he flatters, Robert," said Matilda. "You may be a scholar but Stephen has the more ready tongue."

"My utterances, coming from the heart, take longer to reach my lips," said Robert.

"Oh, come," cried Stephen in the friendliest manner, "do you mean then that I speak falsely?"

Matilda laid a hand on each of the men's arms.

"No harshness, please. I would not wish that over me." She was smiling, her eyes dancing. Stephen thought: There is nothing you like better, my Matilda. And if I flatter you and lie a little then we are pair. We were meant for each other. This worthy bastard is different from us. "I know," went on Matilda, "that you will both serve me well. And that gives me great pleasure."

They talked of the arrangements for the ceremony and the matter of precedence was not openly discussed, though Matilda referred to it obliquely. Both of the men knew it to be too dangerous a topic for discussion and refused to be goaded.

Matilda enjoyed this rivalry between them. She referred constantly to Robert as her good brother and Stephen as her dear cousin; and all the time Stephen knew that she was urging him to declare his passion for her. What then? Did she not realize that this was as dangerous now as it had ever been?

But this bold adventurous woman liked danger; and had always wanted to be the centre of it.

Stephen wished that he could have been a faithful husband to his dear, good, dull Matilda. He wished that he did not feel this irresistible attraction for his cousin which could, if he allowed it to, take possession of him, bring him to disaster.

The two men surveyed each other cautiously. Robert of Gloucester knew full well that Stephen had believed it possible that he might follow his uncle to the throne. Now he would have to stand aside. This he was prepared to do but not so far back that Robert of Gloucester should take precedence over him.

Stephen remembered the advice of his wife and his brother Henry. The Empress might be trying to goad him to folly, but those two had only his good at heart.

* * *

Roger of Salisbury said to the King, "This matter of precedence has become one of great moment, my lord."

"It is of little importance."

"To Stephen it is of the greatest."

"Oh, come, Roger, why shouldn't my son come before my nephew?"

"Because your son is a bastard."

"What a difference a ceremony makes. I loved well his mother. Never did I love a woman as I loved her. And I love well my son. He is one to be proud of."

"But a bastard, sir, and I fear Stephen will be mortally offended if you set Robert before him."

"Stephen will be offended! By God's death, have I not done everything for that boy? Where would he be without me? In Blois...the third son of a Count. All his lands, his riches, his wife...all these I have provided and he is going to be offended with me!"

"Stephen is an amiable young man. He will take the oath and swear fealty to Matilda, but I have it on good authority, that once the ceremony is over he will ask your leave to retire to Boulogne as there will be nothing to keep him here."

"I see."

"Stephen has fought well for you, my lord. He has been loyal and loved you as a son would a father. Of course he has had hopes. He would be a fool if he had not. Now the Empress has returned and he will be her supporter. But if you allow your bastard to take precedence over him he will regard that in the light of an insult. It will undermine his position here at Court. He will sooner or later return to Boulogne. Do you wish that, my lord, with the Clito at large over there, looking for those who no longer feel the same loyalty towards you as they once did?"

"You are suggesting that Stephen would turn traitor?"

"Not at once. But if he went away....If he stayed in Boulogne. My lord, it is only recently that he fought the Clito on his own borders and inflicted defeat on that young man. Stephen will stay here. He will be your good servant and if ever the day should come—which God forbid—when Matilda should need that support, he will be at hand to give it. I hope, my lord, you will consider well before you inflict this indignity on your nephew."

The King was thoughtful for a few moments and then he said: "Very well. Let them kneel before the Empress in this order. The Archbishop of Canterbury first, then you Roger, followed by the King of Scotland and then shall follow Stephen and after him Robert."

Roger bowed. "Ah, my lord, as usual you show your wisdom to us all. I see your motive. You wished Stephen to ponder. The bounty he enjoys comes from you. But for you he would be at his home in Blois...with few possessions, a third son. Now he comes after the King of Scotland. He will serve you with his life as he was prepared to do. He will stay in England. He will be at your right hand as in the past. He will remember this day."

The King nodded. Roger was right of course; and this tiresome business of precedence was settled.

In the great hall of Windsor—the pride of Henry who had transformed a fortress which was little more than a hunting lodge into a magnificent castle—Matilda was seated on a throne-like chair, there to receive the oath of loyalty from those who were intended to be her future subjects.

Matilda sat there, proud and regal. All was going as she had dreamed. She was home; and her stepmother was barren; and her father had named her heiress to the throne. This was the fulfilment of her ambitions.

Windsor, beautiful Windsor, which had excited her mother so much because she hoped that by the time the King returned from the Normandy wars she would have his magnificent apartments ready. Her thoughts went back to the days before she had been sent to Germany. It had been Whitsuntide and they had celebrated the feast at Windsor—the new Windsor; and it was in this very hall that her father had sent for her and there, with her mother beside him, had told her that great honour had been done to her, because the Emperor of Germany was asking her hand in marriage.

Beautiful Windsor, with its forests and legends of King Arthur from whom her mother must have descended. It was appropriate that she should be back in this hall where she had been told of her destiny years ago and now she could see herself at the pinnacle of her desire—or almost. Not until the crown was on her head would that be so. Yet she was almost there. One more step, she thought. She studied her father. He was ageing fast. His servants said he suffered from indigestion and they could not tell how great the pain was because they dared not approach him when he suffered from it. How many years...two, three. Five at the most?

And as she watched that array of knights she thought of

102

other ceremonies—at Utrecht when she had been betrothed to the Emperor Henry and at Mainz when the Archbishop of Trier had placed the Imperial crown on her head. She had thrilled to such honour and had tried not to see the old man at her side who had made it all possible. If it had been young Stephen who had been her husband then how differently she would have felt. But the pomp and ceremony had compensated her to a great degree. Homage, rank, power—these were the real goal, she knew. But love was important as she had realized since she grew older.

And then she thought of a poor old man with wild eyes and trembling hands, rising from his bed and wrapping himself in an old woollen garment and padding barefoot through the castle.

He is dead, she told herself. That is the end of him. Was he not buried with all the ceremony due to an Emperor? That phase of my life is finished. The Empress will in due course become a Queen.

Her father sat beside her, his eyes watchful. There was her stepmother, poor Adelicia whose barren state made this ceremony necessary. I for one shall not complain of that, thought Matilda wryly.

One by one they came and knelt. Archbishop William of Corbeil first, followed by Roger, Bishop of Salisbury. There was a man she must watch. If ever there was trouble in the country she would want him on her side. And next David the First of Scotland, her mother's brother, who had recently become the King after the death of his brother Alexander. The King was wise; it would be well, in the event of any trouble, to have the oath of the King of Scotland. And then the moment for which she was waiting. Stephen. A triumphant Stephen because he had won his battle with Robert of Gloucester and came before the King's bastard.

She thought: How handsome he is! The others are insignificant beside him. And passionately she asked herself why fate could have been so cruel as to marry her to the old Emperor when she might have had Stephen. It would have been so reasonable if her brother William had already been drowned on the White Ship before her marriage. Cruel Fate, that had given her to that senile old man and then taken William.

But Fate was smiling now. Here she was, an Empress, and a Queen to be; and kneeling at her feet the handsomest man in England, his eyes glowing with passion to which she responded whole-heartedly.

Life was offering a great deal. She must grasp it. It was offering the crown and that was what she wanted more than anything. And Stephen was here to swear undying devotion.

What more could she ask? It was foolish to entertain for one moment these memories of a crazy old man with wild eyes, padding barefoot about his palace.

Stephen had pressed her hand; his lips were on her skin; he lifted his eyes and they smiled at each other.

The Reluctant Bride

Roger and the King were together in Henry's private chamber. Startling news had come from Normandy. The King of France, perennial enemy of England, had offered his wife's half-sister, Jeanne, to the Clito.

"By God's death," cried Henry, "here is a fine state of affairs. They were always allies, but this will bind them so close that they will be as one. He does it to plague me. It is a signal, you will see. Trouble is going to flare up in Normandy."

"When has there not been trouble in Normandy?" asked Roger. "Only your brilliant generalship has kept that troublous Duchy in our hands."

"No peace," said the King. "No peace at all. Moreover Louis is making Clito a present of the Vexin—and that piece of land lying as it does on our borders, has caused me more trouble than any other. I see that I shall soon be leaving for Normandy."

While they were discussing these matters a messenger arrived with more disquieting news. The Count of Flanders had been murdered and as he had left no heirs, the King of France had bestowed his lands on William Clito.

"Louis is putting more and more power into that boy's hands," cried Henry. "Soon there will be no holding him."

"There is also Fulk of Anjou," Roger reminded the King. "Ever since his daughter was returned to him minus her dowry he has been waiting to get his revenge."

"Ah, Fulk. He is the one I fear more than any, Roger. There is a true soldier, a man who is shrewd and ever ready to seize an opportunity. If he were but on my side, I would stand against Louis and Clito—for neither of whom have I much respect."

"There was a time when you and he were friends."

"That was when he believed his daughter would one day be Queen of England. Oh, Roger, how often are my troubles and stresses brought back to the disaster of the White Ship."

"Marriage brought his friendship, then...."

Roger was looking intently at his master.

"He has a son," said the King, slowly. "He is but thirteen years old, I believe. Matilda is twenty-four."

Roger spread his hands. "Age cannot always be a consideration in royal marriages," he said.

"There you speak truth. What then?"

"An alliance with Fulk would change the entire picture."

Henry laughed. "I can picture Louis' face when he heard."

"Remember, my lord, how it helped us at the time of your son's marriage with his daughter."

"I remember well."

"It could change again."

"A boy of thirteen and my daughter. Could a boy of that age get sons?"

"Of a certainty, my lord. You were not much older when your first were begotten I believe."

"I was advanced in such matters."

"A strong woman such as your daughter would be a good teacher."

They smiled. Then the King said: "I believe you to be right in this, Roger. But I must needs think. I had wished that Matilda should marry again but I had wanted an English marriage. As you know there was a hint when I got them to agree to swear fealty to her that there would not be a foreign marriage. The people do not want a foreigner here on the throne."

"The throne would be for Matilda."

"Ay, but a husband, Roger."

"A boy now but he can be moulded into a man. It is better that he should be young."

"We need Fulk's help," said the King. "We need it badly."

"May I suggest, my lord, that we brood on this matter."

"A wise suggestion, Roger. Let me give it thought."

The King sent for his daughter. He wished to be completely alone with her. He had a matter of great importance to discuss.

106

By God's death, he thought, she gives herself airs this daughter of mine. One would think she were Queen and I a subject.

Yet in a way he was pleased with her demeanour. When her turn came she would carry the orb and sceptre with dignity.

"Now, daughter," he said, "be seated. This is a matter which must be resolved without delay. You are now the heir to the throne and your first duty as such will be to provide the heirs the country needs."

She was silent. Her heart had begun to beat very fast. She could not get out of her mind the picture of her husband rising from his bed and padding barefoot to the door. She thought of the news of his death and the funeral. She had not seen the face of the man in the coffin.

"Therefore," went on the King, "the next matter we have to deal with is your marriage. You have no children by the Emperor and that may well be a blessing, but you must now without delay set about the task of providing heirs for the nation."

"Yes, father," she said slowly.

"We have found a bridegroom for you. This marriage will bring peace to the country and to Normandy...."

"So I am to be used."

"My dear daughter, we are all used. I married your mother because she was a Saxon princess and although I had been born and bred in England and was the son of a Norman king, I had to submit."

"My mother always used to say that yours was a true love match."

"I wooed her it is true but I did so because I know what such a marriage would do for the country."

"And secure your accession to the throne."

"That was so. I was wise. And so must you be. The country wants an heir. It is your duty to provide that."

"And who has been chosen to be the sire?"

"Geoffrey of Anjou."

"Who is he?"

"The son of Fulk."

"Your enemy!"

"At the moment. Some time since he was my friend. That was when his daughter married your brother."

"And I am to have the son."

"He will inherit Anjou and as you know this is the most

107

important province in Normandy. He can cause me great trouble if he remains my enemy. If he is my friend everything is turned about."

"And so, because of his father's infidelity this man is to sire my children."

"You know full well that you must have a husband. I have chosen Geoffrey of Anjou."

"I have no wish to marry...yet."

"But I wish you to marry without delay."

"And what is he like, this Geoffrey of Anjou?"

"He is a little young at this time, but that is something which time will remedy."

"A little young. How old?"

"He is approaching fourteen years."

"Fourteen! A child! For me!"

"He will grow up quickly."

"I'll not have him."

The King stood up and assumed an expression which would have struck immediate terror into any of his subjects. But Matilda was his daughter and she also rose. They faced each other.

"It would seen," said the King, "that you are under a misapprehension. You do not rule this land yet, and you, Madam, are as certainly a subject as the lowliest serf in this castle. Remember this! I have raised you up. As easily could I put you down. Ay, and would, if you displease me."

Matilda said: "And when you put me down who will then be your heir?"

"There are others."

"To come before your own flesh and blood?"

"There are other members of my family who could succeed me to the throne."

"My cousin Stephen? Or one of your many bastards? I believe there are twenty of them—perhaps more."

"And more joy they bring me than my legitimate children. One died...and the other a virago who would rule the land before she comes to the throne."

His anger was terrible but her common sense warned her that if he became truly enraged he would disinherit her. She would have to go carefully.

"But father," she faltered, "a boy not yet fourteen."

"It is his age now."

"I am a woman, father. I do not want a child for a husband."

"It is necessary. We need this marriage. We have to placate Fulk or there will be bitter bloodshed in Normandy with God knows what disasters. Clito is rising. I do not fear him, but I do know the might of Fulk. And marriage alone will bring him to our side."

She was silent for a few seconds and he went on: "So, we shall go ahead with the negotiations. They will take a little time. You will have some months before you need to go to Anjou."

"Go to Anjou! Why should he not come here?"

"Because his estates are in Anjou."

"But...."

"You are not yet Queen of England; it would be well to remember. When I die you would return with him and rule this country. In the meantime it would be necessary for you to go to Anjou."

To go to Anjou. To leave England. Not to see Stephen. It would be as bad as being in Germany. Had she escaped from one doom to walk straight into another?

She would not have it. Anything...anything was better than that.

She made up her mind.

"There is something I must tell you," she said. "It concerns my husband."

He looked at her sharply. "The Emperor?"

She nodded. "He...he may not be dead."

"What do you mean?"

"One night he left our bed. I saw him wrapped only in a woollen garment...the sort pilgrims wear. Barefooted he left the apartment. I never saw him after that."

The King narrowed his eyes. "What means this? You did not see him! Did you not attend his funeral and was he not buried in State and was not a monument erected to him?"

"This was so, but I cannot swear that the body which was buried at Spires was his. I did not see him after that night. I was told that he had died."

"But you must have looked on his face. You, his wife...not to know him!"

"I did not."

"This is a wild story and I believe it not."

"It is wild certainly but where there is madness strange things happen."

"Madness?"

"You know full well the Emperor was mad. His usurpation
109

of his father's crown preyed on his mind. He could talk of nothing else. All through the night he would ramble. You cannot know what I suffered with him. He was mad, I tell you. I knew. His ministers knew it. All those close to him knew it. And I verily believe that he either left the palace to become a pilgrim or was spirited away by those who realized that they could not leave the Imperial crown in the hands of a madman."

The King was staring at her in horror. "This cannot be true."

"You know full well that it could be true."

"Why did you not demand to know the truth?"

"Because I did not want to. I had endured that insane old man long enough. I wanted to come home to my true inheritance."

"If he has been buried he can be deemed dead, and there's an end to it."

"And if I married? If I had children and if my first husband were alive what would these children be but bastards."

"God's death," said the King.

"I tell you this," went on Matilda, "that if I were sent to a thirteen-year-old boy I might well refuse him because, since I know not whether my husband be dead or alive, I am in no position to become a wife to another and bear children who would be the heirs to England."

"So you refuse to marry Geoffrey of Anjou?"

"I have told you my reasons. You will admit they are good ones."

"Nay," thundered the King. "I do not call them good ones. You are a widow. Know that."

"How can I be when...."

"Because I say so."

A scornful smile curved Matilda's mouth but the sight of her father's cold fury made her suppress it. She was ruthless but no more so than he was. He had married her into Germany when she was a child; he had brought her back because he wished to make her his heir; and now he was determined on her marriage to Anjou. She knew that if she defied him she would do so at her peril. He had not the same love for her as he had for Robert of Gloucester. She was his legitimate daughter but his love children were closer to him. Her strength was in her legitimacy, not her father's love. Stephen could take the crown, for he was near enough in the succession and the people would prefer a man to rule them rather than a woman.

She must be careful or it might be that she, like the poor Emperor, might be spirited away.

She was playing a very dangerous game.

So she was silent and lowered her head so that her father might not see the speculation in her eyes.

"You have much to learn," he said, and the coldness of his tone showed her the calculating depth of his anger. He would stop at nothing, she knew. "I am the King. There are many years left to me—a fact which may disturb you."

"Nay, nay," she cried and tried to simulate real emotion.

He went on: "I *will* be obeyed. You will have heard what happens to those who disobey me."

"I know that you are just and never hesitate to punish the unlawful."

"No matter who they be," he added. "Understand this, my subjects obey me unquestioningly. You may be my daughter but you are also my subject."

"I know that, Father."

"Rather think of me as your King. What you have told me is disturbing. But I know full well that the marriage I have chosen for you and which will bring much good to your country is distasteful to you. I believe it may be that you have invented this wild story because you do not wish to marry the man I have chosen for you."

"That is not so, Father. The story is a true one."

"That I shall discover. In the meantime you will do as I say. You will mention this to no one and to make sure that you do not, you will not mingle with the Court."

"You are sending me away?"

He was thoughtful for a moment. "I cannot do that. But you are going to need nursing and I shall ask the Queen to care for you in her apartments; and there you will stay with her until I give you permission to emerge."

"Please, Father, I promise that I will not say a word of this. . ."

"There is one thing you must quickly learn, Matilda. Methinks your years in a foreign court have made you forget that I am the master here. Wait here until I return."

He left her. She sat down on the faldestol; she was trembling. What had she done? She was going to be a prisoner here, perhaps. The Queen's prisoner! But perhaps at least she had saved herself from marriage with that odious boy.

111

She was sure he was odious. Thirteen years old. The thought was revolting. To go away from England to Anjou, to leave everything she had come home for... power... and Stephen!

But had she done the right thing?

The King returned and the Queen was with him. Poor silly Adelicia, thought Matilda, she looked alarmed. And well she might be with such a husband.

"I have told the Queen that I wish you to have a rest. She will look after you in her apartments. Adelicia, my dear, take care of my daughter. See that she is undisturbed. I want her to be kept from everyone. You will be her constant companion. Then I am sure in due course she will recover her health."

Adelicia was smiling shyly; and Matilda had no recourse but to go with the Queen to her apartments since the King accompanied them and made it clear in a quietly sinister way that she was his prisoner.

Matilda sat at the window and looked out on the courtyard. They were celebrating Christmas at Windsor but she was not down in the great hall. She must stay up here with only the Queen for company.

In the great hall they would be thinking of her, if they dared not talk of her. They would be careful not to arouse the King's displeasure. What were they thinking? His only daughter just returned from Germany; all the powerful men of the kingdom had been commanded to swear allegiance to her; and now she was shut away from the Christmas festivities although she was in the castle.

It must be a great mystery.

Stephen would be down there with his wife, that other Matilda. Was he thinking of her? But of course he was. Suppose he had been a bold lover caring only for his lady's weal, like those of whom the minstrels sang, would he not have risked all to come to her?

But Stephen was not of that kind. She would have despised him if he had been. Had he attempted to come near her he would have incurred the King's displeasure with who knew what dire consequences. She, whose ambition was to wear a crown, could understand and respect a like desire in Stephen. Oh, the pity of it that they had not married then when they were young. She would have been the Queen and he her consort. Always she would have made him aware of who was the ruler. But what a wonderful life they would have had together!

Dreams! she thought contemptuously. All dreams.

And so she must pass her days with Adelicia and the best thing she could say of her was that she was kind.

There Adelicia would sit over her needlework—Matilda was not interested in such feminine accomplishments—while Matilda paced up and down, or sat looking out of the windows, or talked endlessly of the wrong which had been done to her.

Adelicia always tried to soothe her and to tell her that everything the King did was for his daughter's good. How that made Matilda want to scream. Everything the King did was for his own good, she replied, to which Adelicia made the comment, which was perhaps not unwise, that what was good for the King was good for his daughter, for she would one day rule the country after him.

Adelicia talked of the Emperor for whom she had some affection, she said, because he had helped her father to recover Lower Lorraine.

"He was good to my father," said Adelicia.

"Remember this," retorted Matilda, cynically. "Sovereigns are never good to others. They are only good to themselves. You may depend upon it that it suited the Emperor to help your father and it was for this reason that he did so."

Adelicia shook her head and said she believed there was a great deal of kindness in the world.

Such a companion for me! thought Matilda. Oh, why did not Stephen come to see her?

Everything had gone wrong. A horrible premonition came to her that she might never become Queen of England.

What if her father discovered that the Emperor was not dead? What had they done with him? Imprisoned him somewhere? Suppose he lived for years and years until she was too old to bear children?

What if she never came to the throne after all? Who would? Stephen? She laughed at the thought. She would never allow that. Robert of Gloucester? That was what the King would like but even he knew that the people would never accept his bastard. But her grandfather the Conqueror had been a bastard, and before he became known as the Conqueror he had been called "the Bastard", often slightingly. His father, Robert the Magnificent, had forced his vassals to accept him as their Duke. And what had been the result? Wars throughout his life. And those wars had ravaged Normandy ever since.

It was a horrifying thought.

It must never come to pass.

It was more than eight weeks since she had been placed in Adelicia's apartments. Spring had come; she watched the buds on the trees from her window and heard the mating songs of the birds.

Her father came to the apartment. He sat down and looked at her gravely.

"I'll swear you have had enough of these walls," he said.

"I am sick unto death of them."

He smiled. "And in a mood to be wise mayhap."

"I would prefer anything I believe to staying here."

"I am glad to hear it, for you are going to leave these rooms."

"I am to be received back at Court?"

"I cannot keep my daughter shut away indefinitely."

"People must think it strange," she agreed.

"Well, you are recently a widow and in mourning. They will believe that for a time you wished to be alone. But now that period is over and it is time for you to emerge. There will be a grand celebration at Whitsuntide to mark the occasion of your betrothal."

She caught her breath and waited. He paused for a few moments before adding: "To Geoffrey of Anjou."

He waited for the storm of protest, but it did not come. She knew that it was useless to protest.

He watched her for a few seconds, guessing her thoughts, then he nodded with approval. At least she had learned one lesson.

"So this boy agrees to take me," she said.

"His father insists that he does."

"Poor child, he has no more say in the matter than his bride."

"It is the way with royal marriages. You will have the satisfaction of knowing that you have saved many lives which would otherwise have been lost in the battles for Normandy."

"I and this boy must pay the price I daresay."

"Oh, it will be amusing enough. You can school him. You will do what you will with him."

She shrugged her shoulders. It was useless to do anything but accept. And in truth she was so weary of being shut away that she welcomed any diversion.

So once again there was a gathering in the great hall and there she was solemnly betrothed to Geoffrey of Anjou. Her

114

eyes flashing, her head held high, she took her oaths and there was a burning resentment in her heart.

If her father but knew how she hated him he would be alarmed. He must die, she thought, before I can come back, and I hope that day will not be long delayed. To wish a father dead, that was surely a wicked thing; but not when that father first bartered her to a man forty years her senior, because he needed an alliance with Germany, and now having served that sentence, here she was being handed to a boy ten years younger than herself. It would be understood that she had little love for such a sire. He wanted only the advantage she could bring him and was ready to sacrifice her to attain it; she too wished only for the advantage he could bring her and only his death could give her what she wanted.

So she was betrothed to Geoffrey of Anjou and was to leave almost immediately for Rouen where the marriage would take place.

Once more she received the homage of the principal men of the kingdom. They must accept her as the lady of England and Normandy.

She was glad of an opportunity to have a word with Stephen before she left.

"I trust you have missed me, cousin," she said.

"More than I can say."

"You knew I was in the Queen's apartments."

"Ay, I knew."

"And made no effort to see me."

"It was against the King's wishes."

"Some might have defied those wishes."

"Not the wishes of Henry of England."

"Are you such a coward then?"

"I trust I am brave enough. But I would keep myself comely in my features, for dearly as I should have loved to see you I could not have endured for you to turn away in horror when later you saw me."

"My father is a harsh man, Stephen."

"He is a King who will be obeyed."

"You know I am to go away, very soon. Only a few days are left to me here. I'm to be married to a ... child, Stephen."

"He is the luckiest child on earth."

"Oh, Stephen ... are you thinking what I am?"

"I think so. If they had married you to me how wise they would have been."

115

"And how happy we should have been! Good-bye, Stephen."

"You will be back ere long."

"And when I come?"

"Who knows—everything may be different then."

In a few days time she left. The King had appointed Robert, Earl of Gloucester, and Brian Fitzcount, to accompany her.

Alas, thought Matilda, that Stephen had not been sent. How she would have enjoyed that. But how dangerous that would have been! Always fear of what would happen to them had kept them apart. There were some who would risk all for love. Not Matilda, not Stephen. And Henry would have no mercy on either of them.

She must forget Stephen for a while. At least she had seen him again; she knew that that flame of desire could still flare up between them. It was a comforting thought.

Now she turned her attention to her half-brother Robert, and Brian Fitzcount.

Robert was already her good friend so she set out to charm Brian. He was called Fitzcount because he was the illegitimate son of the Count of Brittany. When he was quite a boy his father had asked Henry if he would take him into his Court and instruct him in the arts of war and chivalry. Henry who had always liked to surround himself with protégés had agreed to do so and Brian had become a special favourite of his. A short while before Henry had knighted him and found a rich wife for him. The King had further shown his favour by sending him with Robert of Gloucester to escort Matilda to Rouen.

Brian was anxious to ingratiate himself with the haughty Empress who, feeling resentful against her father and against fate for separating her from Stephen, set out to charm both Brian and Robert. Before they reached Rouen the two men had sworn to serve her to the end of their days. Any arrogance which had deserted her while she had been her Father's captive now returned, and although Robert of Gloucester brought instructions from Henry that the marriage was to take place immediately she found reasons to delay it.

The first reason was the celebration which must take place in the city which had been decorated for the purpose. This took time to prepare and the people must not be hurried

116

through it, declared Matilda. Through the streets went dancers and heralds and Henry had decreed that there should be a proclamation bidding all rejoice in the coming marriage of the heiress of England to the son of the Count of Anjou. Any who did not join in with great rejoicing would suffer the King's displeasure. The heralds sounded their trumpets and criers at street corners announced the declaration which the King had ordered should be given throughout the city.

"Let no man here present, native or foreigner, rich or poor, high or low, stay away from these royal rejoicings, for whosoever shall do so shall be named guilty of an offence against the King."

So, at the coming of Matilda none dared but rejoice.

The Archbishop of Rouen called at the palace to see Matilda. She received him with that haughty demeanour which was already beginning to be noticed and resented.

"My lady," said the Archbishop, "I have instructions from the King, your father, to perform the ceremony of marriage between you and the son of the Count of Anjou without delay."

"I am as yet unprepared," replied Matilda.

"These are commands from the King."

"You cannot make me take my vows if I refuse to speak," retorted Matilda.

"You have come here to marry, I understand."

"In my own time. I will not be unduly hastened."

"The people are already celebrating this event."

"Let them. I shall say when I shall marry."

The Archbishop was torn between what he had understood the King's orders to be and the stubborn determination of his daughter. When Matilda stood to her full height and her eyes flashed with rage, she was indeed formidable; and everyone knew that the King was an ageing man and that she had been proclaimed his successor.

The Archbishop postponed the ceremony.

When the King heard of Matilda's prevarication he flew into a rage but after calm consideration and discussion with Roger of Salisbury he came to the conclusion that a little delay was not so much to be deplored. The bridegroom was overyoung. Sixteen would be a more reasonable age for marriage; and Matilda had many years before her for childbearing. Fulk had been placated because the King had sent his

117

daughter to Normandy and there was no danger from that quarter.

In due course, Henry would go to Normandy and deal with Matilda's tantrums.

He did this sooner than he expected for a few weeks after Matilda had arrived, fresh trouble broke out in the Duchy and the King's presence was urgently needed there.

He left at once.

In Rouen he demanded of Matilda what she meant by disobeying his orders and forcing the Archbishop of Rouen to do the same.

"I needed time," she said. "This is a serious step, particularly in view of my husband's...."

Henry held up his hand. The Emperor's end was a matter he did not want mentioned.

"Your marriage shall take place when I have settled this trouble," he told her. "I give you till then to come to terms with your future."

She was pleased. It was a victory if a small one.

William Clito in his new found strength, with the King of France firmly behind him, was a greater menace than he had ever been; and no sooner had Henry brought order to one trouble spot than another presented itself.

A year had passed since Matilda had come to Rouen and she was still unmarried.

It was June before Henry could safely leave the battlefield and return to Rouen. Geoffrey was at that time fifteen and Henry decided that there should be no more delay.

Fulk came to Rouen with his son and the prospective bride and bridegroom were presented to each other. Neither was favourably impressed; Matilda saw a petulant boy, Geoffrey an arrogant woman; and neither was of a temperament to pretend otherwise.

The King had much to say to Fulk and he suggested to him that the happy pair should be allowed a few moments alone to "congratulate each other on their good fortune."

When they were alone the happy pair scowled at each other. Matilda was determined to show Geoffrey right from the first who would be in control of their household.

"Do not imagine," she said, "that I want this marriage."

"You could not want it less than I do."

"You should be pleased with your prospects."

"I do not see it so, Madam," he replied insolently.

"I should be the one to complain. You are but a boy...."

"And to be married to an old woman!" he countered.

"Old! I am not old. It is because you are but a child that you think so."

He shrugged his shoulders. "Your father is overeager for this match."

"Yours is not averse to it, I gather."

"They have arranged it between them."

"So there is something to be gained on both sides."

"I do not wish to consider their motives. They are obvious enough."

"You began it, Madam."

"I can see you are going to be a tiresome boy."

"And you will be a shrew."

"Two such as we are are sure to have a happy marriage," she retorted with sarcasm.

"Alas," replied the boy, "it is something we must submit to."

"Then we must needs accept our ill fate."

"'Tis so, I fear."

Then Matilda turned her back on him and went to the window to look out. They were shortly joined by their fathers.

"Alas," said Fulk beaming with pleasure, "we must interrupt this happy meeting. Condolences my son, but you will have the rest of your life to spend with this gracious lady."

Matilda noticed too that the King was delighted. It seemed everyone was pleased about this coming wedding, except the two it most concerned.

Henry was indeed pleased. Fulk had told him that he was contemplating going to Jerusalem. It was time he repented of his sins; and when he did so he would pass over all his possessions to his son Geoffrey who would immediately become the Count of Anjou. He proposed to see the marriage solemnized and then depart.

Nothing could have delighted the King more. His prospective son-in-law was a young man who could be guided. Anjou would therefore be, from every practical point of view, under the King's command. His greatest enemy would be removed; this was to have happened with the marriage but if Fulk cut himself off from his interests in Anjou it would be doubly desirable.

Fulk was happy too. He could now pass to his period of

repentance and make sure he had expiated his sins before he died. He could congratulate himself that Normandy would be brought to his family through his son; and that was the fulfilment of a lifelong ambition.

Once he had seen Geoffrey married to the King's daughter, he could leave for Jerusalem and repentance, knowing that he had gained all he set out to gain in Normandy; and there would doubtless be certain battles in the Holy Land which would be a joy, for there he could practise war with all its attendant cruelties under the eye of God and it would not be a sin but all in His cause and therefore laudable.

There was no longer any reason to delay the marriage.

The King knighted Geoffrey and the royal party travelled to Le Mans and on the 17th June of the year 1128 Matilda married Geoffrey of Anjou.

That the marriage should prove a failure was inevitable since both parties had firmly made up their minds that it should be.

Their dislike did not diminish as they knew each other better and as neither would make the slightest attempt to placate the other they indulged frequently in their favourite pastime which was throwing insults at each other.

Henry had had to hurry from Le Mans because fresh fighting had broken out in Normandy, a reminder that although he had appeased Anjou, the Clito was still a formidable enemy.

It seemed though that fate had decided to favour him. A hint of this came in one of the despatches he received from the battlefield of Alost. At first it had been dismissed as trivial for the wound was nothing but a prick in the thumb from an enemy's lance. When Henry heard that because of this his nephew had gone to the monastery of St. Bertin to recover, he laughed aloud.

"The poor boy is so concerned about a scratch then?" he cried.

But the scratch was no ordinary one. The thumb was infected and the poison spread through the Clito's body.

Within a week he was dead.

Henry could scarcely believe his good fortune. Anjou his to command through the marriage of his daughter and the young Count; and now the Clito to whom so many had rallied because they believed that, with his father a prisoner in England, he was the true heir at least of Normandy if not England as well, was dead.

He was growing old. But it seemed to him that all his wishes were coming true. Now there could be some peace in Normandy. He was in truth now—if one forgot Robert in his prison and all must agree that Robert was unworthy to govern—the rightful heir to England and Normandy.

He would go back and enjoy a little domestic peace. Adelicia did not excite him in the least, but she was good and meek; and he was of an age which did not look for the sensational adventures of youth.

The Lovers

When the King had a great deal to occupy his mind he did not give much thought to the past, but since he had returned to England where State matters could peacefully be discussed and there were no longer the sudden and urgent calls to Normandy he began to look back over the outstanding events of his life.

He found a certain pleasure in sitting with his wife and discussing these. Again and again he recounted the story of the lost White Ship and how his misfortunes had begun with that dire tragedy. He continually stressed that if it had not been for the loss of that ship there would not have been this desperate need to get an heir, for he would have had one already. He would not have had to marry again. Poor Adelicia! she cast down her head as though in apology.

He patted her hand. "You have been a good wife in all but one thing," he told her.

"The most important thing," she answered.

"That was not in your power to supply," he told her and added kindly: "You have been a comfort to me."

It was true. When he meandered on about the past he did not want an intellectual companion. Sentiment suited him much better in such moods and the self-effacing nature of the Queen was exactly what he needed. He could talk to her for hours and she would only answer briefly or nod her head in sympathy. He was therefore able to tell her of his many sins and how he was beginning to feel the need for repentance.

"Fulk of Anjou has gone to Jerusalem. I heard he is to marry Melisande, the daughter of Baldwin. He will follow him as King of Jerusalem. So you see he has found a happy solution. He had a son to whom he could leave his estates in

Anjou. Could I go to Jerusalem? Could I make a pilgrimage to the Holy Land? What of my duties here? What of England and Normandy?"

Adelicia ventured that perhaps God would accept repentance from England as readily as from the Holy Land.

"It is much easier for a man who has lived by his sword. He simply transfers allegiance from ambition and love of power to God. When he fights the Infidel he fights for God; when he respects the Holy Land he respects God. His sins are forgiven and he is rendered pure again. Fulk's sins were great—and think, now he is saved!"

Adelicia thought it might not be as simple as that and Henry had brought much good to England and Normandy so perhaps that would count in his favour.

He liked to listen to her comfort, but his sins still hung heavily on him.

One night she awoke to find him shouting in his sleep. She tried to soothe him, but he sprang out of bed and wild-eyed picked up his sword.

"Henry, where are you going?" she asked.

"I am going to kill them...these men who mock me...they are blind for I have ordered that their eyes be torn out. Their arms are stumps for I have had their hands cut off. Their faces are mutilated...for I..."

"Henry, there is no one here."

He was staring at her wildly.

"Was it just a dream then?"

"A dream—nothing more."

She helped him back to bed. "It was as though they were here...in this chamber...those whom I had long forgotten...the dead...the mutilated..."

"Do not think of them."

"I do not by day, but for long they have haunted my dreams."

"Pray that God will give you peaceful dreams. Pray that he will forgive your past sins."

"I will, Adelicia, I will."

He lay awake long after she slept and his calm and precise mind took control. He had committed sins, yes. He had been cruel and ruthless. But he had done much that was good.

England was a prosperous land. His father would have applauded, and what greater praise could he ask for than that. He would rather have the approval of the great Conqueror than that of any man living.

124

He had lived for sixty-two years. It was a great age. Few men attained it. Even his father had died at the age of sixty. He was suffering now from old man's remorse. Surely not many years could be left. He had built up such treasures on earth and how could he bear to leave them. England and Normandy! They had been life to him. He had them safe, more peaceful than they had ever been, but he himself was old and he had the old man's fear. What happened when his call came, and he could take nothing with him? His great father had died and his end had been undignified for his body had been left to rot. It was as though some mischievous fate had said: "Great dignity you had in life, now in death you shall lose it. You have lost England and Normandy. You would never have lost them in life; but in death they are passed from your hands because you cannot take them with you." His brother Richard had died when hunting in the New Forest; his brother Rufus before whom men had trembled in his life had been trundled to Winchester in a cart drawn by churls and no one had wanted to bury him. When at last they had, the Cathedral tower had fallen down and men said that it was the saints protesting because such a wicked man had been laid to rest in a sacred place.

Kings lost their dignity with death—even great kings.

There was his brother Robert languishing in his dungeon. Should he repent and free Robert? And what would happen then? Robert was a broken man, even older than himself—advancing up his seventies.

We're a long-lived race, thought Henry, when we are allowed to take our full span.

If he released Robert of what use would that be to his brother? Yet it might be that the rebels would rally round him. Nay, leave Robert. He was happier in his dungeon in any case and he could trust that other Robert, his bastard of Gloucester, to look after his uncle.

There seemed nothing he could do to show God his repentance.

But when the morning came he laughed at himself. I have done what I must, he said. None can say of me, Henry I or Beauclerc—whatever they will call me—that I did not leave the kingdom in a better state than that in which I found it.

It was comforting to be with Roger and to talk over events. Never, declared Roger, since the famous year 1066 had there been such peace. Taking Normandy from Robert, the mar-

125

riage with Anjou, had been proved to be the actions of a wise sovereign. The death of the Clito was Fate's seal of approval on all the King had done. Comforting talk, for as God so approved that he had removed the Clito surely too bad a view could not have been taken of Henry's sins.

He could now, said Roger, settle down to a peaceful period. He could improve his relations with the Church; he could found a few abbeys. All that should help to improve his chances of salvation.

This Henry agreed to do and was more contented than he had been for a long time. Then disquieting news came from Normandy. Matilda had left her boy husband and was in Rouen.

"God knows what this means," cried the King. "I must go to Rouen at once."

He set sail with Adelicia and exhausted from the journey and feeling the weight of his years he arrived at the castle where Matilda had installed herself.

She received him coolly enough which irritated him, but Adelicia had warned him that in his less than robust state of health he should be careful about losing his temper. She feared every time he did so that he would do himself some injury.

He sought an early opportunity of being alone with his daughter.

"What means this?" he demanded. "How dare you leave your husband?"

"Husband. That baby!"

"Oh, come, he is no longer so young."

"You do not know what I have had to endure from him."

"We all have to adjust our ways to those of our partners."

"I doubt you ever adjusted yourself to my mother or your second wife."

"My affairs are of no concern to you. It is yours we are discussing."

"What can you hope for when you marry me to such a one!"

"He is handsome enough...."

"Enough! Enough for whom? Not enough for me. I hated his silly face the moment I saw it."

"And told him so, I doubt not."

"I would not choose to lie to my husband."

"You must be the most difficult woman on earth."

"I'm your daughter."

"Now, Matilda, I do not ask of you what is impossible."

"You do since you ask me to look upon that boy as my husband."

"You will have to try to live in peace with him."

"We hate each other."

"Are you so foolish that you do not know the purpose of this marriage?"

"I know it well. It is to make Anjou your friend and not your enemy."

"That was the original purpose. Now there is another...of even greater importance. If you are to be the Queen of England you must have heirs. Have you forgotten that?"

"*You* seem to have forgotten it when you think you can give them that infant for their sire."

"I take it he is capable of getting children?"

"That may well be."

"Then he must get them on you."

"What sort of children do you think they will be?"

"It matters only that there are children. Give me a grandson who will in time be King of England and I will cherish him and you for giving him."

"You ask a good deal of me."

"I ask only your duty."

"There were others to whom you could have given me."

"I made a fine match for you."

"With an old man."

The King looked uneasy as he always did when the Emperor was mentioned.

"Now," he said, "you have a young one and I doubt not he can give you fine sons. It is your duty to forget your differences. Many royal couples have no great love for each other, but they know they must get heirs and they do so. You shall now go back to Geoffrey. You will tell him that you have come to live in peace. You will be a good wife to him and he a good husband to you. You will go at once. That is my command."

Then Matilda played her trump card.

"That I cannot do, Father, for the simple reason that he will not have me."

The King stared at her. "'Tis true," she said. "We have quarrelled much and at last he said to me: 'Get you gone. I never want to see your face again. I regret the day I ever married you and I care nothing for the consequences. I want only to be rid of you.'"

127

The King was nonplussed. He understood Geoffrey's sentiments. Yet how could he order him to take back his wife and get her with child?

It was a sorry matter. His luck had changed. He had quietened Anjou and the Clito was dead. But if Matilda would not get children where was the heir to the throne? The people had reluctantly accepted a woman but would they rally to her if she had no children? If she had a fine, bonny son to follow her, it would make all the difference.

But they would not get children. They hated each other. And Geoffrey had driven her away.

There was nothing he could do but take her back to England with him.

Stephen was excited by the return of Matilda. It amused him that the marriage with Anjou had gone awry. How many times did he rail against a fate which should have married him to Matilda! Then he could have been King to her Queen.

But what was the use? He had his good Matilda and she was as royal as the Empress; and they had two dear children whom he loved. It was difficult to imagine not being the father of young Baldwin and Maud. He was a good father; he liked to play with his children; they were not in the least in awe of him; he supposed later Baldwin would have to go away and be brought up in the household of some chosen knight, to learn the arts of war and chivalry among other nobly born boys. His wife did not wish the boy to go; nor did he.

In the meantime the haughty Empress—now Countess of Anjou—was back at Court, imperious, demanding and exciting as always. Two unsatisfactory marriages had by no means softened her; but to him she would always be the most fascinating woman in the world.

There was a new recklessness about her, a certain gleam in her eyes when they rested on him. Stephen knew that she was tempting him to commit a folly; and he knew that when the moment came he might well be unable to resist.

She did not exactly seek him out; but often he found himself alone with her; it was usually during the hunt, for then they could be most inconspicuous. The King still hunted whenever possible; that was one pastime of which he would never tire. It was said that he no longer chased women as he had been wont to do, though there was the occasional encounter; but, was the verdict, these were of a shorter duration and held nothing of the fierce passion of the past.

The King was indeed beginning to show his years.

Stephen riding with the huntsmen invariably made a point of losing himself; he could be certain that when he did he would come upon Matilda lost in the same manner.

One afternoon they met in a glade of Windsor Forest. He saw her eyes sparkle as he rode up to her.

"Well met, cousin," she said. "I expected you."

He bowed his head.

"You are going to miss the kill, Stephen."

"I fancy I shall miss nothing."

"You always knew how to please women."

"I hope always to please you."

"You do. I know you through and through, Stephen, and yet...."

"And yet you have soft feelings for me."

"I cannot imagine why. You are a laggard, cousin. You do not seize your opportunities."

"Of which opportunities do you speak?"

"All, I dare swear."

"There is one opportunity I long for."

He leaned towards her and took her hand.

"Yet you do not seize it," she said.

He leaped from his horse and was about to tie the creature to a tree when she laughed at him. "Do you think I am some forester's daughter to be rolled in the bracken?"

She touched her horse and was away. Disconsolately he remounted; he turned his horse in the opposite direction to that which she had taken but before he had gone very far she was beside him.

"There is a time and a place for everything," she said.

"Tell me when and where?"

"You wouldn't dare, Stephen."

"You know how it has always been between us."

"Yes, I know. For me as well as for you. Oh, God, if they had given you to me instead of that senile old man and that puking boy."

"Ah, Matilda, what a life we would have had!"

"You are content enough with your Matilda. How dare she have my name."

"It is a favourite one among ladies of high birth."

"They should have named *me* differently. My mother, my grandmother...and that silly little wife of yours."

"Your mother was not Matilda in truth. She took her name from our grandmother."

"Oh, we are close, Stephen...cousins. Perhaps cousins should not marry. There would have had to be a dispensation, would there not?"

"It would have been easily obtained."

"Then why did they not obtain it!" She struck her thighs with her clenched fist. "They have ruined our lives, Stephen, yours and mine. Or perhaps yours is not ruined. You seem satisfied with your silly little wife."

Stephen flushed slightly and said: "She is a good woman. I have naught to complain of in her except that she is not you."

"Yes, you are smugly satisfied. You like your wife and you would wish me to be your mistress. I, the Empress, the Queen to be. That is what you wish, Stephen of Blois."

"What a shrew you have become."

"My little husband would agree with you."

"Poor man!"

"He is scarcely that. They married me to him, Stephen, but I'll not endure it. I'll not go back to him. I'll stay here and you and I will be together as we were meant to be."

The moment of temptation had come. He knew it. If she turned to him; if he touched her he would succumb. He knew that theirs would be a wild passion; it would not be tender as it was with that other Matilda. There was an inevitability about his passion for this proud woman and hers for him; it had been there from the time they were children. There was a hatred in it too, as well as desire. He was not sure that he loved her. He knew she was cruel and ruthless; he knew that she longed for the crown and her father's death. As for her she was aware of his ambitions; she thought him a coward; she knew that there would be something excruciatingly exciting about their union for Stephen would be in great fear. It would be such fear that only an irresistible desire could overcome it. He would be thinking all the time of what would happen if they were discovered. What would his chances be of survival? And hers? But what did she care for her silly little husband, for her tyrannical father? What if he disinherited her? What if he decided to put his bastard Robert on the throne? He might well do that. He would have the excuse if she and Stephen were caught in adultery.

It was this knowledge which made it so exciting.

"Matilda," said Stephen.

"Not here," she said.

"Then for the love of God say where."

"In my bedchamber."

"That would be madness."

"This is madness, Stephen. I shall be waiting."

"If we are discovered...."

"Then we must say to ourselves—for I doubt we should be allowed to say it together—'It was worth while.'"

They rode through the forest. They fell in with the rest of the party; then they rode back to the castle.

When Stephen returned to his apartments in the castle his wife was waiting for him. There was a look of such anxiety on her face that he was immediately full of concern.

"What ails you?" he asked quickly.

"It is little Baldwin. He is sick of a fever. He is so hot and he mutters all the time."

He followed her into the chamber where the boy slept; he was on his bed; his face unaturally flushed; his hair in damp tendrils about his temples.

He knelt down and laid his hand on the boy's brow. It was burning hot.

Baldwin opened his eyes and said: "Father," in such a manner that Stephen felt a lump in his throat.

He looked up at his wife.

"Have you sent for the physicians?"

She nodded. "They will be here shortly."

The boy closed his eyes and Stephen stood up. "How long has he been like this?"

"Since morning."

"It is a childish ailment."

"I hope so."

He gripped her hand and she turned her face away that he might not see how frightened she was.

The King's Saxon physician, Grimbald, came into the chamber. He examined the boy.

"He has a fever," he said.

"Will it pass?" asked Matilda.

"We must wait and see, my lady. I will prepare a cooling draught which should soothe him."

The draught did little for the child. Matilda had drawn up a stool and sat by the child's bed. Stephen sat on the other side.

131

Now and then the boy opened his eyes; he looked from one to the other and smiled.

"Our presence comforts him," said Matilda.

Stephen nodded.

How fragile was the child, how beautiful. Matilda wished that she could bear his pain. Stephen watched her anguished gaze and thought: She has the air of the Madonna. He remembered that other Matilda in the forest—her eyes flashing. She would be waiting for him in her bedchamber. She would have dismissed her attendant women in her imperious manner. She would be expecting him to go to her by means of the secret stairs which he knew and she knew. It would take him almost to her apartment. He would tap lightly on her door; she would be waiting for him.

The great moment was almost upon him.

He had half-risen from his stool and the child conscious of movement opened his eyes.

"Father," he whispered. "Stay."

He sat down again. Across the bed Matilda looked at him; the terrible fear was in her eyes and it was a shared pain.

He sat on, watching the boy, not daring to move lest he disturb him.

A messenger came. The King was without. He had heard of the child's illness.

Stephen rose quietly and left the chamber. Henry was waiting there, his eyes anxious. "Stephen, nephew, I have heard the news."

"My lord, we fear...."

The King laid his hand on Stephen's arm. "I know what it means," he said. "I have suffered myself. Is the child conscious?"

Stephen nodded.

"Let us go in."

Henry stood by the bed but the child was not aware of him, yet his relief was obvious when his father sat down close to him.

"I shall stay with him," said Stephen.

The King nodded. He touched Matilda's head and said: "My thoughts are with you. May God bless you both and save this child."

He left them; and all through the night Stephen and Matilda kept vigil at their son's bedside.

* * *

132

Little Baldwin was dead. The news spread through the castle. The child who had been healthy one day had caught a fever the next and the end had been speedy.

His mother kept to her room and only her husband could comfort her. "She is in good hands," said the King, "for Stephen is a tender husband and a family man. It is best to leave them alone together."

For the next days Stephen thought only of his wife and sought to appease her, for she had loved this son of hers more than any other being. She loved her daughter Maud and she loved Stephen, but little Baldwin with his bright and loving ways, the little son of whom she was so proud, had been the first with her.

At such a time she must be grateful to Stephen. All the finest traits in his character were uppermost: his tenderness, his concern for her, his gentle explanations to little Maud as to why her brother had gone away. What would she have done without Stephen? wondered Matilda. He was not faithful, she knew. She was aware of his passion for that other Matilda; but he was the kindest and most tender husband in the world at this time and she could not have wished for a better.

The child was buried in the Priory of the Holy Trinity, outside Aldgate—that very Priory founded by the King's first wife, the little boy's aunt.

The Court mourned deeply for him, and in particular the King, who remembered afresh the loss of his own son and talked incessantly of the tragedy of the White Ship.

It seemed to Matilda that nothing would go right. Stephen would have come to her and whatever happened afterwards they would have fulfilled their destiny, so she believed. What if he had got her with child? She laughed at the thought. Then she would have gone back to Anjou; she would have forced her husband to spend a night with her if she had to give him a love potion to make him do so and hers and Stephen's child would be the heir to England. The thought excited her. That was how she would have had it.

But he had not come. His child had been sick and died. Fate had intervened. Would he have come if that had not happened at that precise time?

She believed he would. There would be another time. She had never been able to abide inactivity. There must always be drama about her. She wanted to live boldly and dangerously.

133

One day when she was thinking of these matters in her chamber one of her women came to her in a mysterious fashion and said that a stranger was in the castle—a holy man—and he wished to have speech with her.

"You are sure he said with me?" she asked.

"He said he must speak with the Empress Matilda, my lady."

"The Empress. So he called me by that title. And a holy man, you say. You may bring him to me."

The monk was brought to her chamber.

"You are the Empress Matilda?" he asked.

"I am," she answered. "What brings you to me?"

"What I have to say, my lady, is for your ears alone."

She signed to the woman to leave them.

Then she said: "Proceed, good monk. Why have you come to me?"

He looked over her shoulder. "We must be entirely alone."

"We are. Continue."

"I come from the Emperor, your husband."

"The Emperor is dead," she said.

"Nay, my lady, but he soon will be. He wishes to see you before he dies."

"What tale is this! The Emperor is dead I tell you. He was buried at Spires and a monument has been erected there in honour of him."

"This is not so. He has been working in a hospital. For years he has been doing this as penance for great sins, he says."

"Where is he?"

"He is at Westchester. He implores you to come to him. He wishes to ask your forgiveness for his action. He wishes you to know the truth."

"How can I be sure that you are speaking truth?"

"My lady, if you come with me I will take you to him. He confessed his sins to me and has put this burden on me. It is the last request of a dying man that you shall go to him."

Matilda was silent for a moment; then she said: "Wait here a while."

When she returned to the chamber, the King her father was with her.

"Hear what the monk has to say," said Matilda.

The King listened.

134

Then he said: "You and I, daughter, will ride to West-chester. We will go alone with this monk."

There was no doubt that the man lying on the pallet was the Emperor; he was emaciated and dying but there was an expression of tranquillity on his face which Matilda had never seen there before.

"Matilda," he whispered.

Matilda knelt by the bed. The King stood back watching her.

"I am here, Henry," she answered.

"It was good of you to come. This had to be. My sins lay so heavily on me. Forgive me, Matilda...for going."

"You found peace," she said.

He nodded. "Peace," he repeated, "and I believe, the for-giveness of my sins."

"You walked out of the castle that night then...."

"Yes, with nothing. I had already arranged this with my confessor. I took nothing with me but I was brought to En-gland and worked here in the monks' hospital. I served here as the lowliest and I have found peace, Matilda."

"Your ministers knew...."

"They thought me mad. They had wished to put me away.... They took this opportunity to proclaim my death. It fell into place, Matilda...and so I expiated my sins."

She said: "You should not speak. Rest."

"Stay beside me, Matilda. Tell me that you forgive me."

She stooped over him and kissed his brow. "You did right," she said. "You are now at peace."

"It is a great thing, Matilda...to come to peace.. at the end...of one's life."

His eyes had become glazed and he lay back and closed them.

The King came to his daughter and touched her shoulder. "I will send for the priest to come to him," he said.

Henry and Matilda remained in the chamber while the priest administered to the dying man.

The King appeared to regain some of his old vigour during the next weeks. It was always so when there was something important to be done.

He had been deeply affected by what had happened at Westchester; it had been a reminder of his own need for

135

repentance; but there was a matter of greater importance to be settled.

As the Emperor had been living during the ceremony of marriage between Matilda and Geoffrey of Anjou, they had not in truth been married. He was rather relieved now that there had been no children. That could have brought about a very awkward situation, and one which might have stored up trouble for the future, for however much secrets were guarded they had a way of leaking out.

His great concern was to secure the succession. He had failed himself with Adelicia, and Matilda was his only hope. The day she presented him with his grandson a great weight would be lifted from his mind. It was because he had feared the Emperor might be living and Matilda's marriage with Geoffrey no true one, that he had allowed her to stay at his Court and had made no effort to send her back to her husband.

Now he was assured that the Emperor was dead his great desire was to reunite Geoffrey and Matilda and there must be another ceremony so that the marriage was legal and binding; then Matilda must produce a son.

When some major problem had to be settled he always sent for Roger of Salisbury. This is what he did on this occasion. He told him the story, ending with the fact that he had witnessed the passing of the Emperor in his miserable cell but gloriously peaceful in spirit.

Roger said: "At least we can now proceed. It is a mercy that he sent for the Empress otherwise he might have died in obscurity and the mystery never been solved. Let us be grateful for that. Our first plan is to get them together."

"Unmarried," said the King.

"There must be another ceremony. This could easily be performed in secret."

"The trouble is," said the King, "that these two hate each other. Both are delighted to be apart."

"Your daughter, as heir to the throne, must realize her responsibilities."

"It may well rest with Anjou."

"My lord, you will not allow this little Count to flout you. I'll swear. We can put out feelers. You are most displeased at this rift and your displeasure will be felt in Anjou if the young man does not make some move to be reuinted with his wife."

The King nodded. "That is it, Roger. They must come

together. I want to see my grandson. Once I see a healthy boy I shall turn my thoughts to repentance."

"I trust my lord, you will not leave us to go into a hospital as the Emperor did."

"I am too weighed down by responsibilities. I could have concerned myself with my own conscience long ere this if God had not taken my only legitimate son from me."

"His ways are mysterious, my lord. But your efforts have been marked with great success which shows His approval of what you do. The Anjou marriage at precisely the right moment, the death of Clito... and now the Emperor himself. He is dead. Let us go from there."

"You are a wise man, Roger. I knew it the moment I clapped eyes on you in that little church in Caen."

"Gabbling through mass at a speed which delighted my lord."

The King laughed. Trust Roger to raise his spirits.

"Then first, Anjou," he said. "Geoffrey will ask his wife to return. And I shall command her to do so."

"Then the ceremony will take place. They are older now. They will know what is expected of them. I'll warrant that ere long you will see your grandson and you will rejoice at the happy outcome of this matter."

The King smiled with a show of affection on his old friend and wise counsellor.

The King faced his daughter.

"You are to return to your husband. There shall be another marriage ceremony in secret, and you will then live together that you may have sons."

"And if I refuse?" demanded Matilda.

The King flushed angrily. It was at times like this that he wished he had never named her his successor.

"Then," he said, "I shall disinherit you. Do not think that there would be any to support you. The news would be received with joy. You should know that only my insistence made the lords of this land accept you. They have no great wish to be ruled by a woman and in particular one as arrogant and overbearing as you are proving to be."

Matilda was silent for once. She saw the purpose in her father's eyes. She had to be careful.

"So the secret ceremony will take place, and this will be the true one. Then I want sons. Do you understand me? I want sons without delay."

"What of Geoffrey? He may well refuse."

"Geoffrey, like you, Madam, will obey his King or suffer the consequences."

Here was the raging Lion of Justice, the King who had taken over a disordered country from Rufus and by his stern and almost always just laws brought back order and prosperity to the land.

Matilda bowed her head. She knew when she must obey. She must curb her dislike of the boy they had chosen for her husband; she must marry him, bed with him; and do everything in her power to give the King the grandson he insisted he must have.

So the marriage took place in the presence of the King and when it was over Henry showed his great relief to Roger because the first step in their plan was achieved.

Matilda was determined now to get a child quickly. She knew her father and she realized that if she did not soon provide the heir he would consider disinheriting her. He had stressed the fact that the people would be glad to see her replaced and this was the candid truth.

She was not popular with the people—her sex and her character were against her. She knew that the people liked Stephen and that she enjoyed no such popularity.

Stephen had always ingratiated himself with the people— highly or lowly born. He had always courted popularity which was something she had never done. He wanted the people to be on his side because they liked him; she wanted them to support her because they feared to do otherwise.

Stephen was never out of her thoughts, Stephen whom she wanted passionately as a lover and who was yet her rival. For if her father disinherited her to whom would he look but to Stephen? His nephew was the Conqueror's grandson; his wife Matilda was of royal Saxon blood. She was able to bear children. There had been a son, little Baldwin who was dead—but there was a daughter, Maud, who lived and they would get more sons.

Matilda wanted to laugh aloud because the situation amused her. Stephen, the man she desired with a passionate longing was her great rival. She was determined to have Stephen as her lover and at the same time she was going to fight him for possession of the crown.

It was her relationship with Stephen, and that only, which

would make her endure the embraces of the hateful Geoffrey of Anjou.

She had seen the death of her first husband with her own eyes. She was truly married to this boy and no matter how they disliked each other they must get a child.

In the bedchamber they faced each other.

"It is, alas, a necessity that we get a child," she said.

He scowled at her.

"Oh, come, little fool. I am a beautiful woman and when you are not scowling you are not uncomely. Do not imagine that this matter is any more to my taste than yours but we have to get a son."

Geoffrey understood this.

She took his hand and with a show of amiability led him to their bed.

Stephen had joined the King's entourage. He was reckless now and so was Matilda.

"We have missed so many opportunities," she said to him, "that if we miss another we deserve to be parted all our lives."

He was still afraid. What if there was a child?

She laughed.

"Who should know but us two? If there were, Stephen, and he were a boy, he would be King of England one day."

How those words moved him! She was never sure whether they or his passion for her swept away his fears.

The passionate attachment! How delightful it was! There would never be anything like it for either of them again. They could not know how long it would last. At any time the King would settle his affairs in Normandy and return to England.

Each day they feared he would announce his intention to depart. She was delighted that his presence was needed in Normandy. This was the time of great excitement. She and Stephen were meeting whenever possible. A clandestine love affair was all to her taste. It was only the excitement of her encounters with Stephen that made it possible for her to do her duty with the boy they had chosen for her husband.

She glowed with a beauty that she had not possessed before. Whenever she was in an assembly where Stephen was, her eyes would seek him out and a great triumph would fill her. For years she had mourned because they had not married her to Stephen but would she have had it otherwise? Would not marriage have made something mundane of their relationship? Now every meeting was an exciting adventure because they could never forget the fear of discovery; the fact that their passions urged them on to greater daring added such a fillip to their fierce pleasure as could never have occurred in the nuptial chamber.

Only because of this could she endure her relationship with the inexperienced boy whom she despised.

Destiny had brought her and Stephen together, had parted them and brought them together again. Lovers and rivals. And always she wondered: Does Stephen's seed live within me? Shall it be his son or Geoffrey's who inherits the throne?

She was happy as she had never been before.

People—what blind fools they were!—said: "Matilda has grown contented with her marriage."

The King was satisfied. Matilda was living in at least outward amity with her husband; those whose duty it was to keep him informed, assured him that they shared the marriage bed and were indeed endeavouring to make the union fruitful.

With fresh warnings to Matilda that it was imperative for her to get a son, he returned to England.

Stephen, naturally, must return with the Court.

So this was the end of that first passionate phase. The lovers took a long and sorrowful farewell.

"Stephen," she said, "we overcame our fears, did we not, and was it not worth it?"

"I would have willingly died rather than never lived as I have these last months."

"This is not the end, Stephen. Our destinies are entwined. Who knows—I may carry your child. That would not be an impossibility, would it?"

"Is it so, then?"

"I know not," she answered. "I do not even know that I am with child, but if I should be there would be the question, would there not? Stephen's or Geoffrey's? What if that child should become a King of England?"

He embraced her. She saw the speculation in his eyes. He had failed to achieve his ambition but it might be passed on to his son.

She wondered then how often the thought had occurred to him at the height of his passion: "Shall it be my son?"

This was there at the root of the pleasure. The uncertainty, the discovery of each other's minds as well as bodies.

"What shall I do without you, Stephen?" she asked.

"Or I without you."

"Wait," she said. "There will be other times."

So Stephen left for England and Matilda was left alone with her young husband.

A Surfeit of Lampreys

With a more peaceful period the King's obsession with his sins returned. He drew closer to Adelicia who was the one who could best comfort him.

She was accustomed now to his waking at night and calling out to her. The nightmares were growing more and more frequent.

One night he arose shrieking and picking up his sword began to slash at the hangings.

Adelicia, awakening startled, dashed from their bed to restrain him.

"There is no one here," she assured him. "Come back to bed, Henry."

She drew aside the hangings to show him that no one was hiding there. He put down his sword and sat up in bed covering his face with his hands.

"I saw Barré there, Adelicia. You remember Luke de Barré. He was my friend. We went adventuring together in the days of our youth. He wrote verses against me, inspiring my enemies and worse still laughing at me. I ordered that his eyes be put out."

"I know," said Adelicia. "He was punished for his sins."

"But he had been my friend. Somehow I think he meant no great harm. He loved words, Adelicia, and words commanded him sometimes. He would say something and I would challenge him. Then he would say: 'But see how beautiful that sounds. I must say it because it is poetry.' And I ordered his eyes to be put out...his eyes, Adelicia, the most precious thing he had, for he loved the flowers and the trees, the grass and the sun more than most men do. He glorified them. And

143

I ordered his eyes to be put out! He killed himself rather than lose them. And now he comes to haunt me."

"It was but a dream, Henry."

"They come at night... men I have killed. How many men have I killed in my lifetime, think you, Adelicia?"

"It often happens that a King must kill if he will survive. This is not murder. It is statescraft."

"Wise little Adelicia. I have not loved you enough. I have not made you happy."

"You have done your best and I have not been unhappy. My great regret has always been that I have been unable to give you the son you wanted."

"Oh, Adelicia, stay awake. Talk to me until the dawn comes."

It was sad and disquieting to see a great and powerful man so reduced to fear by the terrors of the night.

In the morning Adelicia sent for Grimbald, the King's physician, and at the risk of displeasing Henry told him of these nightly hauntings.

Grimbald wished to speak to the King and Adelicia confessed to her husband what she had done.

"You did it out of your care for me," he said gently. "I will see Grimbald."

He explained to the doctor: "I am sorely disquieted in the dead of night. Sometimes it is husbandmen who surround my bed with their tools in their hands ready to strike me. I have done much that is wrong against them. I have taxed them to pay for my wars. I have taken their homes to make my forests. I have punished them severely for trespassing in these forests and trapping and killing the animals. They are dreadfully mutilated men, Grimbald, who stand round my bed. And I have caused those mutilations. I see knights and fighting men. They come at me and they are so real that I rise from my bed and take my sword."

Grimbald nodded. "My lord, you are beset by a surfeit of conscience. You remember now deeds which seemed to be necessary at the time you did them. Now they return in the quiet of the night to haunt you. If you were not a mighty King I would prescribe a visit to the Holy Land. There you could obtain absolution of these sins which worry you. But you cannot do this for your duty lies here with the country you govern. God would not wish you to leave it."

"My grandfather Robert the Magnificent went on a pilgrimage and left my father but a boy of seven as the Duke of Normandy."

"The great Conqueror could easily have been killed in his childhood had God not preserved him for a great destiny." Grimbald crossed himself and bowed his head since it seemed he had spoken ill of the dead and the sanctified dead at that because all knew that Robert the Magnificent had died during his pilgrimage to the Holy Land and thus expiated the sins of usurpation and murder.

"And I and my brothers would never have been born," said the King. "But I have no son in whose hands I could place my kingdom, only a daughter and I doubt not that were I to go, and leave the sceptre in her hands there would be trouble."

"Nay, my lord, you must stay in that place where it has pleased God to put you. But you could reform your ways wherever you consider it possible. Be a faithful husband."

"I am too old to be otherwise, Grimbald, so there would be little virtue in that."

"Pray frequently. Found a few abbeys. Devote yourself to the Church, for you are suffering not from a sickness of the body but a display of conscience which comes to us all as our years increase."

"I have done much to prosper the abbeys," Henry said. "I and my wives have founded several. Rahere, one of my minstrels, founded the priory of St. Bartholomew and I have aided him in this. He built a hospital adjoining the priory and much good was done to the sick and dying. In the field near Clerk's Well to the north of my city of London, Jordan Bliset founded a priory for Benedictine nuns and there also much that was good was done. My first wife Matilda was unflagging in her efforts to help the poor. She built many hospitals. St. Giles of Cripplegate was one and poor lepers were given succour there. She built churches and even bridges, such as Bow Bridge, and although these might not be said to have been made for the glory of God they brought great comfort to the people."

"This is good," replied Grimbald, "but you still feel this need for repentance. You will do so until you have founded more abbeys and brought greater good to the Church."

The King thanked his physician and went away to discuss with Adelicia what else they could do for the glory of God and the saving of his soul.

* * *

In spite of his efforts to win salvation the King continued to have disturbed nights and these were having a marked effect on him. He looked his age; his temper was even more violent and more easily aroused.

Sometimes he told Adelicia he believed God had deserted him. He had spent his life in making England great and God had taken his only son and refused to give him another. He greatly feared that God was displeased with him.

Again and again Adelicia pointed out what benefits had come his way. He liked to hear them listed and he would nod and say "Yes, yes. There was that." He liked her to keep an account of how many abbeys he and his family had founded. He took a great interest in them and enjoyed going through their accounts.

But again and again his melancholy overcame him. Then one day there came some joyful news.

Matilda was pregnant.

"It may well be," he told Adelicia, "that God is at last answering my prayers."

That Christmas, which was spent at Windsor, he fell sick. He could not leave his bed and there were no festivities. Adelicia herself nursed him, for who but a wife, she asked him, should be at her husband's side at such a time?

He was even more melancholy in sickness. It seemed clear to him, he said, that God had forsaken him. Yet how could he take a pilgrimage to the Holy Land? God must understand that he had a country to govern.

Early in the year a terrible fire broke out in London and more than half of the city was wiped out.

The King lying prostrate on his bed heard the news and groaned.

"This is a sign," he cried. "God is displeased with me."

A few weeks later the picture changed.

Matilda had given birth to a child—a healthy boy.

"We wish to call him Henry after his grandfather," she wrote.

The King rose from his bed, his spirits restored. God was no longer angry for he had given the King what he had prayed for above all else.

A grandson! An heir! A Henry!

He commanded that the church bells should ring. There should be bonfires and rejoicing. All the country must be *en fête*.

At last God had granted England an heir.

He must go to Normandy to see his grandson. Reports that the child was lusty and healthy delighted him and he could not wait to see for himself.

First he addressed the Parliament and ordered that an oath of loyalty to his grandson, the future King of England, should be sworn.

Roger had pointed out that the Queen might yet bear him a son but he shook his head woefully.

"You forget, Roger, that I have become an old man. All my hopes lie in this grandchild."

The oaths were sworn and the King set out for Normandy. Adelicia remained behind in her role of Regent with Roger of Salisbury to assist.

"I shall return ere long," said the King, "but I must see my grandson."

There was some consternation when, as the King stepped on to the royal ship, the light began to fail. The King looked up at the sky. A short while before the sun had been shining brilliantly, for it was a warm August day. It seemed as though a shadow had fallen over a part of the sun.

They set sail but before they had gone very far the darkness had increased and the sailors began to feel very uneasy. One shouted that the face of the sun was being slowly covered.

It was true. The darkness increased so that it was like night. Lanterns were brought. The sailors, the most superstitious people in a superstitious age, were filled with terror.

"An evil omen," they whispered. "We shall never reach Normandy."

The general opinion was that some danger threatened the King. He was an old man and the sea crossing could be dangerous even in summer.

They talked of the calamity which had befallen the White Ship.

The King stood on deck with the sailors staring up at the sky in which the stars were now visible and a great melancholy overcame him. He was in his mid-sixties; his end could not be far off. God had shown his displeasure in some ways, although great advantages had been granted him, and the birth of a grandson surely meant that He was smiling on Henry of England. Yet this was an uncanny experience.

A shout went up. Yes, it was a little lighter. The sun was clearly emerging from the shadow. The stars vanished; there was no longer any need of lanterns. It was once more a summer's day.

"To Normandy," cried the King, "and my grandson."

But as the sailors went about their work they murmured that it was an omen.

"If the King reaches Normandy in safety," they said, "he will never see England again."

How happy he was to hold his grandson in his arms. He examined the child minutely.

"This is a perfect boy," he cried joyfully.

Even Matilda seemed to have become lovable since she was a mother.

The King paraded up and down the chamber holding the child. He thought of all the years he had prayed for a son and now in a way God had answered his prayers.

"This boy will be great," he said. "Do not ask me how I know. Suffice it that I do. God has answered my prayers not as I prayed they would be answered, yet this I know is his reply and I rejoice. Would I could live another ten...fifteen years to see the boy grown to manhood."

Matilda was very proud of the child, too, but there was little of the softness of a mother about her. The King was pleased though to see a certain amity between her and her husband. Geoffrey was delighted to have become a father and this was clearly the reason for his better relationship with his wife. No matter the reason, thought the King, as long as it remains.

The King ordered that there should be feasts and entertainments to welcome his grandson into the world; and all those who did not wholeheartedly rejoice would incur the King's displeasure. So feasting there was and the minstrels and troubadours excelled themselves and sang tenderly of love and the fruits of love of which this beloved infant was an example.

Henry found it difficult to tear himself away from the royal nursery. He doted on the child and became young again as he rocked him in his arms.

England was in safe hands. Roger and Adelicia were reliable; he could dally awhile in Rouen and play the proud grandfather. There he could forget the barrenness of Adelicia. She would never bear him a son now. There he could even accept the arrogance of Matilda. It mattered not. He had his desire and all his hopes were in this child.

148

It was true that Matilda's arrogance was often hard to bear, and as the months passed she became more so. She wanted no one to forget that she was not only the future Queen of England but the Duchess of Normandy; and as she contemplated her ageing father and saw him, nursing his grandson, she thought it was time he left State affairs to those young enough to handle them.

One day she came to the King and told him that she was pregnant.

His joy increased. "Another son," he said. "That is the best news I have had since little Henry made his bow. If this is another boy you are carrying then that is God's seal of approval. Two boys! It is always wise to have more than one as I found to my cost."

Matilda cut him short. "Oh, yes, yes, we have heard all about the White Ship and we know you married Adelicia to get a son which you failed to do. And now there is my little Henry so that trouble is over. And if I should have another son...."

"I shall pray for it with all my heart," said the King, and he thought how hard she was, how unloving; and he wondered he did not disinherit her. He would have done so some years ago. He had allowed no one to displease him in the days of prime—nor later. But he was an old man; and there was trouble enough. If he disinherited her now, with himself so old and the child so young, there could be civil war. That was the last thing a King wanted for his country even if he would not be there to see it.

Nay, he would forgive Matilda, for whatever else she had done, she had given him little Henry.

During a banquet in the castle of Rouen which was part of the celebrations for the birth of the King's grandson a messenger arrived from England. The news he brought plunged the King into melancholy.

His brother Robert had died in Cardiff Castle.

It was twenty-eight years since Henry had seen Robert, who must have changed greatly for he was eighty years old...an age rarely reached by any man.

The King left the banquet and retired to his chamber and that night was beset by dreams more violent and disturbing than any he had known before.

He could not get Robert out of his mind and he sent for

one of his brother's servant-guards for he wanted to know every detail of his brother's last days.

When the man arrived he was closeted with the King for a long time and was submitted to many questions.

"I wish you to tell me the truth," said the King. "If he cursed me, I would know it. Fear not for yourself. However unkind that truth to me I would have it. And you need only fear if you should withhold aught from me."

"The Duke was not a vindictive man, my lord," replied the guard. "He did not revile you. He used to say he understood you and that you were another such as your great father."

"He said that, did he?"

"Ay, my lord. And as the years passed he grew to be content with his prison."

"He was a man of great charm, dearly loved by many, but he lacked the qualities to become a great ruler."

"He knew it in the end, my lord. He liked to hear what was happening in England and he used to say: 'My father would like that. Strange that our young brother would be the only one to resemble him.'"

The King felt happier to hear such sentiments expressed but when men have trembled for fear of displeasing you, can you be sure that they are telling the truth?

"Did he accept the fact that he was a prisoner while I was a King?" he insisted. "Did he never complain that I kept him under guard?"

"Sometimes, my lord, he would say that he was like a bird in a cage who could look out at the green fields and never walk on the grass. There was one oak tree that he used to watch all through the years. He became excited when the buds came and then the leaves; and sad when they fell. 'Another year is passing,' he would say, 'and I am still the King's prisoner.'"

"For twenty-eight years he languished in my castles, my prisoner," mused the King. "Had I released him there would have been those to rally to his banner. His was a sad life. He lost his wife; he lost his son. She died many years ago in childbed."

"A sad tragedy, my lord, one of the saddest in the Duke's life."

"But there were rumours that he wished to be rid of her. It was said that her death was due to poison."

The guard did not answer. He had heard of the King's

melancholy and that his conscience troubled him greatly. He did not believe this story against the Duke but he felt that he dared not defend him at this stage. It pleased the King at this time to remind himself that Robert, whom many would say he had wronged, was no saint.

"It was said that he wished to marry the widow of William Giffard," went on the King, "who was possessed of great wealth, for she had promised that if his wife died and he married her she would rouse up all her powerful kinsfolk and put all her possessions into his hands. And then...his wife did die."

"Yet, my lord, there was no marriage with Giffard's widow."

"There was never time for it," insisted the King. "He was busy fighting."

The guard was silent and the King went on: "And he lost his son. All his hopes must have been in the Clito, as mine were in my heir. How did he take the news of Clito's death?"

"He was in Devizes Castle then, my lord. He dreamed that he was fighting in Normandy and during the battle a lance pierced his arm. He awoke crying that he had lost his right arm. And then he told the meaning of the dream. 'My son is dead,' he said, and 'twere so. We heard that William the Clito had been wounded by a lance and the poison entering his body killed him."

"Life is full of strangeness," said the King. "Who would have believed when we were playing in our father's castles, years and years ago, that it would come to this? Richard and Rufus dead in the New Forest; Robert my prisoner for twenty-eight years and myself master of England and Normandy, yet I have had my sorrows which have been as great as any endured by them. Tell me more of my brother, though. I have kept him as a noble pilgrim worn out with many troubles reposing in a royal citadel with abundance of delicacies and comforts."

"Sometimes, my lord, he would not eat. He used to say he would starve himself because he would not live as a prisoner."

"But he never did. My brother was one to make plans which never reached fulfilment. Did he not have the best to eat? I sent him rich garments."

"He used to say that if they were not well made enough to suit the King they came to him."

"Which was right and fitting. Was he not my prisoner?"

151

"I think, my lord, that he was not unhappy. He was ever a dreamer and he dreamed his dreams in prison."

"Where he did not have the tragedy of carrying them out to find they did not work." The King nodded. "Let him be given a royal burial. It shall be in the abbey church at Gloucester and there shall be an effigy erected to his memory."

He liked to think of Robert's being given those honours in death of which circumstances had forced him to deprive him in life.

But his dreams were disturbed and Robert became yet another phantom to haunt his nightmares.

Matilda was brought to bed in the following May. Her labour was long and her life was in danger. The King waited impatiently to hear that the child was born.

The doctors were grave. "The Empress is in sorry case," they told him. "This labour has gone on too long and she grows weaker."

The King nodded gravely. He would send for the best physicians. They must save his daughter. But the hours began to pass and still Matilda's child was not born.

The King thought: There is death all about us. Robert has gone and is the next to be Matilda? I had thought it was my turn. Is God taking my daughter instead?

But being a King he must think of what Matilda's death would mean to the succession. An old King of more than sixty, a child of one. That would be disaster. Who should reign?

There was Stephen. Stephen was now in Boulogne where he was managing the lands which had come to him through his marriage. There had been a time when he had thought that Stephen might well be his heir. That was when Matilda was in Germany and the Emperor was alive and ruling. He thought then what a pity it was that Stephen was not his son. That young rascal—and the very mention of him ever at this time brought a smile to his lips—had changed all that. Nay, his Henry was going to be King of England. In his mind he already thought of him as Henry II.

But if Matilda died, there was a predicament. "If you take my daughter, oh, God, give me a few more years that I may make the succession safe."

He thought of Luke de Barré who had laughed often at the follies of men and had said more than once that men whe

152

pretended to worship God were constantly telling him how to rule them. "Would you allow your servants to tell you what to do, oh King," he had said once. "Well, that is what men do when they are in need. They constantly tell their Maker."

Then he was haunted by memories of Luke; he could hear his voice crying: "Would you then take my eyes...? Only a monster would do that to me."

Luke had never said such words, at least not in his hearing. But it seemed likely that he had spoken them to some.

Why was he thinking of Luke when this fearful problem was presenting itself to him? If Matilda died, what then?

A baby King with a host of ambitious men juggling for power. Better Stephen. Could Stephen hold the crown until young Henry was of age? To put the crown on a man's head was a dangerous thing, for Stephen would have sons. He had a daughter now for he had lost little Baldwin, but there would be others and he would be ambitious for his own flesh and blood.

Matilda must live.

Oh, God, let her live. Barré was right. There were times when it must be impressed on the Almighty how important certain matters were.

He knelt in prayer. He prayed for Matilda and he had never prayed more fervently. Yet he prayed not for love of her but rather for his grandson and the need to preserve the country he loved from a possible civil war.

His prayers were answered. The physicians were at the door.

"The child is born, my lord."

He lifted his eyes and said earnestly: "And his mother?"

"Exhausted, sir, and very weak, but she is indeed your daughter, and has great determination to live."

"She will recover," he said with a smile. And remembered that he had not asked the sex of the child.

"It is a boy," they told him.

"Another boy. A strong and healthy boy. So I have two grandsons, eh?"

God was smiling on him after all.

The second boy was as lovely as his brother. The King's happiest hours were spent in the nursery. He could not hear enough details of these young lives. As for the elder, Henry, he was certain that he was destined for greatness. He would have the boy on his knee and try to tell him that he was

153

going to be a King. The child appeared to listen intently and was fascinated by the manner in which his grandfather's lips moved. He would put up a hand to grab his nose and the King would laugh and demand to know if anyone had ever seen a brighter and more lusty child.

Matilda, the mother of Henry and Geoffrey, for the new arrival had been named after his father, was even more arrogant than ever. She still called herself the Empress and indeed had never abandoned the title. She had always liked the sound of it.

Her husband had been a little reconciled at the birth of two sons. There were still violent quarrels but now that he was a little older he felt a grudging admiration for his forceful wife. Their stormy quarrels added a fillip to the emotional side of their relationship and he was finding her almost as physically attractive as he had once thought her repulsive. Now that he was more mature the difference in their ages seemed less marked. It was hardly a happy marriage—what marriages made for ambition ever were?—but at least they had two lively sons and he had been put on good bargaining terms with the King of England.

Matilda took a great dislike to her father. She had long thought it was time he died. But he clung to life too firmly to please her. Some people seemed to think that he was immortal and would live for ever. God forbid that, she thought. For what then of her inheritance?

One day when she was alone with Geoffrey he commented on the King's devotion to their sons.

"In particular, Henry," he said. "Their nurses tell me that he creeps into the nursery and watches them when they're asleep. He often picks up Henry and talks to him—as though the boy can understand."

"He dotes on him," replied Matilda. "He wanted a son of his own so badly and when young Henry arrived, he believed his prayers had been answered."

"He should do something for the boy, then."

"He looks upon him as a future King."

"That's a long time away," retorted Geoffrey. "His mother has to inherit first. But what of Normandy? Why shouldn't he give young Henry Normandy now?"

"Give Henry Normandy! How could a baby govern Normandy?"

"He should give it to the boy's father to hold it for him."

"To you!" jeered Matilda.

154

"And why not?" demanded Geoffrey. "Why should I not hold it in trust? It would be some tangible proof of his love for the child. He is always prating about that. He promised me various castles at the time of our marriage. Why does he not give them to me now?"

"My father hates parting with anything. He has always been avaricious. It is a family failing. It was my grandfather's. He clung to everything he won. Everyone will tell you that."

"We should ask your father to keep his promises."

"We should and we shall. We will catch him when he is in the nursery drooling over Henry and we shall ask him since he is always saying how much he loves the boy, to show his affection in a more practical form."

They plotted together as to how they would approach the King; it was such matters which had the effect of bringing them closer together.

They found him in the nursery holding Henry on his knee. Geoffrey was sleeping quietly in his cradle.

"Why, Father," said Matilda, "we guessed we should find you here."

"This little fellow has grown in the last days," declared the King. "Look at him smiling at me. He knows his grandfather. Do you not, young Henry?"

Matilda took the child from her father and held him aloft.

"Come, my son," she said, "you know your mother, do you not?"

She handed the child to a nurse and told her to leave them as they wished to be private.

When they were alone, she said: "Father, you are pleased with your grandsons?"

"You need not ask such a question. I know well my feelings."

"They have compensated you for the barrenness of your Queen."

"They are God's blessings in my old age."

"Then since you love them so, you should give some proof of your feelings for them."

"Do I not...constantly?"

"You are in the nursery often. You dangle Henry on your knee and doubtless will Geoffrey when he is old enough. But that asks little. I should like some real proof of your love for these children and your gratitude to me for providing them."

155

"You have done your duty," he answered, "And these children are God's blessing to you as well as to me. In due course Henry will be King of England. What greater honour and glory could be given him than that?"

"He should have Normandy," said Matilda.

"He shall in due course."

"We think he should have it now," put in Geoffrey.

The King's anger blazed. This was the young boy he had befriended. He had been his sponsor in chivalry; he had given him a Spanish steed, a steel coat of mail, golden spurs and a scutcheon decorated with golden lions. He had taken pleasure in presenting him with a sword made by the greatest armourer of all, great Gallard. He had been pleased by the boy's good looks and elegance. He had not been displeased when he had been obliged to agree to his marriage with his daughter.

And now the boy was insolent—and all because he was the father of the King's grandsons.

"*You* think!" cried the King. "When have I given you leave to think when and how I shall dispose of my dominions?"

"You have made promises to me," declared Geoffrey. "You promised castles in Normandy on my marriage. Where are these?"

"They shall be yours in due course."

"I demand them now."

Hot anger had turned the King's face to purple.

"You demand from me? You upstart! Do you forget that I am your King and you no more than my subject? Pray do not tell me what I shall and shall not do, or you will find yourself the occupier of a castle dungeon instead of its proud owner."

"You needed my father's help once."

"I need no man's help. Forget not that I am the son of the greatest King that ever lived. You are but a scion of a family which because its lands were set in a certain spot were important. That is all. Remember it."

"You were glad of my father's help..." began Geoffrey.

"I made a treaty with him and that treaty included marriage—your marriage with my daughter. Do not fancy yourself too great, Geoffrey. That would not become you."

"You have not treated Geoffrey as you promised," said Matilda sharply.

"Enough!" thundered the King, and strode to the door.

When they were alone together Matilda and Geoffrey laughed aloud.

"A few more scenes like that and he will burst with fury," said Geoffrey. "I have seen it happen to men of his temper."

"And then," said Matilda, "you think you will not have to ask for favours."

"I shall take them," he added.

"Only if I decide to grant them."

Geoffrey laughed. He was certain that when the time came he would make his wife obey him. He was after all a man and even though she was the King's daughter and named as the Queen, he was her master and she would have to learn obedience.

Matilda smiled cynically. She knew what thoughts were passing through her husband's mind.

Let him wait and see. Of one thing she was certain: She and she alone was going to rule.

The King was very much upset by the quarrel with his daughter and her husband.

"As long as I live," he declared, "I will have no one my equal, and certainly not master in my house."

Geoffrey sulked and left Court. Shortly afterwards news was brought to the King that his son-in-law had taken possession of a castle which belonged to the Viscount of Beaumont.

Henry was incensed because Viscount Beaumont happened to have married one of his illegitimate daughters and the King always concerned himself affectionately with the affairs of his sons and daughters.

He immediately ordered that the castle be given back to which Geoffrey replied that if the King would not give him his due he would take it.

Henry's answer was that he would accept insolence from no man and if his son-in-law behaved like an enemy then he should be considered as such. His wife and children should be taken from him and he would find himself an outlaw.

There were always men in Normandy who were looking for trouble and eager to provoke it whenever they saw a possibility of doing so. This they now saw. Sides were taken in the quarrel between the King and Geoffrey of Anjou, and against Henry were two men whom he had good reason to distrust—William Talvas, of the notorious family, and Roger de Toesny.

157

The King had no choice but to gather together his forces and go out to subdue these rebellious noblemen. He did this without effort; but alas, while he was thus engaged news was hurried to him that the Welsh were causing trouble again. They had crossed the border and had taken possession of a castle there.

It was the old pattern. There was no peace. No sooner had he left England than there was trouble there; and as soon as he returned to England there would be risings in Normandy.

He complained to his nephew Warren, the Earl of Surrey, the son of his youngest sister Gundred, "It has always been thus. Since I took the English crown I have scarcely known one year's peace."

He blamed the intransigence of his son-in-law.

"One would have thought," he mourned, "that because I raised him up he would have thanked me, but instead he asks all the time for more."

Now he was in a quandary. Should he return to England to subdue the Welsh insurrection or remain in Normandy? For he knew that as soon as he was away Geoffrey would stir up more trouble.

He made a decision. He would send some of his best soldiers to England and remain with others in Normandy. He could see great trouble looming here.

He went to the nursery to comfort himself by the sight of the little boys. He took Henry in his arms and walked up and down the nursery talking to him.

"To think, my precious child," he murmured, "that your father is at the root of all my trouble, and because he gave me you I must needs be lenient with him. Oh, my Henry, my beloved Henry II, would that you were a man! Then you and I would stand together. With what joy would I contemplate the placing of the crown on this dear head!"

The child looked at him wondering and crowed with laughter.

"There is a bond between us already," said the King and was momentarily happy.

The King had taken William Talvas prisoner.

"Let him be put in a dungeon and there await my pleasure," he said.

Matilda came to him when he was in the nursery and said that she wished to speak to him about Talvas.

158

"I do not wish to speak of traitors in my grandson's nursery."

"He will not know of what we speak."

"I will not speak of him," thundered the King.

"Yet I will," said Matilda. "And I ask for his pardon."

"You may ask all you wish elsewhere and receive no for your answer. But when I say I will not speak of these matters in my grandson's nursery I mean it."

"Take care of your health, Father. Your anger is dangerous to you."

"You will see that it is dangerous to others."

"If a daughter cannot speak to her father...."

"Forget not that I shall decide when I think of you as a daughter and that will be when I see a daughterly attitude towards me. Your insolence and arrogance try me sorely and I will not be tried. Remember I brought you up to your high place. I can put you down."

"Your nobles have all sworn on oath to serve me."

"I can make them unswear."

"So you would disown your grandson?"

"Never."

"I thought you planned to disinherit me and put another on the throne. Who would that be? Stephen?"

"Stephen?" he repeated.

"Why not Stephen? Did you not at one time plan that he should take what is mine? He is your nephew who never offends you...who weighs his words...who says: 'Dear Uncle, clever kind uncle, to whom I am so grateful. Dear Uncle, everything you do is right. I will obey you in all things. I will grovel at your feet....'"

"Be silent."

"I will speak the truth. You are thinking that you dislike my husband so much that you will disinherit me lest he should ever get a hold of your possessions."

The King was silent. He could feel the blood hammering in his veins. It sounded like hammer strokes, too fast, too fierce.

"But Stephen," she said, "is charming. He is so handsome. He knows how to flatter."

The King said slowly: "I thought you and he were friends...."

"Would you expect me to be friends with my...rival."

"Do you hate him so? You should not. He is a good friend to me and would be to you."

159

She laughed. "I believe at one time you thought of marrying us."

"No," he said. "You were for the Emperor and he did very well with Matilda of Boulogne. You should be friends with your cousin, Matilda. He is a good man and would serve you well. He has sworn on oath to do so."

"You would rather he were my husband than Geoffrey."

"How can we plan these things? How do we know how things will turn out? You were always a virago, Matilda. You have not changed."

"You like him well since you once thought to give him your crown."

"That was before the Emperor was dead. I have made you my successor, Matilda. It will be well for you to remember that I can change my mind."

"You never would and I will tell you why. Because of that boy in the nursery. Whatever I did you would always remember him. He is going to be a King of England. You will never let anything alter that."

"Take care, Matilda."

"Then give Talvas his freedom."

"Why? Because he is an ally of my treacherous son-in-law?"

"Because I ask it."

"Don't be so foolish. Remember what I have told you. You will have to learn that I will brook no insolence either from you or your husband."

He left her because he was beginning to feel ill. The violent quarrels which Matilda seemed to enjoy nowadays made him ill. He did not wish her to know how they affected him.

He went to his bedchamber and lay on his bed. His nephew Surrey asked if he would like to see his physician.

"Nay, Warren," he said. "The Empress upsets me. I like not her overbearing ways. I can find it in my heart to be sorry for her husband—as I would for any man married to such a virago."

Warren was silent. It was not good policy to share in criticism of one who might very soon be the ruler.

The King lay on his bed and wished Adelicia was in Normandy. He could talk to her as he wished and she would give him comfort. He supposed he had been fortunate in his marriages. When he thought of what marriage to one such as his daughter Matilda would be like he shuddered. Then he laughed at himself. When he was a young man he would have known how to deal with her. It was merely that now he was an old man and he was tired and he no longer looked for conflict. He wanted peace.

Warren hovered to see if there was anything he could do.

There was a time when Warren had hated him. They had been rivals for Matilda, his first wife. His thoughts were back at the Abbey where she had been under her stern and harsh Aunt Christina who had wanted to turn her into a nun. And he a penniless Prince had come courting her. Warren, his nephew, had been there on the same mission. In those days Warren had been rich and he, Henry, had been poor, with nothing but his prospects to recommend him. But his dear Matilda had taken one look at him and loved him. He had been a handsome man in those days and with his plentiful dark hair, of which he had been so proud, worn long and hanging about his shoulders. And he had known how to charm a woman, having had so much more experience at that art than most men.

Warren had hated his uncle because he was the successful suitor. And he had mocked him when he had hunted in the forest with King Rufus. Rufus had laughed at his impecunious brother and they had called him Deersfoot because he had had to follow the hunt on foot not being able to afford a horse.

Readily had he forgiven his nephew those early insults. When one was successful one forgave. It was only the failures who found that difficult. Now Warren was his man, his good nephew, one of those whom he could trust.

How was it that when a man was old and sick he found a certain sad joy in delving back to the past? He did it so frequently now that he seemed to be as often in the past as the present.

He kept to his bed for a few days after that scene with Matilda and when he rose it was to learn that his daughter had left the castle. She was joining her husband and had taken her sons with her.

When troubles lay heavily upon them it had always been the custom of the King and his family to hunt. There in the forests they could cast aside their cares and for a few moments indulge in their favourite pastime; afterwards pleasantly tired from their exertions they would feel rejuvenated and better able to tackle their problems.

161

"We will go to Lyons-la-forêt," he said, "and from there will hunt."

So accordingly on a misty November day the Court set out.

The King led the chase and he declared that it was one of the best day's sport he had enjoyed for a long time. In good spirits—in spite of the troubles which were hanging over him—he returned to the Castle of Rouen.

"I am hungry," he cried. "It is always thus after the hunt. It restores my spirits and my appetite. I fancy a dish of stewed lampreys."

His nephew Warren said: "My lord, your physicians have said that this dish is not good for you. It always upsets you."

"Doctors will always blame something when they cannot find the true cause of ailments. How could anything which I so much enjoy be bad for me?"

Warren looked dubious and the King shouted for his chief cook to be brought to him and when the man came he said: "Lampreys! A goodly dish of them for my hunger is keen and I have a mind to enjoy them."

That dish of lampreys was to be remembered for years to come. The King ate of it voraciously but almost immediately afterwards became ill. He was helped to his bed and his physician sent for.

The doctors shook their heads when they heard of the lampreys. Had they not advised the King against them? Why had his cooks prepared such a dish when they knew that it always disagreed with the King's digestion?

The cooks protested that they had acted on the King's orders and there were many to verify this. It was reckoned that this was another bout of that indigestion to which in late years the King had become a victim.

But it was not so, for the King did not recover. He had gone out to hunt on a Monday and by Thursday it had become apparent that he was very ill indeed.

He was sixty-seven years old... a great age. Few who led such active lives lived so long. Robert his brother had been eighty; but the Conqueror had died through an accident and so had William Rufus. They were a long-lived family—or would have been but for accidents.

It was obvious now that the King's end was near. Robert of Gloucester hurried to Rouen and Henry's delight in seeing this beloved son was clear.

"My dear Robert," he said, "stay near me. I have need of you."

Robert thought he should send for Archbishop Hugh of Rouen. "It has come to that, then," said the King. "I have known for some time that the end could not be far away."

The Archbishop arrived and urged the King to repentance. Henry was only too eager to do as he asked.

When a man was on his death-bed he remembered sins which seemed to him at the time of committing mere acts of justice.

He saw his nephew William Warren, Earl of Surrey, there with the Count of Perche who had married his illegitimate daughter—she who had been drowned in the White Ship. He was glad to have these near but chiefly Robert.

"I loved you, Robert," he said. "You were indeed my son. How many times have I said to myself 'I would he were my legitimate son'. Your mother was my dearest love. Many happy times did I spend with her and you have always been a constant reminder of her."

Robert knelt by the bed and the tears were in his eyes.

"It is good to die lamented," said the King. "I would the Queen were here. She has been a good and faithful wife to me. I trust that good care will be taken of her when I am gone. She is a young woman yet and has many years left to her."

Robert said that he would carry out all the King's wishes and that he hoped God would strike him dead if he did not.

"Make no strange oaths, my son," said Henry. "It is not always easy to keep them. I see trouble ahead. Matilda....Where is Matilda?"

"She is with her husband, my lord, and knows not yet of your illness."

The King frowned. "I have made her the heiress to the crown. My knights and churchmen have sworn fealty to her. Sometimes I wonder....Was it a mistake? A woman, Robert, and such a woman...."

"Your daughter, my lord."

"Ay, my daughter. If my son William had not died...if you, Robert, had been my legitimate son....Then I would die happy. Sometimes I thought I should have left the crown to my nephew Stephen. He is a good man. He is easy and affable and is loved dearly. I believed he would have been accepted by the people as Matilda will not be."

163

"You disturb yourself, my lord. Should you not make your peace with God?"

"Ay, son. I will confess my sins again for when I look back old forgotten ones come back to mock me. Let me have the Holy Communion and a last anointing. Robert, you have custody of my treasury at Falaise. I wish you to take from it £60,000. Pay my servants and those who have been hired to fight with me and for the rest give it to the poor. Ask all to pray for my soul. Do this for me, Robert, my son."

"I will, my lord."

And so after reigning over England for thirty-six years and over Normandy for twenty-nine, Henry I closed his eyes on the world for ever.

Hugh Bigod

Riding in from the hunt Stephen, who was in Boulogne with his wife, saw a man on horseback galloping towards the castle.

Stephen paused and waited. There was one piece of news which had been expected for some time and he had been on the alert for these many weeks. The purposefulness of the rider, the speed with which he galloped and the fact that he was making straight for the castle implied that he had news of the utmost importance for Stephen.

Could it be? The King had been ill for some time. The news had been that he was visibly declining. His breathlessness had increased; and his temper deteriorated day by day as did his desire for penitence. The number of good deeds he had performed in the last year was ominous. The messenger was slowing down. He had recognized Stephen.

"My lord," he gasped. "The King is dead."

"You are certain of this?"

"I have been sent to you by those who have seen his corpse. He died of a surfeit of lampreys."

"Ay," said Stephen, "but it was more than that. He has been slowly dying these last months."

"The lampreys finished him, my lord. His base-born son Robert of Gloucester was with him at the end. He has given his orders to him."

"I thank you," said Stephen. "You shall be rewarded. Now go and refresh yourself."

Stephen went at once to his wife's apartments. She was pregnant, a fact which delighted him.

"The King is dead," he said.

Matilda looked at him with dismay; she could see the excitement in his eyes.

"What will you do?" she asked slowly.

"I must go to England at once."

"To support Matilda?"

He was silent.

His wife looked at him sadly. She had been at peace in Boulogne; she could never be happy when that other Matilda had been near. She thought of the arrogant handsome Empress and how pleased she had been when she had left England with her young husband and her children had been born. She knew of course that Stephen had been bemused by the Empress; she suspected that they had been lovers; she knew that there was some close tie between her husband and his arrogant cousin but she did not quite understand what it implied though she did know that it was stronger than any other relationship either of them felt—Matilda for Geoffrey, her husband, or Stephen for her, his wife.

And his first thought was that he must go to England; he must stand beside Matilda. He must be at her side when she claimed the throne.

But Matilda did not understand her husband. Nor did he entirely understand himself.

A wild exultation had seized him and it was not because he was going to help Matilda take and hold the crown.

His wife said: "You are eager to go back to England. You want to be with your cousin Matilda. You want to serve her. I have understood for so long your feelings for her."

Stephen looked at his wife intently; then taking her by the shoulders he said: "I am going to England not to put my cousin Matilda on the throne, but to take it myself."

She reasoned with him. "But, Stephen, how can you? Matilda is the King's daughter, the rightful heir. Her father named her so."

"Nay," he said, "she is a woman and the people do not want a woman to rule them."

"You have sworn fealty to her."

"She is no longer in England. She has a husband. Geoffrey of Anjou cannot be King of England."

"Nor would he. She would be Queen and he would be her Consort."

"Nay," said Stephen, "the people do not want them and it is the people who decide."

She had shaken her head; she had wept and entreated,

166

but in Stephen's eyes there was a look of ecstasy. He saw himself with the golden crown on his head. Why was it that a crown should change men's minds? Stephen who had been kindly and gentle, amiable and well loved had become an ambitious man. But perhaps he always had been.

He was going to take the crown although he had sworn fealty to his cousin Matilda and as she was not of a nature to allow herself to be swept aside there would be bitter fighting and bloodshed.

Oh, what happened to a man when he dreamed of fitting a crown on to his head?

"I shall send for you, Matilda, as soon as I am safe on the throne," he said. He embraced her. Then he took a few men with him and rode down to Wissant where he took ship for Dover.

Lightning shot across the sky, followed by deafening claps of thunder. The rain fell so heavily that it threatened to overturn the ship. Men groped about on deck in darkness horrifically illumined by the flashes of forked lightning.

"There never was such a storm," said one.

"It is the end of the world," added another.

Stephen stood staring defiantly up at the sky, looking for portents. What did this mean? A great king had passed on. He had made one great mistake and that was in leaving his kingdom to his daughter. No man wanted to serve under a woman. But Stephen was about to take the crown although he had sworn an oath of allegiance to Matilda. Was this God's answer to a man who was ready to break his oath? Was the ship going to be overturned? Was he, with all those who had supported him in his planned enterprise, to be drowned?

He muttered prayers asking forgiveness of his sins, but he did not mention the proposed usurpation of the throne. He had not yet committed that sin. God would know what he was planning to do though. Why should he have hastened back to England if not for this purpose?

But one thing he could not do; he could not promise not to take the crown if he were spared to do so. No matter what happened to him now he was taking no oaths under that threatening sky to relinquish his dreams and hopes.

He stood therefore almost defiantly while the storm raged round him. He was in terror of fearful reprisals but such was the lure of the crown that he could not give up his hopes.

The storm abated; the ship had come safely through it and the white cliffs of Dover loomed up before him.

What a joyous moment when he stepped on English soil. He had faced the fury of the heavens and emerged safe; now he must face the verdict of the English people and in time the fury of the Empress.

He, with his men, climbed the hill to Dover Castle. Battered by the storm, drenched to the skin, they were cold and hungry.

But the castle gate was not opened to them and they were challenged from the keep.

"Who comes here?"

"Stephen, the King's nephew," was the answer. "Come from Boulogne to claim what is his. Open up and let me in."

"What do you come to claim?" was the answer.

"The crown," answered Stephen.

"We are loyal here to the rightful Queen Matilda. The castle will not be opened to you."

Stephen was depressed. Was this an example of the kind of reception he would get throughout England? One of his men whispered to him. "The castle belongs to Robert of Gloucester. He has placed himself on the side of Matilda."

"A curse on him," muttered Stephen.

"My lord, it just happens that we landed at Dover. It would have been different elsewhere. There will be many to rally to you, for Matilda was never loved as you are."

Stephen looked up at the castle. Impregnable! And he was in no state to make siege.

"We will march on to Canterbury," he said.

Alas, when he reached Canterbury there was a troop of men at the gates, those who supported Robert of Gloucester; and they refused him entry into the town.

"A pleasant homecoming," said Stephen; but he hastily reminded himself that he was in Robert of Gloucester's country.

They refreshed themselves at an inn and after resting they marched on to London.

Here it was a different story.

The news had reached the city that the King was dead of a surfeit of lampreys and that Stephen, his nephew, was coming to claim the throne.

Many knew Stephen—the generous, affable man who for years had lived at Tower Royal near the Chepe and Watling

street. He had endeared himself to the people and his bon-
homie was for the poor as well as the rich.

Stephen had come to claim the crown. They had feared
that the King's daughter would take it. They had seen her
too—a haughty arrogant woman who when she had ridden
through their streets had never shown the slightest interest
in them.

Did they want a woman and that woman Matilda? No.
They would rather see in her stead kind, benevolent, handsome Stephen.

Stephen rode acclaimed through the streets of London.

He called together the leading citizens.

"My friends," he said, "King Henry is dead. It now is for
you to elect your future King. There are some who would set
up the King's daughter on the throne. A woman, my friends,
who has spent the greater part of her life on foreign soil, who
has no great love for the people of this country."

"We'll not have Matilda," cried a voice.

"Ay, we'll not have Matilda." The cry was taken up.

"Then, my good citizens of London, will you take me?"

"We will take Stephen," they cried.

One man said: "There should be conditions."

"Indeed there must be conditions. The people who elect
their Sovereign must know what he will bring to them. Tell
me, good people, what you would ask of me?"

"Peace," said the man who had first talked of conditions.
"Peace that we may live in quiet."

"That I grant. It is my great wish to live in peace."

"And you will swear to pacify the kingdom for the benefit
of us all?"

"I swear," said Stephen.

"Then while you live we will support you with all our
strength."

Stephen replied: "Then I thank you good people of London
for without your support no man can hold the crown. I must
now to Winchester that I may present myself to the people
there; and if they are as good and wise as you then we may
look forward to a peaceful reign."

What did he care for Dover and Canterbury when he had
London with him?

As he rode towards Winchester he thanked God that his
brother Henry had been brought to England and after mak-

ing a very favourable impression as abbot of Glastonbury had been elected to the See of Winchester.

Stephen knew that he could rely for support on Henry and he was not mistaken. As he came to the gates of the city he was met by his brother and an assembly of the leading men of the town.

They had come to proclaim Stephen King.

Amid acclamation Stephen entered the town and his brother took him to his palace which was called the Castle there that Stephen might be refreshed and what was more important, discuss with Henry the next method of procedure

Henry was a devoted member of the Church; at the same time he was a very ambitious man; and he did not mind employing worldly methods to achieve his ends.

With his brother as King and himself in Winchester this could be the best possible state of affairs he believed—for both Church and State.

When they were alone together he said: "We need each other, Stephen." And with that wise comment Stephen was in complete agreement.

"It is most important," said Henry, "that there should be an immediate coronation. Once that has taken place you are indeed King."

"I have my doubts of William Corbeil."

"He is a man of stern principles," replied Henry. "It is a pity he took the oath to Matilda... as you did."

"It was taken under duress," replied Stephen. "That leaves us free to change our minds. The people will not accept Matilda. There would be civil war if she returned."

"Stephen, do you think she will not return?"

"I know not. She is now in Normandy. She has two sons Geoffrey of Anjou will try to take Normandy from me. For that I must be prepared."

"If I inform William Corbeil that you have sworn to preserve the liberty of the Church he may be persuaded," said Henry.

"We must have Corbeil on our side."

"Ay and Roger of Salisbury. It is a pity that all these men have sworn allegiance to Matilda. The King made a mistake in attempting to force her on the country. He knew it and it was for that reason that he made men swear several oaths His family feeling got the better of his good sense. It is a pity."

"Nevertheless we shall succeed," said Stephen.

"I doubt it not," replied the Bishop. "But that coronation must take place without delay. If Matilda were to set foot in England now, it could be disastrous."

"I fear that she may. She is forceful and longs for the crown. It seems certain that she will lose no time in claiming it."

"It must be prevented. There will be nothing but disaster under such a woman. You should bring your wife to England. She, too, should be crowned."

"I shall do that."

"And get a son. There is nothing like a young boy to please the people."

"Henry, you and I together...we cannot fail."

They pledged each other's good health and prosperity, but each spent a restless night. Henry was thinking of William Corbeil and the oath men had taken to serve Matilda. Stephen was thinking of Matilda too—that wild, passionate woman who had dominated his life, the woman he had loved, and still did, and whom he was betraying now. What would she say, what would she *do*, when she heard that Stephen had taken the crown?

He pictured her rage and fury. It would be intensified because of the passion they had shared.

He waited with trepidation for what Matilda would do.

William of Corbeil was a man who did not like trouble. It was said of him that he had come to his exalted position through good luck rather than merit. Yet he was a man of principles and when Henry of Winchester came to him with the request that he should crown Stephen King of England he drew back in dismay.

"How could this be," he wanted to know, "when I have sworn an oath to accept the King's daughter as my sovereign?"

"The oath was taken under duress," pointed out Henry.

"'Twas not so," replied William. "And an oath is an oath however taken. Are you asking me to imperil my soul?"

What a fool the man was! thought the Bishop of Winchester. Did he not see that Stephen was on the spot and that he had the support of the country? Could he not understand that the people would never accept Matilda?

"Stephen has sworn to preserve the liberties of the Church," insisted Henry. "Do you think Matilda would do that?"

"I am not concerned with the liberties of the Church, but with my oath."

"Then you are not doing your duty towards the Church."

"I am doing my duty towards God. How could I forgive myself, if having sworn an oath, I perjured my soul?"

God preserve us from fools, thought Henry of Winchester. But the unfortunate fact was that William of Corbeil was Archbishop of Canterbury and the crowning ceremony must be performed by him. Until it was, there was danger that the ceremony might never take place.

Matilda would soon be making her presence felt.

The situation was saved by the arrival in England of Hugh Bigod.

The Bigods were a rising family, who had come into prominence during the reign of the Conqueror when Robert Bigod had warned the great King of a treacherous attack which was about to be made on him. Robert was rewarded and his son Roger grew up in the service of the King and was given estates in Norfolk. King Henry had found him a useful man and had rewarded him with the castle of Framlingham. Roger's eldest son William was drowned in the White Ship and his second son Hugh inherited the estates.

Hugh was soon looking for means of further extending the family fortune. As a boy the King took him into his service and he became Henry's *dapifer*.

Like most men he had to decide now on whose side he would be. It was a fateful decision. To make the wrong choice could be to lose everything his family had built up over the last fifty years; to make the right one could double everything that had gone before.

Hugh reckoned himself to be an astute man. Matilda did not stand a chance, he was sure. The whole of the country would be against her. Stephen was his hope. Hugh was not content merely to serve Stephen in the manner in which many would. He must call attention to himself in an ostentatious way.

When Stephen arrived in England the position was that he was accepted by London and Winchester; he had his brother Henry, a most powerful man, on his side; Henry had secured the treasury for his brother; but the Archbishop of Canterbury was refusing to crown him.

Hugh presented himself to Henry of Winchester and Stephen. He could set this matter to rights.

"I have something of the utmost importance to impart," he said. "The King disinherited his daughter Matilda. He quarrelled with her just before he died, and named his nephew Stephen as his successor."

Henry was delighted. He said: "This makes all the difference. You must accompany me to the Archbishop of Canterbury and tell him exactly what you have told me."

"I shall do so with pleasure," said Hugh.

Stephen thanked him with tears in his eyes.

"My lord King," replied Hugh, "there was nothing a man of honour could do. I knew this to be so. The King, on his deathbed, repudiated Matilda. He said that such a quarrelsome woman would bring discord to the nation. His successor was to be his nephew Stephen who, after the death of his son in the White Ship, he had first thought to name. But because he had a daughter and she was his own child he named her and men swore fealty to her. But he later saw that the English would never be ruled by a woman and he saw too that she was of a temper that would not bind men to her."

"We will lose no time in going to William of Corbeil. He shall hear this and it will sweep away his doubts."

The Archbishop of Canterbury was pleased to hear what Hugh Bigod had to say. The situation was beginning to make him uneasy and he wondered what he could do if Stephen attempted to force him to crown him.

He was an old man. All he asked was to live in peace and he did not wish to be disturbed now.

But this man Hugh Bigod was ready to swear that Henry had disinherited Matilda so that was clear enough.

Hugh Bigod, calculating that this would win him an earldom from the new King, was ready to swear on the Holy Evangelists that Henry 1 had disinherited Matilda on his deathbed and named Stephen as his successor.

"In this case," replied the Archbishop, "all those who took the vow of fealty to Matilda are now released from it. I believe such vows to be null and void for the English would never accept a woman as their sovereign."

So thanks to the timely arrival of Hugh Bigod the coronation could go forward.

Stephen was crowned at Westminster on the 26th December—St. Stephen's Day, which seemed symbolic. He promised to establish all the liberties and good laws which had existed during the reigns of King Henry and Edward the Confessor, and to preserve the happiness of all classes of men and women.

The King was of pleasant and gentle mien; he had made himself beloved in his youth; he was married to a Queen of Saxon blood who had already born him a son and daughter—the son, alas, had died, but the daughter lived and the Queen was now pregnant with, it was hoped, a boy who would follow his father.

There seemed a good promise that life would continue under King Stephen as it had under King Henry, and that peace and prosperity had come to stay in England.

The King's Mysterious Malaise

Adelicia was surprised to find how deeply she mourned her husband. During his lifetime she had never felt very close to him. The disparity in their ages was great and although Henry had been kind he had never taken her into his confidence. He had married her, she was well aware, for the sole purpose of getting a legitimate son and heir to the throne. That she had not been able to provide him with one had been a constant grief to her. He had not reproached her but she knew that he often thought of his numerous illegitimate children and had believed that she was a barren woman and that it had been great ill fortune which had led him to settle on her.

She had dreaded those nights when he had been beset by nightmares and she had not known how to comfort him. She had been afraid of his bouts of temper. It had been a relief when he was called away to Normandy; and now she would never see him again.

She was astonished when Stephen came back and was proclaimed King in London. How could that be? Had he not sworn fealty to the King's daughter Matilda and was it not the King's wish that Matilda should follow him?

Before he had left for Normandy, the King had been so delighted because he had a grandson.

He had said to her: "Adelicia, I rejoice in the birth of this boy. This will make the people accept Matilda for while they will not like a woman as their sovereign, they will say: 'Ere long we shall have a great King, another Henry who will be as his grandfather and his great-grandfather before him.'"

And now Stephen was setting himself up as King.

It was bewildering.

The King's *pincerna* was asking to see her. She immediately granted an interview. She had always liked William de Albini whose duties to her husband had often brought her into contact with him. As the King's cupbearer he was naturally in constant attendance and as this was a post which his father had held before him he came of a trusted family.

William was a few years older than herself but seemed young since she compared him with her late husband; and on this occasion there was a faintly anxious expression on his face.

"You would speak with me?" asked the Queen.

"My lady, you know there is to be a new king when we had been expecting a queen."

"Yes, I have heard the news. What think you?"

William looked over his shoulder and she said: "You may speak your mind before me."

"I think, my lady, that the people will take Stephen rather then the Empress. But the nobles have sworn fealty to Matilda and there could be trouble."

"I hope this will not come to pass."

"It would mean a civil war."

"I trust not. It is the last thing that the King wanted. He often compared the greater prosperity enjoyed in England to that of Normandy and said that while England lived at peace within, Normandy was constantly trying to tear itself apart."

"I was thinking of your safety, my lady."

"I? What should I have to do with it?"

"In such a war all those in high places could be drawn in. May I make a suggestion?"

"Please do."

"That you retire from Court. It would be understandable. You are in mourning for the King. You could stay for a while in one of the abbeys you have founded, or perhaps in your castle of Arundel."

She was silent. He was looking at her intently and she flushed under his gaze.

"I should like to leave Court," she said. "It may be that the new King would wish me to. He has never been aught but gracious me. But faces change when they are beneath a crown. My husband has never said to me that he would disinherit Matilda. Nor could I believe that he had—when at last she bore a son. His greatest joy in the last weeks he was here was in contemplating the good fortune which had given Matilda a son. He referred to him as Henry II. Yet if Stephen

176

is King he will wish any son he may have to follow him, will he not?"

"I see trouble," said William. "It is for that reason that it would please me to see you leave Court."

"Thank you for your concern. I will take your advice. I shall stay for a while at Arundel. It is a pleasant spot and there I shall feel at peace."

"May I have the privilege of visiting you there?"

"That would be for me a pleasure," she told him; and bowing low William Albini took his leave of the dowager Queen.

The King's body was brought to England. It had previously received a form of embalming. This was done by slicing it and covering it with layers of salt and then wrapping it in the hide of a bull. Thus a certain preservation was assured, which was merciful as the cortège waited at Caen four weeks for a favourable wind.

It seemed fitting that the body should be laid to rest in the Abbey of Reading because the King himself had endowed it some fourteen years earlier.

Stephen arrived at Reading to be present at the burial and there he wept and made a great show of grief for the uncle who had done so much for him. He was not completely insincere. He had been fond of his uncle; and he had been grateful to him. His tears were genuine while at the same time he exalted in the glory which only the death of Henry could bring to him.

After the King had been laid to rest Adelicia went to Arundel where William de Albini came frequently to visit her.

When Matilda heard what was happening she gave way to great rage against Stephen.

How dared he—he of all people! He should have been the first to rally to her support and what had he done—stolen the crown!

How she hated him!

She had discovered that she was pregnant—and after her terrible ordeal with young Geoffrey, that was the last thing she wanted. Her condition was a handicap and she had to rely too much on her young husband.

Although she was reconciled to him she had no great love for him. He gave himself airs and she never failed to remind

177

him that if he had anything of which to be proud he owed that to his marriage with her.

"Your father was eager for alliance with my house," he taunted. "Why should he be if we were so unimportant?"

"As he told you it was merely because of the position of your lands."

It was the constant theme between them. There was no tenderness, no affection. The only bond was a common ambition, for his importance depended on her position and she could only rely on his help to gain and keep it.

People had begun to call him Geoffrey Plantagenet because he had adopted a habit of wearing a sprig of broom in his cap. This was the *planta genista* which they called Plantagenet.

When the name became attached to him he continued with this custom and was never seen without the sprig; and he caused the shrub to be planted on his lands.

Matilda suffering from the discomforts of early pregnancy gave vent to her fury against Stephen. She would go to England; she would have him in chains, she declared; he should have his eyes put out. She loved to remember those eyes close to her own, their expression one of ardent desire. She would teach Stephen of Blois what happened to those who flouted the Queen of England.

"First," Geoffrey reminded her, "we must make sure of Normandy."

"Why did this have to happen when I am with child?" she demanded.

"There we see why women are not meant to be rulers," said the tactless Geoffrey.

She quarrelled violently with him on the spot—and her disappointment fed her anger. It was Stephen she hated, not this foolish young boy. What cared she for Geoffrey? But Stephen had betrayed her.

"No one will follow him," she cried. "They have sworn fealty to *me*. How wise my father was to make them swear on oath."

When the news came that Stephen had been crowned she could have wept with rage. How dared they! Hugh Bigod had dared to say that her father had disinherited her. When had Henry done this?

"Bigod said on his death-bed," retorted Geoffrey. "You shouldn't have quarrelled with your father. You quarrel with everyone."

"You quarrelled with him, too. Who was it who demanded castles all over Normandy?"

"You said they were our right."

And so on. Quarrelling, thought Matilda, when they should be making plans to attack.

She was the Queen though; she was the Duchess of Normandy and if she could not yet go to England—for Geoffrey was right when he said that they must first secure Normandy—at least she could claim the Duchy.

The border towns surrendered to her; but the rest of Normandy made it clear that they would follow the English in taking Stephen for their ruler.

Meanwhile the child was growing within her. It would be born in July, and there was little she could do until the child was delivered. There must not be a repetition of her last confinement, the doctors warned. Special care must be taken to avoid that.

Geoffrey must go out and fight. He was ready. At least he was ambitious and eager for her to be the acknowledged ruler because he believed that he would then rule through her. He was mistaken of course, but she let him make his own dreams, for the more grandiose they were, the better he would fight for her.

It was a frustrating time. What ill luck that she had not been in England at the time of her father's death! What bad fortune that she had quarrelled with him just before he had eaten those lampreys. Geoffrey would say it was her own fault but she regarded it as the greatest bad luck.

Robert of Gloucester had returned to England. He was deeply disturbed by what was happening. He had had a real affection for the late King who had been a good father to him and he was anxious to carry out his wishes.

He was unsure what steps he should take. He did not believe that the King had disinherited his daughter. Trying, she was, and the King had never loved her, but she was his legitimate daughter and as such, surely true heir to the throne.

Some of his friends had suggested that he take the crown. He had quickly refused. That, he knew, would plunge England into civil war—a contingency above all others that the King would have deplored.

"But," they said to him, "You were his beloved son. If he

could have made you legitimate you are the one he would have wished most to see on the throne."

It was true. But he was *not* the King's legitimate son and the King had a legitimate daughter and a nephew.

Some might say that Count Theobald of Blois, Stephen's elder brother, came before Stephen. But Stephen was the King's protégé; he was the one who had been brought up in England and there had been a time Robert knew, when the King had considered making Stephen his heir.

And now Stephen had stepped in and taken the crown.

Roger of Salisbury, Robert heard, had after consideration, given his services to Stephen. The Archbishop of Canterbury had crowned him; Hugh Bigod had sworn that he had heard the King disinherit Matilda; and when Stephen's representative had come to Falaise to demand the treasure which the late King had put into Robert's keeping, Robert thought it advisable to give it up.

But he did not really believe Hugh Bigod's statement and he was certain in his heart that the King wished Matilda to take the crown. This must be so because the King's grandson must follow him. Henry would never have made Stephen King because that would have meant that Stephen would nominate any son *he* might have to follow him.

No, it was that small child in Matilda's nursery whom the King had called Henry II, who proved the falseness of Bigod's statement and the wrong Stephen had done in taking the throne.

Robert must work therefore to win the crown for his half-sister Matilda.

But how? England had gone over to Stephen. Normandy was going. And Matilda's attitude wherever she went did not endear her to the people. Her husband, Geoffrey Plantagenet, was young and inexperienced and, like his wife, too arrogant.

But much could change.

Robert must therefore bide his time and for a while appear to go along with popular opinion.

Stephen sent word to him that he expected him to return to England.

It was not exactly a command; it was a feeler. What was Robert thinking? Whose side was he on? That was what Stephen wished to know. Important men were supporting him; what was Robert of Gloucester going to do?

Robert wrote back that he wished to return to England.

He had, however, taken an oath to the King's daughter Matilda. He had heard that the King had disinherited that daughter. If this were the case he, Robert, would accept Stephen as King of England and serve him well. In return he would wish his estates in England to be left in his hands.

Stephen gave an undertaking that Robert should remain in possession of all lands bestowed on him by the late King.

"Then while this prevails I shall serve you as King," replied Robert.

That Easter he returned to England.

Stephen's wife, Matilda, heavy with child, was glad to step ashore from the ship which carried her to England. She was uneasy. She would have preferred Stephen to have kept his oath to their cousin the Empress rather than take the crown himself.

It was for this reason that she must come to England now. The child she carried might well be a boy and heir to the throne. It was important therefore that it should be born in England.

Stephen was waiting to greet her at Dover—a Stephen with the new dignity of King. When she had last seen him he had had hopes; now he had a crown. Men paid great deference to him although they did not tremble at his word as they had at Henry's. Stephen was liberal with his smiles. He was going to win people to his side, not by fear as the previous kings had, but by his friendliness towards them.

As for herself she was now the Queen of England, a title which sat uneasy upon her. Even her attitude towards the child she carried had changed. When she had first known she was pregnant she had been happy. The birth of the child would compensate for her the loss of little Baldwin; and she cared not whether it were a boy or a girl. Now the child had assumed great importance. If a boy it could be heir to the throne. He would not so much belong to her as to the country.

One of her temperament would indeed have been happier in a less exalted position.

Stephen embraced her. "I feared for your safety," he said, "And the child's."

The crossing was uncomfortable but could have been so much worse," she said. "How are you faring?"

"You will see for yourself. The people acclaim me. They want me, Matilda, for their sovereign."

She smiled and said nothing. Later, perhaps when they

181

were alone she could talk to him. But Stephen would not tell her the whole truth. He was a man of changing moods. At times he believed he could not fail and that the whole world loved him; but he could quickly change and see failure pursuing him and everyone's hand against him.

She knew Stephen's weaknesses better than anyone and she loved him for them.

Now she saw that she must not depress him. She must seem to share their euphoric dream. She must never give a hint of her misgivings. To do so would spoil his pleasure. He saw himself as the elected King. The people wanted him. Even the late King had in time decided that he was the one. Had not Hugh Bigod confirmed this and received an earldom for so doing? It was well to reward one's friends. Stephen was always generous to those who served him. He had always said: "One must make friends with everyone." That had not been the way of the Conqueror and King Henry. They had never bought friendship; they had never sought it. They demanded obedience to their laws.

Stephen rode with her to London, beside her, taking care of her, speaking anxiously of the Queen's condition.

"The people like to see you thus," he whispered to her. "They want the succession assured. It is when it is not that there can be great trouble."

And so they came to London.

Very soon after her arrival she was brought to bed. Her child was born after a short labour—a boy. Stephen was in ecstasies of delight. God was smiling on him, he said. This showed, did it not, that God was with him?

He had only been King for a few months and see, here he was the father of a bonny son.

They named the child Eustace.

Stephen could not honour his wife enough. The Empress who had dominated his thoughts for so long was now an enemy. The crown was between them. If ever they met again it would not be in a bedchamber but on a battlefield. In the meantime he had his wife, that other Matilda, gentle, loving, whose sole ambition was to serve her husband. She had begun auspiciously by giving him a son.

He would look wonderingly at the child. He held it in his arms and marvelled at its tiny hands; he kissed its brow reverently.

"A crown," he said, "and now a son."

* * *

It seemed inevitable that there must be trouble sooner or later. It was while he was congratulating himself on his good fortune that the news reached him that the King of Scotland had invaded England. His excuse for doing so was that he did not understand why there should be a King Stephen on the throne when the lords and knights together with the powerful men of the Church had sworn allegiance to the King of Scotland's niece, the Empress Matilda.

Stephen marched north. As he passed through the towns people came out to welcome him. There were many who were waiting to join his ranks.

During the reign of Henry I, England had enjoyed a long peace and while this was appreciated by many, there were young men who longed for the excitement of war. They joined Stephen; and it was said that never before had such an army been seen. By the time he reached Durham it was of such mighty proportions that it struck terror into the hearts of the Scots and King David immediately sued for peace.

Henry would have taken heavy reprisals for such action; not so Stephen. He wanted all men to love him; even his enemies. When David pointed out that having sworn an oath of fealty to the Empress Matilda he could not do so to Stephen, he was excused from doing so. It was at this time that men began to doubt Stephen's talents as a ruler.

He was affable, true; he was no coward; he would always be at the forefront of his armies; but he could never strike terror into men's hearts because they would know that if they wept and showed their penitence they would be forgiven. It seemed reasonable to them then, to try their luck at displacing him for in doing so there was much to gain and little to lose.

He even decided to take Henry, the Scottish King's son, under his wing and bestow estates on him. Although his attitude to his enemies was questioned, at least he had shown great promptitude in suppressing the northern rebellion and on his return journey south he was treated to such a show of loyalty and affection that the Scottish trouble seemed to him yet another indication of God's approval.

The King wished all to know how pleased he was with his beloved Queen. He would not be satisfied, he declared, until she had been crowned.

The coronation should take place at Easter and there

should be such a celebration of that feast, the like of which few had seen before.

Many were invited; there should be such a display of gold and silver, and jewels and rich garments that all would know prosperity had come to stay. He wanted to impress on them all what a kind and benevolent man he was. His grandfather had been a great Conqueror but he had not been loved; his uncle had been known as the Lion of Justice, but men had trembled at his frown. These two had been wise rulers up to a point, but they had been cruel and ruthless.

Now the people had a king who would rule them wisely and well, yet benevolently. The times had changed and that was a matter for rejoicing.

At the heart of all this magnificence was the coronation of the Queen. His Matilda was to be Queen Matilda and this was to be a ceremony which men would remember all their lives.

Matilda was a little pale and strained but Stephen's great delight to see her so honoured sustained her. She wished that she could throw off her misgivings, and feel as confident of the future as Stephen did. But perhaps it was in her nature to fear.

Stephen took advantage of the occasion to reassure the people of the good times ahead. He solemnly swore that he would serve the country well. As far as the Church was concerned he would not keep the possessions of a bishopric to himself if a bishop died, but would allow these to pass to the bishop who was elected in the place of the deceased one. The tendencies of Rufus and Henry to retain such lands and riches had been greatly deplored. There were constant disputes over the forests. Many people owned forests but to the Kings there was something sacred in these green glades because they harboured the animals they so loved to hunt. Rufus and Henry had made laws that no man was to cut timber in his own forest; he was not allowed to kill a single deer. The forests, no matter who owned them, had been considered to be the sacred hunting grounds of royalty. This was a law which was deeply resented by the people; and when Stephen declared that he renounced that law he was applauded throughout the country. There was another law which the people particularly deplored and that was the levelling of a tax of two shillings on every hide of land. The late Kings had refused to give relief from this tax which had been in existence for many years. It was in fact known as Danegeld.

This public announcement of the King's intention was received with acclaim.

"The new King," said the people, "is greater than all who have gone before. He is as wise as King Henry and he will keep that King's good laws and renounce his bad ones, for in addition to his wisdom he is possessed of sympathy and understanding of all conditions of men."

The reign had set fair. Stephen had never been so happy. He had taken the crown with greater ease than he had thought possible; he had a healthy young son; his wife Matilda was a good woman whose greatest happiness was in serving him well. What more could a man ask?

There was a minor irritation.

At the banquet after the Queen's Coronation the King said that Henry, son of the King of Scotland of whom he had grown fond, should be seated on his right hand.

William of Corbeil, as the head of the Church, was incensed, because this place should surely have been reserved for him.

Archbishop William had been very uneasy since he had been persuaded to crown the King. He did not entirely believe in Hugh Bigod's declaration that the late King had disowned his daughter and because of this he was more touchy than ever. To see the son of a King who had recently openly declared himself to be Stephen's enemy put before him, was more than he could endure.

What reasoning was this that put a recent enemy before the head of the Church?

Nothing could placate the Archbishop. He left the banqueting hall and surrounded by his servants declared his intention of leaving without delay.

The incident was not going to be easily forgotten. It was, said many of the knights, an insult to the Church. And surely the King was unwise to show such partiality for this young man that he set him above the nobility of England?

Stephen was nonplussed. All he had wished to do was help the young man, put him at ease; after all he was a kinsman. He knew the young man's father had recently risen in revolt but he believed in forgiving his enemies.

How difficult it was, even if one was a benevolent man, to please everyone all the time.

The King of Scotland hearing of the trouble which had arisen out of the partiality of the King for his son, declared that he too was offended. Naturally his son as a future King of Scotland should have the place of honour. If this could not naturally be conceded to him then his son Henry must return to Scotland. He should no longer honour a Court with his presence when that Court did not appreciate the dignity due to him.

The matter had become a bit of a joke.

"Did Stephen or did he not subdue David of Scotland?" was the question which was being asked. One would have thought David and his son Henry were the victors.

Was this what came of being too lenient with rebels? William the Conqueror and Henry I would never have behaved in that way. None would have dared to defy them.

One morning soon after these events the Queen awoke to find that Stephen appeared to be in some kind of stupor. She bent over him in alarm to speak to him but although he looked into her face he could not explain to her how he felt, merely wishing to lie still.

"You are exhausted," she said: and gave orders that the King should not be disturbed.

All through the day he lay there; Matilda remained in his bedchamber and would admit no one.

He is exhausted, she told herself. After a long rest he will be himself.

But the next day he showed no inclination to rise. He just lay in bed, a glazed look in his eyes.

"Stephen," said Matilda, "can you tell me what ails you?"

He could not, and she said: "I must send for the physicians."

He made no protest and when they gathered round his bed he showed little interest in them or in anything. They could not understand what had happened to him.

Matilda brought in little Eustace but he looked at the baby with lacklustre eyes. This man in the bed was so different from the energetic, charming man abounding in friendliness that Matilda was—as the doctors were, too—completely bewildered.

He could not eat nor could he sleep. He simply lay still, looking blankly before him.

For a week he persisted in this state; he was growing frail; he had the air of a man who was wasting away.

The doctors had never known anything like it. It was as though he were possessed by some spirit alien to himself.

There were whispers about him.

"The King is mad."

"The King is near death."

They remembered too that he had usurped the throne. Was this God's punishment? All had gone well. He had calmly taken the crown but the late King had commanded his subjects to swear allegiance to Matilda. Everything had appeared to go well. Men such as Roger of Salisbury and Robert of Gloucester, and old William the Archbishop of Canterbury had been won to his side. But was God merely leading him on that when He struck him down the fall should be more marked?

Never had such a state been heard of. Stephen was not an old man or it might have been understood. He was wasting away, slowly being robbed of his mind and his bodily strength.

In a short time there would be a new ruler of England, for God was showing clearly that he did not intend this one to reign.

Matilda was frightened. She would allow none but herself to attend him. She wondered if some subtle poison had been administered; she would not allow any to prepare his food but herself.

She loved him dearly. In spite of his infidelities, in spite of his action in taking the crown of which she could not approve, she would never swerve from her devotion to him. Her presence comforted him she knew, for sometimes when she moved out of his sight he became agitated. It was the only time he showed any feeling but indifference to what was happening to him.

Was it conscience? she wondered. Did he in his heart fear what he had done? She had once believed that he was in love with the Empress Matilda. She no longer believed that, for would he have robbed a woman he loved of that which she, being ambitious beyond all things, would dearly love to possess? There was some deadly fascination about a crown. None could resist it. Stephen had not been able to. Was this the reason why this terrible wasting disease had seized him?

"The King is dying," the cry was taken up all over the country. There was great consternation among those who had supported him.

Hugh Bigod, who had sworn on oath that Henry I had disinherited his daughter, went to Norwich Castle and fortified it. The son of the Earl of Devon, Baldwin of Redvers,

187

raised a revolt against the King and was joined by Robert of Bampton. Geoffrey Plantagenet was about to invade Normandy and Robert of Gloucester had declared himself in favour of Matilda.

Matilda sat by her husband's bed. He turned to look at her and, to her delight, he spoke to her.

"You are sad," he said.

"How could I be otherwise when you are so ill?"

"What ails me?" he asked.

"I know not. Nor do the doctors."

"I feel a great weight upon my body and my mind. I want nothing but to lie here and wait for death."

"How can you do so when you have a kingdom to govern?"

"I am too tired," he said. "Others will do it better than I."

"What has happened to you, Stephen?"

"I do not know," he answered.

"If you could but rouse yourself. . . ."

"Why should I? Because I have a kingdom to govern? Many will say I had no right to it, Matilda."

"You have a wife, a daughter and a baby son. You have a right to protect them."

"You are right, Matilda. I have them. May God bless them."

The tears came into his eyes and fell on to his cheek.

"Give me your hand, Matilda," he said.

She did so.

"Help me to rise."

He stood up, but he could scarcely do so.

"You are weak still," she said. "But you will recover. I know you will recover now."

"I must, my dear wife. For you and my children."

"Thank God," said Matilda. She summoned servants. "Bring the King's garments. He is so much better that he will dress."

He allowed them to put his garments on. They hung about his body for he had lost much weight.

"I shall prepare a meal for you," said the Queen. "None shall do that but myself."

And they sat together and he ate with relish.

Matilda cried: "I thank God we have come through that slough of despair."

Stephen recovered from his mysterious malady as quickly as he had fallen into it. The fact that several of the knights whom he had trusted had shown that as soon as he was laid low they were ready to rise against him seemed to speed his recovery. There was need for immediate action.

It seemed that Hugh Bigod had not in fact rebelled but had merely fortified his castle in his own defence and as soon as the King was known to be well, he removed those fortifications—which seemed a reasonable enough action.

The case of Robert of Bampton was different; he had broken the country's laws so firmly enforced by Henry I, and had ravaged the countryside, robbing and raping, so that in his area there was a return to the terror of the days of William Rufus. Stephen marched on Bampton, seized Robert and he was brought before a court who punished him by forfeiting all his possessions.

It was a different matter with Baldwin of Redvers. Here was a very ambitious man. He had inherited the title of Earl of Devon from his father and with this some extensive lands, not only in Devon but in the Isle of Wight. Having been forced, during the reign of Henry, to suppress his rapacious designs, he now saw an opportunity to give full play to them. The stern Lion of Justice was no more; the new King, some said, was on his death-bed, and certainly too ill to take action; so this seemed the moment for him to rise up and let it be known that he was the ruler of his particular territory. He began by subduing the city of Exeter; no one was safe there after dark; men of substance were kidnapped and held to ransom; they were tortured until they gave up their money, their women or whatever was demanded.

The citizens appealed to the King to come to their aid. This made Baldwin laugh. "The King is half dead," was his rejoinder. "This is an end to the restrictions we have suffered for years."

But he was wrong.

News was brought to him that the King had recovered and that he was going to make an example of Baldwin of Redvers. He was on his way to Devon with a strong force but was sending two hundred cavalry ahead of him.

Baldwin snapped his fingers; but he was uneasy. He fortified Exeter Castle but he had no intention of being starved out in it. He could do better, he believed, by leaving it in the hands of some of his men, making them first swear that they would not submit to the King as they owed their first allegiance to him. As a hostage to his followers he left in the castle, his wife Adelise and his children.

189

Stephen arrived with his army and encamped about the castle. The siege had begun. It followed the usual pattern, but Stephen followed the practice of his uncle and, leaving some troops to continue with the siege, went away for a while to take other castles and rich lands belonging to Baldwin.

For three months the siege continued. Then it seemed to Stephen's followers that God intervened for the wells within the castle precincts dried up and the besieged were obliged to use wine for cooking. Since there was no water Stephen ordered that lighted torches should be flung over the walls for the enemy would have no means of putting out the fires which were started except with wine.

It was clear that the besieged must be on the point of surrender.

A truce was called, that two of the leading knights might come out and parley with the King. They would make terms they said.

Stephen received them and when he saw how thin they were he was moved to pity.

His brother Henry of Winchester was with him at the interview.

"My lord King," said the first of the men, "we have meant no rebellion towards you. We have sworn fealty to our lord the Earl of Exeter and he it was who commanded us to hold this siege."

Stepehn conceded this and was about to speak when his brother tugged at his sleeve.

"I am sure," said Henry, "That the King would wish to consider what you have said."

Stephen dismissed the men and when they were alone Henry said: "They are on the very point of surrender. Did you not notice their sagging and wasted skin? They are dying of thirst. You should not make terms but insist on absolute surrender."

Stephen said: "They are of a certainty greatly suffering."

"Strong men do not make terms with traitors unless it is expedient to do so.

Stephen was at last persuaded and his answer was: "Absolute surrender."

The men went away but they had realized that the King had wavered and it was only the influence of his brother that had made him resolute.

Later that day there was another emissary from the besieged castle. It was Baldwin's wife, Adelisa; she came in all humility, her feet bare, her hair hanging loose about her shoulders. She was weeping bitterly, as she threw herself at Stephen's feet.

"I beg of you, my lord," she said, "Have pity on us. My children are starving. You have children of your own."

There was no doubt that the King was moved at the sight of this beautiful woman and it took all Henry's considerable powers to make him refrain from offering to lift the siege without delay. But Henry did succeed in the end and Baldwin's wife went sorrowing back inside the castle walls.

Stephen called together his advisers and among them was naturally his brother Henry and there was also Earl Robert of Gloucester.

Stephen said: "Baldwin has fled. His men at arms and his servants are at our mercy. I could destroy them all."

"It is what you should do," said Henry.

Robert of Gloucester said: "You cannot destroy so many and it would be unjust to select a few and let them suffer for the sins of all. But what sin have these men committed? They have sworn an oath of fealty to their lord and they have obeyed him."

"That lord had already sworn an oath to me," Stephen reminded him.

"'Tis so, but these men had not," pointed out Gloucester.

Henry said: "If you allow these men to go free all the lords in the land could rise against you. They could leave their men to do battle with you knowing that when they were defeated your prisoners could say, 'Oh, but I only obeyed my lord.'"

"I would be a benevolent king," said Stephen.

"Benevolent kings are for peaceful states," retorted Henry.

Robert of Gloucester was thinking that Stephen for all his charm, good looks and talent for pleasing people was a weak man. He wanted to live at peace. And a strong man was needed to rule this country. It had had the benefit of two strong men, the Conqueror and Henry I, and they had done much; but the task was by no means completed and what had been so hard won could be easily lost.

Moreover Robert had sworn fealty to his sister. This man Stephen was a usurper. He had declared his readiness to serve Stephen for what would have happened if he had not done so? He would have been languishing in a dungeon now. That was not the way to bring Matilda back to England and place her on the throne.

So he urged Stephen to show leniency while Henry of Winchester tried to point out the folly of following this advice.

But Stephen would do what he wished to do; and he could not get out of his mind the sight of that beautiful woman with her feet bare and her hair hanging about her shoulders, and how she had spoken of her children.

He made his first blunder. He would accept the fact that those who had conducted a siege against him were acting on the orders of their lord the Earl of Exeter, to whom they had sworn fealty. *They* were not the criminals; that was their master.

The siege was over. There were no reprisals. The news spread throughout the country. It was possible to rebel against the King and suffer no punishment for so doing. This was an invitation for those who favoured rebellion, to rebel. They would do so with impunity for they were not responsible.

This decision had made nonsense of the oath of fealty. Baldwin in the Ise of Wight was at first amazed and then amused. One siege had failed; so he would try another. He fortified Carisbrooke Castle and from there attempted to set up a new kind of rule. He gathered about him a company of pirates to harry the ships which went between England and Normandy.

Stephen, although lenient to his fallen foes, lost no time in acting against them. He assembled a fleet and went to the Isle of Wight.

The summer had been hot and dry and strangely enough the wells of Carisbrooke dried up as had those of Exeter. This greatly heartened Stephen's followers because they believed it was a sign that God was on their side.

The outcome was that Baldwin was forced to surrender, but here again Stephen made a major mistake. With Baldwin in his hands he did not keep him his prisoner; he contented himself with stripping him of his possessions, and sending him into exile.

And where should Baldwin go?

To Anjou; there to be made much of by Matilda and her husband who were busy with plans as to how they were going to defeat the upstart Stephen.

The Queen Commands

Never in her life had the Empress Matilda suffered such frustration. She had long dreamed of ruling England; during her father's lifetime she had waited impatiently for his death and when it came she was unable to take advantage of it.

Here she lay in childbed; and like the birth of her second son the birth of the third was long and arduous. Then ... another boy.

How ironical life was! How her father had longed for a boy from his meek Adelicia, and the poor thing had been barren! Yet no sooner did she allow Geoffrey Plantagenet to be a husband to her than she was with child and in a short while had three boys. Young Henry was but three years old and here was master William making his appearance—and there was young Geoffrey in between.

He shall be the last, she decided. For I am heartily tired of their father and having got three boys I need not concern myself with getting more from him.

What she would concern herself with was getting the crown.

Stephen was constantly in her thoughts. She loved him; she hated him. If her father had arranged a marriage for them instead of giving him that insignificant Matilda of Boulogne and her the senile old Emperor of Germany and then a foolish boy.... But how many times had she railed in this manner.

Suffice it that Stephen had betrayed her. The thought maddened her, yet delighted her in a way. There had been a time when she had planned how she could seduce him; now she found equal joy in planning how she would outwit him. For the time would come when she would snatch the crown from him, and then she would take the greatest delight in tormenting and humiliating him.

She beguiled these wretched hours of inactivity in thinking up tortures for him.

In the meantime she must recruit as many people as possible to her banner. Stephen was a fool. He was too soft and gentle. He cared too much whether people liked him or not. That was no way to rule. Subjects must see that there was a strong man ruling them, a man who would show no mercy when his laws were broken. Was that not how her father and grandfather had ruled. One ruled by strength, not amiability.

Handsome gracious Stephen! He had some lessons to learn. When he was in his dungeon perhaps she would visit him, remind him of the nights they had spent together—torment him, tease him, perhaps submit to his entreaties to linger with him. And afterwards she would have the chains set on his feet and hands to remind him that, although she might amuse herself with him when the whim took her, he was still her prisoner.

For he had failed her. She had believed when she had seen him so eager for her, when he had told her in the dark of night that there was no one like her, and she had thought of him as hers in all ways, that he would stand with her, as that poor fool Geoffrey her husband never could. She had believed she could trust Stephen. And he had taken the crown for himself!

She would never, never forgive him. Hers was not a forgiving nature. She was not easy and soft as he was.

When she regained the crown people would understand that she meant to be obeyed. She would quickly make them realize who their ruler was. She would follow in her father's and grandfather's footsteps and if some were put to the sword or lost a limb or two or were deprived of their eyes—then they would learn the more quickly.

In the meantime here she was helpless—and Stephen was no doubt thanking God for his achievement. He had actually been crowned. And so had that miserable wife of his. Queen of England! *That* Matilda.

"Stephen of Blois," she said aloud, "you shall pay for this."

She had asked that her case be tried before the Pope. She demanded that Stephen be excommunicated. She was the rightful heir to the throne; she was her father's only legitimate child and the knights and members of the clergy had sworn allegiance to her. All right-thinking men and women must support her against this upstart son of a count—and not even his eldest born—who had usurped her place.

Geoffrey of Anjou came into her bedchamber. She looked at him critically. She supposed some would call him an elegant man. She had never thought so because always she had compared him with Stephen. She did so now and she wished with all her might that it could have been Stephen standing there before her. How she would have jeered at him; she would have risen from her bed, weak as she was, and flown at him; she would have scratched his face and bitten his hands and exhausted herself and him by the passion of her hatred which would she knew, turn to love. And how she would have enjoyed that!

But he was far away, in England, in his palace wearing her *crown* and all that was left for her was this silly young fool sporting his sprig of broom in his hat and calling himself Plantagenet.

"What news?" she asked.

"None."

"Nothing from Rome?"

"Nothing. Innocent does not want to embroil himself with Stephen."

"He is a fool. He should know that no one cares whether or not they offend Stephen." Her lips curled into a sneer. "Stephen is so kind, so gentle. Stephen is so courteous. No one quarrels with Stephen."

"Some of his knights do. He has trouble there."

She was silent, willing the knights to rise against him all over England, all over Normandy, to defeat, but not to kill him. Oh, no, she could not bear that. A world without Stephen would have lost its savour. She wanted to know that he was alive; she wanted to go on dreaming of the day when she would confront him... in his dungeon

"And what are you doing?" she asked scornfully. "A man would have been in England, would have made some attempt to snatch the crown from the traitor who has taken it from his wife. But what can one expect from a boy!"

"What a general!" he said. "She gives orders from her bed! What if I went to England? What of Normandy? You haven't even got that."

"Then why not?"

"Because the people do not love you, that's why."

"Did they love my grandfather?"

"Your grandfather was a great ruler."

"They shall see that his granddaughter is no less."

"Men respected him."

"I shall force them to respect me."

"You may imprison them, torture them, but you cannot force them to do that."

"You have much to learn, Master Geoffrey. If I were not weak from bearing your child...."

"At least I am man enough to give you a boy."

"Scarcely a hero's task you'll admit. Now, Master Plantagenet, I want you to go out and subdue those of my Norman subjects who would rebel against me. If you cannot win my English Crown, for the love of God make my ducal one secure."

"Methinks the people have heard too much of your temper. They like you not."

"I will force them to accept me," she said. "Wait until I am rid of my burdens."

"Then we shall see," he said. "I have news for you. Your cousin is in Normandy."

"Stephen?"

"The King of England," Geoffrey bowed ironically. "He has defeated Baldwin of Redvers and has come that his son Eustace may be acknowledged as the future Duke; he has come to pay fealty to the King of France."

Matilda narrowed her eyes. Stephen in Normandy. The sea no longer divided them.

No wonder she felt exhilarated.

Impatiently she awaited for her strength to return. Geoffrey meanwhile set out with his troops to attempt to regain Normandy for her. This was the reason he had had to make this distasteful marriage. He had undertaken it only because his father had told him that one day he would be the Duke of Normandy. For England he did not greatly care, but passionately he wanted Normandy.

It was not long before she received news that he was besieged by those who supported Stephen's claim and that he needed help that he might break out from the town of Le Sap.

Where was Stephen now? she wondered. Was his Queen with him in Normandy, or had he left her behind as Regent? She would be useless. That silly sentimental creature! What would she know about governing a country? She had always despised the woman; it was the only way in which she could console herself for not being in her place.

She gathered together a troop of men and rode to Le Sap. She would show them that although she was a woman she

196

was capable of taking decisive action. When she arrived with her rescuing force she would have the pleasure of putting Stephen's adherents to flight. It would give her great pleasure to picture his receiving the news of her action.

But it did not work out as she had hoped.

When she arrived at Le Sap, Geoffrey had been wounded and it seemed great good fortune that a retreat was possible. There was nothing for her to do but take him back to safety where he could be nursed back to health.

She was as frustrated as ever.

In the castle of Arundel Adelicia felt remote from the troubles of the country.

She had heard of Stephen's illness and had been very sympathetic towards his wife for she knew how Matilda adored her husband. She had often in the past been sorry for the Queen. Matilda was a good woman, calm and clever in her way. She would have been an excellent helpmeet to any man if she were given the chance to be. She was clever enough to be able to understand statecraft for she had been very well educated in the Abbey of Bermondsey; and at the same time she had acquired a meekness which was becoming. Adelicia had once said to the King her husband: "I hope Stephen realizes what a good wife he has."

It had seemed of late that he did. For she heard that he was often in her company and was eager that all should do honour to her as their Queen. Her coronation had been even grander than his own and he had seemed to rejoice in that.

Adelicia enjoyed tending the flowers in her gardens; she liked to grow her herbs and make them into scents and ointments. She liked to sit at her tapestry. In truth she liked the quiet life of a noblewoman who does not have to be at Court.

If she were truthful she would say that she had come to the happiest part of her life. She had been young when she married Henry the King and the years with him had not been easy ones. He had been kind to her in his way, it was true, but she had always had the terrible feeling of guilt because she had not been able to supply that much-wanted son. She knew that he did not regard her physically with any great excitement. There had been many to tell her what kind of life he had led. This had been conveyed to her in several ways, with suppressed giggles, with shocked allusions, with solemn pronouncements. And she had understood. He had numerous illegitimate children, and his first wife had given him only two legitimate ones. She had learned how he had wooed that first wife and what a love match it had been. It was all long ago and she had always said to herself, "I must be grateful for his kindness and tolerance at least."

Yet, in the quiet of her apartments she could admit to herself that his passing was a relief. No more the labour of trying once more for what seemed to be impossible; no more of those fearful nightmares when his misdeeds had haunted him and he had leaped from his bed to grasp his sword and slash at the hangings. No more irascible bouts of temper. Here she was, not a young woman but not an old one either—for she was but in her thirties and not half way yet and he had been sixty-six when he had died. Yes, she was happy here at Arundel, shut away from the anxieties of life outside and now and then hearing the clatter of horses' hoofs in the courtyard and looking down to see William de Albini there looking up, kissing his hand to her and later mounting the spiral stairs to her apartments when refreshments would be brought and he would talk to her of what was happening at Court—or more often of the pleasures of his estates of Norfolk, and they would enjoy the gardens of Arundel together.

And as she thought of him she heard sounds of his arrival, and there he was just as she had seen him so many times.

A groom took his horse; he dismounted; he came up the stone staircase and he was taking her hands and kissing them.

"I am happy to see you," she told him.

"I have come to say farewell," he answered.

Her expression was suddenly woebegone and she could not hide it.

"Then my absence will sadden you?" he asked.

"Tell me how long you will be away?" she said.

"I trust not long. I am to go to France to celebrate the marriage of the young son of the King of France."

"You will joust, I doubt not."

"I doubt it not either."

"And you will astonish them all with your skill. I know well that that is so. I would I could see you."

"I would ride the better if you did. There is something I would say to you before I go. You will know that I have long been devoted to you. I was aware of you even before the death of the late King. I envied him then."

"Many envy a king his crown."

"'Twas not his crown I envied. And now you are free. I

198

have long thought of what I would say to you and now I find it difficult. You are a queen...."

"A queen without a husband, of no importance in truth."

"I am but a knight...."

"Pray say what is in your mind for it may make me very happy."

He took her hands and kissed them. "Adelicia," he said, "could you forget you were a queen and be the wife of a humble knight?"

"I could only be happy thus," she said.

"Then," he answered, "let us plight our troth for we have both learned the pleasures of the simple life. I know in my heart that you will be ready to exchange the glories of the Court for them."

They smiled at each other. Adelicia thought she had never been so happy in her life; so did William; but they did not mention this. It would have sounded like treason to the late King.

There seemed no reason why Stephen or the Queen should object to their marriage.

What a joy, thought Adelicia, at last to be of no great importance.

They planned to marry as soon as William returned from his mission to France.

Matilda, Queen of England, had changed since her husband had taken the crown. Until the death of King Henry she had seemed insignificant, so meek that she scarcely ever expressed an opinion. Since she had become a queen that meekness had dropped from her. She was by no means arrogant and in truth the change in her had nothing to do with the fact that she had become Queen of England.

From the time she had been brought to the Court of England from the Abbey of Bermondsey to be betrothed to Stephen of Blois she had been conscious of her inadequacy. There had always been that other Matilda. The fact that they bore the same name had seemed significant; and her cousin had always made her feel she had no right to it.

That Matilda, known as the Empress from an early age, for no sooner had she been betrothed to the Emperor of Germany than she began to assume the manners of an Imperial ruler, had dominated her cousin's life. The Empress had ruled the nursery, Stephen had adored her, and of course she, Matilda, who had been brought to the Court for the purpose of marrying Stephen had adored him.

It seemed the most natural thing in the world to love Stephen. She had not been surprised that in her arrogant way the Empress loved him too or at least looked upon him as hers. The Empress could in fact love no one but herself, but Stephen's presence had at one time been necessary to her pleasure. Then she had gone away and Stephen had in due course married Matilda, but always there had been the shadow of the Empress between them.

Stephen was a man who could win the love of others without effort. He was also kind to people and pretended to be interested in their affairs. Even the humblest scullion could be sure of a smile and a greeting from him. This ensured their loyalty. Matilda had never been sure whether Stephen loved popularity so much that he made an effort to gain it or whether he smiled and feigned amiability because he was too lazy to do anything else. She had never fully understood Stephen. He could be brave and energetic—as he had been when he seized the crown. At other times he could become so lethargic as to ask for peace at any price. She deplored the fact that he had allowed Baldwin of Redvers to escape him, yet at the same time she loved him for his susceptibilities which would not let him be hard on those he had conquered.

The truth was that she loved Stephen with a quiet and abiding love which was in sharp contrast to the feelings the Empress had for him.

Matilda knew that she did not excite his senses as his cousin did. She knew that he was not a faithful husband. With that easygoing way of his he slipped into love affairs and there were offspring to prove this. But she was his Queen and there had been times when he had told her that of all the people in the world she was the only one he could be completely sure of.

His light love affairs she accepted as a woman married to such a man and loving him dearly must do. It was the Empress who had cast a shadow over her life. And when Stephen had taken the crown this change had come over his wife. He did not love the Empress. Love as the Queen understood it was devotion, sacrifice, the elimination of self-interest. Yet Stephen, instead of holding the crown for his cousin, had snatched it and held it himself.

In her heart she believed this to be wrong. Stephen had sworn fealty to the Empress Matilda. He had been the first of the knights to do so, and it had been the wish and command of the last King that his daughter should come to the throne. Yet the fact that he had done this filled her with exultation for it showed clearly that he did not love the Empress.

It was for this reason that she the Queen had grown in stature and her true self had begun to emerge. She had discovered strength in herself which she had not known existed. She had wanted Stephen to know that she was beside him; that she would be with him no matter what happened. Whether it was right or wrong for Stephen to have taken the throne was of no account to her. She loved Stephen; she was his wife; and she was going to help him hold what he had taken.

All through his recent illness she had nursed him and they had come more closely together. She had managed to convey to him her absolute loyalty; and he had realized the worth of such devotion. He had told her what it meant to him to have one person in the world who was entirely for him. She knew that beneath his tenderness on this occasion there was sincerity.

When he had left for Normandy he had said, "I go knowing that you will care for my affairs as no one else. These men who have sworn to serve me may well do so if it suits their ends, but only in you can I put my trust."

These words she would treasure. She would die rather than fail to deserve them.

And so those about her saw the new Matilda emerge. The Queen who would stand beside her husband in success or failure; the woman who had no thought in her mind other than his good.

Her task was a difficult one and she knew that it would become even more so. Stephen was in Normandy where there had been continual trouble throughout the years; but since Stephen had taken the throne—and there were many who said it belonged to the Empress—numerous robber barons whose pleasure in the past had been to ravage the land, to plunder, to seize wealth and women and to terrify the countryside while they exercised their cruel lusts, saw the possibility of a return to the old days of William Rufus, which had existed before Henry, Lion of Justice, had brought order to the country with his stern laws. They knew full well that amiable Stephen was no Henry. The fact that he had shown such leniency to the followers of Baldwin of Redvers and to Baldwin himself was an indication of what could be expected.

201

The reign of Henry was over; a new order had begun and the barons were going to make the most of it.

There were disturbances all over the country. Rochester Cathedral was burned down; there were fires throughout cities as far apart as York and Bath. The King of Scotland was preparing to invade and insurgents displaying the banner of the Empress Matilda had taken Dover Castle which they declared they would hold for her until her arrival in England.

The Queen was alarmed. She realized the importance of Dover in the event of an invasion. It was the spot which must stand for Stephen at all costs.

She called her ministers to her and told them that they must with all speed gather together an army and she would march at their head to Dover.

There were murmurs against this project but she with her fierce new-born authority silenced them. She would conduct them there; she would see that Dover was taken and held for King Stephen.

They were sceptical. What could this woman do?

"The country is beginning to turn towards the Empress," they told her. "They are saying that Hugh Bigod committed perjury, that Henry would never have disinherited his own daughter, especially his grandson, young Henry. The King of Scotland will soon be on the march. It might be better for you to join the King in Normandy than attempt to hold Dover."

She dismissed this with scorn.

They did not believe her capable of governing, so she would show them that she was.

Before setting out for Dover she sent orders to her subjects of Boulogne. They were to harass the castle from the sea; they were to prevent any ships arriving with provisions.

Thus began the siege of Dover Castle conducted by the Queen who such a short time ago had seemed a colourless princess.

The besieged might have held out had it not been for the people of Boulogne who, eager to show their loyalty to their Princess, responded with enthusiasm to her call. Attacked on all sides the rebels in Dover Castle were quickly vanquished.

Everyone knew that they must reverse their opinion of the Queen. She had shown herself as a woman of strength and resource, one to be respected.

When Stephen returned, Dover was his.

Like his subjects he was amazed by the actions of his Queen.

"But why?" she asked. "Surely you know that your cause—whatever it is—must be mine."

Then did he realize how kind fate had been to him in giving him such a wife.

There was no time though to celebrate the victory of Dover. He must march north to subdue the Scots.

A Troubadour's Song

William de Albini was impatient to return to England. He had for long been in love with Adelicia—a fact which he had been forced to hide during the lifetime of the King, and now that she had promised to marry him, his great desire was to have done with Court life and settle quietly as far from it as possible. He was delighted to discover that Adelicia was of a like mind.

He was a man of great personal charm. Tall and with very clear-cut features and fine curling hair he was immediately noticed in any assembly. His skill at the joust had made him one of its finest exponents and at any important ceremony he was expected to perform.

It was for this reason that he had been selected to attend the wedding celebrations of the young heiress of Aquitaine to the bridegroom who had recently become the King of France.

This was a grand wedding, for the French were even fonder of brilliant ceremonies than the English and they performed them with a greater dignity.

The bride Eleanor had been declared Duchess of Aquitaine when her father had died on a pilgrimage to Compostella whither he had gone to ask the saints to intercede for him that a marriage he intended to make should be fruitful and yield a male heir.

Eleanor was a vivacious and extremely attractive girl of fifteen, ambitious and delighted with the new honours which had come to her; the dowager Queen, Adelaide, was by no means uncomely nor did she appear to be overburdened with sorrow on account of her recent widowhood.

Before this Queen and her Court, William de Albini had

jousted to the admiration of all who beheld him, and it was not surprising that he won the prize which was awarded for the most outstanding performance.

The trophy was presented at the royal box set up in the field and seated here were the young bride and bridegroom with the Dowager Queen of France.

As William rode up to the box and bowed low he was aware of three pairs of eyes regarding him. Those of the young King were friendly but the gaze of the two females he found disconcerting.

The bride's beauty was startling. Never before had he seen such a lively expression on such a young face. Her beautiful eyes were speculative and he had seen that expression in the faces of women before when they looked at him, but never in one so young. But it was the Queen Mother who filled him with real alarm.

Her voice was low and husky as she complimented him on his performance. Never, she said, had she been so excited by any performance at a tournament, never had she presented a prize with greater pleasure.

He bowed low, accepted the trophy and rode off.

He continued to think of the glitter in the Queen Mother's eyes and the manner in which the young Queen had regarded him. So he was not entirely surprised when he was summoned to the presence of the Queen Mother, although it was strange that she should wish to see a knight who, although he was the outstanding performer in the tournament, could scarcely be said to be of very exalted rank.

When he arrived she immediately dismissed her attendants and came to him; she stood before him breathing deeply, her eyes—alert and glittering—surveying him from head to feet.

"I had to tell you what great pleasure your performance gave me," she said.

"You are gracious," said William.

"And you are brave and handsome. I never saw a man who pleased me as you do."

"I am honoured...."

She laughed at him. "Come," she said, taking his hand, "be seated near me."

She sat on an ornate chair and indicated a stool which he might use. The stool was very close to the chair.

From her exalted position she looked down at him.

"From whichever way I look at you," she said, "I like you

206

more. Come, my good friend, do not look so surprised. You are not going to tell me that ladies have never smiled on you before."

He said, "I am unprepared for such gracious...."

"You will soon be prepared. Such a fancy I have taken to you that I would wish to keep you near me."

He rose and stood before her. "I must ask your leave to depart."

"It is not granted," she answered. "I believe you are afraid of me. Fear is not becoming to a knight."

"I am not easily frightened," he said with dignity. "What I fear is that I may be forced to speak frankly and in doing so, offend you."

"There shall be frankness between us. I like you. There is no reason why you should not stay here in my apartments."

"That I could not do."

"I am a widow," she said. "A King's widow. I might find it in my heart to marry you. What say you to that?"

"I could say that I am sure you would not be so unwise."

She stood up and came very close to him. He shrank from her for he was fully aware that she was a passionate and sensuous woman. There could not have been a greater contrast to Adelicia; their only point of resemblance was that they were both Dowager Queens.

"I would be prepared to be very unwise as you call it for a man like you."

"Then I must warn you against such acts which it could well be that you would later regret."

"I regret nothing. Have done with your coyness. There is one thing I will not endure and that is wasting time in idle talk when acts are so much more to my taste."

He drew away from her in horror.

"I ask your leave to retire, Madam."

"It is not given," she snapped. "You are a fool. Do you not realize what is being offered you?"

"I realize this, Madam, and marvel that you be so generous."

"Oh, come, my handsome knight, you are not so reluctant as you pretend. I like you. From the moment I clapped eyes on you I marked you for mine. You should be marvelling at your good fortune and determined to make the most of it."

It was not the first time William de Albini had found himself in a similarly embarrassing position. His good looks, his equestrian skill, his tall fine figure had brought him constant feminine admiration, but never before had he been confronted by an imperious woman who appeared to regard him as her subject who must obey her wishes no matter what she demanded of him.

Usually fair words cleverly chosen to convey his rejection had sufficed to extricate himself and save the importuning lady from embarrassment, but this Queen was too direct, too blatant in her desire to make him her lover. She needed plain words.

"Madam," he said, "I must tell you that I have recently become affianced. I am true to my betrothed. We have taken our vows."

The Queen burst into loud laughter. "We will forget your little English lady, my lord. You are now in France and it may well be that when you and I have made life pleasant here you will have no will to return to her."

"That is not so, Madam. I have no fancy for another."

"You are mad. Your foolish little virgin cannot give you one tenth of the pleasure I can offer. Come, you waste our time. This night is for enjoyment. I will make a promise to you. . . ."

"I must tell you, Madam, that I am betrothed to the Dowager Queen of England."

That startled her. She narrowed her eyes. "The widow of King Henry!"

"We are pledged. We shall marry on my return. I trust now, Madam, that you understand my position."

"That woman," she cried. "She is barren. The King was in her bed only for the purpose of getting the children she was too barren to have. He sought pleasure elsewhere. And you would put *me* aside for that woman."

William would endure no more. He bowed and hurried towards the door.

"Stay!" she cried.

He turned his head and temporarily looked into eyes which blazed such hatred at him that his one desire was to get away.

The Dowager Queen of France was in a fury. She was not a woman to consider her words once her passions were aroused. She had never sought to restrain them when her husband was alive and she saw no reason why she should do so now.

"That man gives himself airs," she declared. "It is time he was taught a lesson."

Her attendants smirked; they knew the tastes of their mistress. She had been accustomed to beckon and expected the object of her desires to respond with alacrity. Invariably they did; for all knew that the Queen Mother was insatiable in her desires and to have them frustrated maddened her.

Many had noticed the looks she had bestowed on the handsome William de Albini; and the fact that he had refused the Queen was discussed throughout the Court.

The young bride Eleanor was amused by the situation. Her mother-in-law should realize that there were younger and more attractive women at Court. And it seemed that the desirable Albini had pledged himself to another Queen. Her name was Adelicia and she was a Queen Dowager too.

It was worthy of a ballad, said Eleanor.

The Dowager Queen raged in her apartments. The young bride attempted to soothe her.

"There are hundreds of other men, Madam," she said "Why become so absorbed by this one?"

"He insulted me," said the Queen Mother. "He would have none of me."

Eleanor tried to hide her smile from her mother-in-law.

"He is a villain," said Eleanor. "You will have your revenge on him I'm sure."

"I should like to see him torn limb from limb," said the Dowager Queen viciously. "Then mayhap he would not be so proud of his beautiful body."

"You should let one of your lions amuse himself with your handsome knight, since he will not permit you to."

The Dowager Queen narrowed her eyes.

"I have a lion in a cave in my garden...."

Eleanor spread her hands. "There, you see, is your answer."

She was mocking, but the Queen Mother's eyes were blazing with fury.

"By all the holy saints," she said, "I will do it."

Eleanor said to her husband: "She will do it. There is such a fury in her that she will have him put into the cave with the lion."

"Her anger will cool," said the young King of France.

"The deed will be done before it has time to."

"She likes handsome men too well to spoil their beauty."

"Only if she can enjoy it. I saw the purpose in her eyes."

Eleanor was smiling secretly. She too had a fancy for handsome men. She was very young and romantic and she thought the story of unrequited love and the faithful knight who would not swerve from his devotion to the lady of his choice indeed worthy of a ballad. She loved the troubadours. Her grandfather had been a poet and a minstrel and she had learned many of his poems which had been set to music.

She thought how romantic it would be for the young and handsome knight to be thrown to the lion for the sake of his love; but if he were torn to pieces that would be far from beautiful. Such things did not happen in songs, where love triumphed and the bodies of beautiful knights could not become a gory mess. That would not do. Some magic powers were given to them and they overcame the lion and returned to their true love to live happily ever after.

She knew that the Queen Mother was determined on revenge, and would have William de Albini arrested and thrown into the lion's den.

The ballad will be spoilt, said Eleanor with a grimace.

Adventurous, mischievous, liking nothing so much as to meddle in the lives of others, she sent a message to William de Albini bidding him leave for England immediately, for if he did not he would surely die.

William was no fool; he was well aware of the nature of women such as the Dowager Queen. He had seen that blazing hatred in those passionate eyes and he knew that the overwhelming desire for sexual satisfaction would be satisfied in some strange way by his destruction.

He took the advice and left the Court of France without delay.

When Eleanor knew that he was gone she wrote a ballad. A knight loved a lady in England and came to the French Court where he excelled at a tournament. A lady of high rank saw him, and desired him. She offered him honours and riches if he would be her lover. The knight was faithful to his betrothed and in an excess of fury the lady of high rank thrust him into a cave in which was a fierce lion. But virtue triumphed over evil for the knight found himself possessed of supernatural powers and when the lion flew at him he thrust his hand into its mouth and snatched out its heart so that it died immediately.

Its heart, thought Eleanor. Nay, he could not do that. It would not be in the right place. How could he reach its heart?

He tore out the lion's tongue. That would be more plausible. And so the beast died and the knight triumphed and went back to his true love.

Eleanor sang the song. Many had seen the Queen Dowager's preference for the handsome knight, and the knight had disappeared, and the story became a legend and in due course was believed.

From the incident the Queen Mother learned that she would have to be very wary of her daughter-in-law who was preparing to begin on adventures of her own. As for William de Albini, he could only thank fortune for a lucky escape.

When he returned to England he told Adelicia that he thought they should marry without delay. She was agreeable to this. The King had no objection. He was busy with problems of his own. As for the Queen, she had always been fond of Adelicia and could only delight in her happiness.

They settled at Arundel and William assumed the title of Earl of Arundel. The couple were very happy and very soon Adelicia, who had been barren during her marriage to Henry I, became pregnant. In due course she gave birth to a son, called William after his father.

She had never been so happy in the whole of her life.

Matilda's Triumph

It was almost four years since her father had died, the Empress Matilda was thinking, and still England was not hers. She had been overtaken by the most extraordinary ill luck. She had not been with her father when he died; she had been pregnant; she had suffered in childbed; she had an ineffectual husband; she had not even been able to take and hold Normandy, let alone claim England.

But this state of affairs could not be allowed to continue.

Eagerly she awaited news from England; she was constantly despatching messengers. Two good friends she had: one was her uncle the King of Scotland who had played his part in harrying the King; the other was her half-brother, Robert of Gloucester, who had at first feigned to go over to Stephen's side and had ever since kept her informed of what was happening.

She was waiting for him to tell her when the time would be ripe for her to take ship to England and claim her inheritance.

Robert had written to her that the time had almost come. The English were beginning to be very disillusioned with Stephen. They found that although he had been brought up at his uncle's Court he did not resemble Henry in the least. He was weak; this was becoming more and more apparent. Stephen was liked as a man, for he was kindly and amiable, and none could call him a coward, but he was no leader of men; he was too friendly when he should be aloof; he was soft when he should be stern. The verdict was that while men, and women in particular, would always like Stephen, they could not respect him.

Robert wrote: "He has now reached the height of his unpopularity because he has brought in, with the aid of his wife, a host of Flemish mercenaries. These men are there to fight with him if the need should arise and this is a constant possibility. At the head of these men is the adventurer William of Ypres who has great influence with Stephen. He and his band of men are feared throughout the country; they ravage and pillage the land in the name of the King. They have done a great deal to turn the people against Stephen. As soon as you are ready you should leave for England."

This news threw Matilda into a fever of impatience. So Stephen's wife was proving to be not the lily-livered creature she had imagined. Stephen was relying on her more and more. This knowledge increased Matilda's desire to be there, to see Stephen for herself, to take personal revenge.

Even so it was not until the September that she was ready to sail.

Robert met her with one hundred and forty knights.

She demanded: "Where is the army I shall need?"

Robert replied that they would have to muster the army as they marched through the country. Her tardy arrival was unfortunate, for the country position had recently changed and was now in a comparatively peaceful state. Stephen had subdued the rebels and had enriched himself by taking several of their castles. The moment was not exactly appropriate and he suggested that they go to Arundel and there seek refuge with her stepmother and her husband, William de Albini.

As there was nothing else to be done Matilda agreed to do this.

Adelicia was astonished when she was told by one of the men-at-arms that a party was seen to be approaching. She went with William to the topmost tower to see for herself. She did not recognize the riders but in view of the uncertain state of the country was considerably alarmed.

William was in the courtyard when they arrived.

"The Earl of Gloucester!" he cried. "And..."

He stared in dismay at the arrogant woman riding beside the Earl.

"It is Matilda, the true Queen of England," said Robert.

William knelt and Matilda nodded curtly.

"Where is my stepmother?" she asked. "Ah, I see her." Adelicia had come into the courtyard. She too stared in dismay and astonishment.

"I am weary," said Matilda. "I have travelled far. I need food and a bed."

Adelicia replied: "Welcome. I beg of you come into the castle."

Matilda allowed herself to be helped from her horse. Adelicia embraced her, thinking: What means this? What have we done? Has she come to fight for the crown?

And she and William had only that day been congratulating themselves that they had satisfactorily removed themselves from court intrigue and conflict.

"The best room must be prepared for you," said Adelicia. "Orders shall be given. You must be refreshed."

The knights encamped about the castle and an apartment was prepared for Matilda and another for Robert while refreshment was brought.

Matilda explained then to her hosts what her intentions were.

"Stephen usurped my throne," she declared. "I have come to regain it."

"He has held it for nearly four years," Adelicia reminded her.

"I intend that he shall not hold it for another four weeks."

"You will fight, my lady?" asked William, thinking of the hundred and forty knights against Stephen's army and the Flemish adventurers.

"I shall gather an army together and take the crown that it may be set on the head to which it belongs."

Dear God, prayed Adelicia, let her not stay here. Let her go away so that we are not involved in this.

"You will march through the country," she asked. "That is your intention?"

"I have to get my army together. Rest assured I shall do that with ease. Stephen must give up the crown, and that will be the end of King Stephen...and his Queen. Queen Matilda! How dare she take my name. There is only one Matilda who shall rule this land. I am that Matilda."

"If he hears you are here...." began Adelicia.

Matilda laughed. "He will hear soon enough. And he will come here. I shall know how to deal with Stephen."

"If he comes with his armies...." began William.

"Let him come. I have no fear of his armies."

Nay, thought William, but we have, and we are being forced to side with you against the King.

215

Matilda went on: "I should like to see him here. I look forward with pleasure to seeing Stephen again."

Robert said that it would be necessary for him to raise an army to add to his knights. He believed he could do this for there were many people who were weary of Stephen's rule and many more who believed that Matilda was the rightful Queen. He proposed to leave Arundel with the men he-had with him and add to them; when he had an army to fight with him on behalf of Matilda, she could place herself at the head of her troop. In the meantime it would be advisable for her to stay under the roof of her stepmother.

The peace of Arundel was shattered. Matilda was a demanding guest. She made it clear to everyone from the highest to the lowest that she expected immediate obedience. No one's wishes were of any consequence if they did not coincide with her own.

Robert of Gloucester had gone to Bristol and hourly she expected to hear that the people of England had rallied to her cause and were ready to help her oust the usurper from the throne and place herself there instead.

She enjoyed the company of Adelicia towards whom she showed a somewhat contemptuous affection. Adelicia would sit with her tapestry affecting a quiet she did not feel, while Matilda paced up and down and talked of what she would do when she was on the throne of England.

"I trust," said Adelicia on one occasion, "that this will be achieved without bloodshed."

"I shall not hesitate to shed the blood of those traitors who oppose me."

Adelicia shivered. "These wars are tragic. Particularly when men of one country are fighting each other."

"I fear my cousin Stephen's soul is burdened with guilt. The best thing he could do would be to go on a pilgrimage." She smiled, contemplating the picture. "I might suggest that to him when he stands crownless and in chains before me."

The vindictive note which crept into her voice when she mentioned Stephen horrified Adelicia.

"I trust these matters will be settled amicably."

"You are too trusting, stepmother," retorted Matilda. "It is strange is it not that I am once more under your roof? Do you remember when my father gave me into your keeping. Dear stepmother, 'twould have been better if he had given

216

you into mine. But now that I am returned to be Queen of this realm I shall not forget our friendship."

Adelicia did not reply. She wondered whether Matilda would take the crown as easily as she planned to.

"Yes," went on Matilda, "my father put me into your care and do you remember that Christmas when I was kept to your apartments? The King was afraid to let me mingle with the Court for fear of what I should betray."

"I heard it mentioned."

"That my first husband was alive, that he was mad, that he had wandered from his bed! And that, Adelicia, was exactly what he did. He rose from our bed and walked out into the night in nothing but a pilgrim's robe and carrying a staff. He was mad, Adelicia. What they do to us! Does it not rouse your fury? We are married at an early age without our consent. I was twelve years old when I was married to the Emperor. Imagine it, Adelicia. How old were you when you were given to my father?"

"I was eighteen years old."

"You were fortunate. Although my father must have been a demanding husband. He was an old man when he married you, as my Emperor Henry was when he married me. That is not such a bad thing, providing these aged husbands die before we are too old and we can choose for ourselves as you have, Adelicia."

"I am singularly blessed. I have the best husband in the world."

"A consolation after how many years was it with my father?"

"Fourteen years."

"A long time and these were the days of your youth but I will tell you this, Adelicia, when I first came here I would have said you had upon you the bloom of a young bride."

"Mine is a happy marriage."

Matilda clenched her fist. "Would I had been as fortunate. Was it not enough that I had married that senile old man. Then they had to give me to an arrogant young one."

"You have three fine sons."

"Yes, I have three fine sons. They would please me more if I could say they had a father whom I could admire."

"They are your consolation."

"Oh, Adelicia, you see good everywhere. Was it not always so. You are the good wife and mother. All that a man could

217

ask of a woman, for do they not want to see us meek and complying, ever ready to bend our will to theirs?"

"I have my own views on many subjects."

"Ah, but you never force them on others. It amuses me that you have twice sheltered me because you and I are as different as two women could be. Were you in my place you would bow your head and say Stephen is King. It is better for a man to wear the crown. Come, would you not?"

"It is difficult for me to imagine myself in your place."

"And for me to imagine myself in yours. You have a handsome husband and I hear that he braved a lion's den for you. He is a fine strong fellow. And you are his meek and adoring wife. Let me tell you this: I would never allow any man to rule me. I will be supreme."

"Perhaps that is why fate made you an Empress."

"Oh, as an Empress I had to be careful. A foreigner in a foreign land. I was merely the wife of an Emperor—little more than a child. It is different now. I am the Queen of England in my own right and no one is going to take that right from me."

"Stephen will contest your claim. You know that."

"Stephen!" she cried and her eyes flashed with excitement. "Do you think I fear Stephen? I knew him well before you came to England, Adelicia. Then he was my good cousin. My brother was alive—poor William, the heir to the throne. But William died and I was a woman and far away in Germany, so the idea grew in Stephen's mind that he would be King. I often think that they should have married me to Stephen."

"If they had, there would not be this conflict."

"There would always be conflict. Had we married though, it would have been a domestic one instead of a national one."

She was smiling to herself, imagining life with Stephen.

She is obsessed by her own importance, thought Adelicia; but perhaps not entirely so for Stephen plays an unexpected part in her dreams.

The Queen was disturbed. There was no news which could have affected her so deeply.

In the quiet of their bedchamber she watched the King closely. She knew that he was more strongly affected than he wished her to know.

"So...the Empress has landed in England," she said, for she must speak of this matter which affected them so deeply in many ways.

218

"It had to happen sooner or later."

The Queen tried to speak calmly. "It is surprising that she should have delayed so long."

"She dared not come before."

"Robert of Gloucester is her strongest partisan. That disturbs me."

Stephen said: "It is to be expected. He is her half-brother."

"But he swore allegiance to you."

"I believe he did it that he might serve her the better."

The Queen's calm deserted her. "He will grow tired of her arrogance. Her temper is so harsh. She has no gratitude for those who serve her. That is not the way to win adherents."

He was silent. He could not explain to her that although he agreed with her he could understand only too well the power of Matilda. He thought of her passionate rages and he wondered why he found them more exhilarating than his wife's gentle affection. Was Matilda's scornful passion irresistible? He did not know. She had come here to take his crown. They were enemies. Her coming would plunge the country into civil war and yet he felt an exhilaration which he had not experienced since he had last seen her.

"And she has gone to the Queen Dowager," went on the Queen. "How dared she do that! Adelicia has been placed in a dangerous position because of this."

"Adelicia knows that I will understand it was no wish of hers. And what else could she do but receive the Empress when she comes to her as a guest?"

"She could send a message to you and ask your will."

"She knows full well that I will be aware of her arrival and where she is."

"Stephen, you are too lenient with everybody." She shook her head in tender exasperation. "You see too clearly two sides of every question."

"But, my love, there *are* two sides to every question."

"It is not always politic for a King to behave as though there are. For your uncle and your grandfather there was but one side. Their side."

"Then they were wrong."

"But they kept the peace and men feared them."

"Perhaps it is not in my nature to be feared. You should have had a different husband, Matilda."

"You know I would not change the one I have for any man living."

"I have one faithful subject at least," he said with a smile.

219

"Faithful," she replied seriously, "until death. But you must make the Empress your prisoner without delay."

"I must indeed," he said.

"It is to your advantage that Robert had to go to Bristol and leave Matilda unprotected in Arundel. She must never be allowed to join him there. If she did she might well raise an army against you."

"She shall be made my prisoner."

"Without delay," added the Queen.

She was aware of the excitement he was feeling, for he could not disguise the glitter of his eyes.

"Yes," he said, "I will go to Arundel."

"Nay," said the Queen. "You should not go in person. You should send another to make her your prisoner and you should be sure that she is placed in a stronghold that she cannot harm you again. Remember how your uncle treated his brother Robert of Normandy. Once he had him in captivity there was less bloodshed in Normandy. He allowed the Clito to go free and look what trouble that caused him."

"You have become a statesman, Matilda."

"In your cause. So you will send troops to Arundel? You will send one of your most trusted men to take the Empress prisoner. Then we must find a suitable stronghold. It is the only way. She has a son Henry for whom she wants the throne. But don't let us forget our own Eustace."

"As if I could ever do that."

"Nay, nor could you. So you will send to Arundel."

"I will send to Arundel," he said.

Stephen wanted to be alone to think. He could see her so clearly with her eyes flashing; and he remembered how they had softened for him, how they had blazed into triumph, how she had demanded the consummation of their love.

Of late when he had grown closer to his Queen he had thought that his relationship with the Empress was one of the past; he would tell himself that memory had magnified it; that he had never really felt that overpowering excitement and the need to satisfy his craving no matter what the consequences.

But now she was back he remembered.

How could he ask another to arrest her, to make her his prisoner? She would regard it as an insult. If the King wished to make her his prisoner, the only way he could do so was to take her himself. It would be an insult to send anyone to do that.

He would ride into Arundel. He would say: "You are my prisoner." He could imagine her laughing at him, but he would be firm; he would let her know that he, the humble cousin, not even the eldest son of the Count of Blois, was now King of England and she—even she—the proud Empress who believed she had a greater right to the crown of England than he had, must recognize him as such.

The Queen had said he should not go in person. He knew what was in his wife's mind. She did not want him to come face to face with the Empress. She was afraid of what might happen if he did. She did not underestimate the powers of her rival, and she was afraid.

Yet how could he send another to arrest Matilda?

He would face the truth. He did not want to. He wanted to go himself; he wanted to walk into that castle with that assurance which none but a King could have, and he wanted to make her understand that he was the master.

He knew that he would never in his life have enjoyed anything so much as facing Matilda and making her understand that she was in the presence of her King. She had always despised him; nor had she ever attempted to hide this. Matilda never hid her feelings; it was part of her arrogant manner of thinking that if people did not like what she did they must needs dislike it. She would change for none. And even in their most passionate moments when they—she no less than he—had confessed their need of each other, she never failed to let him know that she considered herself his superior in every way.

Proud Matilda, he thought, this is a moment I cannot resist and only you will know how much I savour it.

It was characteristic of Stephen that even while he had been telling his wife that he would send his deputy to take the Empress prisoner he was planning to perform the act himself.

He sent for his brother Henry, Bishop of Winchester, and told him that he intended to leave for Arundel where the Empress Matilda was being given shelter by Adelicia and William de Albini.

"You will take her prisoner, of course," said Henry.

"Yes, I shall take her prisoner."

"Robert of Gloucester is having some success in Bristol."

221

"I know. But when it is understood that I have the Empress, his supporters will fall away from him."

"You will certainly be in a strong position if you hold her," said Henry. "Arundel is not well fortified. You could ask Adelicia to hand her over to you. She could do naught else."

"I have had communication from her to say that the Empress came to her without invitation and that she had no alternative but to receive her. Considering the proud nature of the Empress I fancy she might refuse to be, as you put it, handed over."

"She is a woman who must be handled with care," said Henry.

"In that I agree. It is for that reason that I must myself go to Arundel."

He rode at the head of his troops. The Queen had sadly watched him go. She almost wished she did not understand him so well. There was no sign of that lethargy which since his illness had attacked him from time to time. He was like a young man again.

Indeed he felt it. It was due to the prospect of finding her there in Arundel Castle, imperiously ordering all those about her to do her will, perhaps watching from a topmost tower for his arrival and smiling to herself as she did so.

They would come face to face and it would be as it ever was. All the hate they bore each other, all the love, would overflow and mingle and the emotions each aroused in the other would be the most exciting experience either of them had ever known.

Before the castle his troops encamped. From one of the turret windows Matilda watched. She thought: I am trapped here. He can make me his prisoner if he will and nothing can save me, for this castle is not equipped for a long siege.

Adelicia was distressed. "The King is without," she said. "He is come in person to take you from here."

"And will you let me go? Will you abuse the rules of hospitality? Will you pass over your Queen—yes, your true Queen—to a traitor! Have a care, stepmother. You would not wish to see your husband robbed of his estates, named traitor."

"I beg of you," said Adelicia, "do not involve me in your quarrel. My husband wishes only to do his duty to his lawful sovereign."

"Then that is to me."

"The King would say otherwise."

"And what say you? What say you?"

"I shall obey my sovereign...."

"Your sovereign so-called King or true Queen?"

"Whosoever is my acknowledged sovereign."

"You play with words. Did my father teach his meek wife to do that?"

"I cannot disobey the King's orders."

"Stephen! Bah! He would not make war on women. He is soft and foolish. Tell him I came to you and demanded hospitality and you were obliged to give it. Tell him too, that I would have a word with him."

"You think he will come into the castle to parley with you?"

"I think he may well do that."

"He will besiege us. We shall lose our lands."

"You will lose them when I am in power if you do not obey me."

Adelicia went to her husband. He thought they must deliver the Empress's message to the King. Stephen was reasonable. He would understand that they had not sought to be the Empress's host and hostess. That dubious honour had been forced on them. The Empress asked for the courtesy of a visit from the King. She hoped, she said, he would not be *afraid* to grant this.

He had known that this would happen. He should see her because if he did not she would declare that he was afraid to. He wanted to see her. He wanted to tell her that he was the master now. She was his prisoner. She, who was so proud, so sure that she was right in everything she did, was now completely dependent on his goodwill. He could cast her into a dungeon; he could submit her to any indignity he cared to inflict. Where was her pride and her arrogance now?

His brother Henry said to him: "You will surely not see her?"

"I feel I must."

"Because she demands it? She is in no position to demand."

"She is our cousin, Henry."

"She is your bitterest enemy."

"I fear her not."

"Nor should you while she is in your power. But if she were to escape...."

"She *is* in my power. I wish to bring that home to her."

223

"So you will see her."

"Yes," said Stephen happily. "I shall see her."

Triumphantly she awaited his coming. As soon as she saw him her spirits were lifted. What a handsome man he was. The years had not impaired those looks, rather had they intensified them. All the old charm was there. Again that oft repeated sentiment came back to her. Why did they not marry me to Stephen? If they had only had the foresight to have done that the country would not now be facing the threat of civil war. There would have been no need for it.

It was typical that she should be the first to recover from her emotions and to speak before he did.

"So, it is Stephen, the would-be King."

He felt the old excitement rising. It was a hundred times more exciting than going into battle with any other foe.

"It is your sovereign lord, Stephen the King. You should be on your knees in homage and fear for your life."

"It is you who should do homage and be in fear for yours."

"Now, Matilda, you joke. You cannot forget that you are my prisoner."

"So you enter the house of another as a friend and then announce you will plunder it. Is that your interpretation of kingship, Stephen of Blois?"

"Stephen the King comes in expectation of obedience."

"You always set your expectations too high."

"Come, Matilda, let us be sensible. You are my good cousin but I am the King and you have come here to dispute my right to the crown, is that not so?"

"Your right to the crown. What is that? What right pray have you to my crown?"

"The right of possession."

"Not for long," she cried. "Oh, not for long."

"You are asking me to have you sent to a dungeon."

"Do you doubt that I should not ere long be rescued and you and I would change places? And know this, Stephen of Blois, aught that you did to me would be done a hundred times more harshly to you."

"I doubt that not...if it ever came to pass."

"You are too sure of yourself."

"Nay, you are that."

"Then perhaps we both are. Perhaps that is why we are so well matched." She was inviting friendliness now. He knew that this was the moment to beware. "So, Stephen," she went

224

on, "you are a false friend and lover. You who professed to love me would now be cruel to me."

He seized her by the shoulders and drew her towards him. She suppressed her triumph and smiled at him. "You have forgotten so soon?" she asked softly.

"You know that I shall never forget."

"Those hours we spent together," she said, "they were precious to us both. There was nothing like them for either of us...not for you with your silly Queen who dares to bear my name, nor I with the poor old Emperor and my callow boy husband. Admit it, Stephen."

"I never denied it."

"At least you were true in one thing. And now you talk to me of dungeons. You would never put me into a dungeon, Stephen. How could you sleep quiet at night if you did that to me? How can you sleep quiet at night now knowing that I am here...and we two not together?"

"Matilda..." he said.

"Yes," she answered. "Your Matilda as no other Matilda could ever be."

Their embrace was fierce—reckless on his side, calculating on hers, but nevertheless the overwhelming desire was there for them both.

He was a soft man, this Stephen, and never softer than at such moments.

As they lay together clinging to each other as though by the very force of their passion they could ward off the need to separate, she said to him: "Stephen, what matters anything but that we two are together?"

He sighed. "We shall have to part," he said. His voice broke with anger. "Has it not always been thus? When we were children we knew that we two should be together...and always we must be apart."

"Perhaps one day, Stephen...."

"How could that be?"

"You have your wife—your silly little Matilda. I have my foolish Geoffrey. Who knows...."

"Matilda has been a good wife to me," he protested.

She laughed, all tenderness departed. "She has said Yea, Stephen, Yea, Stephen, through day and night. And never Nay, Stephen. That is why you say she has been good to you. Has she given you what I have? Have you ever felt towards her as you do towards me?"

"You know well that I have not."

"Then an end to your falsehoods. You want *this* Matilda."
She smote her breast with her clenched fist. "You need her—
this one. She who has carried your seed in her womb...who
was meant for you and you for her...."

He had raised himself to stare at her. "You mean...
Matilda.... You mean...young Henry?"

She lowered her eyes and a smile curved her lips. When
she did look at him she was mocking. "You men! How you
preen yourselves when you believe you have fathered a fine
male child. Oh, it must be male. It must be a boy for there
you see yourselves reborn. My Henry is a fine boy, is he not?
Lusty, sharp...all a man could look for in a son."

"And he is mine!" cried Stephen.

"You have spoken," she said. "I have not."

"Matilda," he said and he seized her and shook her. "Tell
me truthfully. The boy...young Henry...."

She shook him off and stood up laughing at him.

"That shall be my secret...as yet," she answered. "I would
see first how you treat me. 'Twas not long ago that you were
talking of putting me into a dungeon."

"I would never allow you to be ill-treated."

"Is it necessary to tell me that? You insult me by men-
tioning it. Have I not but a moment ago surrendered myself
to you?"

"Oh Matilda, did you ever surrender to me? Was it not I
who surrendered to you?"

She seemed well pleased. Then lifting her face to him she
said: "Stephen. Let me go to Bristol."

"Your brother is there."

"Yes, let me join him there."

"Robert of Gloucester is my enemy. You ask me to let you
go to my enemy?"

She put her arms about his neck. "You will let me go,
Stephen."

"How can I?"

"You can because you must. I ask it and you will not refuse
me."

"It will be expected that I place you in the care of someone
who will guard you for me."

"Nay, that would make me a prisoner. Would you make
a prisoner of the daughter of that King who gave you everything you have? My father favoured you. He had you brought
to England. What would you have been had he not done that?
Stephen Lackland! He gave you lands...he gave you a rich

226

wife. Oh, yes, you owe your fond Matilda to him. He gave me life and I have been yours, Stephen. Think what you owe my father. Could you insult his daughter by making her a prisoner?"

"And if you go to Bristol?"

"I will return to Anjou, mayhap. My brother will escort me."

He knew she was lying. He was bemused. He thought of her yielding as she had such a short while before, whispering to him softly of her love for him which was greater than anything on earth, greater than their marriage vows, greater than the crown which hovered over them both.

She put her lips to his ear and nibbled it gently. "Then I shall go to Bristol, Stephen. You will come and see me there. We will make plans for our next meeting. It will be as happy as this one when I am in Bristol."

He sighed and she said, "Thank you, Stephen; thank you, my dear."

She tore herself away from him. She ran to the door and out of the apartment.

She was calling to her stepmother.

"Adelicia. Adelicia, where are you? The King has been gracious to me. He has given me leave to go to Bristol."

Stephen stumbled after her.

You fool! he said to himself. You are mad. You cannot let her go.

He found her with her stepmother.

Adelicia's relief was evident.

"Oh, Stephen, my lord King," she said, "it is noble of you. But then you have always been so."

"I should leave at once," said Matilda, smiling triumphantly. "Dear Adelicia, your fears were without foundation. You were so frightened, were you not? You thought you would offend the King and you see he is our very good friend."

Stephen did not speak. He was trying to still the voices in his head which were telling him what a fool he was.

Inwardly depressed, Stephen went to his brother Henry, Bishop of Winchester, and told him that he had agreed to allow Matilda to go to Bristol.

His brother stared at Stephen in amazement.

Stephen hastened to justify himself. "She is our cousin," he said. "I and you too, Henry, owe everything we have in this land to her father, our uncle King Henry I. How could I make her a prisoner?"

"She would not hesitate to put you in chains."

Stephen shook his head. He was thinking of those passionate moments when they had surrendered to each other and their emotions. How could lovers such as they had been harm each other?

"Nay," he said, "she would remember the kinship between us...even as I do."

Henry was not a man to waste words. His inner thought was: My brother is a fool. But he remained silent.

Stephen seemed relieved. "She is to go to Bristol," he said. "I have given my word."

To Bristol, thought Henry, where her half-brother of Gloucester is raising an army to drive Stephen from the throne and put Matilda there. Yes, his brother was indeed a fool.

"She has not yet gone," ventured Henry.

Stephen looked pained. "I have given my word," he reminded his brother. "I shall send her with an escort and as there is no one in my kingdom whom I trust as I trust you, that escort shall be you."

Henry bowed his head.

He was not displeased. He would relish a journey which would put him in close contact with Matilda, that he might get to know better a woman who was clever enough to outwit his brother. Not that Stephen was a wise man. Henry had become more and more disillusioned with him since he had gained the crown. Yet he had an admiration for Matilda and he felt that in the near future it might be necessary for him to make an important decision.

Matilda rode at the head of the party with Henry, Bishop of Winchester, beside her. She was clearly delighted with the outcome of her meeting with Stephen—and had good cause to be. Henry had no doubt that his brother was now regretting his rash action.

Henry was an ambitious man. He had supported Stephen not entirely out of brotherly affection; he was after all a grandson of the Conqueror and as such must be imbued with the desire to govern. As head of the Church he could have had a say in the affairs of the country, and with a weak man such as Stephen was proving himself to be there was no reason why the Church should not take precedence over the

State. Far-seeing and astute as he was, Henry could look ahead to the days when the conflict between Church and State would be as mighty as that between warring states. As a churchman he was on the side of the Church—particularly when the crown was on an unworthy head. And Stephen's conduct had led him to the conclusion that Stephen was unfit to be King of England. The people were now realizing that he was no Lion of Justice; even Rufus had been stronger. England needed men such as William the First and Henry the First. Its foundations were not yet firm enough to stand against the feeble government which a weak king would bring.

Henry had naturally supported his brother, but he was beginning to wonder whether he had given his allegiance in the wrong quarter.

Many said that Stephen usurped the throne, and this was true. The heiress was the daughter of King Henry—and it was only the fact that she was a woman that had tempted many people to accept Stephen. Had Stephen been a strong man, this would have been the best possible course, but alas, Stephen had proved by his treatment of his enemies that he was not a strong man. And never could he have shown this so clearly as when he allowed Matilda to slip out of his grasp.

For what purpose did Stephen think Matilda wished to go to Bristol? Was he unaware that Robert of Gloucester was gathering men to her banner there? Why had he done this? Because Matilda had bewitched him. She had seduced him from his duty to his country and those who had given him their allegiance. He was in love with her, and weak enough to let that affect his judgment.

Clearly such a man must sooner or later place his crown in jeopardy, and when he did so, Henry wanted to be on the winning side.

Matilda was haughty. He admired the manner in which she took for granted the fact that she had been allowed to leave Arundel. She behaved as though the crown was already safely on her head.

She did deign to talk to him as they journeyed. She asked the distance they had come and how far they had to go.

She said on one occasion: "You are surprised that your brother gave me free passage to Bristol, are you not, my lord Bishop?"

"I admit," he answered, "that the matter did take me by surprise."

"Stephen is a fool," she said.

He flinched. One did not speak thus of the King.

She laughed at him. "You should know that I have no intention of letting him keep what he has filched from me. You are startled, my lord Bishop. Have no fear that you listen to treason. What you should fear is treasonable actions in the past. All those who have helped Stephen to the crown are my enemies."

The Bishop was silent.

"I would forgive those who came to my side now that I am here," she said. "So your cause is not hopeless. I know that I was far away and it seemed politic to stand with the usurper. My half-brother made a pretence of doing that. I doubt not others did the same."

"That may well be," he said cautiously.

"And you, my lord Bishop, you are his brother, but you are my cousin. You owe much to my father. He would be displeased that you had denied the true heir to the throne because your brother asked that you should support him. Come, Bishop. It is not too late. You are a shrewd man, I know it well. Do you think Stephen will long hold the crown now that I am here?"

"He has been crowned King of England."

"By traitors. And what has he done for you, my good Bishop? Come tell me the truth. When old William of Canterbury died did you not hope for the highest office in the Church? You do not answer. Nor do you need to. We know, do we not, that you are an ambitious man. You were the natural successor to William but you did not become Archbishop of Canterbury. Do you know why?"

"The Pope refused his consent."

"Why? I will tell you. Because Stephen opposed it—urged by his silly little Queen. Yes, that woman is beginning to have quite an influence over the man you call King. For that alone he should be deposed. Together they worked against your election."

She laughed. She could see she had struck a vulnerable spot. That rankled with him. He had believed he would be elected to the See of Canterbury. But he was still merely Bishop of Winchester. Was that the just reward from Stephen for one who had helped him to the crown?

"So," she went on, "they elected Theobald."

"The Pope was in fact a good friend to me," he answered. "He made me Legate of England which could well be a position of as great power as that of the Archbishop of Canterbury."

"I doubt not that you are a man of some influence in my kingdom" she replied. "And that you are a wise man. It is for this reason that you will cease to support the usurper and rally to the banner of the true Queen."

"The King is my brother...."

"The usurper is assuredly that, but your allegiance belongs to your cousin. I do not sue for it. It is not in my nature to sue. I demand it. And, my lord Bishop, you would be wise to accede it without delay. I am not of a temper to deal lightly with those who work against me. You do not see in me such a one as your brother Stephen."

"I have learned that, Madam."

"Then when the time comes you will receive me in Winchester."

He did not speak but he had stopped his horse as she had hers and for a moment they looked steadily into each other's faces.

"I see that you will give your loyalty to me," she answered. "And I promise you that when you do this you shall regret nothing. I know full well that you have knowledge of the government of this realm. I should not take one whit of your power from you and I should leave in your hands the preferments to bishoprics and abbacies. We understand each other, I believe."

"Yes, my lady, I am sure we do."

She nodded and rode on, he beside her.

She gives herself such airs, he thought, she could indeed already be the Queen of England. Although she had yet to gain the crown she behaved more like a sovereign than Stephen ever had when the crown was actually on his head.

My brother, thought Henry uneasily. Yes, but a fool. And I believe that but for him and his wife Matilda I should be the Archbishop of Canterbury.

He admitted then what he had known in his heart he was going to do. He was going to change sides and support Matilda against his brother.

Matilda's Prisoner

The news that Stephen had freed the Empress Matilda and that she was on her way to Bristol to join Robert of Gloucester astounded Stephen's supporters. The King was mad, they said. What had that mysterious illness which had attacked him so suddenly really been? The Queen had nursed him herself and had allowed few to go near him. Could it really be that the King had been attacked by madness?

He had been overlenient with his enemies which had proved to be a weakness in him, though his genial temper was well known and he was not disliked for it; but to allow his rival to walk calmly out of the trap in which she was caught it seemed could only be the action of a madman.

Matilda was here and she was indeed the true heir to the throne. A woman, yet by all accounts an indomitable one. Moreover, Robert of Gloucester was supporting her and he was one of the ablest generals in the country. Many had believed that, as the King's son, he should have had the throne. But he was a bastard—favourite son of the King though he had been—and he made it quite clear that he had no intention of taking the throne from the one whom he considered to be the true heiress of England—his half-sister Matilda, King Henry's only legitimate child.

Thus by the time Matilda joined Robert in Bristol many of those knights and barons who were anxious to be on the winning side had thought it expedient to rally to her banner.

After leaving Arundel, Stephen had returned to Westminster and there his Queen was waiting for him. She tried to hide her melancholy foreboding; she had been stunned with horror and grief when she heard that Stephen had allowed Matilda to escape. At first she could not believe that this was possible, but when the implication of what this meant dawned on her she understood perfectly. Stephen had been trapped by the enchantress. What power had this woman? Matilda the Queen knew that her rival was a handsome woman but her character was far from attractive. Haughty, selfish, arrogant she undoubtedly was. And yet her brother Robert, who was a man all must respect, was her faithful adherent, and Stephen—her own husband—was so besotted by her that he put his crown in jeopardy by letting her go free.

Her mind went back to the early days before her marriage when she had been brought from the Abbey of Bermondsey to the Court to learn that she was to marry handsome, gentle Stephen and how happy she had been and thought herself the most fortunate of princesses because such a husband had been selected for her. That other Matilda had been forced to leave her home and go to an old man while she was given handsome Stephen. Had she been so lucky?

Yes, because she loved him. His weakness made her more determined to protect him; and how strange that she, Matilda of Boulogne, as they called her, who had been so quiet and unassuming, now knew herself to be so much stronger than Stephen.

She greeted him affectionately when he came. He was shame-faced, knowing that she would have heard by now that the Empress was on her way to Bristol. Some might have reproached him for being a fool and for being unfaithful to his wife—for she knew he had been—but she did not. It was in his nature to be unfaithful to his wife. There had been other women before the Empress had come back. They had been different. Dear, charming, easy-going Stephen, who could not easily say No, even when his crown was in danger.

When they had dined and were alone in their chamber she said to him: "There is little time to be lost, Stephen."

He nodded.

"I hear that many are rallying to the Empress's banner."

He was silent.

"Depend upon it," she said, "there will be a mighty battle."

"I have many faithful followers," he answered.

She was silent, wondering how many of those had deserted to the enemy since he had shown himself to have acted in a manner unaccountable to those who did not know of the passionate involvement of the King with the Empress.

"Stephen," she said, "how can you know who is faithful?"

He turned to her then and took her face in his hands. "There is but one I know of," he replied.

"On that one," she answered, "you can always depend no matter what should befall."

He laid his head against her breast then and she comforted him as though he were a child. He was ashamed of his subservience to the Empress; he realized fully how foolishly he had acted, for she cared only for herself, the gratification of her senses and her ambitions. She had no love to offer him, only a searing passion which they both found irresistible. It was this Matilda, his wife, who stood with him and would support him no matter what happened. He was a fool. This was where his loyalty lay, with this woman whose cause was his, who loved him selflessly. And he had betrayed her and risked his crown for the sake of a sensational encounter with his beloved enemy, the Empress. No doubt she was laughing at him now, telling Robert of Gloucester of her victory, and with what ease she had tricked her cousin the King into letting her escape.

"Oh, my dearest Matilda," he said, "my Queen, don't leave me. Stay with me."

"I will always serve your cause," she told him, "but it may well be that I cannot always stay with you."

He was alarmed. He raised himself to look at her and a fierce delight filled her heart because the prospect of losing her terrified him. He loved her; she was the steady rock on which he built his life. He could not do without her, and yet he could not be faithful to her.

"Stephen," she said, "there may be little time left to us. A mighty battle is about to break out. There will be civil war in this country. Let us face the truth. Robert of Gloucester is amassing an army. When the Empress meets him she will find men rallying to her banner. They will march on...who knows where? Winchester? London perhaps? And you will have to be ready to meet them."

"Why did they make me King," cried Stephen angrily, "if they did not want me?"

"They wanted you, Stephen, when they put the crown on your head. Men's minds change."

She thought sadly: They would never have changed had you, my dearest husband, acted as your uncle Henry would have done, as your grandfather the great Conqueror would have done, and you would not now be in this miserable dilemma.

But she said nothing. Reproaches would help not at all. It was not brooding on the past which was necessary but planning for the future.

"The people are fickle," cried Stephen.

She put her arms about him. "When they see that you are strong, Stephen, they will support you."

"Then I will show them," he said.

And she thought sadly: You will not do that by giving way to the Empress, by allowing your enemies to escape.

But she said: "You are a brave fighter, Stephen. All know that. None who have seen you in battle can doubt your courage."

"I have never doubted it," he told her. "I will fight to the death, if need be, for my crown."

She was silent and he turned suddenly to her and took her by the shoulders. "They blame me, Matilda, for letting the Empress go."

She could not look at him.

"You blame me, Matilda."

She shook her head.

"She is my cousin, Matilda. We were children together . . . I could not make her my prisoner. What was I expected to do? To put her in some dungeon?"

"Nay," she said, "you should not have done that."

"I remembered when we had played together as children."

She raised her eyes to his and tried to read what those memories were.

"My cousin," he went on. "It is not good to make war on one's own kith and kin, Matilda."

Matilda replied: "It may be necessary if they make war on you."

He nodded and his eyes as they met hers were crestfallen. She felt protective, as she might have felt towards their little boys, Eustace who was now four years old, and baby William.

"Stephen," she said, "let us not think of what is past but plan for the future which indeed we must. The Empress with the help of her brother Robert—and let us not under-estimate him—is raising her standard at Bristol. It is certain that soon they will be marching against you. You must be prepared."

"I will vanquish them," he said, "never fear. And then, my Queen, you and I will live in harmony and peace for the rest of our lives. I want to show you how I love you, how I depend on you, what you mean to me. . . ."

236

She smiled. They were so clearly the protestations of a husband with a need to satisfy his conscience.

"You are fond of me, I know, dear husband," she said. "And we have our children to consider. The Empress has a son, young Henry, and the fact that this boy exists will make her fight the harder for the throne. She will be fighting not only for herself but for her son."

"The Empress would fight as fiercely for herself as for any other."

He was bitter, yet even when he spoke of her in anger there was a lilt in his voice which none other could put there.

"We have a son too, Stephen. Our Eustace. William, too. We shall be fighting not only for ourselves but for our children. It is a matter of who shall inherit the throne...your son or the son of the Empress."

He lowered his eyes. She must not read that particular secret. She knew as so many did that there was a passionate attachment between himself and the Empress. She would guess at what had passed between them when she had so successfully prevailed on him to release her and so place his crown in jeopardy. But what she must never know was that Henry of Anjou, that bright and lusty boy, who had been the pride of his grandfather's heart, could well be his.

My two sons then, thought Stephen. Henry...Eustace. Was Henry his son? Who could say? Perhaps even the Empress was not sure.

He was filled with a sudden hatred towards the Empress. He thought of her always as the Empress because his Queen was Matilda. Her son should not inherit the crown. That must be Eustace.

"Eustace shall have the crown," cried Stephen. "I will stake my life on it."

He meant it. He had a resolution. He would never again be tempted by the Empress. He knew who were his true friends. The love his gentle wife had for him was worth everything; his passion for that other Matilda was but a destructive force and it always had been.

"We must think ahead, Stephen," the Queen was saying. "There is Normandy to be considered. We should consider placating the King of France. If he were our ally, Normandy would be safe and you could give all your attention to England."

"You should have been a statesman, Matilda."

"We learn what we have to. I shall be as your first min-

237

ister, Stephen, for whom else can you trust and our position is desperate. I have thought long of this. We have a son, a fine boy who will one day be King of England. If the King of France would consider a betrothal between his young daughter and our son that would be the best alliance we could hope for. Such an alliance would strike fear into your enemies."

"You are right. But how can I leave England now to parley with the King of France?"

"You can send an ambassador."

"Who?"

"The only one who, you can be sure, has your cause at heart. Your wife."

"*You,* Matilda?"

"None other. I will go to France taking Eustace with me. I will persuade the King of the good this alliance will bring us both."

He stared at her.

"Why, my beloved Queen has indeed become a statesman," he said.

Those were bitter months which followed. Stephen had never wanted to fight. He was no coward; he was ready enough to face death if the need should arise, but he had always liked to be on good terms with all men; and it grieved him that there should be some who hated him and wanted to take the crown from him.

If it were not for his cousin Matilda, they would have been content with his rule. He was not like his uncle and grandfather. They had been harsh men. They did not care whether their subjects loved them; they only cared that they obeyed them.

There were so many happier ways of passing one's time than fighting.

And Matilda his Queen was in France where she was proving herself to be a worthy ambassador. She had been received with honours at the Court of France and indeed it was to be expected that she would be, for she had taken with her a large dowry which she would pay to the King of France for his daughter. This was custom in reverse since it was the bride who usually brought the dowry to her husband; but the situation was desperate. Matilda knew that the fact that Stephen and the King of France had become allies would be worth many a soldier and his arms to her husband's cause.

Robert of Gloucester and the Empress Matilda would receive the news with dismay; and the Queen was determined that they should receive such news.

The King of France believed that Stephen would defeat his cousin because he could not conceive that any country would accept a woman as its ruler. The bargain was made. Eustace, son and heir of King Stephen, had become the son-in-law of the King of France through his marriage with Constance, the French King's daughter.

Stephen was heartened by the news. The Empress and her followers were dismayed by it.

In his palace Stephen thanked God for his clever and faithful wife.

It seemed impossible that it was but six years ago that the stern Lion of Justice had reigned over England. Then it had been possible for travellers to walk the roads after dark unharmed. Their purses were safe enough, for any who dared rob them and be discovered in the deed had suffered the terrible penalty of mutilation. The law of the Conqueror had prevailed and with it came justice. A purse of gold was not worth the loss of a man's ears, his nose or his eyes; he did not want to have his feet cut off for the sake of the contents of some traveller's pocket.

The Conqueror had declared he would restore law and order to the land by severe penalties for those who defied those laws, and so terrible were these penalties that few incurred them.

Henry had followed the rule of his father. But now Stephen was on the throne.

He had shown by the treatment he meted out to his enemies that he was no Conqueror. There was no need to fear Stephen it was said. A man who allowed those who had taken up arms against him to escape and come back to plot against him once more could not very well inflict a harsh punishment on a mere thief.

The customs had changed. Castles were springing up all over the land. Every man who had the means to do so built himself a castle and this he defended against all comers. Those who had enough money to build themselves strongholds did so and from these fortresses they ravaged the land about them. They would take any man they found on the roads and bring him to the castle that he might be forced to

239

work there. Those who had goods and lands were captured and tortured until they gave them up.

New methods of torture were invented; and not only to extort but to give a fearful sadistic pleasure. The roads had become unsafe. Unwary travellers were captured and taken to the castle to be made sport with; and if a man had a quarrel with another he might well be taken from his home one night and within the cruel walls of some fortress meet his lingering painful end.

No one was safe; the most terrifying instruments of torture were devised such as the *sachentege* which consisted of an iron collar attached to a beam of wood. This collar was fitted with hideous spikes. It fitted round a man's neck so that he could not move without bearing its weight. There was the *crucet house*, a short narrow shallow chest in which a man would be forced; sharp stones would be crammed in on top of him and great weights put upon the chest so that the man's limbs were crushed.

Men were hung up by their feet and fires were lighted beneath them; knotted rope was twisted about their heads and pulled until it entered their brains. They were thrown into dungeons full of toads, rats and snakes. Nothing was too fearful for these sadists to do to their victims.

The orderly land of which William and Henry had been so proud was now the home of anarchy.

The Queen had sent mercenaries from Boulogne to fight for the King and what had at first seemed a blessing proved the reverse for these men roamed the country pillaging the land.

Civil war, the greatest evil which could befall a country, had broken out.

The good old days of the late King Henry were over.

More and more of the knights and barons were turning from Stephen. He had proved himself to be a weak king, and because of his weakness law and order had been lost and its place taken by anarchy. But Stephen was determined to fight for his crown or die in the attempt. Often he thought of his Queen Matilda who had stood by him so staunchly and even at this time had arranged the match for their son which had done so much good. He roamed the country and laid siege to those castles the owners of which had gone over to the enemy. At least he proved himself to be a valiant general.

He did achieve certain successes and it seemed that the war was going in his favour; and it was not until Stephen and his army came to Lincoln on Candlemas Day of the year 1141 that the decisive battle was fought.

Rannulf, Earl of Chester, hearing that Stephen was marching on to Lincoln and realizing that his intention was to lay siege to the town and castle, decided that he must immediately get help, so he left the castle in the charge of his young wife and brother.

Rannulf knew that Robert of Gloucester would come immediately to his aid because his wife, whom he had newly married, was Robert's youngest and much loved daughter.

The situation was desperate, for Stephen, although his popularity had waned considerably during the last months, was still the King and possessed of a well trained army; and although his opponents had stood out against him with some success, their efforts so far had been confined to minor forays. By the time Rannulf was able to reach Gloucester where Earl Robert was with the Empress Matilda, Stephen was already encamped on the outskirts of Lincoln.

Both Robert and Rannulf were anxious as to the fate of the young woman who was daughter of one and wife of the other. They gloomily discussed what an effect the siege could have on the inmates of the castle, and they were thinking of her. They pictured her growing emaciated, her beautiful golden hair growing lustreless—worse still, she might contract some fearful disease which many did in such circumstances, or even die.

Matilda listened to Rannulf's account of Stephen's army and cried: "We must defeat him here. This is our chance. I want him brought to me in chains. Then he will see what it means to take the crown from me."

Robert replied: "You will not be so lenient with him, my lady, as he was with you."

"I am not a fool, brother," she answered shortly.

"We must somehow raise an army," said Robert. "If we can trap him in Lincoln we have a fair chance. What have we now—a handful of desperate men."

"They will fight well," said Rannulf. "They have everything to gain and nothing left to lose."

"Except their lives," replied Robert grimly. "Before we march on Lincoln we must raise an army."

Rannulf looked alarmed, and Robert knew what he was thinking. How long would that be? Would the castle hold out? And what of his bride who was a prisoner there in the castle?

Robert understood his son-in-law's fears and indeed shared them. This would not only prove to be a vital battle in the campaign for the Empress, it must be won—and speedily—for the sake of his beloved daughter.

The Empress watched the two men leave at the head of their followers. Her eyes glittered. She was glad that girl was a prisoner in the castle of Lincoln. Those two men would fight for her more fiercely and determinedly than they would for a cause.

She smiled Briefly. Something told her that victory was near. What a triumph that would be when Stephen was her prisoner.

She felt a sharp pang of fear. They must not kill him. That she could not bear. A world without Stephen would be robbed of its savour. Even a crown could not compensate for that. She wanted to hold him her prisoner, to inflict indignity upon him; she wanted to show him what a fool he had been to think he could triumph over her. Never, never—even during their passionate interludes—had she submitted to him. Always he must be the suppliant. He had made her so happy when he had allowed her to escape. Not because she was free to go to Bristol but because he had shown her and the world what a fool he was. Never had he been so completely hers as that moment when she rode out of Arundel and rarely had she been so happy.

And now this fight after which he should fall into her hands. It must be so. So she was thankful that those two men who had left grim-lipped to raise an army had that added incentive of a loved one in danger.

She waited impatiently for news. Each day she would be at the turret watching for that messenger who would bring it to her. Stephen, her prisoner.

Robert of Gloucester with his son-in-law at his side had greater good fortune than he dared hope for. The state of the country had sickened so many people. It had been brought home to them that Stephen was not as his uncle had been. They had complained about the harsh laws of Stephen's predecessor; now they saw how their very harshness had preserved the peace. England needed a strong king and it was clear that she had a weak one in Stephen.

The alternative was a woman but she was guided by Robert of Gloucester who was a man of courage and integrity. He would be beside the Empress when she became Queen; and even the King's brother, Henry of Winchester, had shown that he was ready to desert Stephen for Matilda and Robert.

Men fell in readily behind Robert and by the time he approached Lincoln he had amassed a considerable army.

It was the end of January and the rainfall had been heavier even than usual. This was the marshy district and when they reached the River Witham it had become so swollen that they could not cross.

Stephen meanwhile had forced his way into the town and was encamped about the Cathedral and the siege of the castle had begun.

On the second of February, Candlemas Day, Stephen, knowing that the battle must soon begin, went to the Cathedral to hear mass. Here there occurred one of those incidents which men such as the Conqueror could turn to their advantage. Not so Stephen. During Mass the candle which he was holding broke suddenly in his hand. There was a deep silence as Stephen stood looking at the stump he held in his hand while the lighted portion rolled on the floor.

All those watching said: "This is God's sign. The King's light will go out as surely as that of the broken candle."

Stephen took another candle and attempted to shrug the matter aside, but those watching were sure it was a sign.

Meanwhile Robert's army was determined to attack and, wading their way over the marshy land, they forded the swollen river.

Chilled to the skin the soldiers stood in formation while Robert of Gloucester addressed them. He was a man of great eloquence and was able to communicate his fervour and determination to them all. He hinted at what they could gain and made it clear to them that their lives would assuredly be worth very little if they lost.

So those men, who had joined the banner of Matilda, the Empress, in spite of their long march and their exposure to the damps of the marsh and river, stood determined to fight.

Stephen heard that Robert was addressing his men and had by so doing brought out great heart in them. He sent for one of his followers, Baldwin Fitz-Gilbert, a man with a voice of thunder, and commanded to him to cheer the army and abuse the enemy.

This Baldwin Fitz-Gilbert did, and reminded the soldiers that Robert of Gloucester was a bastard and that Kings' bastards were dangerous men. "Will you fight under Robert the Base-born General?" he yelled at the opposing armies. The answer came back echoing over the marshes: "We will."

Stephen was in a position of advantage for he was on a slight incline whereas his enemies were on the flat ground. There was only one aspect of his position which might be dangerous and that was that if the enemy drove him back he could become penned up within the city walls.

He considered the position. He was now coming face to face with his greatest enemy, for Robert of Gloucester was undoubtedly that. If Robert had not given his support to his sister she could not have established herself as firmly as she had. She owed a great deal to him.

Yet Stephen could not forget that this man was his own cousin, Matilda's half-brother and the beloved son of the late Henry I.

How close they all were! Kinsman fighting kinsman. When Stephen thought of that he had little heart for the fight. He wished that they could live in peace. And so they could if he would hand over the crown to Matilda.

Oh, God, he thought, what an evil fate it was that gave me the wrong Matilda for a wife.

Again he let himself think of what the future would have been if they had married him to the Empress. Stormy, without doubt, stimulating, exciting in the extreme. Every moment lived to the full. And she would never have lost an opportunity of letting him know that she had the greater right to the crown.

He pulled himself up. This was no time for dreaming impossible dreams. She was his enemy. His life and future were at stake and that of his good faithful wife and his beloved son.

So he would go out and meet Robert of Gloucester in combat.

He gave orders. They would move forward. Yes, he knew he had the advantageous position; but he did not want Robert of Gloucester to be able to say when the fight was over that fortune had favoured Stephen.

He would throw away that advantage. The armies would descend to the plains. They would fight fairly.

His men marvelled at him. The King must indeed be suffering from madness. One could not be so magnanimous in war. He had thrown away the greatest opportunity he had when the Empress Matilda was in his hands. Now they were fighting to regain what he had thrown away. And because he had the advantage he was giving that away too.

What could an army think of such a man? Had not the candle broken in his hands? Fate would not go on giving him advantages if he showed his lack of appreciation of them by throwing them away.

The battle was brief. Robert had been right when he said so many of those who followed him had little more to lose than their life; they fought for those lives with all the skill and fury of which they were capable.

Stephen's followers had already begun to doubt him; they had lost their belief in his ability to rule before the battle started. It seemed impossible that those men, cold and wet from their journey through the marshes, should have fought with such spirit, but they did.

Moreover they were led by one of the most skilful generals of the day, Robert of Gloucester, and for him there were two great reasons why he was determined to win the battle of Lincoln. He believed his cause to be just; he had sworn to Henry I that he would support the accession of his daughter Matilda. Stephen had sworn that too, and broken his word. The other reason was that Robert's daughter was in the castle of Lincoln.

Spurred on by these reasons Robert was the greater general on that day.

At the first indication that the battle was going against Stephen one by one those who had supported him for what they hoped to gain began to slip away.

Stephen realized what was happening. He was losing the battle. He could hear all about him the sudden cries of men as they fell from their horses or were run through by the enemy's lances. The tumult was great and he knew the shouts of triumph came from the enemy.

Matilda, he thought, you are winning. You said you would always subdue me. But not if I can help it....

Then he thought of that other Matilda. She would not hear of the battle for some time because she was in France. He was filled with remorse. He must fight for her and their son Eustace. He must never surrender.

About him his supporters were dwindling. Could they really be so false? Why should men desert him for Matilda? Had he not always been kindly, affable? He never wanted trouble and had tried hard to please all men. Matilda was arrogant; she would be cruel. Why should they support her against him? Because her cause was just, because she was the King's daughter and Stephen merely his nephew. Because they had sworn fealty to Matilda...as he had.

Now he could see the enemy clearly. He was surrounded. "I will never give in," he cried. "Never, never, never."

There were only men on foot now to fight with him. Closer and closer came the enemy. He slashed right and left with his sword. He saw blood everywhere as he struck down man after man.

He was fighting with all the strength and skill he possessed. All those who beheld him were astonished at his courage and skill.

One after another men fell before him but he was not so blind that he could not see the terrible toll the enemy was taking of his supporters. They were thick on the ground now. Slaughter all about him and only he erect on his horse fighting on with a courage born of desperation.

He saw a man's face close to his. Murder was in his eyes. Stephen ran him through. But his sword had broken.

His horse was down. This was the end. It must be. The enemy were everywhere and there were so few of his supporters now to surround him and fight with him.

Someone had thrust a battle axe into his hands. He grunted his thanks and began striking to the right and left of him.

He was fighting like a madman. But it was useless.

Rannulf the Earl of Chester was bearing down upon him. No doubt seeking the honour of capturing or killing the King. He struck at him with the axe. Rannulf avoided the blow but was thrown to his knees.

"Die, traitor," cried Stephen, but before he could deliver the fatal blow a stone struck him and he himself fell to the ground.

His enemies were upon him.

Someone had snatched off his helmet.

"The King!" The cry went on. "We have the King."

And so was Stephen brought a captive to the Castle of Gloucester where the Empress Matilda waited to hear news of the battle.

She saw the messenger approaching and went down to the courtyard to wait for him. He leaped from his foaming horse and threw himself at her feet.

"My lady, the battle is over. The King has fallen. He is your captive."

She stood erect, smiling. Stephen a captive! On the way to Gloucester!

She took the rider into the castle and herself offered him the goblet which would refresh him.

"Tell me what you know."

The messenger gasped out that the battle had been fought at Lincoln and that the King's forces had deserted him when they saw the battle going against them.

"Ere long," she said, "my brother will be here and with him will come the King. King no longer though, merely Stephen of Blois, my prisoner."

She saw them riding towards the castle. Robert was at the head of the cavalcade and among that band of riders was Stephen the defeated King.

Into the courtyard they came. Robert her good and faithful brother and Stephen....

She wanted to laugh aloud. How different he was! No longer the proud King.

She waited for her brother to come to her and when he did she embraced him warmly.

"Robert, good brother, you have done well this day."

"I have brought the traitor to you."

"He is below," she said, a smile playing about her lips.

"Ay, he is below."

"I am glad you brought him alive." Her expression was fierce suddenly. She thought: I would never have forgiven you if you had brought him to me dead.

"He fought like a lion," said Robert. "He amazed all who beheld him. Never did I see a man fight as Stephen fought this day at Lincoln."

"It availed him little," she cried scornfully.

"Nay, but it was none the less brave for that. It was as though a devil possessed him. There he stood in the midst of his followers and one by one they fell. Yet he remained and none could bring him down."

"But he was brought down."

"Ay, at last. But he fought with such valour as I have rarely seen on any battlefield. Men looked at him and said that a god had come down to earth."

"And then our god was taken captive. I must decide what I shall do with him."

"You will put him under honourable restraint, no doubt."

247

"He is my captive. He shall have his chains and his dungeon."

Robert looked at her with astonishment. "Doubtless," he said, "you will remember his leniency towards you."

"I remember his foolishness," she said. "This man has usurped my crown. He has set himself up against me. He deserves death."

Robert said: "I had thought there was an affection between you."

She smiled at him. "Have the captive sent to me," she said.

"Matilda, I ask you...."

She looked at him in surprise. He did not seem to understand the implication of this victory. He was her good brother, it was true—half-brother and base-born she would have him remember—but she was the Queen and she would give orders.

"You ask me!" she cried. "I would have you remember, brother, that I shall say what shall and shall not be done. Although you are my good brother and have done your duty in a becoming manner, I am your Queen and this victory means that all in the country will acknowledge me as such. Bring the prisoner to me."

There was colour in her cheeks. She loosened her beautiful hair and shook it out so that it fell about her shoulders. Rarely had she been so excited in her life.

They brought him in—a guard on either side. It made her want to shout with triumph to see him thus, the stains of battle on him still, dejected, the prisoner.

"Leave us," she commanded the guards.

They hesitated. They feared to leave her with a man who might well be desperate.

"Leave us," she repeated her voice sharp with anger. They dared not disobey, so she was alone with Stephen.

He would have come towards her. "Matilda...."

"Stay where you are, prisoner," she commanded.

He stopped short. "Why, Stephen," she said, "you are weary. You fought well, I hear. You may be seated. Take that stool."

He sat down, his head lowered. He dared not meet her eyes. She was like some avenging goddess.

"I was afraid," she said, "that my friends might have killed you."

He lifted his head, for there was a tremor in her voice as

248

she spoke, one which he had never heard before. It sent a wild hope surging through his heart. There was some softness in her then, some compassion, and if this was so who would be more like to benefit from it than himself.

"I am glad they did not," she said. "I wanted to see you here like this. Your corpse, my dear Stephen, would have been no use to me."

He smiled at her but she did not return his smile. Then he stood up and once more came towards her. He wanted to take her into his arms, to tell her that he cared nothing for the battle when he was with her. As ever when they were alone thus, little else could be of importance.

"I did not give you permission to approach me," she said.

"Nay," he answered, "so I will do so without."

"You will obey me," she said. "Forget not that I am the Queen."

"When you and I are together it is Stephen and Matilda, man and woman. King or Queen, what matters that?"

"It mattered to you when you took my crown."

"They should have married us."

"But they did not, so you took what did not belong to you, you thief. Do you think I will ever forgive you for taking my crown?"

"Matilda, you were far away. The English would not accept a woman."

"They are going to accept their Queen. They are going to be ruled by a woman who will be as strong as ever her father or grandfather was."

"You will not rule by harshness."

"Will I not? Shall I rule as you did and make myself a laughing stock to both my friends and enemies? You are a fool, Stephen."

"You loved me."

"I liked your body. I despise your mind. You fool, Stephen. You let me go. I could have been standing before you as you are standing now and you let me go."

"I let you go because of what there was between us."

She burst out laughing. "A crown was between us, Stephen, and we both stretched out our hands for it. You were slow and foolish, Stephen. You had it within your grasp and you let it go . . . you let *me* go. You had lost from that moment. And I shall never allow you to lay your thieving hands on it again. You are my prisoner now and you will see that the Queen of England is not the fool the self-styled King was."

"What will you do with me, Matilda, now that I am in your hands?"

"You will see, and you will not like it. I shall not allow the people to laugh at me for a foolish woman."

"You will keep me near you?"

"I will keep you where I know you are well guarded so that you will never escape. You shall have your dungeon, Stephen. It is what you deserve. My father kept his brother prisoner for more than twenty years. It was necessary. For while he was free there were misguided men who would rally to his banner and try to wrest Normandy from my father's rule. There might be foolish men who would rally to you, Stephen. Though I doubt it for now all men know your weakness, your lack of kingly qualities. But I shall take no chances. When I lie in my warm bed at nights, Stephen, I may think of you... in your cold dungeon... lying there on the straw with perhaps a rat to keep you company. And I shall say: That was Stephen who desired me as he never desired another woman. If he had loved me and had kept the vows he made to my father and had served me as his Queen, which was what he promised to do, then he should have had a place of honour beside me. I would have given him lands and power and now and then a place in my bed for he is a handsome man and his body pleases me. But he deceived me. He worked against me. He stole my crown and for that he shall pay. Prepare yourself, Stephen."

She clapped her hands and a page appeared.

"Call the guards," she said.

They came to her bidding.

"This man is to be put in chains," she said. "He is to be taken to Bristol Castle and there he shall be put into a dungeon of my choosing. He shall stay there until it is my will and pleasure to release him."

She watched the horror on his face; she saw the appeal in his eyes.

"Matilda..." he began.

But she waved an imperious hand.

"Take the prisoner away," she said.

Robert came to Matilda, his expression subdued.

"He has gone, our captive?" asked Matilda.

"He is on his way to Bristol with an armed guard."

"I am glad of it."

"Was it necessary to put him in chains?"

250

"Necessary! Our enemy! The usurper! I should have had his legs strapped under the belly of an ass and let the people come out to jeer at him as he passed."

"He is our cousin, Matilda."

"He is the man who swore on oath to support me and who took the crown instead."

"'Twas so, but there were men to swear that your father named him as heir on his death-bed."

"Lies," snapped Matilda. "All lies. And I bid you be silent on that subject, brother, or I shall suspect you of traitorous thoughts."

"Could you do that in view of the manner in which I have served you?"

"Nay, Robert, you are a good brother, but I am determined to have my way. I shall let all know how I deal with traitors."

"Perhaps a little generosity would not come amiss."

"You have seen where a little generosity brought Stephen."

"He was indeed over-generous to you."

"The fool was indeed and look where it has brought him. Do not fret for him, brother, or I might well dislike your feelings of generosity towards our enemy."

Robert was uneasy. She was not Queen yet and her arrogance was becoming unbearable.

He said: "Your first step now will be to go to Winchester and there take possession of the royal crown and treasury. When you have them we should then make our way to London for the crowning at Westminster."

"This I know well," she said sharply. "And we shall set out for Winchester without delay."

"We have to remember that Winchester is in the hands of its powerful Bishop, who happens to be Stephen's brother."

"I spoke to Henry of Blois on our journey from Arundel. Like the fool he was, Stephen sent his brother to escort me. I think I shall know how to handle Henry."

"He is a man of great power. We must not forget that."

"I shall subdue him," she answered.

Robert was growing more and more uneasy. Matilda had always been overbearing but her manner had changed since the capture of Stephen. She seemed determined to remind everyone with each gesture she made and every word she spoke that she was the Queen. But a queen was not a queen until she had been crowned at Westminster and he must remind her, as tactfully as he could, that she had not yet attained that goal.

Bishop Henry in his stronghold of Winchester was aware that Matilda was marching on the town. He was in a quandary. He had long decided that Stephen was not strong enough to hold the crown and he had implied this during his journey from Arundel with Matilda. At the same time Stephen was his brother and he was well aware of the arrogant nature of his cousin Matilda.

He was not prepared to defend Winchester against Matilda and Robert of Gloucester; on the other hand he was not going to hand over Winchester to her without some show of reluctance.

He called a meeting of the members of the clergy who served under him for the purpose of discussing the matter with them.

"Stephen is my brother," he said. "I feel the brotherly bond between us urging me to act in one way while my conscience dictates another. My first loyalty is to the Church rather than to the Crown, and yet it appears to me to be a most unseemly act to yield to my brother's enemies while he still lives."

His fellow-churchmen assured him that they understood his desire to serve the Church and they were sure he would do so even to the exclusion of any family feeling he might have for a man who had, it must be admitted, shown himself to be unworthy to rule.

He believed that his best plan was to parley with the Empress outside the city and if he could convince himself that it was in the interests of the Church and the country to place the city of Winchester in her keeping, this he would do.

Matilda, having realized the power of the Bishop, agreed to meet him in a field outside the city and at the chosen spot on the end of March, a month after the battle, the meeting took place.

It was dull and dark; heavy clouds obscured the wintry scene and the rain was falling intermittently.

She rode out some little distance from her escort and the Bishop rode forward from his.

He bowed to her. She thought: He is a shrewder man than his brother though not so attractive. This man would never make my heart-beats quicken.

"Well, Sir Bishop," she said, "what have you to say? I had

thought you would have had the bells ringing to welcome your Queen, and not ask her to parley without the city walls in a windy field."

He said: "My brother is your prisoner. Forget not that he is my brother."

Ay, she thought, and my lover; and still I put him in a dungeon with chains about his hands and feet.

'Your brother," she said, "who has proved himself unfit to rule."

The Bishop admitted: "He has shown some weakness."

"Rest assured, lord Bishop, that I shall show none. I shall be as my father and grandfather before me and men will tremble at my name as they did at theirs."

"I would have to be assured that the Church would suffer in no way."

"Why should I wish to subdue the Church?"

"There are monarchs who believe it is their right to subdue all about them."

"And what would you ask for the Church?"

"That I should control matters of chief account in it. That the Church should not be subservient to the State. The bestowal of bishoprics and abbacies should be in my control."

"And if I said yes to this?"

"Then I would open the City of Winchester to you and welcome you there. I would receive you as the lady of England and when you are crowned as the Queen, I would escort you into the city with monks and nuns. I would do this myself so that all would know that I supported your claim to the throne."

She disliked being dictated to, but her brother had assured her of the importance of Henry of Winchester. Moreover he was Stephen's brother; it was due to Henry that Stephen had been able to proclaim himself King.

To be escorted into Winchester by him would be a triumph. She laughed to herself as she thought of Stephen in his wretched cell hearing the news of his brother's treachery.

She would see that such items of news reached the wretched prisoner. They would make his misery more complete.

"I agree to your conditions, Henry of Winchester," she said.

And so the Empress Matilda entered the City of Winchester.

* * *

253

Matilda held the crown in her hand. Some had called it a glittering bauble. It might well be that but it was the symbol of power. She placed it on her head and felt ennobled—regal, in truth a queen.

That same crown had once encircled Stephen's head. How she wished she could go to him and show him that she was wearing it now.

But she must be crowned, for until she was she could not be called Queen; and now that the crown was in her possession she must go to London with all speed. She would brook no delay. She would know no peace until that crowning ceremony had been completed and she was proclaimed throughout the land as Queen of England.

Henry was trying to explain his actions to the assembly of churchmen.

It was not easy. Whatever he said he had deserted his brother at the time of his greatest need; and yet he must justify himself; he must carry the assembly with him and convince them that they must all swear fealty to Matilda.

He pointed out that they had all sworn allegiance to Matilda. Henry the King had insisted on that. So they had made their oaths. It was true that when Henry had died Matilda had been far away in a foreign country. She had made no attempt to come to England and claim the crown; and there had been men who had sworn that the King on his deathbed had named Stephen as his chosen heir, and they had been deluded by this. Matilda had delayed coming and so the crown had passed to Stephen.

"It vexes me greatly to dwell on the manner of king my brother proved to be, but we are all aware that there is no longer justice in this land. No man is safe from the vicious attacks of those whose actions go unpunished. Anarchy has come back to the land such as had not been known since before the days of William the Conqueror. While I love my mortal brother and it gives me great grief to take cause against him, I esteem more highly the cause of my immortal Father. God has handed my brother to his enemies, for he has shown himself to be weak and they are strong; and I know now that God commands me to do His Will and to accept the Lady Matilda that this kingdom may not totter and fall without a ruler."

There was a silence all about him. It was so hard to make out a good case for his actions. But it was true that anarchy

254

prevailed in England; and this was due if not to Stephen's weak rule, to the civil war which was brought about by the rival claims to the throne.

"It is a prerogative of the clergy to choose and consecrate a sovereign prince," he finished. "God has chosen for us this lady of England and Normandy, the daughter of a king who was a peacemaker, a glorious king, a rich king, a good king without peer in our time, and we promise her our faith and support."

He paused. He looked anxiously at the faces about him. There was a moment's hesitation before the applause rang out. These members of the clergy realized that Matilda was here with an army which was growing in strength every day.

They were with him.

Winchester was now open to Matilda. Her next step was London and Coronation.

Flight from London

In Arundel Castle, Adelicia anxiously watched the progress of events. She was pregnant. It seemed ironical that she who had been unable to give her first husband, the King, an heir when it had been so desirable should, in her second marriage, prove to be so fruitful. She had already borne two children—little Reyner being conceived very soon after William was born, and now she was expecting another child. She often thought how happy she and William could have been but for the fact that William must be in attendance on Stephen and that had come to mean that he must constantly be engaged in battle.

She was frequently reminded of that period when Matilda had been her guest at Arundel—not one of her inviting it was true—but it had been a trying time for surely her stepdaughter was the most imperious and demanding guest any hostess could have.

William had been afraid at that time that Stephen would ask them to keep her there, where she would have lived as a kind of honourable captive. His feelings had been mixed when Stephen had allowed her to leave for Bristol. He could not but be relieved to be rid of her, yet as he stood firmly beside Stephen he must marvel at the King's action in letting his rival go free. It had proved to be a major error, for ever since there had been conflict throughout the country.

Adelicia was in a perpetual state of anxiety; every time a rider came to the castle she would fear what news he brought. She prayed daily that this terrible conflict would soon be over and that her husband would be restored to the domestic circle. How happy she could be then! How different was life with a man such as dear William after that with a

King of England. Henry had never been unkind to her but he had never cared for her either. He had relied on her to a certain extent, particularly when darkness fell and his conscience troubled him. There had been an affection between them but how different was that from the tender devotion of William. How wonderful life would have been if she could have come from Louvaine as a girl to marry William and they could have lived in peace with their family. At least she must be grateful that she had finally found William; and she could only pray that he would come through these fearful wars in safety.

It was a chilly February morning when her women came to tell her that a party of horsemen was riding fast towards the castle. She rose and hurried down to the courtyard. To her intense joy the party was led by William. His garments were muddy and it was clear that he had ridden far but a great gladness swept over her, for he was not sick or wounded.

He leapt from his horse and embraced her.

She led him into the castle; she took off his boots and sent for water and unguents that she herself might bathe and anoint his stiff limbs.

She did not ask immediately for the news and she knew it was not good because he did not hasten to tell her.

But at last it came: "Stephen has been defeated at Lincoln. He is Matilda's prisoner."

She closed her eyes and her first thought was: What will this mean to William? How would Matilda behave towards those who had been faithful to the King?

"I hear that she has sent him in chains to Bristol," went on William.

"In chains!"

"She is a vindictive woman."

"And yet...."

"I know," he answered. "There was a tenderness between them. What a terrible mistake he made when he allowed her to go free. Methinks it has cost him his crown."

"And if it has...."

William pressed her hand. "We shall see. We must wait for that."

She turned away to hide her fear but he was beside her. "Adelicia, you must not worry. It is bad for the child. Come, I would see the boys. Tell me, is young William the rogue he was when I went away?"

"We should have warning if she decided to act against

me," William told her later. "I have good friends. And remember there are many in this country who believe Stephen to be the true King."

"There was the oath that was sworn to her. Henry made them swear. I remember so well his insistence."

"But forget not there were those who said he changed his mind on his death-bed. He had quarrelled with his daughter. Who would not quarrel with Matilda? And he had discovered that men would not follow her...not only because she is a woman but because she is an imperious and vindictive one."

"William, you do believe that Henry chose Stephen on his death-bed?"

"I do and I regard him as my King."

"And you will never serve Matilda?"

"I shall fight for Stephen as long as I live, for, although he has not proved to be the strong man his uncle was, still I believe him to be the true King. He has been solemnly crowned. He is our King and master."

"But if he is in chains at Bristol...."

"He may not always be. He shall not always be."

"Oh, God," she cried, "how I wish there could be an end to this fighting."

"It will not be until Stephen is back on the throne, my love, and the Empress driven from this land. In the meantime I am here with you and our babies."

"Are you safe here?"

"As safe as anyone is in this land."

"She may send her guards for you. She will know you fought with Stephen."

"I have good friends and I shall have warning of that. Come, let us forget conflict for a while. We are here together. Let us remember that."

So they were together, but the shadow was there. Every time she heard a clatter of horses' hoofs in the courtyard, Adelicia was alarmed. Every time she passed a window she would look out, straining her eyes to see if there were riders on the horizon. It was an uneasy existence.

News came to Arundel of Matilda's entry into Winchester and of her acceptance by Stephen's brother. This was the biggest blow which could have befallen Stephen's cause, said William. Not only was Henry Stephen's brother but a man of great influence throughout the country. If he had turned against Stephen then it seemed he had little hope left.

"What will become of us?" asked Adelicia.

"We must wait and see. Matilda has not yet been crowned."

"But she is in London. Surely that ceremony cannot long be delayed."

"Once it is then I fear for Stephen's life. I do not think he will be allowed to live long."

"She could not have him murdered. I never understood her feeling for him. He was important to her in some way."

William looked tenderly at his wife. How could she in the innocence of her uncomplicated nature, understand the tempestuous character of a woman like the Empress?

There was another visitor to Arundel, and Adelicia knew then that try as they might they could not escape involvement in the conflict.

Stephen's Queen, Matilda, returned to England.

She came first to Arundel with a small escort, there to learn the true state of affairs from William de Albini whom she knew to be a good friend of her husband.

Adelicia welcomed Queen Matilda with great compassion. She knew how dearly this Matilda loved her husband and she knew too that his unfaithfulness had caused her great grief which had in no way shaken her devotion. She had often said to William of the Queen: "There is a perfect wife. If Stephen has had ill luck in some ways the gods were smiling on him when they married him to Matilda of Boulogne."

The Queen had changed. In fact every time Adelicia saw her she seemed to have become more serious, more statesmanlike. Adelicia remembered her in the early days of her marriage to Stephen when she had been so quiet and unassuming and overawed by her good fortune in being married to the most handsome and charming man at Court.

She had never wanted to be Queen. Like Adelicia she would have preferred a life of domestic felicity in some quiet country house. But Stephen was ambitious and had seized the crown and she as his loyal wife was beside him in everything he did.

She wanted to hear from William all that had happened. "Spare me nothing," she said. "I must know all."

She knew of course that Stephen was the Empress's prisoner and she shuddered to think of him in chains in some filthy dungeon being treated as a felon.

"Oh, how dare she!" she cried. "How can she do this to Stephen?"

But she knew. Matilda could hurt and humiliate him because in some way she both hated and loved him.

When she heard of Bishop Henry's defection she was stunned. This was the greatest blow, for Henry had turned against Stephen, and that was something she could not understand.

"If he has changed sides," said William, "it is because he is sure that Stephen is on the losing one."

"This is one battle lost," replied Matilda. "A war is not lost through one battle."

William was silent. Stephen in chains! Matilda in London about to be crowned! And the wily Bishop of Winchester acclaiming the Empress as Queen. What hope had the Queen of bringing Stephen back to power?

But there was something about her; it was almost a superhuman quality. "We *shall* win," said the Queen. "Stephen shall be released. He shall be proclaimed King of England. I swear it."

To see the hitherto mild Queen so vehement was an inspiration which even the prosaic William was aware of. He found his opinions swerving a little. He did not see how this woman could raise an army and fight the forces of Robert of Gloucester and the Empress Matilda. She was no great general. She had to raise an army. Who would support her? The Empress was all but crowned.

"She is not crowned yet," cried the Queen. "I know that if I could raise a standard many would rally to it. You would, William, I believe."

"I would serve the King with my life."

"I knew it well," said the Queen; "and William of Ypres has sent word to me. I will join him in Kent."

"Where is he now?" asked Adelicia.

"He is in Kent, biding his time. He has sent word to me that his men were routed at Lincoln and that he fled the field seeing the impossibility of being of use to the King. He thought it wiser to reserve his strength for a better opportunity."

"Can you rely on him?"

"I must," said the Queen firmly.

Adelicia was of the opinion that if William of Ypres could be trusted he was indeed a worthy ally, being an adventurer and a man well skilled in battle. He was the son of the Count of Ypres by a village girl of Flanders who had carded wool for a living. He was a name to be feared and while such as he were ready to support Stephen's cause there was a hope that everything was not lost.

"The people of Kent are loyal to Stephen," she went on, "and the citizens of London always loved him. We had many friends there when we lived at Tower Royal and Stephen would go and mingle with the traders. They knew him and he always had a smile and word for both men and women, however humble they were."

So certain was she that she would succeed that she had been able to inspire Adelicia and William with her optimism. Of one thing they were certain, and that was Stephen's hopes had brightened with the return to England of his Queen.

The Empress was now installed at Westminster. She had been proclaimed Lady of England and Normandy at Winchester in April, two months after the defeat of Stephen; she had made her progress through Wiliton, Reading, Oxford and St. Albans and at all of these places she had been received with honour. It was midsummer when she entered London.

So certain was she of her welcome that it did not occur to her for one moment that the people of London might not readily accept her. In any case, she was not concerned with her subjects' feelings towards her. They were of no account she would have thought. She was the Queen and all must realize it.

Indeed, imperious as she had always been, since her arrival at Winchester her arrogance had become intolerable. She could not forget for one moment that she was the Queen and the fact that she had not yet been crowned made her determined that everyone must proclaim her as such in every degree, however trivial. She was brusque with her friends, and even her brother Robert and Henry of Winchester were irritated by her manner of addressing them.

Stephen's wife, Queen Matilda, had taken up her abode at Tower Royal and her servants there and the people in the streets of London expressed their sympathy for her. They knew that they dared not openly support Stephen, but at the same time they wished to show their sympathy for the Queen.

As for Queen Matilda herself, she was convinced that William of Ypres would be successful in raising an army and she was not going to rest until she had brought about her husband's release. At the same time she believed that if she pleaded with the Empress she might prevail upon her to free Stephen.

She called at the Palace of Westminster and asked for an audience with the Lady of England.

The Empress laughed when she heard that the woman calling herself Queen Matilda was without. At first she declared she would not see her.

"I have no time to see all the supplicants who call at the palace," she said.

Then it occurred to her that it might amuse her to see this woman who was Stephen's wife, so she ordered that Queen Matilda be brought to her.

She kept her waiting and even when she was brought in she was forced to stand until the Empress deigned to notice her.

The Queen could not believe that a kinswoman who had been a playmate in the royal nursery could behave in this manner. She could understand a certain ceremony on public occasions, but not when they were alone together.

"Matilda," she began. "I have come to ask you...."

The Empress raised her eyebrows. "Do not forget," she warned, "that you are addressing the Queen."

"I did not know the coronation had taken place, and I, Matilda have been crowned Queen of England."

"You would be wise not to remind me of that. You and your husband took the crown to which you had no right. He is suffering for his sins. You are bold. I should have you punished in like manner."

"I have come to ask you to release Stephen."

"Release the man who usurped my crown! Why should I?"

"Because he is your cousin. Because your father named him as his successor."

"That is a lie. Those who speak treason shall suffer the traitor's death."

The Queen had one thought. To bring about her husband's release. If she must submit to the arrogance of Matilda in order to bring this about, then so must it be. She therefore decided to ignore the rights and wrongs of the matter and to appeal to the Empress's tender feelings if such existed.

"Stephen lies in a dungeon," said the Queen. "He is treated there like the meanest felon. He is your cousin. I beg of you move him to a comfortable prison, if in prison he must be."

"In prison he must be and there shall remain and prisons are not meant to be comfortable, cousin."

"We were all children together. You were friends once, you and Stephen...."

A smile curled the Empress's lips. Friends! Oh, more than friends, you good and faithful wife to Stephen. He was my
263

lover. He could not resist me. He desired me as he never did you, you silly feeble creature. Some would say you are comely enough, but you lack my fire. Only I could kindle Stephen to deep passion. He was ready to risk everything for me... as he has shown. But what I cannot forgive is that he took the crown and did not come to me when my father died. For that he shall lie in his dungeon. I have not finished with him yet. He shall wish that he had never been born because he betrayed me.

"This has nothing to do with the nursery," said the Empress. "And I have no time to talk to you. Pray leave me now."

The Queen knelt before her and raised her eyes to the Empress's cruel face. They were bright with tears and her hair had escaped from its coif. She was a beautiful woman. The Empress thought of her with Stephen, their embrace... the children they had.

"Go from me," she cried angrily, "or I will call the guards to take you away. Go quickly before I throw *you* into a dungeon. But it would not be that in which your husband now spends his time. Do not think that."

It was no use pleading with the Empress and to remain was dangerous. Of what use would she be to Stephen if she became Matilda's prisoner?

The Queen left the palace where once she had held state with Stephen. She came out into the street and wrapped her cloak over her head. Even so some people recognized her.

"It is the Queen!" she heard the whisper.

"Come from the Lady where she had been pleading for her husband."

"Poor lady. She was always good to us."

"Different from...."

One man came forward and taking the Queen's hand kissed it.

Deeply moved she passed on. The Empress's indifference to her sufferings and that of Stephen had shocked her; but she was comforted to remember that she and he had always had the affection of the people of London.

The Queen could not forget the baleful light in the Empress's eyes when she had talked of Stephen and she decided that she would leave London for Kent, and there join with William of Ypres.

She had received disquieting news from Normandy. Since

Stephen was a prisoner and Matilda had been accepted as the Lady of England in Winchester and Bishop Henry had sworn allegiance to her, the Empress's husband, Geoffrey of Anjou, had had little difficulty in persuading the Norman barons that Stephen's cause was lost and all those who had so recently sworn allegiance to Eustace and accepted him as the heir of Normandy, should now transfer their allegiance to the Empress Matilda and her son, Henry.

This was yet another blow, but the Queen realized that the important thing was to bring about Stephen's release without delay and set him back on the throne. Once that was achieved Normandy would naturally return to him.

But in the meantime the Empress was installed in London about to be crowned Queen of England while Stephen remained in chains in Bristol.

Only a supreme optimist could hope in such circumstances, but the Queen's grew out of desperation.

When she reached Kent she had a pleasant surprise. Far more men than she had dared to hope had rallied round William of Ypres who delightedly told her that the overbearing conduct of the Empress was turning many of her onetime friends against her.

This was a small comfort but the Queen was pleased to clutch at any hope.

The Queen's visit had upset the Empress more than she would admit. There was no doubt that Stephen's wife was a beautiful woman. She was far more feminine than the Empress could ever be and she was proving herself to be more than ornamental. She had proved herself something of a stateswoman in France when she had married young Eustace off to the King's daughter; and her devotion to Stephen was constantly mentioned.

It was said: Stephen could hardly be called a lucky man except in one respect. He could not have a better wife.

Such remarks angered the Empress who was far from happy, though about to be crowned Queen of England; she had had her revenge on Stephen, but she was bitterly dissatisfied. Her temper could be aroused by the slightest matter and it was often out of control.

Robert of Gloucester warned her to curb it. "You will lose friends unless you treat them with more respect," he warned her.

"Lose them!" she cried. "It is not for men and women to

decide whether they shall take their friendship from me. They will be grateful that I choose to honour them."

"They may feign to be honoured, but resentment will smoulder in their hearts," said Robert.

"You presume too much," she retorted. "Forget not that although you are my half-brother you are my father's bastard."

To speak thus to the man to whom she owed almost everything she had gained was such ingratitude that he was speechless with dismay. He could only withdraw from her presence and ask himself whether he had been wise to support her. Stephen was a weak king but he was courteous and kindly. Matilda was becoming more and more of a virago every day.

The Bishop of Winchester who was at Westminster and whose task it was to win the citizens of London to her side was also resentful of her treatment of him. She seemed to have forgotten that these men held great power in the land and that without them she could do little. She was so obsessed with her own royalty that she could see nothing else.

Her servants disliked her and tried to keep out of her way. In the streets of London they were saying that the Lady of England was "a niggish old wife." She was a shrew, a virago, and completely different from Stephen's sweet-faced Queen who had always a smile when she walked through the streets and never passed a poor beggar without giving him something to ease him.

"Why," demanded the Empress of Robert, "does my coronation not take place immediately? Why should there be this delay?"

Robert explained as patiently as he could that it was necessary to win the favour of the people of London.

"Win it! The Queen must win the favour of London! Winchester hailed me. Other cities have accepted me."

"This is the capital city," said Henry. "If London were against you and refused to accept you it would not be easy to hold the rest of the country."

"Call together an assembly of the leading citizens," commanded Matilda, "and I will address them."

"It would be advisable to let them know how gratified you are to be received in their city."

"*Their* city. This is *my* city. I am the Queen."

"They will not call you that until after the coronation," said Henry.

266

"Then for the love of God let us have this coronation."

"We shall need money that it may be celebrated with the pomp that is due to your rank," explained Robert.

"Then we must have money. Why do you delay? I declare I must insist on your obedience. Call an assembly without delay."

Robert and Henry exchanged glances and Henry said: 'I will let your wishes be known."

When she had left them the Bishop said: "If she continues in this way I fear the people will revolt."

Robert bowed his head in consternation. Neither of them knew then how soon the Bishop's fears were to be realized.

Henry spoke to the assembled citizens. He presented to them the Lady Matilda, the daughter of the late King whom they all revered. He had been a king who had made good laws and had been strong enough to see them carried out. They would find in his daughter such another ruler. She was the true heiress of England.

This was somewhat reluctantly acceded. She was in truth the direct heir, but she was a woman. They remembered the reign of the Conqueror and that seemed like a golden age. Rufus had followed and those had not been good years, but Henry had followed—Henry, Lion of Justice and the Conqueror's youngest son; he had restored his father's stern, just laws and England had been a better place for that.

The citizens conferred together and their spokesman said that they would be ready to accept her but first they wished to know if the charters which had been granted by Matilda's father would stand.

Matilda's eyes flashed with anger. Were they making conditions to her? These people who had given their support to Stephen! Had she not always heard that London had been the first to accept him! London had favoured Stephen and his Queen. And now that she was here they were offering her conditions.

"You are impudent to mention privileges to me," she declared, "when you have so recently been helping my enemies."

There was a hushed silence. The Bishop was exasperated; Robert was clearly alarmed. But Matilda was so certain of her power that she went on to tell the assembly that she needed money and that she was about to impose taxes on the people of London to provide this. When they had given her the money she needed they should have a grand spectacle of a coronation and she wished there to be no delay.

The spokesman asked leave for the assembly to be dismissed as he and his friends wished to confer together to discover the best way of meeting her demands.

Matilda inclined her head. "But let there be no delay," she cautioned. "I am an impatient woman."

Robert tried to reason with her.

"I fear they are offended," he said.

"Offended. Let them be. As long as they find the money what care I if they are offended or not?"

"Sister, it is always necessary for a ruler to please the people."

"Are you telling me how to be royal, you...bastard?"

She is drunk with power, thought Robert. I must caution her.

"You will see," he said, "that it is necessary to please the people."

"You are as weak as Stephen. That was his way, was it not? Please everybody. Smile here, smile there, forgive your enemies. Let them get away to fight another day. You are a fool, Robert."

"Can you say that? Have I not provided you with an army?"

"Oh, you are a good brother to me, but you do not know what it means to be royal."

"Our father kept me at his side. I was with him often when he was concerned in matters of State. He taught me much."

She said almost gently, "I know, Robert, and you have served me well, but I am royal. Understand that. I am the daughter of a king. I was the wife of an emperor. I know that a ruler must be strong. Do not anger me, Robert, for I do not wish to lose my temper with you. I forget not that you are my good brother and you shall be rewarded."

"Reward me by taking a little care, Matilda. That is what would please me."

"You are like Stephen...all of you. And look where his softness brought him. To a dungeon...in chains."

"It does not please the people that he should be there."

"Nay, brother, but it pleases me and that is all that matters. I am hungry. I trust they have some good meat on the spit. If not...."

"Oh, come, Matilda, they are too frightened of you not to cook your venison to a turn."

"Then we will eat and I will confer with you and the Bishop, and we will plan the coronation, for my frightened subjects will give me what I ask. Doubt it not. You will see I am right when they come tomorrow with their bags of gold. Now let us to the hall."

She felt pleased with the day's work. She would laugh at Robert and the Bishop when those burghers came cringing. She would say to them: "You see I know how to rule."

She smiled when she saw the board laden with good meat and she took her place at the head of the table but as she was about to be served there was a violent clangour from without and it seemed as though every bell in the city started to peal.

Robert started up in dismay. "What is happening?" he asked.

One of the servants came running to the table, trembling so much that he could scarcely speak.

"The people are gathering in the streets. Some have swords, some other weapons. They are marching on the Palace."

"We have no time to lose," said Robert.

He seized Matilda by the arm before she could protest and indeed she had no mind to. She knew suddenly that the whole of London was rising against her. Those men in the hall had hated her. They had decided that they would turn her out.

As she hastily followed Robert out to the stables and obediently mounted the horse he was holding, she knew she was in great danger.

Robert leaped into the saddle and by that time others had joined them.

Matilda knew that if these people caught up with her they would tear her to pieces. She could expect no mercy from them. They hated her, these people of London. Reluctantly they had received her but they wanted Stephen and his wife Matilda.

No sooner had she and the little band left the precincts of the palace than the mob broke in.

As they could not find Matilda, they plundered the rooms and carried off all the treasure they could find. One thing was certain, London had rejected Matilda.

The Funeral Cortège

The news of the Empress's flight from London soon reached the ears of Queen Matilda and she lost no time in riding into the city with her son Eustace beside her.

How the people cheered her! They kissed her hand and they told her they were delighted that she had come. They would not have that niggish old wife back on any conditions.

"Good people," cried the Queen, "I thank you on behalf of my husband the King. He is a prisoner now. The prisoner of that woman whom you have rejected, but it shall not be for long."

"Not for long," echoed the people.

"My good friend, William of Ypres, has gathered together an army and we shall march on Winchester where the niggish old wife has taken refuge. If any of you will join us...."

"Ay, we will," was the cry.

And thus the Queen marched out of London with many an able-bodied man in her train; and when she joined with the army gathered together by William of Ypres they were a formidable force.

For two months the Queen's army encamped outside the gates of Winchester. Inside the besieged city was the Empress. It was difficult for her to believe that the tables could have been so quickly turned. Her brother told her frankly that she was to blame. Her treatment of the Londoners had turned them against her, he pointed out. If she were going to win and hold the affection of her people she must curb her temper and not treat her subjects as though they were serfs.

Matilda stormed and raged. To what a pass had she come? She had relied too much on others. She should have acted alone. She looked round for scapegoats and those who served her dreaded to be near her.

Her consolation was that Stephen was in a less comfortable position than she was. If she was in a besieged city, he was in a dungeon. She wanted constant confirmation that he was still there.

Heartened by events the Queen asked for an audience with the Bishop of Winchester, who had clearly shown that he was beginning to regret turning from Stephen to the Empress, whom he had left in his castle while he himself retired to another of his residences on the outskirts of his town.

Being fully aware that the position had reversed and that the Queen was now head of the winning party, he agreed to see her and they met at Guildford.

He tried to justify his betrayal of his brother by explaining that his main duty was and always would be to the Church and it was only on that account that he had gone over to the Empress. He had been led to believe that the oath he and others had taken to King Henry to serve his daughter should be adhered to. He now realized that he had been mistaken and that it was indeed true that the King had named Stephen on his death-bed.

The Queen was not deceived but she needed the help of her brother-in-law too much to quibble. Henry was a powerful man and one of the greatest blows she had to suffer was when he had turned his coat and gone over to the Empress. That he now wanted to turn back again was a good sign, for Henry was a shrewd man—far shrewder than Stephen would ever be—and it was clear that he now saw that Matilda would never be accepted by the people of England.

Therefore Henry and the Queen could make a pact together. They stood firmly with Stephen and the next step was to defeat the Empress and release Stephen from captivity.

The Queen's hopes were high as she joined her army outside the gates of Winchester.

Enraged, sickened with exasperation, the Empress stormed through the castle. In the streets buildings were being destroyed, houses were burning; fire-balls were thrown over the walls of the city each night and the smell of burning constantly in the air. Food was growing short; there was sickness among the people.

The Empress cursed and raged against the fate which had

brought her here just at that time when she was on the point of being crowned Queen. Robert could have told her it was her own fault but that would not have eased matters. She raged against the people of London and declared what she would do to that city when she was free. She would hang those citizens who had refused her money and had roused the mob against her; she would set her soldiers loose in the streets and let them pillage until they were satiated with the spoils. All this she would do when she had broken out of Winchester and made her triumphant march on London.

"First," said Robert calmly, "we have to break this siege."

The weeks passed. Even the Empress was growing listless. There was little food left and much sickness in the town. The fire-balls were still raining down on them by night and there was the stench of death and destruction all around.

She called Robert to her with her good friend Brian Fitz-Count, who was as a brother to her.

"I cannot go on in this way," she said. "Something must be done."

"If we surrendered you would be the Queen's prisoner," Robert reminded her.

"Not that!" she cried. "Anything but that!"

"It would mean the restoration of Stephen."

"And I his prisoner! That shall never be."

"Then perforce we must endure the siege."

She went to the window and bade him come to stand beside her.

As they looked out on the devastated buildings she pointed out a man who was propped against a wall.

"He is dying of disease or starvation," she said. "It is a plight it seems to which we all must come." There was silence and she went on: "If we could break out. . . ."

Brian Fitz-Count said: "We could attempt it. It is either that or waiting here until we are too weak to withstand further."

"For two months I have been confined in this castle," said Matilda. "By God's faith I cannot endure it longer."

Neither man reminded her that she had none but herself to blame and that there was no reason why she should not have been received in London and crowned Queen of England—none but that her own arrogance was intolerable. Her followers were deserting her. The only men she could rely on were Robert and Brian—Robert held to her by the ties of blood and by his certainty that it had been his father's wish

273

that she should rule; and Brian because he had known her as a child and her father had given him everything he had.

It was strange, they both admitted to themselves, that they should feel some affection for her, but they did. She was intolerable, reckless in her arrogance, her own worst enemy, but there was a magnificence about her. She was handsome too, and although there was little that was soft and appealing about her, she aroused in them a desire to serve her.

Both men knew that to whatever pass she brought them they would remain faithful to her until the end.

A funeral procession came along the street—a small party of mourners and two men carrying a roughly made bier.

"Another death," she said. "I wonder how many there are in this city and how many more there will be before there is an end to this siege. Why look, they are taking it through the city gates."

"The Queen's instructions are that safe passage shall be given to those who wish to bury their dead outside the city walls."

"She is as soft as her husband," said Matilda contemptuously.

"Nay, she is a strong woman. It is hard to believe, remembering her as we knew her, but since Stephen's adversity she has shown a fire and determination which few women could equal."

"He is fortunate to inspire such devotion in a wife."

"The Queen is a good woman, we must grant her that."

Matilda was bitterly resentful. She hated the woman now; before she had despised her; and the hatred was harder to endure.

She thought: I must get out of here. If I do not in a short time, she will be victorious; and I shall be her captive.

She could not endure that. She must be free. She would take any risks to be free. Her smouldering eyes rested on the funeral party, the wasted body wrapped in winding sheets, the bowed heads of the mourners.

"I have it," she said. "I shall become as a corpse. I shall be wrapped in my shroud and bound to the bier...."

"Nay, nay," soothed Robert, thinking her to be hysterical.

"Ay! ay!" she cried. "I see what shall be done. I shall be carried out of this city on a bier and I shall have one or two stalwart mourners to follow me. I shall be as that poor man who is being carried out now...only I shall not be dead."

The two men stared at her.

"Is it possible?" asked Brian.

"Of course it is possible. It is going to be possible. For I will not stay here to starve to death nor will I give way and become the prisoner of Stephen's wife."

Robert was thoughtful but Matilda knew by the glitter in his eyes and the pulse which throbbed in his temple that he was considering the escape in all its aspects.

"I could not be one of the mourners," he went on. "I should be recognized. They know me too well. You, Brian...?"

"I must be there. One of us must be with you, Matilda. I will disguise myself so that none of you will know me but I will be there."

"And when you have carried the bier through the gates?" asked Robert.

"There should be horses waiting for us."

"How?"

"Ah, how! That is the question. We shall be in the enemy's camp."

"It may be necessary to carry the bier into Gloucester."

"Then if that must be done, then so it shall."

"Could Matilda survive the journey?"

"I tell you I will endure anything...anything but that I should fall a prisoner into that woman's hands."

"It is worth an attempt," said Robert, "for there is no other way out of this. It is either death or surrender if we do not attempt to escape."

"And you, Robert, when I'm gone?" asked Matilda.

"I shall not stay here. I shall attempt to break out in some way."

"You will use a bier?"

"Nay, they would not allow that to happen more than once. I shall rely on my sword."

"I thank God," said Matilda, "that we have at least made plans. To stay here is driving me mad. When shall we do this?"

"There is no point in delay. Tomorrow. At dusk. It will be growing dark by the time we pass through the camp. The night will be our friend."

"Then tomorrow," said Matilda.

Wrapped in a shroud the Empress climbed into the roughly made coffin. Those watching her shuddered. Superstitious as they were they were looking for all kinds of omens. She herself felt better than she had for weeks. Inactivity had always

275

irked her. She was sure that her plan was an excellent one. Soldiers who were constantly facing death had a great respect for death. They would never attempt to disturb the shroud and see who was hidden there. Why should they? But once they learned that the Empress Matilda had escaped in this manner they would examine every coffin which was carried out of the city, or perhaps they would give an order that none other must be brought out.

Alas, so many passed out to the burial grounds in these last months. Doubtless the besiegers rejoiced and believed that the city was almost on its knees. Matilda could imagine the joy of the Queen. Was she writing notes of comfort to her husband, telling him that the Empress who had put him in a dungeon would soon be occupying one herself?

She disliked the smell of the shroud and the wood of the coffin. She hoped she would not have to stay long inside it. As the ropes were bound about the rough box she almost felt that she was indeed dead and was being taken to her grave. That day would come—oh, but it was a long way off, she had many years to live yet...to live and reign, she told herself fiercely.

They were ready; the coffin was hoisted on to the shoulders of four stalwart bearers and the journey began.

Cowering under her shroud she listened to the voices about her. She knew that people were making way for the procession, that they crossed themselves and murmured: "Yet another one. How long before I am carried out of this city in such a box?"

Free! thought Matilda. I shall soon be free.

Out through the city. She could see very little for her face was half covered; Brian had said that none must recognize her if they should decide to look at the corpse. She with her heavy-lidded eyes and her striking features would be quickly identified.

"Halt!" It was one of the guards speaking—the Queen's guards.

"Another poor soul going to her grave," said someone.

There was a brief pause. Her heart was beating so fast that she thought it must shake the coffin and betray her. How long that pause seemed to go on! What if someone had betrayed her? What if they should say: "We wish to see what you are carrying"—and finding her, take her to the Queen.

She almost rocked the coffin in her fury to think of that woman. How she hated her! Stephen's wife who loved him

276

and served him and was determined to save him from his dungeon.

The cortège was moving forward. All was well.

They were beyond the camp now, out in the burial grounds. The coffin was lowered to the ground.

"And now," said Brian.

"And now we must go on our way. We must be well away by daybreak."

"If there were horses."

"Horses! Where are the horses here? We must continue with the funeral procession, and carry the Empress on to Gloucester."

To Gloucester, her bearers on foot, herself wrapped in a shroud and carried in a coffin!

It was the only thing to be done. She had come through the enemy's camp; she was free; but she had to travel to Gloucester in a coffin carried on the shoulders of two strong men.

She would never forget that long journey; she was sore and bruised from the buffeting she received in the coffin. She was cold and hungry. She felt too weak even to complain and felt sick and faint when at a lonely spot she emerged from the coffin to stretch her limbs for a few brief moments. But always there was the biting fear that the Queen's soldiers would appear and take her prisoner and do to her what she had done to Stephen.

I will never be that woman's prisoner, she thought. I will never give her that satisfaction. She has Stephen. She shall have nothing more, certainly not the satisfaction of giving him *me* as her prisoner.

So she lay in the coffin and was jolted on and on through that wearisome journey; and her joints stiff, her limbs bruised and herself sick and weary, she arrived within the comforting walls of Gloucester— her half-brother's territory where she could for a while be safe.

She had only just arrived at Gloucester Castle when she received the news which was one of the greatest blows possible to her cause. Robert of Gloucester battling his way out of Winchester had been captured. He was now Queen Matilda's prisoner.

Escape Over the Ice

When Robert of Gloucester was brought before the Queen, she could not disguise her great delight, for she knew that without her brother the Empress would be lost. What a fine man he was. No wonder the King had doted on him. There was a rare nobility about him; such a man must be treated with the utmost respect.

"You are my prisoner," said the Queen, "as the King is that of the Empress. Tell me, have you news of my husband?"

"I have not seen him but I know that he is in close confinement."

"I fear for his health."

The Queen looked at him searchingly and she saw that he believed she would do to him as the Empress had to Stephen. He was a man of action and the prospect of spending long weeks or perhaps months, even years in a dungeon appalled him. He did not show his apprehension, but it was there and she was aware of it.

"I did not see the King," he said, "but had he been ill I should have heard of this."

She lowered her eyes, for she was thinking of the terrible time when Stephen had been attacked by that curious lethargy which she had feared bordered on madness.

"The Empress has treated him cruelly," she went on. "I know full well that it was not your wish that this should be. Do not think that I would treat you in like manner. I shall place you in the care of William of Ypres and you shall have as much freedom as it is possible to give you in the circumstances. You understand that you are my prisoner and so must remain."

"I understand this," he answered, "and I thank you."

She signed to the guards to take him away and when he had gone summoned William of Ypres.

"He is a noble gentleman," she said. "We must treat him with the respect due to his rank and character."

William of Ypres had no objection to that. "As long as he is in our keeping and can be of no further use to the Empress that will be well. She will be lost without him. He has been her strength. Had it been left to him she would never have been turned out of London. Without him she will be defeated and forced out of the country."

"One cannot be sure," replied the Queen. "There were those who said that *our* cause was lost when Stephen was captured."

"They did not know what a clever and devoted wife he had."

"How do we know who will spring up to take the place of Robert of Gloucester with the Empress?"

"There is Brian Fitz-Count of course. He is still with her."

"So thought I. This conflict is not over because of the capture of one man however important he is."

"But the loss of this man is the greatest blow they could have suffered."

"It is true and our greatest gain, for I am going to offer him in exchange for Stephen."

William of Ypres was silent. The Queen had proved herself an able general. She was strong and had a good man in William of Ypres to help her. They had come out of disaster under Stephen to the beginning of triumph under the Queen. The Queen knew what he was thinking. They could continue the war; they were in a strong position; but if Robert of Gloucester was returned to the enemy, they would gain in strength; and it may be that the Empress had learned a lesson and would not be so rash in future. What would they gain from the exchange: the presence of the King, a figurehead.

The Queen said firmly: "I shall immediately begin bargaining for the return of Stephen."

"And give up Robert?"

"Do you not understand that Stephen is in that miserable dungeon! Who can say what is happening to him? He may be ill. He may be dying."

"We shall give them back their greatest general."

"No price is too high to pay for the freedom of the King."

She spoke as a woman; William of Ypres was thinking as
280

a commander. He knew that she would have her way. She had proved herself to be a forceful woman.

The Empress stormed up and down her chamber. That woman wanted her husband returned to her...in exchange she offered Robert!

We must have Robert, she had been told. We need him. Not only for his generalship but for the effect it will have on our supporters.

"Of course I know we must have Robert, but I will not give up Stephen."

"It is the price the Queen is asking."

"Leave me alone. I tell you I will not give him up."

They left her; she clenched her fists and hit them against the wall until she bruised them. She pictured their return, the loving embraces.

"No," she cried. "He shall not go. I'll not let him return to that woman. Let him stay in his dungeon. He shall be chained to the wall. He shall be kept there in filth and squalor until he no longer looks like her handsome Stephen...or mine."

She sent for her advisers.

"Offer the Queen a large sum of money and twelve of Stephen's captains. And in exchange we want Robert."

"She will not listen."

"Convey my wishes to her. Tell her she had better listen."

"We are in no position...."

"Do not tell me what position I am in. Go and do what I say or you will find yourself a prisoner."

There was no reasoning with her, but as they had known it would be, the answer they received was No. The exchange must be Robert for Stephen.

The Empress stormed and raged but even in her most violent moments she knew that she could not do without Robert.

At length she gave way.

What a joyous moment it was for the Queen when she beheld her husband, even though his appearance shocked her. He was so thin, emaciated and sick.

"I will soon nurse you back to health," she assured him.

"What you have done is miraculous," he told her. "I could not believe that any could bring about such victory. Why,

Matilda, I knew you to be gentle and loving, but you have proved yourself to be a great general."

He told her of the treatment he had received in his dungeon. At first he had suffered great hardship and privation but when his jailer, the lord of the castle, had gone to the wars his lady had been less severe. Although she could not release him she had had the chains taken from his ankles and seen that comforts were brought to him. Women had always been affected by Stephen; the Queen knew this and in this instance was glad of it.

"We must now make plans," he said, "to bring an end to this war."

"We must succeed in driving the Empress back to Anjou," replied the Queen; and she watched him somewhat furtively, for she wondered what his feelings were now regarding her rival, who ironically enough was his, too. She would continue to fear an encounter between them; and she wondered whether he would be strong enough to resist her.

Many would have reproached him for allowing the Empress's escape from Arundel—which had brought him to this pass. But not the Queen.

He had suffered enough and if he had discovered that the Empress was his enemy, however desirable she was, then the Queen must be content.

For some days she nursed the King, who showed signs of a return to that illness which had attacked him so alarmingly on a previous occasion. For a few days he became lethargic and could not remember where he was. The Queen kept him confined to his chamber and his condition as secret as possible, and herself nursed him, but the news leaked out that he was dangerously ill and many were predicting his death.

But as before, the malady passed and the King was ready to take to the battlefield.

The Empress was delighted to see Robert, but she greatly deplored the need to free Stephen. She rebuked Robert for allowing himself to be captured and Robert was stung to reply: "My dear sister, do you think I wished for it! You know how we were placed. You had escaped in the coffin. Could I have remained in the castle? I should either have been killed or captured. At least it was better to make a bid to escape."

She knew that he was right but it eased her to give vent to her temper. Aware as she was that she had lost many of her adherents through her outbursts, still she could not control them.

"We must attack them," she cried. "Why do we hesitate?"

"Because we are not in a position to attack," replied Robert with a hint of weariness. "They have the advantage now."

"Because we have freed Stephen."

"It always raises the spirits of an army when their leader is restored."

"A curse on those who took you and a curse on that woman who would not take an alternative."

"You can scarcely blame her."

Matilda laughed. "Doubtless she is cooing over him now. She is besotted about him."

"She has been a good wife to him. What he would have done without her it is hard to say."

"He would have been in his dungeon, I'll dare swear. Oh, he must be very grateful to her. And I have my useless spouse. There he stays in Anjou while I am fighting for my kingdom. He should be here at my side as the Queen is at her husband's. Robert, he must be sent for."

Robert considered the suggestion. He could bring troops with him, and the fact that the Empress's husband had come to her aid would have a good effect on the morale of their army.

"Yes," he said. "He should be here. The Queen has made use of her son Eustace and there is nothing like a young boy for arousing the people's enthusiasms. She has been clever— let us not deny that, but the fact that she has often ridden at the head of her army with her son beside her has brought her sympathy."

"My Henry should be here, then. He is a finer boy than her Eustace and older too. Yes, Geoffrey should be here and Henry with him. I will send a message without delay to Geoffrey bidding him come to England and my aid."

Geoffrey snapped his fingers when he heard that Matilda wanted him in England. Join that old shrew? Not if he could help it! He was enjoying life too much in his province. He liked to live at ease. Fighting could be uncomfortable.

No, he had no wish to come to England. If he did come he would want Robert of Gloucester to come and fetch him.

When Matilda received this message she raged against her husband. So he was afraid to come without an escort. "The lily-livered boy," cried Matilda. "Go and get him, Robert, and tell him that I despise him. I want him only to fight for me and for no other reason. He should not think it is affection that inspires me."

"It would be better not to say so," warned Robert; but he had become so certain that it would be a help to have Geoffrey at the side of the Empress that he decided he would leave at once for Anjou.

"First," he said, "I must assure myself of your safety. The castle of Oxford is well nigh impregnable. There is not a stronger fortress in the country. I believe you would be safer there than in any other place."

"Then to Oxford I will go and await your coming."

"Rest assured," said Robert, "that I shall return with all speed and when I bring the Count of Anjou and your son Henry, we will plan such a campaign that will bring down Stephen and his army and place the crown where it belongs, on your head."

Matilda took an affectionate farewell of her half-brother and settled in at Oxford Castle, there to await his return.

She hated the life of inactivity. Often she brooded on the last meeting with Stephen. She wished that they would bring him back to her...in chains preferably. She longed to see him, to have him humble before her, and perhaps she would kindle that passion which was ever ready to flare up between them.

She continued to think of him, to need him, to desire him to love him and to hate him. How fiercely she hated him! If only he had come to her when her father died and offered her his affection instead of taking the crown. They could have been together now. There would have been no war. She would have been crowned Queen and he would have been her best loved, her favourite. His wife and her husband would have been as nothing. She and Stephen would have been together. That was what she wanted.

Oh, it was ironical that they should be fighting each other.

Below her window flowed that river which wound its way through meadows and vales to London, the scene of her humiliation. She cursed now to remember that undignified and hasty exit from Westminster. Whenever she smelt roasting meat she thought of it.

She often sat on the window-seat looking out at the countryside which grew more and more bleak as the days passed. Winter was coming.

And not only winter. Robert had been gone but a few weeks when news was brought to her one day that Stephen's army was approaching. Their object could only be to lay siege to the castle.

Once more she was besieged and this time by Stephen. The winter had come and fierce blizzards swept the castle walls; the Empress wrapped herself in her fur-lined cloak and still she shivered.

For three months Stephen's army had been encamped about the castle and there was scarcely any food left. She would sit at her window looking out on the frozen river and wonder how long they could hold out.

Stephen would never let her go again. He would remember what she had done to him. He would never again run the risk of allowing her to capture him. He was soft; he had always been soft with everyone and more especially would he be so with her; he would never behave to her as she had to him. Yet her pride would not stand the humiliation of becoming his prisoner. And yet...how long could they hold out?

She raged against Robert. He should not have left them. Where was he now? Enjoying life in Anjou with that feckless Geoffrey! What did they care that she was cold and hungry and the enemy was at her gates? She forgot that she had commanded Robert to go to Anjou. She could only upbraid him for—as she called it—deserting her. It did not occur to her that her attitude was unreasonable and unjust. Matilda saw herself as the Queen, the supreme ruler; she could only see others in relation to herself and as, in her estimation, she towered above them—for she saw the sovereign as divine—she gave way to her passions of the moment without considering the effects they would have on others. She had not learnt the lesson the Londoners had attempted to teach her, although it was clear for everyone to see. That she was in her present state was due entirely to her own actions, but she was too obsessed by her importance to see it and would have been too arrogant to admit it if she had.

So she raged against her evil fate, her slothful brother, her careless husband; and chiefly against Stephen who had dared take what was hers and had forced her to put him into a dungeon, so that now she feared he might be prevailed on to treat her in a similar manner.

She talked to Brian about their position which grew daily worse.

Gloomily he listened and tried to soothe her. He was very patient, more so than Robert; he understood her better because they had been in the nursery together and in spite of her vindictive nature and her fierce unreasoning temper he was always gentle with her, always eager to placate, always making excuses for her outbursts to those who complained.

He was not such a fool as not to know that she was a mistress whom it was impossible to please and that her own unfortunate nature was at the source of her troubles; he loved her and had admired her from the days when she had made herself queen of the nursery.

One day he came to tell her that several of the household were sick and some were dying. They were suffering from starvation. Food was so low that there was not enough to go round and he did not believe they could hold out much longer.

"Then what do you wish to do?" she asked.

"If we do not get help soon we must perforce surrender."

"Surrender to Stephen, never!"

"In a few weeks time we shall be dead. They may well storm the castle before that. They will know what state we are in and that we cannot hold out against them."

She clenched her fist and beat it against her breast—a habit of hers when she railed against fate.

"I will not be taken by him, Brian."

"There is no other alternative. The weather is growing worse. The snow is falling thick and piling up everywhere. The river is thick with ice. It is one of the worse winters men remember."

"It is hard for them as well for us."

"They have food and wood for fires. The winter is their ally and our foe."

"Why doesn't Robert come?"

"He would if it were possible. We know that."

"He should be here with Geoffrey. If they came with an army and surprised Stephen from the rear...."

"In this weather! It would not be possible."

"I will not be taken, Brian. I said I would not before and I will not now."

"We had luck on our side when you escaped in the coffin."

"I will escape again."

"How? Not in a coffin this time! They are not letting anyone out. And how could you in this weather?"

"You have no spirit. You are all the same. No, no, no, you say. You would stay here I suppose and let Stephen take you."

"I do not see what else we can do."

"We must do something. I tell you I will not be his prisoner...I swear I will not."

Brian shook his head. He asked leave to depart.

"Go," she cried, "since you bring me no comfort."

She was shivering with the cold. Was there no way of feeling warm. She was fully clad as she lay on the straw pallet but an icy wind whistled through the castle.

It could not be long. There was little food now, even for her. I'd rather starve, she told herself, than be his prisoner.

She could see herself being brought before him.

"It is my turn now, Matilda," he would say.

Perhaps that woman would be there...for safety. To protect him against her because Matilda the Queen would fear what he might do if Matilda the Empress beguiled him. Matilda the Queen was no fool. She had brought about the defeat of the Empress and the release of Stephen; she would never allow him to fall under her spell again.

And Stephen, weak, handsome, desirable Stephen, who was loved by his wife and desired by the Empress, what would he do? He would obey his wife because she would be there beside him and he was weak...a clever woman could do what she would with him. And his Queen was clever.

She, the Empress, would have no chance unless she saw him alone, and the Queen who had proved herself shrewd was statesman enough not to allow that.

She rose from her bed and wrapped the fur-lined cape more closely about her. A crescent moon shone a little light on the icy scene. Everything was quiet and softly white.

The ice on the river would take weeks to melt unless the weather changed to summer heat, for it was thick enough to carry men and horses.

Then the idea came to her, as that other had when she watched the dead man being carried out of the town.

If she were clad all in white, if there were clouds across the face of the moon, if the snow fell, then no one would be able to distinguish her.

She could do it. She must do it. It was the only escape from a position which would be so humiliating that it was intolerable to her proud nature.

She did not wait for morning. She called one of her servatns and told her to bring Brian Fitz-Count to her without delay.

He came sleepily from his bed.

"Come to the window," she commanded.

He did so.

"Look at that river. The ice is so thick it would hold a troop of soldiers. Look! The snow clouds are passing across the face of the crescent moon. See, it is dark. If I were clad in white...the colour of the ice and the snow banks no one would see me."

Brian was alert now. She laughed triumphantly. "It is a way. We will try it. You, I and a few picked men. We will wear white garments. You will lower me by means of ropes and all follow me. They will not see us because we shall be in white from head to foot. Do not dare say it is impossible."

"It is...just possible," said Brian.

"We must be ready...as soon as the time is ripe we must do this. Tomorrow night mayhap, for who knows when Stephen will storm the castle."

She was excited now. She had chosen those whom she would take with her, all trusted men. They must work in stealth. How did they know what spies were in the castle? She herself would find the garments she would wear—warm enough to withstand the bitter night air and over them a white cloak. That was imperative.

Brian was eager now. He realized that escape might well be effected. It was as ingenious as Matilda's escape in the coffin.

It was going to be a stormy night. "This must be it," said Matilda. Ropes had been secreted in her chamber. She dismissed her women early so impatient was she, and immediately Brian and the eight knights who were to accompany them came into her room. They were all wearing white cloaks with hoods which covered their heads. Matilda donned hers and they were ready.

Impatiently she waited while the first two knights slid down the rope. Then it was her turn. The ropes were secured about her and she was lowered down the walls. To her joy she was soon standing with the others and in a short time the rest of the party was beside her.

It was an anxious moment when they scrambled down the

river bank and tested the ice. It seemed firm and with the Empress in their midst they began the crossing of the river.

The bitter wind cut her face and made her eyes smart but Matilda felt nothing but triumph.

Stephen would storm the castle and find that she had flown.

It was dangerous going, but she felt strong and sure of success. It was more risky than the coffin adventure but she would succeed now as she had then.

Brian seized her arm as they came to the edge of the river, for now they were very close to Stephen's camp.

As swiftly as the treacherous ground allowed, they passed along. Brian held her arm to steady her lest she slip. Everything about them was still and their footsteps made no sound in the deep snow. It was exhausting but the need to get as far as possible from the camp was imperative, and spurred on by the urgency of the situation, they did not stop until they were two miles from the camp.

Then Matilda paused to look back. She could see nothing in that white world; but she knew that for the second time she had made a miraculous escape and she applauded not God nor her followers but herself for her cleverness.

Through the night they walked and the six miles to Abingdon seemed like twenty. It was dawn when they reached the little town.

She felt half dead with fatigue and longed for hot food and a warm bed but Brian said it would be unsafe to stop as it might well be that their escape had been discovered so they must press on to Wallingford.

He did manage to get horses at Abingdon so that the journey to Wallingford was made in a little more comfort although the blizzard raged about them and the horses threatened to slip at any moment.

At last they reached the castle of Wallingford and there Matilda was helped from her horse. Her feet were numb, her hands so cold that she could not feel them, but hot food was brought to her and a great fire was kindled that she might rest before it.

She ate voraciously and almost immediately fell into a deep sleep.

When she awoke it was afternoon; the fire was blazing and outside the snow was still falling.

She could hear voices in the castle. She called: "Who is there?" And in a few moments a boy came into the hall.

For a few seconds she looked at him; and then she stood up and cried: "Henry, my son."

He came to her and a sudden and rare tenderness swept over her. Her first-born! The boy who had so delighted her father. Her nine-year-old son Henry!

"Mother," he said, "I am here to fight for you."

She embraced him.

What triumph. She had escaped from Stephen by crossing the icy Thames; she was free and her son Henry had come to fight for her.

Robert of Gloucester came into the hall.

He knelt before her.

"News was brought to me that you were here and we came with all speed."

"I escaped on the ice," she cried.

"I know it. Brian has told me."

"Stephen was encamped round the castle. He was unaware of us."

"It was a clever idea. You completely foiled him."

"You were coming to our aid?"

"As soon as I had gathered an army."

"That would have been too late. Is Geoffrey here?"

"No. He would not leave Anjou. He sent your son instead."

"Henry will be a greater help to me than my miserable little husband ever would be."

She turned to her son and laid her hand on his shoulder.

"Together, my boy, we will regain the crown of England," she said.

Departures

Matilda's hopes were not realized and although the weak rule of Stephen was deplored and the evil practices which the rapacious barons had set up continued, it seemed to many the lesser of two evils. Matilda's arrogant nature, her immediate attempt to levy taxes on the people of London had made the country feel that it would not have her at any price.

Yet under Robert of Gloucester the young Henry sought to win his mother's cause. He was a boy of great energy and it was seen that he had inherited many of the Conqueror's characteristics, so while Matilda had such a fine general as Robert of Gloucester she was a formidable force.

Civil war progressed and the years of wretchedness continued. The roads were unsafe for travellers; the robber barons could not be controlled. The country needed peace and while Matilda with her son and Robert of Gloucester attempted to gain the crown and Stephen with his Queen were determined to hold it, the strife would go on.

Stephen could not forget what his Queen had done for him and his affection for her grew. He marvelled at her statesmanlike quality and he wondered that he could have known so little of her that he could have thought of her as merely a pleasant but somewhat ineffectual woman.

Soon after their reunion another child was born to them. They called her Mary.

If only the war could be brought to a conclusion, the Queen believed that she would be completely happy. She had ceased to fret about Stephen's absorption with the Empress. She heard that she was becoming more and more ill-tempered and that even her faithful adherents like Robert of Gloucester and Brian Fitz-Count were often so exasperated that those in their circle believed they would desert her. They never did; and such was her magnetism that however intolerably she behaved they still adhered to her.

But surely, thought the Queen, Stephen must realize that she could bring nothing but evil to him. That lesson must have been driven home.

The Queen was deeply involved in the war; she advised Stephen and he was only too ready to listen to her. At the same time there were occasions when they could be with their family and these were the happy times. Eustace was ambitious; and Stephen and the Queen were ambitious for him.

Stephen said: "Rest assured. I shall remain King until I die and only then shall I pass on my crown and it will be to Eustace."

They would plan together. England for Eustace, William should inherit the earldom of Boulogne through his mother. And little Mary. She was too young to be planned for.

And then in the midst of their happy domestic circle a messenger would arrive to say that the Empress's army was attacking some stronghold which for the sake of the crown it could not be allowed to take.

That would be a reminder that the war still continued.

The Empress was weary. The years passed by; she was growing old and nothing was achieved. She blamed those about her; she tried to urge them on to action; but in spite of the fact that she had one of the best generals in Robert of Gloucester, there was no success. There were those occasions when Stephen's army was defeated but then the tide would turn again. There was no decisive battle for either side and the wretched war dragged on.

There was one consolation for her and that was her son Henry; he had spent three years under the guidance of Robert and was learning to become a soldier. He would need to be if he were to defend his dominions, for there was Eustace who was as determined to hold the crown of England as Henry was to take it.

Her husband the Count of Anjou was getting restive. It was three years since he had seen his eldest son and he sent messages to his wife that he wished Henry to return to Anjou.

Matilda raged against him. What had he ever done for her? What was he but a profligate upstart? She was ashamed to own him as husband. What a bitter mistake they had made when they gave her to him. What did he ever do but swagger round with a piece of broom in his hat calling him Geoffrey Plantagenet.

But he was her husband and he had some say over Henry's future. He wanted him back in Anjou. What was the use of the boy's frittering his years away in a hopeless cause?

Robert thought that young Henry should go back to Anjou. "He has learned a great deal about warfare," he said, "and that will stand him in good stead in the years to come. There is little he can do here and he can return when he is older. He might bring with him then an army from Anjou. Let him go."

So Robert accompanied the twelve-year-old Prince to Warham where a party of Angevin nobles was waiting to escort him across the Channel.

They took an affectionate farewell of each other, for Henry had become very fond of his uncle and he was grateful for all that he had taught him.

He was however glad to be going back to Anjou; his mother, although she had fierce and possessive love for him, was difficult to live with.

"Uncle," said Henry, "when I come back it will be with my army. Then we will fight together and put an end to this war."

"So be it," said Robert. They embraced and Robert stood watching until the cavalcade was out of sght.

Robert of Gloucester was a disappointed man. He knew that the Empress would never be accepted by the English and he now admitted to himself that it was entirely her own fault.

If she had been benevolent as Stephen was, or just as her father had been, strong and determined mainly on the good of England, he believed she would have succeeded in taking the crown. She was the true heir. There could be no doubt of that since she was the daughter of the son of the Conqueror who had no other legitimate children. And Stephen although the Conqueror's grandson had descended through his mother and was not even her eldest son. Stephen was a usurper and a weak king and because of this the good laws of William I and Henry I were gradually being lost.

What we need now, he often thought, is a strong king.

His great hope was in young Henry whom he had come to know well. A lusty youth, dedicated, wise beyond his years, too fond of pleasure, but that was a fault of the young.

It was because of Henry that he, Robert, had had the heart to continue the fight. He saw Henry following Stephen and bringing back that law and order which most men now realized was the way to prosperity.

Eustace he believed to be weak, over ambitious; he even lacked the charm of his father, the tolerance and good sense of his mother.

Robert, who was more than a soldier for he was a statesman and scholar, believed that England's salvation would be under the Plantagenets and if Prince Henry of Anjou could become the second Henry of England all his efforts would not have been in vain.

And as he watched the dwindling figures in the distance he was thinking that there at their head rode the hope of England.

He made his way back to Bristol where the Empress was staying, there to report the departure of her son.

She talked with pride of young Henry and with distaste of her husband; but she no longer railed against the delays in putting her on the throne. She had come to realize the hopelessness of her position; but her obsession to battle with Stephen still smouldered, ready to be kindled.

What she wanted more than anything, it seemed, was to have him brought in chains before her.

"The next time," she would say, "there shall be no escape for him."

Robert doubted that there would ever be a next time.

That autumn he caught a chill which developed into a fever, and it soon became clear that he was very ill indeed. His widow and their six children were at his bedside when he died. They mourned him sincerely for he had been a good father and husband.

It was not only his family who grieved for him, for he had been a good man and had never ill-treated those whom he conquered. In fact their conditions had often improved when they fell under his rule—except of course that he imposed taxes on them that he might build castles for his defence and provide means to carry on the war.

To the Empress his death was disastrous, and she now realized that she had not fully appreciated his genius. Her mainstay had been removed and she and her cause immediately began to totter. She had lost not only a faithful brother but her general, her adviser and the man whose skill and wisdom upheld her cause.

Very soon after Robert was laid in his green jasper tomb in the Benedictine Priory he himself had founded outside the walls of Bristol, Matilda saw that she had no recourse but to leave England to Stephen.

With great reluctance she left the country to join her husband in Anjou.

There was great rejoicing in the household of Stephen and his Queen. Bells rang throughout the country. It was peace at last. The enemy was vanquished.

At Lincoln that Christmas they celebrated Christmas with great pomp and splendour.

"At last," cried Stephen, "the enemy has flown. Now I can begin to govern my realm."

In Arundel, Adelicia had followed the civil war with great concern. Her husband was constantly away fighting in the cause of Stephen and the strain of constant anxiety had sent her more and more to religious meditation.

During the years she had given birth to seven children. William and Reyner were followed by Henry, Godfrey, Alice, Olivia and Agatha. She was devoted to them but even her affection for them made her wonder how long it would be before her elder sons joined the fighting.

William her husband was a faithful adherent to Stephen's cause and when Matilda went back to Anjou he looked forward to spending his days in peace with his family.

For some years Adelicia's favourite brother, Henry of Louvaine, had had a desire to go into a monastery. He had visited his sister at Arundel and they had talked often of the meaninglessness of the pomps of the world and how the only life worth living was that spent in seclusion.

Henry was determined to become a monk and Adelicia listening to him felt a great desire for such a life.

"I am very weary," she told her brother, "of the stresses of the world. When I was the King's wife I was tormented by inability to bear children. I believed that I would find peace with William. He has been a good husband to me. I have a great love for him and for my children, but I am beset by fears. When he goes away I never know when I am going to hear that he has been killed or is suffering torture in captivity. I fear that my sons will spend their lives in fighting, for that would seem the lot of the noblemen of this country. Then I long to shut myself away from the world and devote myself to prayer and to God."

It was only with her brother that she could talk of these things.

William returned when Matilda went back to Anjou, but he sensed the change in his wife. She was loving and kind but remote and he often wondered what had happened to change her.

In the year 1149, two years after Matilda's departure—years of peace from the civil war but during which the terrible outrages imposed by the barons on any who fell into their hands continued—Henry of Louvaine wrote to his sister that he had become a monk and was in the Monastery of Affigham at Alost in Flanders.

Adelicia knew the monastery well for it was one which her father had founded.

Her husband was with her when she received the news and he saw how her face lit up.

"Henry has become a monk," she cried. "How happy he must be!"

"Why," William had replied, "you speak as though you envy him."

"Think!" she answered. "He will know perfect peace. All the troubles of the world will pass over him; he will come closer to God and the saints. Would you not envy a man who had that blessed experience?"

"Adelicia," replied William, "I believe the sequestered life would make you happier than you are here with your family."

"I love you all dearly," she answered, "but I have longed for peace. It has never been mine. Always there are anxieties. This country is in a troublous state. The King is too weak to rule. Each day I expect trouble. You will be called from me to defend this castle or that piece of land. I am fearful that William will soon be old enough to join you. In the courtyards they practise with swords and their lances. I can hear them at their archery. War will come again."

"So you would be happier in a convent?"

"It is not possible for me to leave you all."

"I want you to be happy," said William.

He knew that her health was impaired. It was for this reason perhaps that she found the stresses of life harder to bear.

It was William who made the decision for her.

Why did she not go into a nunnery for a while, to rest, to see if she could find that peace she sought?

So not long after her brother entered the monastery of

Affigham, Adelicia herself entered a nunnery of a similar foundation.

She died there nearly two years after her entry.

With the Empress returned to Anjou, Queen Matilda looked forward to a life in which she could enjoy domestic peace.

Stephen could not express his gratitude to her enough; he insisted that she accompany him on all State occasions and that as much honour was done to her as to himself. He wanted to make up to her for his obsession with the Empress which now that imperious lady was far away seemed to him incredible. He believed he had been under some spell. Matilda was an enchantress; she had summoned up powers of darkness. How else could he have been so foolish as to have allowed her to escape him and for his folly paid the bitter price of humiliation and discomfort in a prison dungeon?

Now he was happy with his beloved wife and their three children.

"We must make up for all the years of separation," said Matilda. "We have come through a great ordeal and God has been good to us. He would wish us to show our appreciation of his goodness by enjoying that which he has given us."

The manner in which thanks to God were shown was invariably in the building of some monument to His glory; and what better monument could there be but a religious house in which He could be eternally praised.

Faversham was the site chosen and Matilda herself decided to preside over the building of an Abbey. For this purpose the Court moved to Canterbury where she would be close at hand to supervise the work in person for, as she pointed out to Stephen, it was not enough to provide the means of building such a place; they must take a great interest in it and be in actual fact concerned with its construction.

The work was put in progress and she and Stephen were happy discussing the plans and going to the site to see how the building progressed.

In spite of her new won contentment Matilda was feeling easily tired and was forced to admit to herself what a heavy strain the last years had put on her. So assiduously had she worked in her husband's cause that she had been unaware of the tensions. It was now that there was a respite from them that their effect began to be felt. She was conscious of a breathlessness, a tendency to catch colds from which she could not easily recover; she felt limp and was attacked by giddiness.

Her nature was such that she tried to hide these disabilities from Stephen and it was only her intimate attendants who were aware of them and watched her with increasing concern.

She was a little anxious about Eustace who was growing into a headstrong boy. He had inherited none of his father's attractive qualities; he completely lacked the ability to make friends for he was inclined to be arrogant. Matilda often thought of how Stephen, in the days when he was merely the son of the Count of Blois had endeared himself to the servants by his affability.

Eustace had heard stories of the young Henry of Anjou when he was in the country. There was a boy who was wild perhaps but had a way of attracting people to him. Even those who were fighting against his faction would tell stories of his exploits and there would be a grin of amusement on their faces.

Henry of Anjou had made a good impression—young as he was. He was reckless but a boy should be reckless; he was quite a fighter too; moreover people could not forget that he was in the direct line of succession being the son of Matilda, the Conqueror's only legitimate child.

Eustace liked to show his authority. He swaggered and reminded everyone that he was the son of the King. So there again was an anxiety. William, the other son, was inclined to be wild too, although, as he knew that he was not destined to be King of England, he was less eager to remind people of his rank. Little Mary took after her mother; she was a quiet, obedient child and had already declared her eagerness to go into a nunnery.

It seemed therefore that the period of peace for which the Queen craved could not be hers, for she knew that her health was deteriorating and she could not help wondering what would happen when Eustace grew a little older.

Stephen was a man who liked to believe that all was well. He could never face trouble until it was close to him. He did not wish to see the manner in which Eustace's character was developing and when Matilda contemplated the future she grew really uneasy.

When she began to believe it would be a future which she might not be there to see, instead of shrugging her shoulders, this made her the more anxious. She knew what Stephen owed to her; she was aware of her own mental strength. Stephen was the weaker of the two and he needed her beside him. One of her great worries was what would happen when she was no longer there.

It was for this reason that she decided to talk to him about their eldest son and point out the alarming signs she detected.

"Eustace is the heir to the throne," said the King, "yet because of Henry of Anjou he fears the people may attempt to set him aside. That is the source of his trouble."

The Queen agreed with him. "Oh, God," she cried, "I hope he does not have to fight for the throne as you have had to do."

"Nay," said the ebullient Stephen. "We have done with that. Henry will take Anjou and that will be an end to it."

"I wish I could believe it."

"Why, my dear, that is a very worried frown you are wearing. I tell you all will be well."

"We must not forget, Stephen, who Henry is."

Stephen could not meet her eyes. Could it be indeed true that the Empress's son, of whom everyone spoke so highly, was his also? He believed it. He wanted to believe it. He could not help it if he felt a twinge of pride every time he heard of his exploits.

The Queen went on: "He is in the direct line of succession, Stephen."

"He would have been so had the Empress gained the crown. But she did not. And Eustace is my direct heir."

"I greatly fear...."

"That when I am dead young Henry will make an attempt. Nay, my dear wife, your son shall be my heir and none other. I tell you what I will do and I know this will please you. I will call together the barons and knights and they shall swear an oath of fealty to Eustace. They must swear to accept him as King when I die."

"Do you think they would do that, Stephen?"

"You forget I am their King. They shall be commanded to do so, Matilda. We will go to Lincoln and there I will call them together. Let us make preparations to leave without delay."

They travelled to Lincoln and there the King called together the leading noblemen. When they heard for what purpose there was a certain reluctance among them to do as the King asked.

William de Albini pointed out to the King that they were remembering the oaths they had taken in the reign of the last King and of all the trouble these had caused. No knight had been sure whether he should remain true to the oath he had taken to support the Empress when it was said that Henry had changed his mind on his death-bed. Civil war had been the result of that oath.

Stephen agreed. "There is one answer to that," he said. "We will crown him as heir apparent. There shall be a ceremony and the crown shall be placed on his head. Then there will be no doubt of my wishes."

"My lord," replied William, "I doubt the nobles will agree to that and it is unwise to place a crown on the head of a new king when the existing one still lives. The Prince is but thirteen years old and you are in your prime. It is a matter which should be put aside for the time."

Stephen declared he believed this was true.

He explained to his Queen.

"You see, Matilda, they are right and it would seem that instead of becoming more restrained, more modest in his bearing Eustace would be more inclined to arrogance."

Matilda did not protest but she thought that the late King Henry would have insisted on obedience to his wishes; and she was certain that Henry of Anjou would come to claim the throne when Stephen died.

He did not wait for that. While Matilda and Stephen were at Faversham, news was brought to them that Henry of Anjou had arrived in England and that David of Scotland, who had always favoured the Empress, was preparing to march across the border in support of Henry.

Stephen immediately gathered together an army and, because the people had no intention of allowing the Scots to invade the country and they were heartily tired of war and they had heard that Henry of Anjou had brought but a small force with him, they decided to rally to Stephen and end the conflict with all speed.

Good luck was with Stephen. The King of Scotland retired behind his border and young Henry went with him. The threatened war did not take place. The people of England rejoiced and Stephen was complimented on the quick firm action he had taken.

"We must be watchful," he said. "We know our enemies

300

are above the border. They must not be allowed to think that we shall let them stay there."

He was astonished to receive a communication from Henry.

Henry was in a quandary, he stated, and he believed his uncle might help him out of it.

This was an extraordinary notion, since a short while before Henry had boldly marched on England.

He had too small a force to attack, explained Henry. He was not in Scotland but wished to return with his troops to Anjou. His predicament was that he had no money with which to pay his men and to get them back. He knew well the King's generosity. He was therefore asking Stephen for the means to ship his men back to Anjou.

This request from an enemy was considered not only audacious but absurd. This irrepressible young man who had come to take Stephen's crown was now asking for money to get his men back to Anjou.

Stephen was amused.

"He cannot be serious," said the Queen.

"He is."

"He is an impudent young man. To ask *you* for help."

"How will he pay those men and get them away without my help?"

"That is surely his affair. Let them see what a Prince they have. They may not be so eager to follow him in future."

"He is headstrong," said Stephen. He could not help it but he felt a tenderness for this young man. Eustace was his own son, he reminded himself, but was Henry also?

He felt almost certain that he was. And who should a boy appeal to but his own father?

No one could deter him. Money was sent to Henry of Anjou, a note of thanks came from Henry; and he and his troops departed for Anjou.

Was the King mad? This was a question people were asking themselves. They all knew of his generosity, his desire to live in amity with everyone. But this impudent boy was the enemy.

They remembered how he had let the Empress slip through his hands. He certainly behaved in a very strange manner now and then.

With Henry back in Anjou there was peace again.

The recent events, however, had worried the Queen a great

deal. The refusal of the barons to acclaim Eustace king, the arrival of Henry of Anjou and Stephen's strange behaviour towards that young man...all this had been a great strain on her health.

The news of Adelicia's death was very upsetting. She felt she understood her need to retire from the world and shut herself up in a nunnery. Poor Adelicia, she had not lived long to enjoy that peace.

They were of an age and she, Matilda, was very, very tired.

She fell ill and on this occasion was too weary to pretend otherwise.

Stephen was horrified. It was characteristic of him that he had preferred to believe that there was nothing seriously wrong with her and when the truth could no longer be avoided he was bewildered.

She could not rise from her bed and asked that her confessor be sent for.

"I do not think I shall leave my bed again, Stephen," she said.

"Nay, nay," he cried, in panic. "I beg you, do not talk so."

"It's the truth, Stephen."

"How can you be ill...so suddenly?"

"It is not sudden, Stephen. It has been coming for some time...more than a year ago I knew."

"I did not. Why did I not? No, Matilda, it is not so. What shall I do without you?"

She smiled gently. "You have given me great happiness, Stephen. I have lived but to be of use to you."

He kissed her hands fervently. It was as though he were pleading with her not to leave him.

"It is no longer in our hands, Stephen," she said.

Her children came to her, Eustace, William and Mary.

"Oh, Stephen," she whispered, "I would I could stay with you to care for you all...."

Stephen wept openly. How could he live without her? He had not known, in spite of everything that had happened, how much she meant to him. Why had he not been a better husband to her?

"If I could have another chance," he whispered.

She could only smile at him.

For several days she lay between life and death and on a beautiful May day of the year 1152 she died.

302

They buried her at Faversham Abbey which she and Stephen had so recently founded. Stephen knew that he would mourn her all his life for he loved her more in death than he had believed possible while she lived.

The Last Meeting

The King was melancholy. He was overcome by remorse. She was dead, his good and faithful wife, and he could never tell her now what she had meant to him. He brooded often on the past; he thought of the women with whom he had betrayed her; he had forgotten half of them now. There was one, though, whom he would never forget and he often wondered how much the Queen had known of that affair.

She was a saint; there would never again be anyone to care for him as she had done. His loss was irreparable. Sometimes he thought he was going to have another bout of that mysterious illness which had brought him close to death and had plunged him into such lethargy, that he could do nothing but lie on his bed so limp and indifferent to the world that if his enemy were storming the castle he would continue to lie there. And if he did? Who would nurse him then? Who would keep the secret of his illness? His guardian angel was gone forever and only now did he know how much she had cared for him.

He longed for a chance to explain to her, to tell her that he was aware of all she had done. He wanted to explain how that other Matilda had put a spell upon him and that it was nothing but witchcraft which had seduced him from his true and loving wife.

News came of the death of Geoffrey of Anjou. Stephen wondered then how Matilda was taking the death of the husband she despised. She cared little for Geoffrey, that had always been obvious, but his death was bound to affect the future.

She was constantly creeping into his thoughts though he did his best to banish her from them. Yet he remembered her in her various moods; and he hated himself and assured himself that this was not so, but in his heart he knew that more than anything he longed to see her again. He wanted to see Henry—why, he would be twenty years old, a young warrior, as ambitious as his mother. Let us hope he has not inherited her temper, thought Stephen. Ever since she had hinted that Henry might be his son he had been overwhelmed by an interest in him. He would glow inwardly with pride when he heard of his exploits. Eustace was his and his Queen's legitimate son but he could not help it if he tingled with pleasure every time he thought of Henry.

Sometimes when a spell of lethargy came over him he would let himself dream that he had married the fierce Matilda instead of the meek one and that Henry was their son, the future King of England. Such a grand boy, bold, puckish, lusty, everything that a young man should be.

Then he would return to reality and understand that this Henry was the enemy as the Empress had been.

Geoffrey's death was hardly likely not to have its effect. The reason the Plantagenet had refused his wife's plea for his presence in England when Robert of Gloucester had gone to fetch him was that he was far more concerned in taking Normandy, for Stephen so deeply involved with holding England had been unable to defend the Duchy. Now that Geoffrey was dead, Normandy had passed to young Henry who had placed himself in a strong position by making an advantageous marriage.

That this marriage shocked many, would of course, mean nothing to the gay adventurer. Eleanor of Aquitaine, twelve years older than Henry, had been married to the King of France. Eleanor, wild, adventurous and completely immoral, had become so enamoured of the dashing young Plantagenet, that Louis VII had now divorced her. It was this woman whom young Henry had now married and he was proudly calling himself Duke of Aquitaine and Normandy.

Stephen could imagine his dead Queen's concern at this turn of events. Normandy today, she would say. England tomorrow. Eustace is the Duke of Normandy, not this son of the Empress.

Eustace was furious; he strutted about the Court telling the King what he would do if he could come face to face with Henry Plantagenet.

His best plan was through negotiations, said Stephen. Eustace should go to the Court of France with his young wife

Constance. Louis was powerful enough to give him his support and to declare Eustace, Duke of Normandy. This meant that Eustace must swear fealty to the King of France and then it seemed certain that Louis would agree. His sister was the wife of Eustace and his wife had deceived him with young Henry. Certainly Henry should not inherit Normandy. That should be for his brother-in-law, young Eustace.

So Normandy was won back. His Queen would have been pleased with that. That was a clever piece of diplomacy to have sent Eustace to France at the time when the King of France had divorced his wife and she had married Henry of Anjou.

Stephen had sent a message to the King of France to the effect that this young man who seemed to have such an opinion of himself had attempted to rob him of Normandy as churlishly as he had robbed Louis of his wife.

The King of France was very serious and replied that he was well rid of his wife and glad to pass her over; he was sure that she would cause as much trouble to her new husband as the Duchy of Normandy did to its dukes.

Stephen wondered what the Empress was thinking and guessed she was in one of her violent rages over the manner in which Normandy had been returned to its rightful owner.

Stephen was eager now to assure the succession as his dear dead Queen would have wished it. He made up his mind that he would insist on the crowning of Eustace, for, once a king was crowned, he was accepted as such and it was a very different matter displacing a man who was the recognized King from ousting him from his place when he was merely the heir apparent.

He had failed once but he was going to succeed this time. It was what Matilda would wish.

He called together the leading men of the Church and told them his will.

They would not agree, he was told.

"You shall agree," he told them. "I am the King and I will be obeyed."

The churchmen conferred together. It was true he was the King but many of them still looked upon him as a usurper. They had seen the way Eustace was growing up and they had also had a glimpse of the young Plantagenet. The latter was the true heir to the throne; he was the grandson of Henry I whereas Stephen was only his nephew. They had accepted

Stephen as King because there had been a bloody civil war fought on the issue and the Empress Matilda would have been an even less attractive sovereign. Stephen had certain qualities; he was not a strong king, but he was not harsh and cruel. They would accept Stephen but not his son.

This was their verdict and although they would not have dared give such a decision to Henry I, they did not hesitate to give it to Stephen.

For once Stephen was wrathful. He would imprison them all, he declared. They should all be shut up until they bowed to his will. He was determined that Eustace should be crowned King.

This he did but it was no rigorous confinement. It merely meant that he shut them up in one house, which was characteristic of him.

No one was very much surprised when the Archbishop of Canterbury escaped from confinement. This made nonsense of the whole affair because a king could not be crowned without him.

Stephen was only faintly disturbed when news reached him that the Archbishop had escaped across the Channel and was with Henry Plantagenet, urging him to make an attempt to secure the crown of England.

Henry lost no time in setting out for England. His marriage to a forceful wife, his certainty that he was the true heir of England and the haranguing of his mother made him determined to secure what he believed was his inheritance.

Stephen rode out to meet the invading army with a feeling he did not himself understand. He was coming face to face with this young man who was often in his thoughts. Matilda's son! Naturally her son would be no ordinary young man. Stephen laughed inwardly to think of Henry's seducing the wife of the King of France, marrying her, and their son being born about two months after the wedding. It was clear that this young man was not going to follow an orthodox pattern.

They were now going to face each other in combat and Stephen could feel that lethargy creeping over him. No, it was perhaps not the old illness. It was a strong conviction that it was wrong for him and this young man to stand on opposite sides in a field of battle.

The weather was cold and the roads icy, and as Stephen rode with his army his horse slipped and he was thrown.

There was a hush throughout the ranks for this sort of

incident was regarded with great superstition as an evil omen
and more particularly when it happened on the verge of going
into battle.

Stephen picked himself up and mounted his horse. He had
not his grandfather's gift for turning such an incident which
could well be a bad omen into one which was a good one.

His horse slipped almost as soon as he had mounted and
again he was thrown. He mounted again and the horse
slipped as before, and for the third time Stephen was thrown
to the ground.

Once would have made his followers apprehensive, twice
would have been alarming, but three times appeared to be
an undoubted sign.

Many of those men who stood waiting for the beginning
of the battle were convinced that Stephen had lost the day
before it started.

It was dusk. The battle would begin with the dawn. The
King wandered round the camp fires and talked to his men.
He talked to them of victory but his heart was not in the
fight and they knew it. He wondered how many of his men
would have deserted by morning.

William de Albini came into his tent and asked for a word
with him.

"My good friend," said Stephen, "I can see you are dis-
traught. You fear the outcome of this battle."

"I fear, my lord, the effect of a long and arduous war on
the people of this land."

"You think it will be such?"

"I think that unless some understanding is reached there
will be no end to these wars. My lord, you see how the country
suffers from them. When the last King died we were prosperous, this was a law-abiding land. Since then it has been
torn by almost continuous civil strife. Put an end to it, my
lord, before it is too late."

"That is what I am trying to do."

"Not through battle. We have had enough of battle."

"Do you fear battle?"

"Nay, my lord. You know that well. I have spent so many
years since my marriage away from my home."

"You could be said to have been guarding that home."

"I would there had been no need to do so. Nor would there
have been had we had peace. You know how my beloved wife

Adelicia could not endure the strife of the world and shut herself away in a nunnery. She is now dead and I a widower."

"As I am. We married saints, William."

"They were wise women, my lord. They wanted peace. They craved peace. They knew that the country needed peace. In their memory we must bring about that peace."

"When I have defeated the enemy it will come."

Albini shook his head. "Nay. It will not come through war. My lord, you know that Henry Plantagenet has a claim to the throne as the direct heir of Henry I. Could you not enter into a contract with him?"

"Give up the throne! You do not mean that. If you do you are a traitor."

"I have ever been your faithful servant. It is because of this that I make so bold as to suggest to you that you make a treaty with him. You to be King until your death and then Henry Plantagenet should be your heir."

"And my own son...?"

Albini shook his head. "I have put this to you, my lord. I beg you think on it. If you could make this treaty there need be no bloodshed on the morrow. Think what this would mean to this land."

William de Albini bowed and went silently from the King's tent.

He could not rest. He thought of tomorrow's battle. He was getting old—forty-six. He had spent so many of those years in battle. He had no heart for bloodshed.

And yet to betray his own son Eustace!

A voice seemed to whisper to him: "But is Henry your son?"

One of his men came into the tent.

"My lord, there is a woman without who would have speech with you."

"A woman! Who is this?"

"An old gipsy woman. She says she must speak with you. She has something of the greatest moment to say to you. It is of the utmost importance...to you, sir."

"What should I want with an old gipsy?"

"She will not go away, sire."

"Bring her to me."

She was wrapped in a long cloak; her hair hung loose about her shoulders; there was mud on her boots.

"Why do you come to me?" he asked.

"Because I must speak to you, Stephen."

There was something in the way in which she said his name that made him start.

He said to the soldier who guarded the tent: "Leave us."

When they were alone, he went to her and took her by the shoulders. "Matilda," he cried.

"You know me then."

"Could I ever not do so? What do you here?"

"I came to see you...."

"How.... You... in my camp."

"This disguise is good," she told him. "All soldiers like to have their fortunes told. I am with my son's men and I broke through into your camp disguised in this way because I had to see you. It is not the first time I have broken through your lines. Once I was a corpse, then I escaped on the ice and now I come as a gipsy."

The old excitement was creeping over him. Her fascination was as potent as ever.

"Why, Matilda?"

"To see you. It may be the last time, Stephen.... That is why."

"Are you prophesying my death?"

She shook her head. "But we have been parted for so long and so many times. Our lives have been ones of brief meetings and long separations. Alas, Stephen, do you regret that?"

"Never anything more. If they had given you to me...."

"Much of the spice would have been taken out of life. Who knows I might have come to despise you as I did my poor Geoffrey. But I waste time. I have come to ask you not to fight tomorrow. I want you to call off this battle. I fear that if you and Henry come face to face one of you will die. I love my son, Stephen. That surprises you. You did not believe I could love anyone. But in a way I love you and I love Henry. He is going to be a great king... a greater one than you could ever be. You are too kind and gentle for a king, Stephen. You are too eager to be friends with all men and that could mean you are no true friend to one. I have changed over the years, mellowed. I have accepted defeat for myself... but not for my son. So I ask you not to fight but to meet to parley, to make a treaty. Give him the crown after your death. You know it is his by right. You knew it was mine by right. I forfeit it to you, Stephen, if you will give it to my son when you die."

"Ah, Matilda, you forget. I had a good and faithful wife and she bore me a son."

Matilda uttered an oath. She was the old Matilda again in her hatred of his wife. She had never forgiven that Matilda for being not the fool she had once thought her but a clever woman who could scheme for her husband.

She said angrily: "This battle is a cruel and unnatural thing. Is it fitting that a father should slay his own son and son to kill his sire?"

"You are telling me that Henry is my son?"

"You know how it was between us."

"Then he *is*!"

"I will say no more," she answered. "But I tell you this. If you fight tomorrow it will go ill with you and if my son killed you I could not forgive him and if you killed him I could not forgive you either."

"Matilda, you must tell me the truth."

"The truth. What is the truth? Who knows the truth? There are so many sides to all questions that the truth is hard to find. For so long I could see but one point of view and that my own. And look to what that brought me. I lost London. My triumph was turned to failure. Stephen, do not fail as I did."

"Matilda, I would know...."

"We would all know everything that were possible. I shall go now. Think on what I have said. Do as I say. If you do not there will be such bloodshed for this England which my father and our grandfather made that they will never forgive you...and nor shall I."

She lifted the flap of the tent and went out.

He started to follow her but changed his mind.

He sat down on his straw. Matilda, he thought. There was never one like her. She still spoke in the same arrogant manner, yet she had changed. What had changed her? Her love for her son...their son?

He buried his face in his hands and so remained for some time.

When he lifted his head he went to the door of the tent and called one of his soldiers.

"Bring William de Albini to me," he said.

When William came he said: "I have thought of your words. Let a message be sent to Henry Plantagenet. Tell him that I would parley with him in person at dawn. We will meet between the two armies and will ride out to each other singly."

William fell to his knees. "I thank you, God," he said, "for Thy great mercy."

The End of an Era

When Eustace heard of the Treaty of Wallingford a wild fury possessed him.

He screamed in his rage. How dared his father dispossess him in favour of Henry Plantagenet! His father was a coward who feared to fight. His father had given away his inheritance.

He shouted to his troops. "Shall we allow this? Let us march on the King. Let us march on the upstart Henry Plantagenet."

But they fell away from him. They were as sick of war as others.

There were a few though to stand beside him then, for there were always malcontents in an army. There were many who were looking for the spoils of battle.

With a band of followers Eustace marched on to Bury St. Edmunds and there he entered the monastery.

The Abbot received him and offered him and his men shelter.

"What we want," cried Eustace, "is money that we may carry on the war against the King who has given my inheritance to the Plantagenet."

The Abbot gently replied that he could give them nothing but food and shelter. To which Eustace answered roughly that it appeared to him there was much treasure in the Abbey and this could be used to provide an army.

Raging against his fate, Eustace was in no mood to reason. He wanted to vent his anger on someone. Had his father been at hand he would have tried to kill him. As it was he turned his fury on the monks.

Crashing into the chapels he took the gold and silver ornaments from the altars; he tore down the rich hangings for their gold and silver embroideries. He ordered that his men should take the corn from the Abbey granaries and in the meantime others should cook a feast of which he and his men should partake in the refectory.

The vaulted ceiling echoed to their ribaldry and Eustace thus attempted to ease his outraged feelings.

So violent had been his anger that while he was eating he choked suddenly and fell to the floor in a fit.

He was carried from the hall in a state of stupor and the next day he died.

This was retribution, said the monks, for his desecration of their abbey.

He was buried at Faversham beside his mother; and Stephen mourned him deeply.

He had, after all, been his son. He had long known that Eustace had not the qualities to make a good king but he could not forget the days of his infancy when he and the Queen had delighted in him.

And yet, thought Stephen, this makes the way clear for Henry.

He believed that it was right that Henry should follow him.

Stephen returned to his palace of Westminster and there he shut himself away for a while to think of all that happened and, as he said, to make his peace with Matilda his Queen.

He would talk to her as though she were with him, explaining why he had acted as he had.

"It was peace, Matilda. No country can prosper without it."

That had always been a belief of hers.

And Eustace? She would understand. "He would have been no fit king, Matilda. You will see that. And what happens when a country such as this one falls under the sway of a weak man?

"You have seen what happened under me. I was no match for them all. I was no Conqueror, no Lion of Justice. I lacked their strength. They cared nothing for the approval of men; I craved it. They were prepared to be hated. I wanted to be loved.

"That was my downfall. And now this young Henry is waiting, to leap into the saddle. I have confidence in him, Matilda, as I could never have had in Eustace."

He was proud of the boy. How could he be otherwise? He would be a good king.

"England will be as she was in the days of her greatness. This young man, this Henry, will lead her back to that path from which under a weak king she has strayed."

He was living quietly, often in the past. But he had learned a lesson just as Matilda had learned hers.

They had one aim now and that was the success of the next King. They did not meet but he felt that their spirits were in accord.

Was she at peace? It was hard to believe that she ever would be.

Was he? Hardly that. But he was now quietly waiting for the end.

A year or so after the Treaty of Wallingford a sudden illness attacked him.

He thought: "It has come." And he was ready, even eager, to go.

He lay in his bed. He had said good-bye to William, his young son, who had been concerned in a plot to assassinate Henry and had mercifully been discovered in time. His young daughter Mary prayed at his bedside.

William de Albini was there.

"Farewell," said Stephen. "This is my end. Do not grieve, I am ready to go."

"You are too young to die," said William.

"I have lived for fifty-one winters, that is enough," said Stephen. "I shall go and join my dear wife and we shall lie together in the Abbey of Faversham which we built to the glory of God. Good-bye, William. Live in peace. Go to Boulogne and there care for the estates your mother left. That would be her wish. And Mary, my child, you should go to Rumsey and there you will discover whether it is indeed a life of seclusion you wish for. Fare you well. I go in good heart. My sins are great but God will forgive me."

The priests were at his bedside and gratefully he took the cross which was thrust into his hands.

There were many to grieve for him. He had been a man who was greatly loved. The people in the streets mourned for him. The Londoners remembered that he had always had a friendly word for them. He had been a good man as men were, but a weak king in an age which needed a strong one.

So while they mourned for him the people of England looked to the future.

This was the end of the Norman Kings; the Plantagenet era had begun.

BIBLIOGRAPHY

Appleby, John T.	The Troubled Reign of King Stephen
Arnold, Ralph	A Social History of England
Aubrey, William Hickman Smith	The National and Domestic History of England
Bagley, J. J.	Life in Medieval England
Baker, Timothy	The Normans
Brooke, Christopher	From Alfred to Henry III
Brown, R. Allen	The Normans and the Norman Conquest
Bryant, Arthur	The Story of England Makers of the Realm
Davis, H. W. C.	England Under the Normans and the Angevins
David, R. H. C.	King Stephen
Green, J. R.	A Short History of the English People
Page, R. I.	Life in Anglo-Saxon England
Pine, L. G.	Heirs of the Conqueror
Poole, Austin Lane	From Doomsday Book to Magna Carter 1087–1216
Potter, K. R. Translated from the Latin with Introduction and notes by	Gesta Stephani (The Deeds of Stephen)
Round, R. H.	Feudal England
Stenton, F. M.	Anglo-Saxon England
Stephen, Sir Leslie and Lee, Sir Sidney (edited by)	The Dictionary of National Biography
Strickland, Agnes	Lives of the Queens of England
Tomkeieff, O. G.	Life in Norman England
Wade, John	British History
White, R. T.	A Short History of England

319

NEW FROM FAWCETT CREST